Copyright © 2010
by Scott Pruden

FIRST EDITION
April 2010

10 9 8 7 6 5 4 3 2 1

ISBN: 978-0-615-34825-4
Library of Congress Control Number: 2010921735

Designed by
Wayne Lockwood

"I think there are innumerable gods.
What we on earth call God
is just a little tribal god
who has made an awful mess.
Certainly forces operating
through human consciousness
control events."
...
William S. Burroughs

"Ah ha ha!
Ever get the feeling you've been
cheated?"
...
Johnny Rotten

D
E

IMMAC

SCOTT B. PRUDEN

LATE

NATE~
GREAT TO MEET YOU
AT ComicCon! ENJOY!
~ Sean P

ION

Codorus Press | NYC

acknowledgements

It would be impossible to thank everyone who has contributed to the creation and completion of this work. However, there are several who helped me mightily in forming ID into the book you now hold in your hands.

Don and Brooksie Pruden, in bringing me into this world, were perhaps the primary contributors. But they are also to be thanked for always being supportive of their son's writing aspirations, for having old manual typewriters and bond paper hanging around the house in the days just before computers and for throwing me in with artistic folk at an early age. Should every author be blessed with such wonderful parents, there would be far fewer sulky memoirs in the world.

To my grandparents, I extend utmost thanks for material, financial and emotional support, even though they might not have been quite sure what I was up to most of the time.

I am indebted to those friends who have read and critiqued ID over the years, most notably Dennis Shealy, Chris Martin, Tom Joyce, Tracy Vogel and Wayne Lockwood, the mad genius behind Codorus Press. This is a far better work for having passed through their hands.

I'm also grateful to the Brandywine Valley Writers Group of West Chester, Pa., for simply existing to give writers a place to be with their own, for encouraging and indulging multiple public readings and laughing in the right places. Also, thanks to John Powell and John DeVlieger for their visual help.

And thanks most of all to the lovely Miss Kelly, the object of my undying love and affection (even though she still doesn't like the way Jon dies). This one's for you, my love.

disclaimer

For purposes of this story, I have taken the liberty of extending the range of the carnivorous Venus flytrap beyond what is considered its native habitat.

Also, the scuppernong grape, though represented here as being ripe in July, typically is not fit for eating in South Carolina until late August or early September. What you choose to do with it up until then is your business.

chapters

PART ONE

EXODUS

Jon Templeton remembered the exact moment he decided to sell his soul. It began with a question in a bar.

"So, Mr. Templeton, what now?"

The cherry of Jon's cigarette flared red as he pulled on the filter, considering the question while trying to ignore the enviro-drone perched on the wall next to him. Everything had happened so fast Jon hadn't had much time to think about the future. The guy from building security – the one Jon had nodded to and exchanged pleasantries with every day for the last five years – had been too busy trying to hurry him out of the office, patting him down to make sure all company-issued items were accounted for and that he wasn't absconding with a shoulder bag full of office supplies.

Now, the din of Murphy's Pub distracted him with the white noise of people enjoying themselves, but it didn't help eliminate his thoughts about just being fired from one of the most prestigious newsgathering organizations in the Southeast. Jon Templeton was seated next to his now ex-city editor, Buck Mays, taking his share of their third round with Buck's question ringing in his head.

"Hell, I don't know. Freelancing maybe?"

As Jon stubbed out the butt and lit up another Camel, Buck gave him the same "Why did I hire you?" look he gave borderline incompetent rookie reporters.

"Well, there'll be no shortage of work if you don't mind some two-bit assignments here and there. But two freelancers in the same house? Hell, son. You'll go broke spending the little bit you manage to earn on a marriage counselor. Then again, y'all make me ill with all that snookie-bear shit, so maybe you'll make out alright after all."

They both chuckled. "Of course, it would give you two a little more time to work on baby-making. I have to say that would definitely be an upside."

"Absolutely," Jon said, waving his cigarette hand in front of him to set the scene. "From ten in the morning till noon, we casually work on our respective high-paying, low-effort assignments, then after a light lunch retire to the boudoir to rut like weasels."

Buck nudged him in the ribs and nodded toward the passing waitress with the painted on jeans and a black tube top that exposed her bountiful cleavage. "Speaking of rutting like weasels, I think I found the candidate for wife number four."

Murph's was a dive off the beaten tourist path, but its true appeal lay in the absence of TVs, Web terminals or holo ads anywhere in the building. The overabundance of stunning twenty-one-year-old waitresses made up for the presence of the frat boy customer base and those pesky drones that followed you around sucking up your second-hand smoke. "Wanna know a secret?" Buck asked. Jon nodded yes in mid-sip, thinking he was about to hear one of Buck's exploits related to busty young waitresses. "My brother-in-law, the pizzeria magnate of Aiken County? He just bought into a Cleaver's franchise down in North Augusta. Now, you want to talk about some great job interviews? Said the girls just come in and practically strip without him even asking."

Jon paused in the middle of inhaling. "What, he's supposed to ask?"

"Well, hell. They sling those wings and rubbery little shrimp with just a thong and pasties on anyway. Why shouldn't they have to strip down to get the job? Hardly anyone but those CNR girls work there, and we know what they're like. Get this: He said once they get hired, there's a special section of the orientation teachin' them how not to get their titties burnt from the grease spatters when they serve the Mamasita Fajitas."

"Tell your brother-in-law I might be coming down to see him for an interview soon," Jon said with a laugh. "He won't ask me to take my clothes off, will he?"

"Damn, I hope not. That's enough to puke a dog off a gut truck." Buck took a long draught. "But seriously, man. What's your plan? I got people I can call. You know I'll do anything for you."

"Jeez, Buck. I really have no idea. We don't want to move."

"Hell no. And start paying a mortgage like the rest of us? Your Aunt Lil sure took care of you two leaving you that house. It'd be stupid to blow that. But your news options are pretty limited. Every operation in the state is either in bed with Garland or one of his cronies."

It was true.

Twenty years of media consolidation had left him with few places to go to ply his trade now that he had offended one of the major players.

He took a thoughtful drag. Jon then fixed his former boss with a mock-serious gaze and assumed the deep baritone he used in his voiceovers. "Maybe now's the time to jump into the noble and high-paying field of public relations."

Buck rolled his eyes and leaned to his left where Nancy Higgins, the Charleston Gazette's state government reporter, sat with one hand high on the inside thigh of a sports intern who had just turned twenty-one, the other holding her pint glass. Jon watched Buck say something into her ear. Whatever it was prompted her to break off her attempt to corrupt a recent minor, place her beer on the table and turn to Jon with steely eyes.

"Jon Templeton, you are the best damn investigative reporter I have ever seen. You're like a ..." She struggled through the alcohol haze to find the words. "... A combination cobra and a pit-bull."

She had picked up her cigarette and was punctuating syllables by jabbing it in the air. The drone scurried back and forth trying to keep up with the shifting stream of smoke. "I've never watched anyone work sources or stay with something they had a gut feeling on and actually watch it break into an honest-to-God story like you do. And just because this Senator Garland thing turned around and bit you on the ass, do not let it sour you on this business."

She dropped her now spent butt in one of several cast-off glasses, reached across Buck's broad chest and grabbed Jon by the necktie, pulling so their faces met in the middle. "Jon, you know I love you, but PR is for pussies."

Just like that, she released Jon, downed the remainder of her pint and resumed her seduction.

Buck's laugh could fill the wide-open expanse of a newsroom. Now it filled the entire noisy bar. "I'm sorry I had to do that to you, brother, but you know she's right. PR, man … That's some soul-sucking shit right there."

The whole conversation, regardless of the fact that it took place four months earlier, kept playing itself over and over in Jon's head. Now it echoed in the near silence of the Carlton-to-Charleston maglev on a blazing hot July morning.

"Soul-sucking shit" about covered it. It was as if a slow, deliberate vacuum was pulling the very spirit out of his body. And the things that fed that spirit – the desire to see the hypocrites brought low and justice done, the craving for caffeine, alcohol and cigarettes – they were gone, too. Now, all that was left was an eight-hour hole in five weekdays and a sizeable chunk missing from his soul, with only a substantially larger paycheck to justify it.

Worst of all, it was now nearly impossible to explain to people what he did for a living. It had been mentioned to Jon on several occasions by those outside the media business that his name was conspicuously absent from the letterhead of Hampton DuBose and Associates, the largest and best connected "image handling" firm in Charleston. His standard reply was, "Of course my name's on the letterhead. I'm one of the associates."

Inevitably his attempt to deflect the question, as well as those regarding why he no longer worked for the Gazette, failed and he had to explain what exactly he did as the agency's "media liaison." Depending on his patience and level of alcohol consumption, it went something like this: While other employees were busy formulating advertising campaigns for major corporations or remaking the images of local politicians, he was responsible for fielding calls from his former news colleagues and telling them bald-faced lies based on the work of his associates. His job was to perform for his clients as a lurid combination of press secretary and spin doctor without the perk of knowing he would one day land a spot as a highly-paid political pundit who could eventually earn even more for trashing his former employers on a Sunday morning chat show.

Every time he had to trudge through the convoluted explanation, he remembered how easy it used to be for him. "I'm an investigative reporter," he'd say. People just knew, and many of them looked upon him with a sense of awe as a result. They could form in their minds an image of the job, whether it was from books or movies or personal experience. If he happened to mention stories he'd written, the awe deepened. "You were the one who brought down EnterTec for selling U.S. security secrets in videogames?"

Yep, that was me, he'd say, trying to not look overly proud. Pride kills, he'd tell young reporters. Pride makes you lazy. In this business, we don't have time to be proud, because there's always another story and another deadline looming. Until, that is, one of those stories turns around and bites you in the ass. For the sake of the neophytes, he always left that bit out.

The maglev eased to a stop at the Meeting Street station and Jon disembarked, the sodden Lowcountry air hitting him in the face like a wall of fat man's sweat. Heading for the office, he tried to remind himself of the reasons for the choice he had made. The pay was stellar – almost twice what he was making at the Gazette. The benefits plan was obscene, including his choice of memberships to three different country clubs. There was also the implied Gold Key service from several high-end escort services. And there was very little danger of being shot, incinerated, beaten, blackmailed or the target of a contract killing, all of which were risks of his previous life.

He wanted to be around when the baby he and Linda were trying to create finally arrived. Hell, he'd even let Linda convince him to stop smoking, cut back on the beers and show up with her at the gym a few times a week. Honestly, he thought, there was no limit to the sacrifices he was willing to make.

Jon made his way through the office, giving a cursory wave to a few coworkers on the way to his cube but otherwise keeping his eyes locked forward. He greeted his computer, which upon hearing his voice logged on just in time for Maxine, the e-receptionist, to appear in the screen's tiny intercom window with a call from Paul at the Columbia paper. He popped in the tiny earpiece, asked Maxine to connect the call and murmured his name.

"Jon, Paul at the Messenger. What's the story on Senator Garland's affair with the underage strippers?" he asked without any pleasantries.

Garland. That name immediately set Jon's teeth on edge. And Paul Godfrey, originally of Vineland, New Jersey, but late of Columbia's seemingly boundless western suburbs, knew it. He knew the history. Everyone at every news org in the goddamn state – maybe the country – knew it. It was still being discussed in online forums and media gossip sites, whispered about over beers after deadlines, roared about over cocktails at parties and turned over and over by veteran editors and rookie reporters alike as they paused in the office break room. And Godfrey, the bastard, seemed to love to rub it in to Jon every time he could.

"That's alleged affair, Paul," Jon said automatically. "And the women in question are interpretive dancers, not strippers." Jon tried to hide any inflections that would show he knew otherwise. Inside, though, having to cover for the corrupt bastard as a part of his job almost made him heave his sausage biscuit.

"That's not a denial, you know."

No fucking kidding, Jon thought. I'm not here to deny, just misdirect. "Look Paul, the girls were staying with the senator and his daughter at his house in Hilton Head. They're friends of his daughter's from school. They are dance students at the university who she met in church," Jon said, sounding like he was reading from a script. He thought about giving Paul the impression he was getting something no one else had, when in fact he'd told the same story to two upstate orgs, the AP and Trump News the night before. It wasn't necessary, though. As usual, The Messenger was lagging behind so it wouldn't be the first to embarrass any of the publisher's powerful and influential friends, Garland among them.

5

It was what Jon didn't say that was important. Especially the bit about the girls meeting at the Church of the New Revelation. Oh, and then there was that part about the senator's daughter also being an exotic dancer. He also seemed to forget to mention the daughter leaving her friends alone with her father over the July Fourth weekend, their palatial beach home stocked with half a dozen sex toys, pint-sized bottles of lube, a library of porno feelies, a case of vodka and several strips of transdermal hallucinogens, stimulants and depressants. They were just minor details. But if Paul were worth a damn at his job, he'd already know those things from the State House scuttlebutt and wouldn't be depending on someone like Jon to tell him. It humbled Jon to remember that he had once been worth a damn himself and was now stuck covering the ass of the man he tried so hard to bring down.

"You know anything about a video of the weekend that might be floating around, Jon? We keep hearing rumblings about one but nothing's popped up on-line yet."

Jon had heard about it. Turned out one of the girls wasn't as churchgoing as everybody supposed and was apparently working for one of Garland's opponents in the November election. The rumor was that she had set up micro cameras in her body jewelry, so that depending on the edit, you got frightening close-ups of Garland doing things to her no one wanted to see the pasty, overweight senator doing to anyone. But at this point it was only rumor, verging on urban legend. Everyone seemed to be positive it existed but no one could actually produce it.

"Not a thing. And if I did, do you really think I'd tell you, Paul? Come on, give me some credit."

"Well, all right. Had to ask, you know. But can I go with your comments so far?"

"Sure, just don't use my name. You know the drill. Call me if you have any more questions," he said. He was interrupted before he could hang up.

"Hey, hold on. Off the record, how are things going down there, anyway?"

Jon was stunned by the question and answered carefully. "Honestly, Paul, it's not what I'm used to, but I'm doing okay."

"That's good to hear, but I tell ya', we all really miss reading your stuff around here," Paul said.

Jon softened a bit, but still wondered he was up to. "Um, thanks, Paul. That really means a lot. Tell all your folks up there I said hey, okay?"

"Will do, buddy. Be talking to you soon."

Jon sat there stunned for a moment after disconnecting. He and Godfrey had been vicious competitors since their first jobs at paper dailies, working sources and setting up exclusives to deny each other stories for almost a decade. Now he wanted to get all concerned? Jon chewed on it for a minute. What was his angle? What did he want?

Then it came to him. That bastard was showing *pity*. Son of a bitch made it sound like someone in the family had *died*. He didn't need that. He was better than that – better than Paul Godfrey or any of his punk colleagues up in Columbia would ever be, and the little worm knew it. He was just twisting the knife, and it made Jon madder than hell.

Even worse, Paul knew he could twist all he wanted. It wasn't like Jon could scoop him, or call up one of his editor friends to make sure Paul's stories stayed off the front pages for a few weeks. He was trapped. Emasculated. Powerless. In another time, it would have been a cigarette moment. Instead Jon popped two Nicachews from their bubble pack and bit down hard. His mouth went numb with the almost excruciating burst of mint as he waited for the buzz to kick in.

With no other accounts on his desk, he spent the next forty-five minutes swimming in a high-dose nicotine haze and mechanically running searches to see what anyone had to say about the lies he told the day before.

All of them picked up on the Garland story, but apparently no one was able to dig up any more than Jon chose to give them. Most were limited to saying the rumor they created in the first place was untrue and that Garland was still an upstanding member of the Senate and was not, in fact, compelled to have carnal knowledge of vodka-soaked young strippers. Being a surreptitious member of the New Revelationists, though, meant Garland was compelled by God to have carnal knowledge of just about everyone he could, and the same went for his young companions.

Jon was in a position to know such things better than anyone since the last story he'd written for the Gazette said all those things and more. It recounted, in excruciating detail, every one of the underground ties, front companies, backroom deals and shady pieces of legislation Garland had created or been a part of during his 25 years as a South Carolina senator. The highlights were his sneaky development projects. Jon had found at least three Garland-owned front companies designed to take advantage of legislation that loosened restrictions on coastal development. The kicker was that Garland introduced and helped pass the legislation.

By the time Jon's story ran on every arm of the Gazette media network – Web, TV, radio and the few printed products it still manufactured – Garland had already closed on a deal to build a resort on the formerly pristine Palm Island off Beaufort. He was also busy offering huge buyouts to Myrtle Beach homeowners who found the trifecta of hurricanes Boris, Kirsten and Nigel two years earlier had turned their third-row cottages into beachfront property. The big tip on that came from Jon's own mother, who called him to ask why a man from a development company had just offered her three times the appraised value on the family's Surf-side Beach cottage and what kind of God-awful piece of tourist trash were they planning to build in its place?

In the end, even in the face of all the evidence against him, Garland prevailed. His party controlled the Legislature, so no one was willing to bring charges against him or even investigate the claims in Jon's story. Jon's own bosses, fearing for their jobs, had turned against him, refusing to stand by their reporter in his most dire time of need.

Jon's story did manage to slow the developers' pursuit of fresh oceanfront property – his family's included – and nature itself ensured the slippery senator would stay away from Palm Island. The hurricanes had already knocked out all the bridges to the staging site, nearby Dewees Island, and it was later discovered that Palm Island was one of the last places to find the carnivorous and nearly extinct Venus flytrap. The federal government subsequently declared it a national park, leaving only one privately owned parcel – a historically significant plantation – on the island

So karma of a sort had come around on Garland, but not nearly as much as it should have, especially given the extensive misdeeds Jon had catalogued as part of his former life.

But it was useless to think about that sort of thing anymore. Now he had a new job and what he hoped would be a family to support, so he needed to focus on the big picture.

He forced himself to move ahead with his day, hoping that the tedium of lying for the rich and powerful would occupy him instead. Checking his e-mail, Jon found a message from his cohort Andre Nelson, lately of the Myrtle Beach paper. Andre was supposed to be on vacation in Jamaica, but as with so many Type A folks, he couldn't help checking in. The fact that Andre was in paradise and Jon was stuck in the office didn't make him feel any better.

"Hi, Jon. This is Andre. Tanya and I are having a great time here, but a couple of things came up that I wanted you to check on for me," he said. He was dictating into his handheld while reclined in a chaise lounge on the beach, the tiny wide-angle lens giving everything a slightly fish-eye appearance. Andre's café au lait complexion had turned even darker in the tropical sun, and the buildings of the resort behind him looked to Jon like the gates of heaven. Palm trees swayed in the breeze, and what he at first thought was some sort of interference turned out to be the ocean's roar in the background. Another figure – darker skinned and dredlocked – appeared briefly. Jon heard Andre say, "Thanks," and realized it was likely a waiter delivering drinks. Andre, he thought, you are indeed a bastard.

"I checked in and heard about the rumors going around about Garland and figured you were on it, so I was wondering if you could do a little research for me before I get back. If you could, I'd just like you to get me a list of names of other political leaders affiliated with the CNR who've come under scrutiny this year. Go ahead and make a copy for yourself, since I'm sure the news outlets are slobbering over this one and you're already getting calls. Have a great rest of the week, and I hope all is well."

"That's it, hon," Maxine said, appearing in the e-mail window. "Anything you need me to do with the message?"

"Just save it, please," Jon replied.

"You got it," the image said, winking at him before minimizing itself to the corner of the screen.

He looked at his schedule and noted that he didn't have any appointments until after lunch. He rose, tried to stop thinking about Garland or Jamaica, then crossed the hardwood floor of the cavernous Hampton DuBose and Associates offices to the reading room.

Any moisture that might have remained in his clothes from making the sweaty trip from the maglev station was instantly wicked away by the dehumidifier that kept the room at an optimum humidity for preserving old newspapers, books and magazines. Though most of the stuff in the room was on file or online somewhere, the agency took extra precautions by keeping hard copies of most of the resource material it used. Jon was looking for information on the New Revelationists to help maintain the front on the Garland account. He had some books in mind, as well as some print articles back from when the church gained its first popularity.

He scanned the titles in the "Religion" section, his head cocked at an angle he reserved these days for vintage book stores. There was an electronic click and the massive ventilation fan left over from the building's industrial days kicked on, drawing out all the contaminated air he brought in. It was like standing inside a jet engine, but the drone was perfect to drown out the thoughts that plagued him. Kneeling, he found one book he knew he could use – "Humping Towards Grace: Christianity and Paganism in the 21st Century" – pulled it from the shelf and began paging through it.

Then he felt it. A long-fingernailed hand trailed down the back waistband of his pants, over the seam in the seat, up between his legs and finally found a resting place right below where his zipper began. It sent a shiver through him and flicked an immediate switch of recognition in his mind.

"Find what you're looking for, Ashley?" he asked flatly above the noise of the fan just before it clicked off. This wasn't the first time for such surprises from his coworker. Ashley DuBose's reputation for conquering rich and influential men all over the state was legendary in some circles, and since Jon's arrival at her uncle's firm he had somehow been added to her "men to do" list.

"Come on now, Jonathan. You've been playing the good little husband since you got here. Don't you think it's about time you realized you're not going to get away without satisfying me?"

She was close, tickling his ear with tiny puffs of breath from the pronunciation of each consonant. He recognized her perfume as one Linda disliked, which made perfect cosmic sense. Still, the scent was intoxicating on Ashley, drawing Jon's mind away from the fact that he needed to remove her hand from his crotch as soon as possible.

"Aha, now we're getting through," she whispered as she felt him begin to harden. "I was almost worried married life had caused some muscles to atrophy, but it seems like everything is working just fine."

Jon reached behind him and roughly removed her hand from his crotch as he turned to face her. Despite his motivation to keep the situation from getting out of control, he had to admit that she looked particularly fine. Her boyishly cut blonde hair and fair skin were a striking contrast to his wife's dusky complexion and feminine curls. Her short skirt rose high on her toned thighs, its black material looking stark against her smooth, bare alabaster legs. Her lipstick was freshly applied, glistening a deep ruby.

"Ashley, please just give it up," he said, still holding her by her wrist. He was trying to sound firm and resolute rather than whiny and pathetic but wasn't quite sure if he was succeeding. "If I was at all interested, don't you think I would have done something about it by now?"

Jon released her and Ashley seemed to accept her defeat. She sat on the floor and pouted, her locked knees suggesting non-existent modesty. At the same time her almost completely unbuttoned blouse - a barely opaque white creation with faux jewels up the front and around the collar – slid down one shoulder to expose a full, lace-encased breast. "Shit, Jon. You know you want me and I know I could make it worth your while. You're just scared. You know the only reason people like you get married is to be safe from people like me."

"And a hell of a lot of good it did me," he said as he stood, brushing the wrinkles out of his trousers while trying to gauge the extent of his visible arousal. It was extensive enough for Ashley to take note, and a devilish look crossed her face once more. She unhooked the clasp on the front of her bra and pulled it away to expose herself to him, her nipples stiffening as they met with the cool air. She then rose up on her knees and placed her mouth precisely at the level of Jon's crotch.

"Jon, honey, there's a world of good I could do you if you'd only just let me. You'd be a happier man for it," she said as she gazed up at him, her hand now snaking up his thigh and her mouth dangerously close to the tent-pole in his trousers.

He pulled away, still not deterring her hand's journey. "I'd be a quickly divorced man for it, and I think I'd be a lot happier if you got dressed before someone comes in and finds us and we both get fired. I might hate it here, but I'd like to have this job at least long enough to clear my probation."

Her hand reached its destination and lightly grazed the hardness there, prompting Jon to shudder slightly and pull away again, this time completely.

"Mmmm. Your resolve's not as strong as you think. Admit it. I'm getting to you," she said in a girlish singsong. Now she was languidly running a finger up and down between her breasts.

God, she was good at this. He turned away and walked towards the door. Yes, she was getting to him and he was determined not to let this business go any further. Jon took a deep breath.

"Last time, Ashley. You put your clothes on now so we can both walk out of here and forget this happened," he said as he concentrated on the grain of the wood in the door.

Jon heard her sigh deeply, apparently indicating she was resigned to failure. He then heard the rustling of material and the click of her fingernails against the buttons on her blouse.

Assuming she was once again dressed, he turned to find her standing, slipping a pair of peach-colored thong panties off from under her skirt and down her long legs.

"Jon, sweetie, your intentions are good, but you know what they say about that road to Hell. I only wish you could see in your heart how much I want you," she said matter-of-factly, the satin underwear now dangling from her manicured forefinger. "And just so there aren't any hard feelings, I want you to have this little parting gift to remind you the offer's always open."

She tucked the hip-hugging part of the elastic in between the buttons of his shirt and gave his left nipple a little pinch. "Now you just go on back out there and we'll pretend like none of this ever happened," she said with mock seriousness. Jon saw what she was doing. Now that she had been rejected – and nobody rejected Ashley DuBose – she was trying to humiliate him. So this is how she works. Sleep with me on demand or prepare to have your manhood called into question. He wouldn't be surprised if right about now she was assessing whether he was gay.

Jon went to open the door but was stopped by her hand firmly on his wrist and the all-business look in her eye. "But just remember Jon. What I want I get, and I will get you one way or another."

Jon considered kneeling to gather the items he had gone in after but thought better of it. No reason to put himself on the defensive again, and he really had no idea what Ashley might do if given the physical upper hand. He had the door opened halfway before remembering there was a pair of peach panties dangling from his chest. He snatched them away, stuffed them in his pants pocket and calmly walked back into the main work area, past at least two fellow employees who looked bewildered at his stunned expression – thankfully not noticing his diminishing erection – to the lobby and out the front door.

Outside the building he found the shady spot on what used to be the warehouse loading dock where he once took surreptitious smoke breaks. Now seemed like a good time for a cigarette, but he fought the urge. He spat out his gum, popped another three NicaChews into his mouth and bit down hard. He looked at his hands and laughed at himself. He was visibly trembling. His knees were weak and he was sweating before he ever stepped out into the brutal heat of the waning morning.

Innocent flirtations he could handle. Even lighthearted come-ons were no problem. But Ashley's brutal onslaught was more than Jon could bear. Yes, Ashley was attractive. And yes, she exuded sex appeal from her pores like musk. That would be enough for some men, he supposed. Jon, however, knew he couldn't be happier than with what he already had in the form of Linda, and also knew that Linda wasn't the type to put up with the extracurricular activities Ashley had in mind.

Anyway, his appeal to Ashley would be fleeting at best. He would have been used up until he was spent or discovered, then cast aside like a toy that had lost the favor of a fickle child. Admittedly, being used up in the way Ashley planned wasn't an entirely terrible thought, but he much preferred the idea of a lifetime of happiness with Linda to a few weeks of exhausting intensity with Ashley.

Better not go back in right now. Somehow it wouldn't be as easy getting his mundane tasks accomplished knowing the one-woman sexual SWAT team was waiting just a few cubicles away. He opened the door and peered back into the airy lobby where the holographic image of Maxine sat ready to assist visitors.

"Maxine, I've got to step out for a while to visit some clients and run some errands, so if Dub asks for me could you just tell him I'll be back soon?"

"It'd be my pleasure, hon," she said. By the time she appeared on Dub's screen to pass the message along, Jon was halfway down the street to soothe his soul with caffeine and saturated fat.

The block-and-a-half trip to the old Market Street Cafe gave Jon just enough time to start trying to mentally sort out his predicament and work up a good thirst. When he arrived, he felt an immense sense of calm upon hearing the genuine, non-electronic cowbell rattle over the establishment's door.

By the standards of a tourist strolling past looking for a quick lunch, the place was a dive. The sign on the window was small and easy to miss, and the antique feel of the place wasn't the prepackaged, old-shit-on-the-wall nostalgia that came with so many chain restaurants. The café was just old, and everything about it said old. But Jon liked it that way, if only because it kept the tourists away and spared him from overhearing imported ignorance when there was plenty of local ignorance to go around.

The place was empty this morning save for the cook, a waitress who Jon knew only as Betty and an elderly gentleman in a pork pie hat and Hawaiian shirt. The old guy sat on the far stool mumbling to himself about damn Commie Cubans and how their efforts toward statehood were really a Castro-planned plot. Never mind that Castro had been dead for 15 years and that the only plots going on in Havana were for new casinos and an expanded Navy base.

As Jon sat, the man grew louder and more agitated. He then started reciting what Jon recognized as 20th century movie titles, suddenly fixing Jon with a direct gaze and blurting out in a spray of toast crumbs.

" 'Dead Man Walking!' "

"Archie, hush up," Betty said. She looked at Jon and shook her head in a way that said "poor old thing."

"'Dead Man Walking,' Sean Penn, Susan Sarandon, 1996. Three stars from Siskel and Ebert," he said before returning to his Cuba rant.

"Lord, it's bad to get old," Betty said without specifically acknowledging her other customer.

Over the grill a compact sound system played an old reggae song — "Pressure Drop" — Jon recognized by its chorus. For the moment the artist escaped him, but the beat was infectious and moved Jon to tap his fingers in time on his knee. The pressure was indeed dropping on him, and all at once, it seemed.

Betty reached into the cooler below the counter and produced one of the few vices Jon could still lay claim to – an icy, green pinch-waist glass bottle of Coca-Cola.

"Whatcha want today, baby?" She popped the cap off the bottle using an old-fashioned counter-mounted opener and placed it in front of him. She then looked at her dainty ladies watch, which seemed microscopic on her huge, coal colored arm, and regarded him suspiciously. "Kinda early for lunch, ain't it?"

"Yeah, I guess. Just some chili cheese fries, I think. I can't stay away from work too long. It looks like it's going to be one of those days."

She scribbled the order on a blank white pad and clipped it to the vent hood where the cook, a caramel-complected man as skinny as Betty was huge, was monitoring the grill and deep fat fryers.

"This early in the day and already having trouble? That's a bad sign, baby. Don't say much for what's to come."

"No, it sure doesn't. Almost makes me want to head to the beach and not come back when they start off like this," he said as he chuckled softly and contemplated the marketing genius of the Coke bottle's not-too-subtle female shape.

Jon found women like Betty, though friendly enough to make customers feel welcomed, always maintained a good-natured sense of detachment. So he was taken aback when Betty turned from shaking a basket full of fries with a truly concerned look on her face.

"Lord, child. You did have a bad time. Ain't never seen you look this down. Bad fight with the boss?"

"Worse. A woman at my office came on to me," he said, not meeting her gaze. He then held up his left hand and rubbed the thin gold band with his thumb. "Apparently this wasn't enough to ward her off."

Betty wiped down a length of the counter with a wet cloth and shook her head. "It never is, baby. Don't mean a damn thing to some people if they don't want it to. They just scoot around diddlin' every cute thing they see. She knows you're married. She knows better, too. Sounds like you got trouble to me."

"Well, honestly I don't know what the attraction is," he said after a long, cooling swig of Coke. "I mean, I've been hit on by my share of women, even after I got married. Getting stuck with women who are that forward, though, that'll just make a guy feel … helpless."

"Oh, honey, don't sell yourself short. You're a nice looking fella, and you don't even have a bad little butt for a white boy." That raised his eyebrows, knowing this woman had at some point assessed his ass. "Lemme see a picture of your wife," she said, one hand on her hip and the other leaning heavily on the counter.

Jon looked into her eyes and tried to gauge her motives as he took another drink and pulled his handheld from his pants pocket, turning it on the counter for Betty to see.

The picture he kept there was taken a few years before at Carlton's annual steeplechase. For the ladies, part of the event's tradition was wearing a new sundress and hat, and Linda wasn't one to go against traditions that involved clothes shopping. Jon caught her by surprise when he took the picture, but it looked as if it had been perfectly posed. Her dark hair flowed out from under the wide brim of the straw hat, her shoulders showing a hint of sunburn in the afternoon light. Someone must have just said something funny, because when she turned at Jon's call she was beaming, her face alight with the pleasure of reveling with close friends and a few very strong mixed drinks.

"Lord, child. That's a pretty girl. I know you fell for her hard."

"Like a brick," he said as he turned the picture around so he could look at it. "I ask myself every day what she's doing with me, but she never leaves, so I'm happy not knowing the answer."

"Child, I've gone through three husbands asking the same thing. I'm big as a house, ugly enough to scare mice and ain't got no money worth talkin' 'bout, so what's a man who's worth anything want with ol' Betty?"

The cook muttered something and she turned to pick up Jon's order, sliding it in front of him and continuing.

"It never fails. Every time one of them dies or runs off, sure as I'm standing here another one will come along right behind him. It's like they're looking for someone to take care of them before they go and they know my heart's too big to turn 'em away. Momma always said I was bad about pickin' up strays," she said with a wry chuckle as she leaned on the counter, her heavy arms crossed over the bosom of the chili stained apron.

"I don't think this woman's intentions were that noble."

"Right with you, baby," she said, lacing her thick fingers together and looking thoughtful.

"Did she show you her titties?" Betty asked straight-faced.

Startled by her candor, Jon had to struggle not to choke on the cheese and chili laden French fry he was in the middle of swallowing. Confused, he admitted she had. Betty then fired off questions with the skill of a seasoned lawyer looking at a hefty percentage of a harassment settlement.

"And you said this was in the office? Was it a small room or somewhere private?"

"Yeah, it was in the reference library. It's basically just a little room with a bunch of old books and magazines."

"Closed off from the rest of the office? Nobody else could see you? And she followed you, right?"

Jon nodded yes to each query and ate another French fry, waiting for what the woman would deduce from such sparse information. After a thoughtful pause, she suddenly tossed her dishcloth over her shoulder, put one hand on her hip and pointed a finger straight at Jon.

"Baby, you in big trouble."

"Why 'big trouble?'" Jon said with his mouth full. "She's been flirting with me for three months and I've been blowing her off the whole time. I never knew it was going to come to this."

"That's exactly the trouble, honey. You didn't stop it when you should have and now it's outta control. I'd bet my last money those other women, they hit on you on the spur of the moment 'cause you're cute and nice and they thought you might be a good lay …"

"A what?"

"I ain't finished," she said with the gravest sincerity. "This girl, she's bad news. She sat down and planned to trap you in there. She knew what clothes she was gonna wear, how she was gonna fix her hair, what color to paint her nails, what underwear she'd be wearing and how much to wax her cootchie before you rolled out of bed this mornin'."

"So what does that mean? It didn't work, that's all. She should deal with that. Jeez, what does she expect? I'm married."

"That's just it. She don't care about 'married.' For her, marriage ain't nothin' more than … Lester, whatta they call those paintings where everything's all cattywhompus?"

The cook didn't look up from his work, simply muttering, "Abstract."

"That's it, honey. Marriage ain't nothing but an abstraction to this girl. That's why she's so in a snit. She fixed herself up like filet mignon and from where she's standing, it looks like you're passing that up to go home to leftover meatloaf. Beforehand you were a challenge, but this was her big play and you shot her down and now you can bet she's feelin' some kinda way. She might've been thinkin' about Mr. Johnson down there before," she said as she pointed towards Jon's crotch, "but now that girl's workin' on revenge."

Her diagnosis complete she turned to the grill and mumbled to herself as she noisily reloaded the basket of fries. "Showed him her titties and the boy didn't crack. Ain't a woman in the world don't think she can put the mojo on a man by showin' him her titties. Somebody must be looking out for you, baby."

"Who you talkin' to, Betty," Lester the cook asked. "I hope it ain't that fella at the counter. He blew outta here soon as you turned around."

Betty turned, thinking he was joking. She found only a barely-eaten basket of fries and the screen on her pay pad blinking a $20 credit.

"Lord, keep him safe," she said as she shook her head and rang the order up, running her cash card through to collect the change and tucking it back inside her bra. "That boy's goin' into Babylon."

Jon huffed back to the office against the thick heat. As the sweat rolled down his face and back, he found himself wondering what devious plot Ashley was hatching. Several movies that might lay suitable groundwork came to mind. Unfortunately, all of them involved spurned lovers wielding kitchen knives and other assorted implements of death. Those thoughts didn't make him feel any better.

As he entered the lobby and dabbed his face dry with a hankerchief, the cool air felt more like the approach of the icy hand of doom rather than a sanctuary from the heat. Things towards the back of the building were bustling as usual, the sound of telephones chirping intermingling with conversation and the tapping of computer keys.

Maxine maintained her computerized watch, recognizing Jon the minute he entered.

"Welcome back, hon," she said.

Jon assumed the gravest, most sincere face he could and approached her station with shoulders hung low, knowing each interaction with the image was recorded. "Maxine, I'm in a big hurry. There's been a family emergency, so could you just tell Dub I won't be back for the rest of the day. Thanks."

As he turned to leave, he heard her speak again. "I'm sorry, Jon, but I have Dub on the line for you. Should I put him through?"

Jon contemplated running, but knew it was too late. The ultimate downfall of the computerized holographic receptionist was that there was no amount of flattery, flirtation or chocolate that could convince one to lie for you.

"Yes, Maxine. I'll talk to him."

Somewhere a processor whired and connected Dub's intercom to the lobby, but to Jon it looked exactly as if the fashionably retro woman behind the desk, accurate right down to the henna tint of her beehive hairdo and the beaded chain on her glasses, was pressing a button on an intercom console to accomplish the same thing.

"Jonnie! I was wondering where you were. Come on up here and see me if you don't mind. Ashley and I have a couple of things we'd like to talk to you about."

Jon cringed. Where the icy hand of doom had simply been hovering before, it was now slowly wrapping its long, cold fingers around his throat and squeezing. He had no idea what the two of them might want, but he had serious reservations about being in the same room with both of them without a lawyer present. He breathed a deep breath and made his way up the metal stairs, his footsteps echoing ominously through the huge room.

Aubrey "Dub" DuBose was the living distillation of what most from outside the south expected a southern man to be. Jon's term for the type was the "huntin'-fishin'-hey, Bo-back slappin'" man - the kind who grew up learning to hunt deer with a 30.06 and a fifth of bourbon and learning to hunt women with a 12-pack of cheap domestic beer and a foreign sports car his daddy bought him. In fact, he was the kind of man who, at 46, still called his father "Daddy."

Dub came from the well-to-do means that were afforded his father, who ran a lumber company in Dillon County. Upon graduating from Auburn University and leaving the vaguely misogynist brotherhood of the Pi Kappa Alphas, he created for himself and his appropriately lithe and blonde former Tri-Delt of a trophy wife an empire built on bullshit and obsfucation. And most disturbingly, he was the type of boss for whom Jon long ago swore he would never work.

The agency offices filled a rehabbed warehouse and were all exposed brick and hardwood floors updated with the latest in high-tech office design. Dub occupied what was once the warehouse supervisor's office, perched high above the main work area to provide the maximum view of the activity below and the least amount of contact with the worker bees. The arrangement left him free to discreetly come and go to Rotary meetings, "business" golf outings and nooners with his mistress at her Isle of Palms condo – owned as a tax write-off by none other than Hampton Dubose and Associates.

As Jon approached Dub's office, the quiet ring of the metal catwalk seemed to toll his gruesome fate. He saw through the office window that Dub was in the position he usually used to emphasize his power: Reclined in his high-backed executive chair, the buttery red leather cradling his seersucker-suited, blond-haired, six-foot frame. Dub had his feet propped up on the heavy oak desk among photos of his Stepford family – all of them appropriately blonde and tan, right down to six-month-old baby Wade – and the mementos of his many personal triumphs. Ashley was primly seated beside him on what Dub called his headshrinker chair, a monstrous leather chaise culled by his wife from the antique shops of Charleston's King Street shopping district.

When Jon knocked, Dub looked up and pretended to be surprised, then rose and motioned him in.

"Hey theah, Jonnie," Dub said as he stood, using the trumped up tobacco country accent he usually reserved only for clients whose business or background was agriculture.

Jonnie. He could barely describe to anyone how much he hated being called that. His parents spent the better part of his first five years instructing relatives and friends against using the nickname, not only because it was demeaning, but because southern men being referred to by a diminutive into adulthood had the effect of making them seem as if they were permanently trapped in adolescence. While many were, Jon didn't consider himself one of them. As a result, the only way Dub got away with it was because he was the guy who signed the checks.

As Jon closed the door Dub came around the desk to give his employee a fatherly slap on the back as he directed Jon to a chair that was a few inches shorter than it should have been. "Siddown, son," he said as he resumed his position, minus the feet on the desk. "We got a lot to talk about. How's evuthing goin' at home? That pretty wife of yours still doing that freelancing work?"

"Yeah, Linda," he said, fully aware that Dub had both made note of her physical assets and forgotten her name. "She has a piece going in Southern Home next month."

He spoke as calmly as he could. Dub was busy studying something on the ceiling above Jon's head, not really paying attention, while Ashley just sat with downturned eyes, refusing to look in Jon's direction. After a few moments of uncomfortable silence, Jon spoke again, trying to fabricate a suitably realistic lie. "Dub, is there anything in particular you need to discuss? I've got some appointments after lunch and I don't want to be too late."

"All right, I'll get right down to it," Dub said as he leaned forward on the desk and began nervously twisting his thick gold wedding band. Jon observed as the ring moved up and down Dub's finger that there was no tan line underneath. He wondered if Mrs. DuBose had noticed.

Dub looked as if what he was about to say caused him physical pain. "It's come to my attention that there's been some difficulty lately with the working relationship between you and Ashley, heah."

Jon felt every muscle in his back tense at the frightening prospect that Ashley had actually told her uncle about the library incident, but managed to cover with a serious look and a nod.

"Now, what my employees do with their personal lives is really none a' my bidness. Hell, as many of those New Revelation folks as we got runnin' around, they could be slappin' 'dermals up and down their arms and having Roman orgies in their back yards for all I know. But what goes on at home don't bother me, just as long as they show up sober on Monday, get the job done and make sure my clients and I look good. The problem, though, is when it spills over into the office. Now it'd seem somethin' between you and my niece has spilled and is making a big ol' puddle across the kitchen floor. To me it looks like we either got to clean up the mess and move on or see what other arrangements we can make."

Jon was determined to not let Ashley get away with whatever deception she was fabricating and forced his face into his most innocent look, an expression he'd perfected as a reporter when he was discovered somewhere he wasn't supposed to be. "Dub, I wish you could be more specific. I think Ashley and I have always worked very well together." He hoped she was squirming with each pleasantry he uttered.

His brow furrowed, Dub sat up and pulled a pack of Marlboros from his jacket pocket, tapped one out and lit it with a huge Chamber of Commerce desk lighter. He inhaled deeply, regarded something on the ceiling behind Jon, then exhaled a long plume of blue smoke. Before the dormant enviro-drone on Dub's desk came to life and began silently sucking up the second-hand smoke, Jon breathed in the scent of the freshly lit tobacco like the perfume of an old lover. He fought the urge to ask him for one, though.

"Okay, Jonnie. We're all grown ups heah and I don't see any reason to tippy-toe around this. Ashley said while she was in the reference library you followed her inside, snuck up on her and tried to … well, sexually assault her." Ashley broke her silence and began to cry softly, her face still turned down. Dub immediately turned to her with a concerned look and gave her a handkerchief with his embroidered monogram. "You okay, honey?"

She sniffed and nodded yes, prompting Dub to turn back to Jon looking more furious than distraught now. "Now I don't know what the nature of this relationship was before, but it seems in view of her accusation I'm faced with a coupla choices. The first one is to fire you and call the police." He pronounced it *po*-lice. "The second is to let you resign, save yourself some embarrassment and some job prospects, then beat your ass six ways to Sunday. Which would you like?"

So it had come to this, Jon thought. He had every idea he could probably beat the rap and maintain his dignity if he went with Option A, but at the same time Linda would have to be dragged into the whole mess. That he couldn't stand for, especially for such a bogus accusation. Given his slim prospects and the fact that he was getting particularly pissed about being fired twice in three months, Jon decided to throw discretion to the wind.

"Gosh, Dub. Considering you're jumping to groundless conclusions based on the accusations of such an upstanding person, you make both choices so tempting. So in view of the fact I haven't done anything wrong, I think we'll go with Option B. Consider this my formal resignation." Jon then rose in the hopes of making a hasty exit.

The grin that crossed Dub's face was the most malicious Jon had ever seen on the man. He stood and leaned across his desk on his whitening knuckles. "You don't know how glad I am to hear that, Jonnie. I was hoping to be able to defend my niece's honor all by myself."

That did it. Jon had resigned and was determined to speak his mind. After all, what was Dub going to do? Fire him? He turned back towards Dub and leaned in close.

"Honor? You must be kidding. For her, honor is putting so many notches on her bedpost that the damn thing snaps in half. Dub, the sooner you realize your niece has laid every man in this town – no, in this state – with a shred of influence you might find your friends don't make quite as many jokes about you behind your back. Because she's had your friends, buddy. I guarantee every golf foursome you play in, you're the only one she hasn't serviced. She's even had your enemies. Hell, she'd probably have their wives if she thought it would get her anywhere. Why don't we ask her?"

Ashley had turned off the water works and was now staring dumbfounded, redness rising in her face like an old-fashioned mercury thermometer. "Ashley, honey, gone down on any senator's wives lately?"

There was no response, just a small choke. Dub, meanwhile, seemed ready to erupt. Still, Jon continued. "I just want it made very clear that I did no assaulting. You ask her again whose hand was on whose crotch and see what she says. The truth is the only way I touched her was to keep her horny little paws off my equipment. I was just another on her list of conquests and it drove her absolutely crazy that I would do something so ridiculous as remain faithful to my wife rather than screwing her in the library like she so desperately wanted me to. So in the future, Dub, instead of assuming Ashley is the virgin princess you think she is, maybe you should start thinking of her as the office bitch in heat and keeping her on a shorter leash!"

Jon's bravado had gotten the better of him, the last comment sending his boss over the edge. Dub immediately rounded the desk with fists clenched in rage and his voice little more than an animal growl. Jon was ready for him, though. He wasn't a fighter – his drill instructors during his two years of compulsory stateside military service recognized that early – but the hand-to-hand combat training they required, along with three decades of well-honed cowardice and 11 years of publicly pissing people off, made him an expert at evasive tactics. As a result, Jon had only to move his head about four inches to the right to avoid Dub's approaching right hook, which slammed into the reinforced glass of the office window rather than Jon's jaw. The crunching noise included not only breaking glass but likely the sound of a few shattering fingers.

Dub looked more shocked than injured when he gingerly pulled back and stared at his limp, crimson-covered hand as if he was very disappointed in its performance. Ashley rushed to stop the bleeding with the handkerchief as soon as she realized what had happened.

Now that things had plummeted to such depths, Jon decided he couldn't let the moment pass without one final stand. While Dub stood there and watched his bodily fluids ooze from his hand, Jon grabbed the lapels of the man's suit coat, held him steady and stared him directly in the eyes.

"And Dub, my name is *Jon*."

With that Jon let Dub slump into a pale, dazed heap, turned and walked out the door.

Again the blessed cool, this time in the kitchen of his own home in Carlton. The fact that he'd made it this far without calling Linda to let her know what had happened wasn't a good start. He'd tried during the half-hour maglev ride from Charleston to go over in his head what he should say, but couldn't come up with anything better than to just tell Linda the truth. And it definitely wasn't the sort of thing he would feel comfortable discussing while surrounded by strangers on a mid-day train.

She was nowhere to be seen - he imagined she was upstairs working on the computer, no doubt on another home piece for one of the high-end home and garden magazines. He could almost hear her fingers ticking quickly along the keyboard as he leaned against the counter trying to compose himself. He imagined her sitting there, her face showing her concentration as she tapped out something clever and poetic about the Victorian furniture and oriental rugs decorating the home of some local celebrity or government personality. One reason she relished such assignments was that her subjects were entirely too rich and snooty to consider inviting Linda into their homes for anything other than shameless publicity on just how rich they were. It gave her a certain sense of superiority knowing that she needed no publicity to validate the worth of her home.

Their first apartment was so small she did most of her work in their bedroom, the computer set up in a corner they fashioned into a small office. Many nights, he would prepare for bed and sit up reading while she continued to work. That was when he learned the most about respecting another person's space and work habits. She didn't mind him being there, but he knew to stay quiet and not bother her with unnecessary conversation until she asked for it or indicated she was finished for the night. He didn't mind. Many times he would quietly put down his book and simply watch her work, relishing the pauses during which, consumed with thought, she would bite her lip or brush her hair over her left ear before resuming her typing. It was at moments like this that he wished he could return to those simpler days. Instead, he imagined that the days ahead would become much more difficult for both of them.

Jon dropped his bag into one of the chairs around the breakfast table.

"Hello," he called.

"Jon? Is that you?" Linda said from the stairs, stopping to make sure he wasn't some midday intruder.

"Yeah, hon," he said, trying to sound as if nothing was wrong. He wasn't very successful.

"Well, isn't this a surprise. How'd my handsome man

manage to get off so early today?" she said, standing on her tiptoes as he leaned down to accept a kiss, which was delicately sweet from the apple she was still chewing. "You should have called me from the maglev and we could have made some lunch plans. I'm about burned out on trying to make this latest mansion sound like something besides a testament to the owner's Napoleon complex. Everything in the place is about one-quarter larger than it needs to be."

She sat in the straight-backed chair opposite Jon, pulled one leg up and tucked it under the other thigh. He was momentarily distracted by her red soccer shorts, which were always just loose enough for him to see farther up her thigh than decorum should allow. She paused her munching to wipe her fingers on a slightly soiled T-shirt from a concert the two of them attended while they were still dating. She was barefoot and unconsciously popped her toes while she took another bite.

Jon sat across from her and leaned forward as if in prayer. "I've got something I need to tell you. Promise you won't get mad?" he said tentatively.

He looked up and saw her eyebrow arch. She momentarily stopped chewing and regarded him with a gaze that said "I know it's something bad, but I don't want him to know I know that."

"I can't promise anything," she said around a mouthful of apple. She made a motion with the apple as if to pull the information out of him. "Tell me anyway."

"Well, I quit my job today."

She was playing it cool. He knew she would be upset, but he wasn't sure how much. She continued chewing and said flatly, "And was there any particular reason for this? I mean, other than the fact that you've hated it since day one?"

Jon took a deep breath and began. Linda knew of Ashley's flirtations. Jon had filled her in early so there would never be any danger of him being accused of keeping something from her. But recounting the morning's events made him feel as if he had really cheated, even though he had done everything in his power to avoid anything approaching impropriety.

Her face betrayed what he could only call amused disappointment. "Sometimes I ask myself why in the world I had to marry such a hot hunk of a man," she said straight-faced. "Am I just going to have to send you off to a monastery to work?"

"So maybe the bad feelings I was having about Hampton DuBose weren't so off base, huh?" he said, trying to lighten the mood a bit.

"Seriously, is this going to be a problem for us? Aside from Dub wanting to beat the snot out of you, of course."

"I don't think so. Knowing Ashley for this long, there's no doubt she will have had sex with somebody today. I just know for a fact that it wasn't me. If the lawyers get into it, I'll just ask for a full genetic screen and I'll be cleared."

Linda got up to drop the apple core in the sink garbage disposer. "So what are you going to do to support me in my luxurious lifestyle now, Mr. Templeton?"

He grinned weakly. "I don't know. I thought I might try freelancing for a while."

"Perfect. That's all I need, competition from my husband, the out-of-work

PR hack." She punctuated her comment by flicking the switch on the disposal.

Jon rose and crossed to her and tried to catch her gaze, which she was doing her best to deny him. "So how mad are you?"

Linda sighed heavily. She was trying to draw the most out of whatever guilt equity she might have built up. "Not too mad. I just wish we could go through a few years without something completely screwing things up for us, that's all. I mean, first the thing with Garland and the Gazette and now this. Are you going to have an even harder time finding a job now?"

"Of course not," he said as he picked up a napkin from the holder on the counter, then placed it on his head like an old-timey paper hat. "I've got my sales pitch down: 'Would you like fries with that, ma'am?'"

"Stop it," she said, pushing him away. She was trying not to, but she couldn't help but laugh.

Finally she looked at him. He could tell by her expression that she wanted to be somewhat understanding, but felt obligated to be angry simply because it was the sort of thing she was supposed to be angry about. And there was that small matter of having one less income for a while. Yes, he thought, she should really be angrier than she is. Thank God she isn't.

"First off, you need to go to church with your mother this Sunday and say a nice prayer to Aunt Lil, thanking her for our cozy situation," she said, indicating their house.

"I'll be on the phone to Mom this afternoon. I suppose I'll have to break the news to her, too."

"Good luck with that. I'm behaving and leaving all the guilt-tripping up to her." Jon silently agreed that he was in for a maternal passive-aggressive onslaught. "And I suppose I'll be able to stand having you around the house a bit more, just as long as you stay out of my way, understand?" She was trying to sound playful, but Jon could tell she was deadly serious.

"Yes ma'am."

"Good. Now go upstairs and get changed. Since you're here I might as well put you to work," she said. As he left her side and went to collect his bag, she stopped him and regarded the front of his trousers. "Did you stop off at that grease pit this morning? You've got a huge chili stain on your pants. Come and take them off and I'll take them to the cleaners with my things. I swear. I send you to school dressed so nicely and you always come back a mess. What am I going to do with you?"

At the top of the stairs Linda went to her office - actually one of two spare bedrooms converted into her own private workspace - to continue working on her story. Jon went into the master bedroom and changed into a pair of paint-spattered and grass-stained khaki shorts and a T-shirt from a Gazette picnic several years earlier. He left the trousers spread out on the bed so he wouldn't forget to add them to the dry-cleaning pile. "Okay, hon. What do you need me to do?"

"I was going to get one of the kids down the street to trim the hedges around the back porch, but I figure now that you're desperate and destitute you might be able to do it. Is that all right?"

"No problem, my love. It's the least I can do for my sole source of financial support," he said on the way downstairs.

It was dark and cool in the tool shed, the smells mingling in a distinctive petrochemical-and-rotting cellulose sort of way, producing a scent as familiar and recognizable as his wife's perfume. Jon took a moment there to pause and be thankful he told the truth and that Linda hadn't been too upset, then slid his feet into a nearly petrified pair of canvas sneakers, took the hedge trimmer from its recharger and went to work.

When Linda appeared on the porch, he had already shaped three of the adjacent shrubs into neat flattops, each one a few inches higher than the preceding one.

"What's up, hon?" he said after switching off the noisy device, taking the moment to wipe the sweat from his brow with the back of his arm. "Not hip to the trimming job?"

"The shrubs are fine, but I would like you to tell me why there was a pair of panties in the trousers you wore to work."

"Holy shit" was the only thought his mind could form. There she stood one hand on her hip and the other dangling the strange underwear out on finger as if it were radioactive. Jon could at first only burst out in nervous laughter then fumble for a response, producing only confused guttural noises instead. How could he have been so stupid? The whole story ... He told her the whole damn story, except for the panties. And there they were, stuffed down in his pocket like a time bomb, waiting to take his honesty and explode into what seemed like an awful fabrication.

"Whose are these, Jon? They certainly aren't mine," she said as she examined them. In the midst of her inspection, she began to cry, her face remaining calm but tears flowing from her eyes like little spigots had been turned on. Then she found the monogrammed letters. What was it about that damn family and monograms? The twisted smile that crossed her mouth was one of ironic realization rather than amusement. "Oh, here we go. It has 'A.D.' monogrammed right here on the front." Then, making direct eye contact with him, as if she hadn't already broken his heart with each word she'd already spoken, said, "Gee, Jon, who could that possibly stand for?"

Her sarcasm cut into him. Again Jon could only sputter and gesture, looking very much like a sign-language interpreter going through some sort of fit, as Linda stood there looking at him as if he were something disgusting she'd just scraped off her shoe.

"Linda, I can explain about those, really..." he managed to blurt out, his insufficient words sounding only like the desperate bleating of a man who knew he was guilty as charged. Before he could say anything else, her hand was up to demand his silence, the free-flowing tears now making rivulets down her beautiful cheeks.

"No, no ... You listen to me, Jon. I have trusted you more than any other man ever since the day we met. I have always believed that you would always be faithful to me. But even fooling around on me wouldn't have been as bad as this –

as assaulting someone." She paused and bit her lip, again attempting restraint. "You know how I feel about this sort of thing, Jon. You know there's nothing worse in this world you could do." This time she failed, and the resulting sob was to Jon like the sound of his marriage dying before his eyes. "... And you lied, Jon. You lied to me and you've never done that before. You did get fired because of this, didn't you?"

"Yes ... I mean, no! I mean, yes, but it's not what you think, really. Linda, if you'll just let me ..."

"No, Jon," she said, sniffing and wiping her nose on the back of her hand. "Before you start lying again, I want you to leave. I don't want you here tonight. I don't think I can deal with it. I just hope getting into these was worth everything you've all of a sudden put us through," she said, balling the panties up and throwing them at the screen that separated them. "And frankly, you're lucky I don't call the police on your sorry ass."

Jon had been fighting back tears already, but her last comment pushed him over the edge. Again, there was the fucking nervous burst of laughter - would he ever learn to control that? - and the tears began to flow from his own eyes. He put down the trimmer and walked toward the porch's screen door. "Honey, please let me explain. I promise it's really not what you think."

"Promise? Don't talk to me any more about promises, Jon. And don't you come any closer to this house," she said. She meant business, and Jon didn't want to take any chances at making the situation worse. He stayed where he was as Linda began to sob, her face contorting and reddening into a heartbreaking mask of sadness. "You know, after all these years you are the last person I ever thought would be capable of this. Now I'd suggest you find a place to sleep tonight, because you're sure as hell not sleeping in the same house with me."

"Linda, it's nothing like that. I promise. Please, just let me explain," he pleaded, now pressing his face against the locked screen door and beating on the frame with his fist, but it was no use. Linda had already turned and walked into the house, closing the door behind her. Just when he thought she might come back out, seeing her walk towards the French doors again, he realized how strong her resolve was. A few quick motions, an electronic chirp and the house's alarm system was activated. Jon was rewarded for his honesty with one last withering glance from inside his home.

Stunned, he stood there beginning to cry himself. After a few moments his brain switched to auto pilot. He wiped his eyes, returned to the shed and hung the trimmer back in its place. His keys were in the shed hanging from a pegboard hook where he left them after unlocking the building. Jon took a long look out the shed door back toward his house, now a fortress barricaded against him, and accepted his lot. The gravel crunched beneath his feet as he walked down the driveway to the street.

"Hello, Jon Templeton. Please state your destination," the ticket terminal's holographic ticket agent said, leaving a brief pause between the "hello" and his name as it processed the information from his eye scan.

Destination? Was it absolutely necessary he have a destination? Would it really do him any good to go anywhere? He thought not, though he had a few ideas about at least one eternally hot place Linda might suggest were she here.

On his way to the maglev station he had considered several options which he might choose as his destination. He decided the only truly viable one was a hasty retreat to the family beach house in Surfside, which he knew to be empty that week thanks to an anonymous call to the rental agent. Its viability was mainly a product of it being free, unoccupied and easily accessible for Linda should she try to find him. Fat chance of that, though. Still, he wanted to give her an easy opportunity should she take leave of her senses and for some reason want to forgive him.

"Surfside Beach," he spoke to the image, which immediately responded with a barrage of times and numbers for trains, the transfer to the Holiday Express in Florence and his anticipated arrival time at the Surfside station. The transaction then completed, Jon took his receipt and repaired to a row of empty plastic seats where he proceeded to lie down and moan quietly to himself.

He was still operating in a haze, not quite grasping that what he always considered a wonderful marriage might very well have ended just a short time before. Out of the corner of his eye he caught a small boy pointing to him and posing an unheard question to his mother. She quickly told him that it wasn't polite to point and that it was none of their business if that man in the dirty clothes was sick.

His train to Florence was as sparsely peopled as the station, allowing Jon to resume his reclined position and the accompanying moaning.

While waiting for his transfer at the Florence terminal, Jon attempted to start up a wordless game of tic-tac-toe with the boy beside him. That is until the child's mother, who was engaged in a heated French-English conversation with one of the human ticket agents, spotted Jon and ran toward her child saying "non, non," dragging the youngster with her so she could continue her argument.

Feeling even worse over his appearance as some rail-riding molester of Quebecois children, Jon shuffled to the terminal duty-free shop and bought a twenty-ounce Coke and a pint bottle of Captain Morgan. In the men's room he poured half of the soda into the sink, refilling the bottle with rum and giving it a little swirl to mix the booze. He returned to his seat and quietly swigged as he waited for his train.

The Holiday Express, in contrast to his earlier train, was a cacophony of throaty hawking noises and trilled Rs, which reminded Jon why he so hated the obsessively correct pronunciation demanded by his high school French teacher and later began to dislike the culture from which the language sprang. It used to be the Canadians would reserve their visits south for March and April when no right-thinking Southerner would venture into the ocean. Nowadays, though, the Quebecois took advantage of every break in the dispute with the radicals along the New York border to swarm into the U.S. on holiday. The only noticeable differences were the timing of the visits and the evidence of heavy armor on their Winnebagos and Itascas.

The last image in his mind as he drifted into an inebriated nap was that of a fat Quebecois woman in a thong bikini arguing with a Myrtle Beach high-school student manning a McDonald's counter. The teen, who looked suspiciously like Linda, was aggressively enforcing the ubiquitous "No shirt, no shoes, no service" rule, if only to save herself from the sight of the cellulite-pocked gargantua trying to order "*un* Big Mac."

At the announcement of Surfside as the next stop Jon jerked awake, looking around quickly to remind himself of where he was. With some disappointment, his new reality settled in. He attempted to compose himself a bit before the train stopped, but the rum-and-Coke mixture left a peculiar taste in his mouth, which he decided could only be alleviated with more of the same. When the train slid to a stop outside the hotel lobby Jon staggered off, the half-full rum bottle making an obvious liquor bottle-shaped bulge in his shorts pocket. In a remote corner of the passenger platform he repeated the emptying and filling process. He weaved down the stairs to street level and then to the beach, trying to look like he had his wits about him when he had in fact left them somewhere between Carlton and here and wasn't really sure at what stop they had disembarked.

The warm sand and blinding sun were at once comforting and devastating. While he always felt most at home with the roar of the ocean in his ears and the humid breeze blowing in off the water, this place also reminded him of the many times he and Linda had vacationed here together. Both enjoyed simply sunning and reading during the day, occasionally pausing to take a dip in the ocean. Linda termed the swim breaks "the pause that refreshes," both after the old slogan for Jon's favorite drink and because the two of them had more than a few times ended up in a surreptitious aquatic coupling in view of several dozen sunbathers. In the evenings, they would go out to eat most times, with Jon occasionally boiling some crabs or shrimp. If they were there with friends, they would go enjoy some of the nightlife that struck a happy medium between the manufactured pap of "family" promoters and the sanctified sex of the Church of the New Revelation.

Regardless, Jon remembered this place for the good times they had here together, and he found it making the already bleeding wounds in his soul just a bit deeper.

The thin sliver of beach was packed as he passed the few high-rise hotels that were being rebuilt. Occasionally he came upon a bare spot where no one had set up camp, warned off by signs erected after the previous year's hurricanes sucked the first three rows of houses and hotels out to sea. Many of the buildings' foundations and broken pilings remained, and the signs alerted beachcombers to the dangers of protruding cinderblocks and splintered posts. It was the same series of storms that resulted in the tripling in value of the Templeton beach house, which had previously been on a bad lot on the fourth row. As Jon later explained to his wife and mother, one hotel owner's $145 million loss is a beach cottage owner's $5 million gain.

Jon gradually began to spot landmarks indicating he was nearing his destination. It was about time, too, since the intense sun combined with the effect of the alcohol in his system was doing nothing to help him along his way. He finally decided to stop for a moment under an abandoned rental umbrella before he made the last leg. As he took another swig of the warming Coke-rum mixture, he though he heard his name being called out by a female voice.

Another sip, and there it was again. He turned and looked up the beach, spotting someone calling his name and waving. Walking toward her, he realized it was Regina Holiday, whose grandmother lived in the cottage next to Jon's. The last time he had seen her was just before her senior year of high school. Jon and Linda had always assumed Regina was so hopelessly shy and plain and uninterested in boys she would have no hope of surviving in the bustling academic and social community she was hoping to join at the University of South Carolina once she graduated.

Jon's first up-close glimpse of the young girl immediately blew his assumptions into millions of very tiny pieces. What had been a plain wallflower of a girl had turned into a self-confident and beautiful woman. Her mousy, boyishly cut hair had grown out into a honey mane that seemed to radiate in the intense sun, and the braces she had worn entirely too long had been removed to reveal a smile as straight and white as a Steinway's ivories.

She was lying on her back and propped up on her elbows, her tanned torso serving as a toasty brown and wholly waxed platter on which the sun feasted, with her various sunning accoutrements spread out around her on a USC beach towel. A precise measurement might have indicated her bikini covered more actual surface area than many others on the beach, but the two-inch crucifixes cut out of the sides of the tops and directly in the middle of the bottoms made the suit a hundred times more provocative.

Even in his inebriated state, Jon recognized their significance. She had joined the Church of the New Revelation, probably as part of one of the group's active on-campus recruiting drives, and it had made a very visible difference in everything about Regina.

"Hey Jon. I didn't know y'all were down here this week," she said as she rose and, before he could stop her, gave him a warm hug. She smelled of botanical shampoo and sunscreen. He found he was at a loss as to where to put his hands to return the hug. He settled for a few fatherly pats high on her back. "It seems like forever since I've seen you guys."

"It's just me this weekend, actually," Jon said, thrown by the unexpected display of affection. "Linda had to go out of town for a story, so I decided to take a couple of days off." He tried not to look as drunk and dejected as he felt telling such lies. He was having trouble standing, so he thought intentionally sitting in the sand next to Regina's spot would be far less embarrassing than collapsing unintentionally a few moments later. She followed suit, but Jon could tell she noticed all was not right. "It has been a while since we've seen you, hasn't it? It looks like college life is agreeing with you."

"Absolutely," she said as she crossed her legs yoga-style and leaned toward Jon, giving him more of a view of her cleavage than he felt comfortable with. "My grades were pretty good the first semester, so that helped a lot. Of course, one of my classes was Human Sexuality, so that made the homework a lot more fun." She placed a delicate hand on his knee to emphasize her point.

Jon, in the middle of another swig from the bottle, almost allowed the rum and warm, flat Coke to fill his lungs rather than his stomach in surprise, prompting him to cough violently to keep from suffocating.

Regina obligingly slapped him on the back to help him get his breath back, then grinned at him mischievously.

"Did I embarrass you, Jon? I'm sorry. It's just that I've become so much freer with my sexuality since I started going to church with the CNR group on campus. Sometimes I forget not everyone's as used to hearing people be so open."

"No, that's okay," he said, the color gradually returning to his face. "I know all about the church. We handle a lot of its marketing and PR at my firm. It's just that I never really figured you for a potential convert. I guess that was my mistake. I actually picked up on it before because of the cutouts in your suit. Is that something new?"

She had extracted a bright yellow plastic spray bottle from her beach bag and was pumping a fine mist of water over her arms and chest, as if to somehow accentuate what Jon had already taken very detailed inventory of.

"Yeah, isn't it great? Sister Veronica just came out with these this year. She said she came up with the idea during one of Reverend Whitaker's sermons. He says the secret to maintaining holy grace is to channel all your lust back into the church where everything is done in an atmosphere of love and forgiveness. That's why she designed these with the cross cutouts. She says nothing helps your partner keep his mind on Jesus more than having a sign of His love tanned on your primary erogenous zones."

"Well if the services are as - inspiring - as I've heard, I guess that sort of thing might come in handy," he said, feeling the effects of the booze intensify as his brain seemed to float around inside his skull like the bobber in a toilet tank.

"Mmmm, yeah. They definitely do. With all the music, the dancing and the sacraments I can hardly make it through half a service without dragging someone off to the meditation rooms," she said, suddenly looking tingly and excited. The water mist had beaded into tiny droplets on her skin, shiny with tanning oil, accentuating the curves which seemed to have become much more pronounced since he last saw her. "Once I got so filled with the spirit I took two guys from my campus group to a chamber at the same time. We really did feel God's power that night."

Thoughts of the spirit, not to mention her two male friends, filling someone he earlier thought of as a relative innocent made Jon's head swim even more. He thought it best he leave rather than to continue contemplating young Regina sharing her body in the name of the Lord. He got up with some difficulty, steadied himself and told her it was very nice to have seen her and he was sure they'd see each other again before he left.

She then surprised him by standing and giving him another powerful hug and, this time, an enthusiastic, tongue-filled kiss on the lips.

"Oh, Jon. You've always been such a sweetie, and I'm so glad you're here. If you feel like it, our services are Saturday nights at nine, but the fellowship portion starts at seven. I like it when I come to stay at Grandma's. Then I can go to the big service at the Ocean Cathedral and see Reverend Whitaker preach. He's incredible, and Sister Veronica is really hot," she said with a wink, letting a finger delicately trail down the length of his arm from where it had rested an uncomfortably eternal few seconds on his shoulder. "I'd be really glad if I saw you there."

"Thanks Regina. I'll certainly keep that in mind," he said, gently breaking the clinch she didn't seem eager to leave. He then said his goodbye and hurried the rest of the way to the cottage. Once inside, he tried to purge his mind of images of Regina and her multiple "meditation" partners and collapsed on the battered naughahide couch. He swallowed the contents of the Coke bottle and the remainder of the rum, then drifted into a noisy unconsciousness.

Mako Nikura couldn't breathe, and the tension in the air of the Nikura International board room — the board room from which he would soon be expected to lead his father's company — didn't make him feel any better. The suit and tie they had stuck him in were more confining than any neoprene wetsuit he'd worn by choice, and the air in the building was stuffy and recycled. He could just imagine the army of microbes, grown strong and virulent in the condensation of the building's climate-control system, gathering along the lines of his immune system readying their attack.

He wished they'd never found him, but it was a little late for wishing now.

He almost regretted ever trying to find out what happened. After a friend told him about seeing the story about the bombing on NewsLink, Mako did something he rarely ever did – he checked the news. He had to, since the word of many of his friends was usually well intentioned but not always reliable. Besides, the last thing he wanted was for some plastic-haired TV geek telling him as part of some "every hour, on the hour" update that his dad had died.

S
I
X

Since he didn't own a FlexReader, he had to buy one of the cheap disposable ones they had at the Quick Mart down on the corner. Ten bucks for the reader and a buck seventy-five for the download later, he watched the pixels form themselves into a front page. But in Florida, his father's death wasn't front page news. It took him clicking through to the National page before he got anything, and even then the story was buried under another about some guy named Zabarra whose work as a labor activist in South Carolina's tobacco country got him gunned down in broad daylight. When he found out it was true — the story was thorough enough to include a photo of the mangled pile of metal that was his father's private Mercedes — he reviewed his options.

The first was to hide, easy enough considering the marginal existence he already led among some of the best and brightest malcontents on Florida's Atlantic coast. The second was to continue as if nothing happened and let them find him, which he knew they could do with almost blinding speed. The third was to show up at company headquarters in Philadelphia and accept the CEO position his dad had attempted to groom him for over the last fifteen years.

He opted to wait, and just as he expected, the company goons showed up at four the next morning. Yoshi was standing in the darkness at the foot of his pallet. The huge, ponytailed security chief had gained entry to the apartment without waking any of the others sprawled like a human minefield on scattered mattresses and blankets on the floor in the front room.

He wouldn't have known Yoshi was there himself if Dina, who he'd met at a surfing competition in St. Augustine the previous weekend, hadn't gotten up from their makeshift bed to pee. When she returned from the bathroom, she was met by Yoshi standing over him like a fierce temple statue, prompting her to make a small, frightened noise. Mako was awake immediately, motioning for the half-naked and trembling Dina to come to him after he recognized Yoshi.

"Don't be scared. He's a friend of mine," he said, using "friend" in the broadest possible interpretation – that being "not an enemy."

"I have to go away for a while, okay?" he whispered to her, holding her and stroking her hair, bleached golden from long hours of monitoring surfers along the Florida coast. "I'll be all right, and I'll try to be back soon. If anybody asks, tell them I left here by choice. Don't worry about me." He then kissed her softly, pulled on pair of baggy shorts, a T-shirt and nylon sandals and followed Yoshi back through the room of prone, snoring figures.

He was driven to a small airstrip where a company jet waited, its engines already whining. Once inside, Yoshi pointed to a cabin at the rear of the fuselage and told him to change into the clothes he would find there. He was also instructed to slick back his bangs, which dangled down to the high cheekbone on the left side of his face, and keep his topknot tied. No questions were asked. Mako knew where they were going.

Stepping inside the private cabin he found it was roomier than he expected, given his gangly, almost absurd height. That and an inborn skepticism for authority were compliments of his Caucasian mother. The height his dad forgave him for, but the skepticism was a constant source of irritation. It was after his mother's death when Mako, fifteen and fresh from the company school in Japan, disappeared.

At first he didn't know where to go. Ocean and the earth crumbling beneath it were rapidly reclaiming California. Central America was tempting, but his ambiguous politics and distaste for violence would surely arouse suspicion there. So he chose Florida, at first teaching himself to hustle and scam well enough to survive, then deciding to turn his talents to something more constructive and lucrative — surfing.

He managed to live by doing delivery work – both legit and not – and winning the occasional surfing competition, saving his substantial company allowance, which accrued quietly in Switzerland, for emergencies. He used the money mostly to help friends on the skids. A little here for the guy who lost his board using it as a bullet-proof shield when the Costa Rican regulars thought he might be working for a drug cartel. Some for a buddy's girlfriend to get an abortion so she wouldn't have to explain how the baby wasn't his (and how the father could have been any of four of his housemates). Usually no more than a few hundred at a time, and always very quietly. The last thing he needed was to be thought of as the First National Beach Bum Savings and Loan.

Hanging in the jet's compartment was a charcoal gray Italian suit with subtle blue pinstripes, a starched white shirt of Egyptian cotton, silk designer tie, leather belt, dress socks and leather shoes, which the goons hadn't even had the courtesy to break in for him. Exactly the kind of outfit he would never wear. As if to reinforce that thought, as soon as he had the socks on and the top button of the shirt fastened he felt himself being closed in upon. At that moment he knew it would be a long hour before they got to Philadelphia.

Yoshi didn't look happy with what Mako had tried to do with his hair, but Mako didn't care. He silently watched dawn break over the Chesapeake, the sun glinting off the raked wing as they dropped out of sonic and prepared to land at yet another private airstrip somewhere in Delaware. From there, he was hustled behind the tinted windows of a company aircar limo, which would speed them into the city in a little under ten minutes. Inside, Yoshi scanned the morning shows for developing news of the bombing.

"I thought for sure you'd be in on this one yourself, Yosh," Mako said, trying to force some conversation out of the stone-faced man. "Getting too old for all that double-oh-seven shit?"

Yoshi, expressionless as always, flipped back to NewsLink, typed a series of subject cues into the keyboard to alert him if something pertinent should be mentioned and then muted the sound.

"My instructions were to find you first, then allow the proper authorities to investigate the incident," he said as he stared ahead, seemingly studying the windshield in front of him for his voice cues.

"No kidding? So when did Dad start letting the proper authorities do anything? He forget to pay somebody off? The mayor? Hey, maybe it was your old buddies in the Yakuza? He always liked having the bully boys on his side, anyway."

Yoshi suddenly looked as if a small rodent had crawled into his mouth and died. "I see your respect for your father has not increased with his untimely death. Perhaps you will not run the company as well as he thought you might."

"Perhaps I'm not going to give myself the chance to find out," Mako said, staring out the dark window as the early morning maglevs, full of commuters oblivious to his plight, made their way into the city below. He almost wanted to join them in their bland existences of waking up, going to work, coming home and sleeping then doing the same thing over again. It would have made things so much easier if he had been born into that life instead, he thought.

Now he was sitting in an over-stuffed swivel chair upholstered with the hide of some unfortunate livestock animal, suffocating as he listened to some chalk-stick company lawyer whose name he couldn't remember drone on about shareholders and boards of directors and controlling interest. The fellow, who someone had yanked out of bed upon Mako's arrival, might as well have been reading from the phone book. All Mako could think about was getting out of the oppressive room and back into some real clothes.

Finally the lawyer took a breath.

"So basically what this document means is that in the event your father dies or is somehow unable to conduct the affairs of the company as a result of death, injury or mental illness, all the controlling shares of stock go to you, Mako Nikura.

So in effect, you are now the primary stockholder of one of the largest multinational corporations on the globe. Of course, as I'm sure your father discussed with you, he also made sure it would be very easy for you to replace him as the head of the company. I've spoken with the members of the board of directors, and they've indicated they will be willing to hear any presentation you would like to make on the subject."

Mako steepled his fingers and pursed his lips and tried to look like he gave a damn. He spun the chair around and stood to look out the picture window at the bustling expanse of the City of Brotherly Love. Below, the mirrored roof of the neighboring skyscraper reflected the early morning sunlight back up to the heavens, from where his mother was no doubt gazing down on him wondering what he would do. What was left of her body was in a memorial park in the suburbs, soon to be joined by the ashes of his father. Apparently, there was just enough left of him after the car bombing to cremate.

Farther below, he spotted the tiny figure of William Penn standing atop the old City Hall building. Mako remembered his father telling him how buildings in Philadelphia once couldn't be built higher than Penn's statue. Later in life, he saw a movie in which the characters discussed how, if viewed from the correct angle, the rolled document Penn held appeared to be a less than impressive erection. The two moments then became eternally connected, Mako never again being able to think of William Penn without wondering who was the first to exceed the limits of the state's founder and his sad little boner.

"As of the end of last quarter, what was the total net worth of Nikura?" Mako asked, still gazing out the window.

The lawyer muttered something quickly, waiting a nanosecond for the requested information to appear in the lens of his glasses. "Would that be including global holdings or just U.S.?"

"Don't waste my time, Skippy," Mako said, trying to project his sneer through his voice.

"Spivey, sir," said the lawyer after nervously clearing his throat.

"Right, Skippy. Just give me the grand total."

Spivey muttered some more. "As of March 31 of this year, Nikura's net worth was calculated at $983 billion and change."

"And the Costa Rican GNP for last quarter?"

"Sir?"

"Yes?"

"Would that be with or without consideration for the drug cartels?"

Mako laughed to himself. "With, of course. Can't leave an entire segment of the economy out of our calculations, now can we?" The fashionable drugs came and went, but cocaine and its many derivations somehow remained eternal.

"Um, that comes to about $23 billion," Spivey said after another quick burst of muttering. "That's just an estimate, though. None of the cartels actually release their financial information."

Mako scanned the city below once again and saw it in a much different light. Richer than a fucking country. Who would've ever thought he'd end up like this, after years of pissing on everything his father believed in. Here he was, forced to run an organization that stood for everything he thought was wrong with the world, and with no way to change it without putting half the planet's work force on the street. He might not have known much about global finance, but half a semester of economics before he ducked out of school had taught him that much.

Mako turned quickly and looked the lawyer in the eye, which caught the nervous fellow off guard.

"Skippy, if my father was sitting in this room and asked you if you thought I could run this company well enough to keep it from going into bankruptcy, what would you tell him?"

The little man cleared his throat again and cut his eyes towards Yoshi, who sat silently in the corner as if none of this was really going on.

"Being honest, sir?"

"Being brutally honest, Mr. Spivey."

Spivey locked eyes with Mako and seemed to summon all the courage he hadn't expended when whoever called him upstairs told him what he would be doing there. The guy was obviously not used to operating at this level.

"I'd tell him I had all the faith in the world that you would quite effectively run this company into the toilet, sir."

By his expression, the statement even seemed to surprise Yoshi, who made a profession of not being surprised by anyone or anything. That sight prompted Mako to burst into hearty laughter.

"Good answer, Skippy! You'll be executive material before you know it," Mako said, looking elated. He crossed the room and stood behind Spivey, one hand on the little man's shoulder and the other reaching out before them on an imaginary horizon. "Just think about it. Mister...mister what?"

"Jerome," he squeaked.

"Mr. Jerome Spivey, vice president of legal affairs. Nice, plush office with lots of Argentine leather. A harem of assistants with nice legs and really tight little asses. And power. I'll tell you what, my man, that's what sets the girls on fire. You do like girls, don't you?"

"Well … Yes, of course."

"And all it takes is to keep being honest. Just like a minute ago. Keep that up and you'll be up that corporate ladder before you know it."

Spivey sat dazed, still staring out at the invisible horizon at his dazzling future with Nikura International.

"Now you just keep thinking happy thoughts. Yoshi, you can sit tight. I'm just going to visit the executive washroom."

As the wood-paneled door slid open, Mako called over his shoulder. "And keep rattling off those dollar figures, Spivey. I don't know about you guys, but all that money talk got ol' William Penn down there a little excited."

After the door sighed closed behind him, Mako immediately pressed the "Lock" key on the small keypad on the wall, then turned to the assistant seated at a low kiosk in the center of the suite.

"Can I borrow this for a second," he said, his hand already on the heavy, molded plastic tape dispenser. He said thank you without giving her the chance to reply and bashed it into the keypad, sending tiny chips of plastic shrapnel across the room.

Returning the now damaged tape dispenser to its spot on the desk, Mako spotted a ballpoint pen coated with a rubber grip. He plucked it from its holder and stabbed it into the damaged control panel, where it sent up an eruption of blue sparks. He then returned the partially melted pen to its previous location.

"Sir, I really don't think..."

"Oh, that's okay. I really don't think, either. I find things run much smoother that way," he said with his most ingratiating smile. "May I borrow your intercom?"

"Uh, yes. I suppose."

"Then open a hailing frequency, Lieutenant. We're going to try to negotiate with these creatures."

The assistant grinned suspiciously and pressed a button on her desk console, prompting an absurdly fish-eyed image of Spivey and Yoshi to appear on her computer screen.

"Excuse me, guys. I hate to disturb you while you two look like you're having so much fun, but I've got to tell you, Spivey, those are the swankiest johns I've seen in a long time. My first apartment wasn't that big, and I shared it with four people."

After noticing Mako's image on the conference room's central display screen, both men moved closer and into a more normal field of vision. Neither laughed at his joke.

"Anyway, Spivey, are we still being honest with each other?"

"Oh, absolutely, sir," the lawyer said enthusiastically. Getting a more close-up view, Mako noticed the man must have had a grotesque case of acne as a youth. No wonder he preferred being stuck down in legal.

"Good, because in that case I don't feel so bad about telling you I've locked you both in the conference room for the time being. Yoshi, I know this is kind of humiliating for you, being head of security and everything, but Father always said a little humility was good for the soul. Mr. Spivey, I'd like you to send my regrets to the board of directors and tell them I won't be taking the CEO spot, but I would love to keep my majority interest in the company. I'd also like the senior vice president to continue running things, since she seems to be doing such an excellent job. You can also continue to deposit the same amount each month in my personal account, if you don't mind."

Mako stepped back from the screen to finish, then remembered something he forgot to add. "By the way, Yoshi, I'd appreciate it if you didn't try to find me again. And Spivey, I'm making you VP of legal. Have a nice day, guys."

He pressed the button marked "Drop" and the image of the two bewildered men disappeared.

"Mako, right?" the assistant said as he stood up from ending the call. "Your father always told me you were a troublemaker."

Even though she was sitting, Mako could tell she was tall. She was in her early thirties, her white-blonde hair cut in a neat, short, executive style that revealed an elegantly shaped alabaster neck. Though she, like Spivey, was one of the Chalk People, he found himself regarding her pale, lithe form with deep appreciation.

"You worked for my father?"

"More like I did your father's work. I'm...well, was his personal assistant, Andrea Martin."

"Oh, man..." His voiced trailed off. Suddenly all the flip antics seemed to mock his father in the face of this woman whose sadness, though well hidden behind her professional mask, was clearly evident.

"It's okay, really. It's just been a little quiet around here for the last day or so. I keep thinking I'm going to see your father walk in with a flower for my desk," she said, concentrating on controlling her breathing so she wouldn't cry, the tears filling her eyes like water running onto sapphire. Mako had noticed the yellow rose next to her computer terminal, and now realized it had already dropped two petals around the circular base of the narrow bud vase.

"I'm just having some trouble reminding myself that won't be happening again." She inhaled deeply and dabbed at an eye with the corner of a tissue, then tried to smile. "But that's my problem. How are you doing?"

"Hard to tell right now. I was too busy getting scooped up by the corporate commando squad to think too much about it. I guess it's kinda hard for me to believe the old man's gone, too. Now I'm just trying to figure out where to go from here." He chuckled at the absurdity of it all. "One thing for sure is that I have no desire to run this company. I think leaving it to me was father's idea of a sick joke."

"Your father missed you very much, Mako. He was always disappointed you didn't have any interest in the company. He just wished you had found something more … legitimate to do with your life. I think he felt that for your mother's sake more than his own. I know you didn't agree with many of the things he did, but he really did love you."

Mako hadn't thought much about his father at all in the last few years, content to live without acknowledging his connection to Nikura International or the man who ran it, and he found the conversation quickly getting too intense for his low tolerance for emotion.

"Yeah, well, that's all old news now, isn't it? We'll just have to leave the rest of the questions up to the authorities. I appreciate the use of your desk supplies, Andrea, but I think it's time I headed back to my illegitimate life. Good luck," he said as he turned to walk towards the elevators.

To his surprise, Andrea followed him, a large silver-colored envelope in one hand. She gripped him firmly by the forearm with the other just before he could press the "down" button.

"Mako, I don't think you understand what's happening here. Yoshi has been forbidden to investigate this. I'm sure he told you that. But the problem is that if it's left up to the authorities, they're not going to find anything. They'll say it was some neo-Luddite nut or random violence by a white power gang, but they'll never really get to the bottom of it."

"So what do you expect me to do about it? You seem to have the mistaken impression I care about what happens to this company," he said, trying unsuccessfully to release himself.

"Maybe so, but I know you're wondering what happened to your father as much as I am, and damn it, somebody's going to find out the truth." Her eyes were full of tears now, the redness growing around them in tiny increments, the tightness of her grip increasing like that of a blood pressure cuff. "And my friend, you've been nominated."

She held up the envelope for him to see. "Your father had me checking on some things a few weeks before he died, and I think he might very well have known who killed him. Everything I collected is here. There are no copies. The police won't get it, and as much as he might try, that little shit uncle of yours won't get it either. I'd give it to Yoshi, but he was crammed so far up your dad's ass he won't even defy him after he's dead. Instead, you've got it," she said as she handed it to him, holding it out until he took it. "What you do with it now is your business. I just have to convince myself you're going to do the right thing."

She released his arm, the blood once again flowing to the fingers that had been gradually growing numb. He shook it to speed the process. "I don't know what you expect me to do. Other people get paid to do this sort of thing. I don't even know where to start."

She reached around him and pressed the elevator button, giving him a gentle nudge into the heavily paneled car once it arrived with a hydraulic whoosh.

"You can start by thinking about somebody besides Mako. It's time to do what's right," she said as she wiped tears from her face with the tips of her fingers. Then she laughed, as if the absurdity of the situation was finally sinking in for her. "Now get out of here so I can call building maintenance to rescue our head of security."

"But what if I can't find anything?"

"Your parents don't care, Mako," she said as the door began to close. "All that matters to them now is that you tried."

39

If Jon Templeton had been wearing a watch and had the strength to look at it, it would've said 6:03 a.m. The sudden burst of sunlight from over the Atlantic horizon was an adequate substitute, telling him that whatever time it was, it was too damn early to be awake.

Gradually the light bled through his eyelids and managed to struggle past his retina and on to the optic nerve, where dazed neuroreceptors sluggishly transmitted the information to his brain, still woozy from the effect of the previous day's rum intake.

During the night Jon had slid from his reclined position on the couch to an absurd fetal pose on the cottage's coarse carpet, the emptied bottle of rum lying beside his face. That was, of course, the worst place it could be.

Jon stretched and breathed deeply, the scent of the few drops of liquor left in the bottle activating the part of his brain that handled retching and vomiting, sending him crawling with half-opened eyes toward the master bathroom, where he planned to be violently ill. Then all was blackness.

Jon awoke again at 10:23 a.m. between the cool, clean sheets of the bed he neglected to use the night before. He was content to lie with his eyes closed listening to the muffled sound of the ocean outside. For reasons he couldn't quite remember, he felt as if his entire body had been put through a meat grinder. He tried to recall what he and Linda might have done the night before to warrant such a brutal hangover, but memory wasn't serving him too well yet. Instead of focusing on last night's drinking, he chose instead to attend to this morning's snuggling.

Lying on his stomach, he reached over to Linda's side of the bed, expecting to feel the smooth skin of her thighs or the thin cotton of her favorite nightshirt. If she felt up to it, she'd murmur softly and let him wake her with soft kisses and caresses, then they would slowly make love before he got up to get their breakfast.

But there was no one there. Jon opened an eye and saw that Linda's side of the bed didn't even seem to have been slept in. He called to her and, hearing nothing, sat up. His head throbbed. Apparently what they had done the night before involved him being kicked in the temple by a bull.

Then it came to him, the pain prompting memory to come crashing down on him like a series of bank safes dropped from thirty stories by some malevolent cartoon character.

Thump! Gee, did you forget about Ashley trying to make you another notch in her increasingly scarred bedpost? Wham! Oh, and don't forget about your job. That went down the toilet right after Ashley accused you of raping her and your boss tried to deck you. Squash! And by the way, your wife probably still thinks you

S
E
V
E
N

are a lying, sexually deviant son of a bitch. Too bad you have very little evidence to the contrary.

And as always happened in cartoons, he wasn't killed mercifully by the first safe, only left bruised, bewildered and accordion-shaped.

Jon lay back down and covered his face with his hands, instantly recalling all the ugliness of the day before. His eyes went to the bedside phone. No messages. Damn. He was really in the shit.

"I should call," he said out loud. But what good would that do? It had been fewer than twenty-four hours, and it was unlikely Linda's seething had subsided enough for them to have a rational discussion. He would give her more time, hoping that she would at least be somewhat curious about how feeble his explanation might be.

Getting vertical wasn't the ordeal he'd expected, but it wasn't a picnic. After a moment to stabilize himself at the bedside, he shuffled into the kitchen. Nothing was left in his stomach, but he still wanted to avoid anything that might prompt further evacuation. Breakfast was a glass of water and three ibuprofin. From the kitchen he spotted the rum bottle lying on the floor, a tiny puddle of liquor left on the carpet. He downed the water and tried not to think about the remaining booze in case his body decided to grant him a case of the dry-heaves on top of all of his other discomforts.

The water was just what the doctor ordered, so he had some more as he thought about his next move. He was inclined to keep a phone handy so Linda could easily reach him. On the other hand, he wasn't sure if that would be any time soon. Looking out the ocean side of the cottage, he could see it was a beautiful day. Hotter than hell, probably, but the sky was perfectly clear and there was just enough of a breeze to kick up small breakers along the sand. The beach would help him think. It would provide some clarity. And if there was anything he needed in his addled state, it was clarity. Just in case, though, he clipped the phone to his waistband. No reason to further endanger his marriage because of laziness.

On the screened porch he grabbed the folding chaise beach chair usually claimed by Linda. The salt-cured boards of the walkway down to the beach already felt like hot rails as Jon walked barefoot to the beach, so much the better to punish himself for ... well, everything for which Linda thought he needed punishing. It was more crowded than when he had arrived the afternoon before. This morning the thin sliver of sand was covered with acres of oily, tanned bodies, frolicking children, umbrellas and colorful pop-up shelters. Just at the wave line, a dreadlocked surfer paddled away from shore, his muscles taut with each stroke into the waves. Their worries were few compared to his. Those sunning were probably occupied with nothing more than improving their tan lines, while the children's main concern seemed to be sitting in tidal pools and seeing how much sand they could trap in their bathing suits. Jon and Linda had hoped by this time next year to be watching their own child collect sand in his suit, but that was about as likely now as Jon giving birth to the child himself.

Practically blinded — his sunglasses were sitting on his dresser back in Carlton, assuming Linda wasn't in the process of destroying everything that was his — he set up the chaise and sat, his body angled dangerously toward the intense sun. The heat and slight breeze served to clear his mind as they always did, and as a result Jon painfully remembered all the events of the previous day. Upon reflection, they seemed even worse than he recalled. Under Ashley's accusations, he lost his wife, who was surely visiting a lawyer at this same moment. His job was little more than a memory, which wasn't much of a disappointment aside from the loss of a regular paycheck. He was likely once again the subject of a series of rumors far more extraordinary than the truth.

Jon could feel his skin burning already. His time at the beach had been minimal this summer, with only the Memorial Day weekend and a week over the Fourth to build anything resembling a base tan. The umbrella was in the storage room in the garage under the cottage. It wouldn't be more than a five-minute trip to get it. Still, he decided ending up with excruciating sunburn might take his mind off his other miseries.

He concentrated only on the sounds of the ocean and the breeze blowing across the sand. That low roar of the ocean, mixed with the sounds of a crowded beach. Snippets of music and conversation drifted by on the wind like seagull feathers – a bit of an old Motown song here, one side of a conversation about Clemson's prospects for the upcoming football season there. Then, almost without realizing it, he found an unfamiliar reggae song dominating the soundscape. It was close, probably from the speakers on someone's handheld, but Jon couldn't remember seeing anyone that close to him when he arrived. When a shadow fell on him, Jon opened his eyes to see where the cloud had suddenly come from to interrupt the sunburn he was working so hard to acquire.

"You're gonna get the living hell burnt out of you laying there like that, white boy," said the silhouette of a person, its head surrounded by a corona of sunlight like the scene was planned by an accomplished cinematographer. His voice had a distinct Caribbean lilt not often heard in these parts.

"Pardon me?"

"I said you're gonna get burnt. Layin' there with no lotion on, lookin' like a frog belly, you're gonna be one burnt brotha, and that's no way to have a good vacation."

Jon shielded his eyes and moved to try and get a glimpse of the stranger's face.

"Thanks, but I'm not on vacation. Do I know you?" Jon said, still trying to see without having to stand.

"No, but I've seen you around. I surf around here sometimes."

The fellow moved out of his cinematically perfect position and sat on a large purple and white towel laid out next to Jon's beach chair. His appearance took Jon aback. He was amazingly fit and his hair was a mass of matted dreadlocks reaching down to the center of his back. The style was much the same as Jon had seen on younger surfers, except for the abundance of silver in the old man's dreads. Aside from form-fitting neoprene surf pants and several more layers of muscle tissue than Jon, he wore nothing else. Beside him lay a surfboard decorated with six-pointed stars, crucifixes, yin-yangs, Arabic and Hebrew writing and a dozen other symbols and letters Jon didn't understand.

"Weren't you out in the water a few minutes ago?" Jon asked.

The old man nodded in agreement, his dreds bobbing as he continued along with the beat of the music. "The surf's gonna kick up real nice with that low pressure system moving in from the west, but we're gon' to have one hell of a thunderstorm" – it sounded like tundahstom – "later in the weekend."

"Thanks for the tip. I'll remember to take an umbrella," Jon said, returning to his reclined position in the hopes of ending the conversation.

"You ain't goin' nowhere but to the hospital if you stay out here with no lotion on, boy. Somebody might think you were *trying* to get burned."

Frustrated, Jon turned to the old man again. "Look, I appreciate the advice and your continuing concern, but I'd really be very happy if you could mind your own business and go back to whatever you were doing. Thanks."

"Hey. No problem. You wanna cook yourself up like a T-bone just because you lost your job and wife in the same day, don't let me stop you."

Jon felt his heart play the quickest-ever game of hopscotch in his chest, sat up to place both feet on the sand and turned to confront the old man.

"Would you mind telling me how you knew that?"

"Saw the whole thing," Eli said. Then he used a T-shirt to dab the beads of sweat from his shiny forehead. "Saw that dirty business start up with Ashley and just go downhill from there. That Ashley, she's a ver' bad girl," he said as he grinned and shook his head.

"My wife hired you to follow me, didn't she? You're some sort of private investigator?" Jon's fists clenched. Unlike his encounter with Dub, he was now quite prepared to go on the offensive.

"No, mon, but you think what you want. You're not going to like the truth anyway." He cut a sidelong glance at Jon, noting his body language. Jon hoped it dissuaded him from trying anything.

"No, please. I'm good friends with the truth," Jon said through clenched teeth. "It just hasn't been doing me a whole lot of good lately."

"Eli," the old man said. He extended his hand for a proper handshake, locking eyes with Jon and maintaining an annoyingly placid expression.

"Great," Jon said. This was no time to be cornered by this old freak, having serious sulking to do. "Whatever you are, you can tell my wife that if she'd let me explain I could've cleared everything up. It's not too late."

"Well, that's kinda why I'm here. I'm afraid it is a little late."

Jon was dumbstruck, the full weight of the previous day's events suddenly falling on his shoulders like a sack of cement. He had to fight to keep from choking up in front of this stranger. "Jeez. I figured she'd take some kind of action, but … She really wants a divorce?"

His chest ached like someone had punched him. God damn you, Ashley. God damn you and your relentless libido and your conniving, evil soul. He could feel the tears welling up in his eyes and there was nothing he could do to stop them.

The stranger – Eli – was suddenly sympathetic. "Hey, hey, boy. Relax. It's not your wife, boy. It's you. You're dead."

43

Jon wiped his eyes with the back of his hand. "What? What the hell are you talking about?"

"Slipped in the bathroom and knocked your head on the edge of the toilet. I think you were still conscious for a minute, 'cause you still had time to empty your stomach and ended up face down in the bowl. Not a pretty sight, but not everybody gets to die like a rock star." He let slip a little smirk, as if the thought amused him.

"You're nuts, old man," Jon said as he gathered his things. He didn't know how this guy knew about him, but he wasn't in the mood for any more of this torture that was bordering on mockery. Dead? Dead to Linda, maybe, but otherwise the old man was full of shit.

Jon rose and folded up the chaise. "And if you're lucky, I won't call the police to come haul your ass off this beach for being a public nuisance."

"And if you're smart, you won't go back in that house, boy," Eli called after him. "It won't make you any less dead."

Jon slammed the screen door shut, dropped his chair on the porch and went straight to the bathroom. There, he saw a body wearing the same T-shirt and shorts he now wore. It – he – was kneeling on the floor, head in the toilet bowl and arms hanging limp and turning a ghastly pale.

Jon shuddered with the creepy feeling he got visiting crime scenes during his newspaper days. Seeing a dead human, so devoid of the animation of even the most comatose living person, was something he had never gotten used to. Knowing that the person's life had been taken though violent means made it even worse. The expressions frozen on their faces, the odd angles at which their bodies had fallen or been left were the stuff that haunted his nightmares and woke him thrashing and sweating. But there had never been a chance of the dead body being his own.

The electronic chirp of his phone interrupted him as he reached to gingerly lift the head from the bowl. He dropped it with a splash and grabbed the handset from his shorts, pressing the talk button and looking forward to hearing Linda's voice. But the phone wouldn't activate. It was like the button just wasn't registering the pressure of his thumb. He was tempted to hurl it across the room in frustration, but he needed to hear the message if she had decided to leave one. As he waited, he looked around and tried to reconstruct what might have happened to him. There was no blood, but the toilet was full of the contents of his stomach. A thin towel bathmat was scrunched up against the side of the shower where he imagined he had slipped. He examined the back of the head and found it was swollen up like an ostrich egg. There had been just enough life left in him to realize he still needed to puke up a stomach full of rum. Great. Nothing like dying with dignity.

Jon palmed the phone again and spoke the words "voice mail." Just one message, the computer voice told him, so he played it. There was a pause that seemed to go on for several eternities, and then the heartbreaking sight of his wife's tear stained face on the phone's tiny viewscreen.

"Jon, if you're there and you get this, please call me back." He so wanted to talk to her, to explain, to see her loveliness behind the tears. "I know I jumped the gun a bit yesterday, and I wanted to give you a chance to explain. I love you and I don't want us to have to go through all this unless there's a really good reason. Please call me." She sniffed once, wiped her eyes and nose and hung up.

Feeling the fury at his forced helplessness rise up inside him, Jon stormed back onto the beach to find the old man supine, tapping his fingers on his chest to the beat of another reggae tune.

"Would you mind doing some quick explaining ... what did you say your name was?"

"Eli," he said without getting up or even bothering to benefit Jon with an open eye.

"Would you mind explaining that, Eli?"

"Which part? Me knowing all about you? The body in the commode? Your wife on the phone?"

"All of it would be nice."

"Okay," he said, sitting up and crossing his legs. "I'm a physical incarnation of ... I don't know – I like to call it the universal essence," he said, moving his hands as if to encircle an invisible globe in front of him. "The body in the bathroom is yours, and your wife has obviously chosen to give you a second chance to explain why some other woman's panties were in your trousers."

"The universal ... God? You're saying you're God?" Jon's emotions were being yanked in entirely too many directions. He didn't know where to focus. First he was concerned about losing Linda forever at the hands of a pit-bull attorney. Then he had just seen tangible evidence of his untimely – and unbelievably stupid – demise. Now this.

"Not God, really, if you mean Yaweh, head of the standard Judeo-Christian religions. I'm higher on the totem pole than the Kid. The highest, as far as I know."

Jon paused and shook his head as if the thoughts now trying to penetrate his brain were some head vermin he could just dislodge.

"The Big Kahuna, boy. That's me. Supreme Being, Master of All Creation, all that crap. I just don't travel with all that churchy baggage."

"And you are making a personal visit to me because?"

"Because you're freshly dead, and I need your help."

Jon decided he'd better sit down, in more like a barely controlled fall.

"Look boy, I know this is a lot for you to handle right now," Eli said as he placed a hand on Jon's shoulder. "But it's ver' important that you help us out. We've been watching you for a while, and when this little mishap came about we had to grab you before it was too late."

"Too late for what? Are we on the verge of the Second Coming? I had a one-way ticket to Hell? Things weren't going badly enough for me yesterday?"

"Well, not exactly. Let's just say that if you had ended up going where you were supposed to go, it would've been a trick to get you out without raising some suspicions, let alone contact you in the first place. Then I'd have to sit around waiting for another candidate to kick off, possibly a far less qualified one."

"I'm dead, and instead of letting me go on to my heavenly reward, you're offering me a job," Jon said with his face in his hands. "Where were you when I was being fired?"

"Oh, I was watching. Nice move with that hand through the window, by the way. That boss of yours, mon, 'dat was a wanker if I ever saw one. Now look, I can't even pretend to know what you're going through right now. It's just not within my sphere of experience. But once we get where we're going, I'm going to give you some help with that, understand? We've got a lot to do and a short time to do it, and the last thing I need is you being distracted."

Jon's mind reeled. Fifteen minutes earlier he was simply on the verge of divorce. Now he was dead and being recruited for God knows what. But if what the old man said was true, God did know and was about to tell him.

"Mind if I ask how we'll be traveling?"

" 'Das a little hard to explain, even for me," Eli said as he zipped up the top part of his wetsuit and untied his dreds so they fell loose around his shoulders. "It might help if you just lie 'dere. I'm just going to grab some lunch for us and then we'll go back to my place."

"My place?" Jon thought. Why did he get the feeling he was going to a surfer crash pad instead of the Kingdom of Heaven?

But just as he settled in and got comfortable on the hot sand, he felt the warmth envelope him. Then suddenly there was cold blackness, and the bottom quite surprisingly fell out of the universe.

The Nikura building's parking garage was deceptively cool compared to what it must have been like at ground level, but the smell of stale urine made it hard to enjoy.

As Mako walked toward the limousine, taking care to make sure he wasn't being followed, he thought about what a shame it was they couldn't have basements and other such underground structures in Florida without them turning into indoor swimming pools. The place was as solid as a military bunker – all the high-rise garages were – but still somehow couldn't keep the homeless folks from using them as public restrooms.

The locks disengaged at his command with an electronic thunk and welcomed him in the ubiquitous sultry female Nikura computer voice. Earlier, when he'd doubled back up the elevators to the roof hangar where he had originally arrived, he found it odd not having to break out a window and hotwire what was essentially his property. The concept of owning big-ticket items rather than committing grand larceny to get them had yet to completely sink in. A few moments inside and a random destination request sent the limo on its way to Trenton without him. He was sure that once Yoshi got free he would be after him, so Mako figured a decoy wouldn't hurt.

This limo was one of the long, black aircar hybrids designed to be flown or driven. In Florida you had to head down to Miami to see them, but here in Philadelphia they were everywhere. It was true what they said about the place turning into New York, but between the island's rapid reclamation by the river and the combat-zone mentality, he couldn't really blame Gothamites for fleeing. Nobody wanted to live under martial law conditions, even if no one ever officially called it that.

Mako slid into the luxurious faux-leather seat as the gull-wing door hissed closed. After he sent the first limo on its way, he alternated elevators and stairs for 68 floors, hoping that if he were being tracked he'd at least confuse whoever was tracking him.

It wasn't until he hit the lower floors, rushing through the mezzanine-level food court and down into the grand atrium, that he realized how hungry he was. The food smells finally caught up with him and beckoned him to the assorted stalls. There was even a Cleaver's outlet with a more discreet version of its sign – a woman's naked torso, her breasts barely obscured by the two huge hamburgers she carries on a platter and the slogan "Bone-Suckin' Good."

Mako was impressed that the crew of nubile waitresses looked fresh and perky even at this early hour. What he wouldn't give to be nestled up to one of them in a booth as she performed the chain's trademark up-close-and-personal greeting, the push-up bra doing its work while her denim micro-mini rode up high, giving him a little peek of the signature Cleaver Girl thong (available at the gift counter for $24.95) he knew they wore underneath.

But fear of recapture moved him on. He tried to keep his cool, strolling casually through the glass atrium and out into the heat. Instead of a Cleaver's girl he decided to settle for a mystery-meat breakfast sandwich from the Greek food cart and its cook with the bushy mustache. He kept his back to the silver trailer to better watch for pursuers. Except for the occasional holographic pop-up ad approaching him to push a feelie salon or a nightclub, no one paid him any mind.

His hunger sated, Mako allowed himself to relax into the limo's rich leather. He loosened the tie, but was still dressed like all the other corporate trained monkeys around him. Even if he wasn't who he was, dressing the way he normally did on the beaches of Florida wouldn't wash in the bustle of a downtown Philadelphia workday. His ability to blend looking like he did was about the only thing that made him glad about the way he was dressed.

Mako still held the silvery sheath, turning it over and over in his hand. It was nothing unusual. It didn't hold about it the aura of destiny. Just an envelope handed to him by his dead father's assistant. Probably nothing, anyway. In the vast labyrinth of global corporations – this corporation in particular – what could she really have found that would help him?

He was a moment away from tossing it out the window and accepting his father's death as an unsolvable murder. But then he thought of Andrea. Father wouldn't have hired her if she weren't on the ball. He knew that. As a boy he'd witnessed weaker candidates for such jobs leave in tears after fewer than ten minutes. He knew what kind of man his father was, and he knew that it took a special type of person – and particularly a special type of woman – to work for him. And as such, anything she gave him to help him find his father's killer was likely legit.

He broke the seal and slid out a half-inch thick sheaf of papers and several computer sticks. The top page was a memo to his father from Andrea, informing him that she had copied the documents from company records and then secured the originals in a safe place. He paged on. As he did, a complicated network of cover corporations and shipping routes came to light, with the intent seeming to be to illegally transport Nikura-manufactured weapons everywhere except their intended destinations. Loads that were supposed to go to Tampa for shipment to the Costa Rican government had been systematically hijacked by a variety of thieves and self-styled domestic terrorists. He recognized some of the acronyms – the Ludd League, Quebec Liberation Front, the Aryan Ascension – but some were unfamiliar. The acronym SHAG showed up a lot where the hijackings were concerned, but Mako had no idea what that might stand for. Some shipments to more distant places like the Balkans and some of the smaller eastern European republics were simply over ordered, with the surplus re-routed within the company to small subsidiaries that then hauled the goods to unknown sites. Manifests showing missing shipments included everything from the newest personal armor and hand-held assault weapons to complex tracking equipment, which sounded like the type of stuff that was only used in aerospace applications.

Damn you, father. It was bad enough that the company was legitimately supplying most of the major armed conflicts on the planet. What made it even worse was that a huge proportion of the goods were being rerouted to pissant terrorists before they even got on the boat.

The packet also contained copies of several news articles about a low-rent domestic terrorism organization called SHAG, which had allegedly used some military equipment manufactured by Nikura in several later attacks on — of all things — dance clubs in the southeast.

Of course, had the information not been organized, front to back, in a manner in which someone unfamiliar with the scheme could understand it, the entire packet would've been inscrutable. Andrea had arranged the information so anyone viewing it would instantly be able to grasp the level of corruption within the company. And from the indication of signatures, work orders, shipping manifests and accident reports, his uncle Hiroshi was at the top of the pyramid this little scheme came together to create.

That also meant, as heartbreaking as it was for Mako to admit to himself, that his uncle probably had a shitload to do with the death of his father.

Mako placed the envelope and its contents in his lap. He let his head loll back against the seat and closed his eyes. Father was dead. Yoshi was forbidden from investigating and Uncle Hiroshi was the prime suspect. It was likely Hiroshi, as the acting head of the company, had personally issued the order to Yoshi, knowing the huge Okinawan's tenacity and devotion to duty. Yoshi would have wanted to track down his father's killer. At one time, Nikura's head of security would have also acted as judge, jury and executioner for said killer. But Yoshi had assured him that those days were long past, and any effort on Mako's part to dig them up would be futile.

Andrea was right. He was the only one who could help. That didn't mean he would succeed in the attempt, but the least he could do was try. As much as they disagreed, he owed that much to Father.

"Driver," he said with as much authority as he could muster.

"Yes, Mr. Nikura. What can I do for you today?" the car replied in its sultry voice.

"I'd like to go to …" He consulted the manifest listing the next weapons shipment, the one due to be sent out in the next few hours. "The Nikura Armaments facility in Bristol, please. And let's stick to the ground."

"Very good, Mr. Nikura. With traffic, our estimated time of arrival will be 9:47 a.m."

The limousine powered up and slid smoothly up the exit ramp. Flashing lights and a polite little alarm heralded their arrival at the garage's street level entrance, both of which were ignored by passing pedestrians. Finally the limo was able to pull into traffic and onto JFK Boulevard, then proceed to I-95.

As he rode, he scanned the news channels as Yoshi had, still seeing nothing but short updates on what happened and the fact that the police, in all their investigative wisdom, were still completely clueless.

"I know who's paying your salary, boys, and it sure isn't the City of Brotherly Love," Mako muttered to himself as he rode into the Philadelphia suburbs, finally switching to a music video channel and lowering the volume. He recognized the particular clip as one by Soiled Syringe, one of the latest post-post-grunge bands, part of a growing revival of turn-of-the-century music. He half-watched the small TV as he dozed. Sleep and consciousness blended together. Images of exploding condoms and rabid cartoon viruses from the video mingled with those of Andrea Martin pleading for him to do what was right.

So far he was doing what he knew was right but that didn't make it any easier for him to do it. He was so used to doing what was easy or profitable or would win him another surfing competition that any thoughts of right and wrong were noticeably absent from his line of reasoning. Even during the days when he was doing courier work for some small-time operators around Orlando and Daytona, he never took any jobs he knew would put him in immediate danger, particularly of getting killed. Now, here he was throwing himself directly into the line of fire, pretending that the fact that his father had already died over this wasn't warning enough to stay away.

Mako dozed for a while, the car eventually alerting him to the fact that they were about two minutes away. He knew they were close to their destination when the lines of trees broken only by the occasional overhead maglev track were joined by a high, razor wire-topped chain-link fence running parallel with the highway. Moments later, the car announced they had arrived. Almost as an afterthought, the car also informed him a biometric scan would be required for entry.

The rear window was already in the process of descending as a guard approached with a DataPad. He looked surprised when he finally recognized Mako.

"Morning, Mr. Nikura," he said in a thick Jersey accent. Dude must live across the river and commute, Mako thought. "We weren't expecting you to visit this soon."

"Just decided to drive around and look things over, Tony," Mako said, having gotten a glimpse of the fellow's nametag as he approached. "After being on the beach all those years, it's tough staying inside those office buildings too long."

"Know what you mean. Sorry to do this to you, sir, but the scan is required for everybody coming onto the property," Tony said as he sheepishly indicated the device he held.

"No problem. It's been a while, but my pattern should still be on file," he said as he pressed his thumb onto the screen and repeated his name. A generic female computer voice announced the confirmation of his identity.

"You're all set, Mr. Nikura," Tony said, offering Mako a laminated visitor's pass to clip on his lapel. "If you have any questions, feel free to ask anyone in the building."

"Thanks Tony. Have a nice day," Mako said as the limo pulled through the gate. If someone had, at this point, asked Mako if he had a plan concerning what to do next, he would have answered them with a yes. Of course, he would have been lying.

The limo approached the front entrance to the main warehouse on the compound at a brisk pace. There was no one outside, most of the employees no doubt avoiding the heat by staying inside as much as they could. Almost without realizing he did it, and certainly without having a clue why, he instructed the car to go around the building to the back. There it was even more desolate, and there he decided to get out.

He returned the documents and sticks to the envelope, tucked the package into the waist of his trousers then mentally prepared himself to hit the pavement and roll. As soon as he opened the door, the car's safeties began to smoothly stop. Mako leaned out and shouted back into the car for it to return to the front of the building and park.

The car was down to about fifteen miles per hour as Mako propelled himself out the door so the rear wheels wouldn't catch him as the car drove on. He hit the ground with his right shoulder and absorbed most of the impact in the momentum of the tumble. With as much muscle as he'd built up on his gangly frame while surfing, stunts like that still left him feeling like he'd been run over by a truck a few days later.

As soon as the car rounded the building, he scrambled behind a stack of discarded shipping pallets. He knew there were cameras everywhere, and he scolded himself for not assessing their locations. Here, though, he imagined he would be safe for the moment. He dusted off and inspected himself for damage. The suit jacket had sustained a four-inch rip down the right sleeve, which had lightly dirtied the white shirt underneath, but it was of little consequence. He didn't feel bad about damaging a suit he didn't like, even if it had probably cost more than the monthly salary of most of the warehouse employees. Otherwise, he was in excellent shape. The envelope had remained where he hid it.

Near the corner of the building, just next to the immense garage door used by entering trucks, was a smaller doorway designed for human use only. Right outside it, there was an area peppered with discarded cigarette butts – the smoking lounge. These guys were lucky. Most places north of Washington, D.C., smoking anywhere on company property would have gotten them fired.

He looked at the sky and figured the time at around 10 a.m., so he could expect a few workers to sneak out for their mid-morning drags at any time. He sat and waited, listening intently for the sound of the door opening or footsteps or human voices.

It was time to formulate some sort of plan, but his mind drew a blank. The heat, his lack of sleep and the speed at which the last 24 hours had moved all served to render him completely incapable of thinking of anything that might save his lousy half-breed hide. The sun rose higher, and the heat from the tarmac seemed to rise by tenfold with each passing minute. Sweat saturated the collar of his shirt, where he still wore the loosened necktie. He tasted salt on his lips from the flowing perspiration and he was convinced he could feel the heat penetrating the soles of his shoes. Squatting was growing uncomfortable, and he shifted his weight back and forth from one foot to the other to keep his legs from going to sleep.

Finally, as Mako's legs were beginning to cramp from kneeling behind the pallets, two workers in blue Nikura jumpsuits stepped out of the door. They propped it open with a stick apparently left there for that purpose and lit up.

Mako peered over the stacked goods and wondered how, with so many years of viewing bad feelie action shows, he could have absolutely no idea what to do at this point. What he really needed was some sort of distraction. He looked around as much as his squatting position would allow him, finding even less outside his direct vicinity. No rocks, no metal, no nothing. For a moment he considered launching both his expensive Italian wingtips, but the prospect of sneaking across half-molten pavement in his sock feet was almost as unpleasant as getting caught.

At last he spotted what he needed. Inside one of the wooden pallets, a few slats had broken and were dangling by nothing more than a badly hammered nail. A few seconds of industrious manipulation broke one free, and Mako instantly hurled it toward a storage shed, where it struck the metal siding with a clatter sufficient to send the men hurrying off to see what was wrong. Mako rounded the barricade of pallets and slipped in the door, pulling the makeshift doorstopper in behind him.

He found himself at the end of a short corridor lined with offices. All the doors were closed except for one. A paunchy man in a short-sleeved dress shirt, who he assumed to be a supervisor, sat at a desk. His feet were propped up casually and his back was to Mako. He spoke to another man whose face was boxed in the upper right hand corner of the projection.

"You heard the new boss man is on the site today, dincha, Ed? Kid's touring around in the company limo nosing into his old man's leftover business. Far as I know, he hasn't even gotten out of the car. Been sitting out there in front of the building just watching," the man in the office said.

"Maybe he's waiting for you to carry him in on a sedan chair or something," the man on the screen said, chuckling lightly. "It's not like you guys do a damn thing over there, anyway. Jeez, what does the kid expect to see?"

Good question, Mako said to himself as he stepped quietly past the office door. He really didn't know what he expected to see or find, or even what he was looking for. The more he thought about it, the more he realized he was doing something very stupid based on very little information and even less planning and resourcefulness. But that never stopped him before, so why should it now?

At the end of the corridor was the end of a tractor-trailer in the midst of being loaded. Mako had memorized the final manifest number in his father's file, and the weapons the truck was supposed to carry were scheduled to be shipped today, so he figured the truck they were leaving in would still be here.

Mako moved quickly beneath the trucks, dodging workmen and forklifts by hiding behind the huge wheels. On his way, he examined each truck for something that might give it away as being the one carrying the shipment. So far, there was nothing. All were the same anonymous silver, only the mudflaps carrying the blocky-type letters NDP, the abbreviation for Nikura Defense Products. He was on his third truck and moving on to the fourth when he spotted a set of mudflaps that wasn't like the others. They bore the bright, stylized logo of Sunrise Moving and Storage, a van line owned by one of Nikura's smaller subsidiaries.

His back ached from all the bending. Still, Mako propelled his lanky frame under the trailers at a pace surprising even to him, checking between each set of trucks for anyone who might stop his progress. When he arrived at the cab with the Sunrise logo — a barely disguised Japanese rising sun — he checked again to make sure no one was in the immediate vicinity, then quickly moved to the rear of the trailer where the manifest hung on a clipboard. A forklift roared by. He ducked back, pressing his body against the side of the trailer and hoping somehow his pinstripe suit would blend with its polished steel. His sweat now wasn't from the heat, but from the fear.

The forklift passed without anything other than a brief increase in blood pressure for Mako, giving him enough time to check the manifest more thoroughly. The printout listed the cargo as the personal possessions of Mr. and Mrs. Ernie Brabbage of Hackensack, on its way to their new home in Atlanta. The number, though, exactly matched the one Mako had memorized. The forklift lumbered past again as Mako hid once more and tried to consider his options.

A bright shaft of sunlight from the front warehouse door made him realize those options were severely more limited than he originally thought. As the door rose, he saw two figures duck under it and come in gesturing angrily.

"Who the fuck locked us out the back door," he heard one say over the surrounding noise. "Who's trying to be the goddamn wise guy, huh?"

The voices rang in Mako's head has he frantically looked around for some other avenue of escape. He looked under the line of trucks and found the way he came in was blocked by a forklift, the driver of which was discussing something with another man, probably the supervisor he overheard earlier. Ahead of him he had at least four hundred pounds of angry Teamsters ready to dismember whoever was responsible for ruining their smoke break. Meanwhile, everyone was wondering why the new head of the company was content to sit in his cushy limo outside the warehouse while they slaved away inside. He couldn't say that he blamed them.

Mako quickly ducked back under the truck and moved toward its cab. He could see little from his vantage point, so he was forced to estimate the location of the angry smokers and hope they wouldn't spot him. He paused, gathered his courage and silently counted to three, then bolted out from behind the cab. He put one foot on the running board and one hand around the side rail and pulled himself up, opening the cab door and sliding in with the clumsiness of a truly desperate man. To his ears, it sounded as if he couldn't have made more noise if he'd had aluminum cans tied to his ankles. It wasn't until he was in the cab with the door closed, lying on the seat and trying to control his rapid breathing, that he realized how lucky he was that the truck's door was even unlocked.

Getting in was easier than he expected. Getting the truck and himself out intact was going to be a different matter. It had been a while since he had driven a truck, and it was a much older and smaller Volvo delivery model. Compared to that clunker, jury-rigged from internal combustion for a cell, driving this thing would be like flying a transcontinental shuttle. But even among all the technology, it didn't take him long to spot the key dangling from the ignition. Though it seemed far too obvious among all the other controls, when he sat up and turned it he felt the massive cell whine to life.

The two smokers immediately made eye contact with Mako in the driver's seat, pointing at him and motioning for him to get out. It didn't take long for the other workers to notice, many of them rushing toward the cab, apparently in the hopes of stopping him with their own bodies. When he put the huge machine into gear, however, they dispersed quickly. Flooring the accelerator, he rumbled past the crowd, which stood there watching helplessly.

Mako figured he cleared the large door by three inches at best, since it was still being raised after the smokers' entrance. He thought he heard an alarm sound as he cleared the warehouse, then spotted Tony and his colleague running toward the center of the closed gate, both preparing to draw their sidearms. The threat of gunfire only prompted Mako to press the accelerator harder, bearing down relentlessly on both men. When they saw he wasn't going to stop, they both scurried aside, clearly unwilling to give their lives for the company.

The gate itself gave a millisecond of resistance, then ripped from its hinges on the metal posts. Mako was out, and on his way to visit Uncle Hiroshi with a trailer full of evidence behind him.

The last time Jon awoke face down in grass was his freshman year of college, when polishing off a bottle of cheap whiskey with three friends was still considered a valid form of group interaction. After the grass, the next things he had seen were the corduroy slippers of the university president, on whose lawn Jon was prostrate. That being the case, when Jon awoke staring at Eli's bare toes he had to remind himself there probably wouldn't be campus trash duty or other such acts of required public service to follow. At the same time, however, Jon considered that knowing he would spend a few days spiking gum wrappers in a parking lot might be a bit better than going blindly into service for the Supreme Being.

The grass was thick and green, lush beyond anything that would be growing in his own dry yard in the heat of a South Carolina July. There was also a pleasantly cool breeze blowing over him, offsetting what felt like a harsh sun beating down on his back.

"About time you decided to wake up, boy. I don't think I've ever seen a dead person sleep as much as you do," Eli said.

Jon sat up and evaluated his physical condition — whatever that might be for a corpse — and found it to be acceptable. Eli sat stretched out before him, two bags marked "Weenie on the Beach" sitting beside him. But there was no Weenie on the Beach anymore. It had been efficiently bulldozed to make way for the latest Cleaver's franchise, burdening yet another part of the state with the wink-wink nudge-nudge "Bone-Suckin' Good."

"You hungry?" Eli asked as he passed one bag to Jon. "Jumbo weenie with chili, mustard and slaw, right?"

Jon peered in the bag and nodded his head in agreement and approval, suddenly realizing he was much hungrier than he thought he would be, especially considering there were no other metabolic functions to fuel. After unwrapping the hot dog, he ate with increasing enthusiasm regardless. The damn thing might as well have been filet mignon.

Looking around as he chewed his first bites of solid food in what seemed like days, Jon tried to place himself and his surroundings. It was going to be tough. All he saw was grass. Low, rolling hillocks of it everywhere. If he didn't know better, he'd think they were in Central Park before the doomsday people sprayed it with defoliant just out of spite for the world not ending when they said it would. That, along with the distinct absence of gang rapists, religious cultists, public copulation, military police, smog and bombed-out skyscrapers led him to the conclusion he was elsewhere.

Behind them stretched a line of immense trees. Above was a squall line that Jon imagined would be what the anxious doomsday folks hoped they would see when the four horsemen really did

55

make their fateful ride of pestilence and war and all that. Even during the most severe hurricane conditions, when the sky seemed to turn green with sickness from the swirling winds, Jon had not seen the ominous, foreboding color of the distant clouds. As they boiled like a grotesque celestial stew, flashes of lightning shot down and exchanged charges between the heavens and the earth. Afterwards, however, there was not the expected thunderclap, indicating the area over which the weather hovered was farther away than Jon estimated. What most confused him was that even with all the atmospheric turmoil so close, above where he sat the sky was a perfectly clear, deep blue, the sun shining down brightly on his face.

Eli, who was stretched out on the grass and using his fingers to scoop up from his wrapper bits of fallen chili, was the first to break the silence.

"You might want to start finishing up there, boy. We've got a lot to do and not much time to do it."

"Where are we?" Jon asked as he shoveled the last clump of coleslaw onto the remainder of his bun.

"No need to worry about that. You'll only be here for a bit, anyway," Eli said. "Next up for you is orientation and briefing. Plus I've got a couple of people I want you to meet." Eli stretched and yawned, then balled his trash up inside its bag and tossed it over his shoulder, where it landed in a large blue trash container which had apparently appeared there for that sole purpose. Jon took a final slurp from his take-out cup of half-lemonade, half-sweet tea and placed his trash in the same bin. When he looked again, it was gone. It was then that Jon realized with some relief – and a little disappointment – that he hadn't wanted a cigarette since his arrival.

Eli had already gained a substantial lead, and Jon had to move at a slow jog to catch up. They seemed to be following no predetermined path even though Eli was certainly positive of his direction. They were headed up a small incline, as grassy as everything else in this place. So much so, in fact, that Jon almost expected to crest a hill and find a sand trap or a tee green on the other side. Instead he spotted a brightly colored tent which, based on their current course, he presumed to be their destination.

The tent turned out to be smaller up close than it had appeared from a distance, Eli held open the heavy canvas flap and guided Jon in.

"Welcome to Mission HQ, boy. Head on in and grab a seat. The show starts in five minutes."

It was dark and cool and smelled faintly of old canvas and sawdust inside the tent. Two antique wooden folding chairs had been set up facing a classroom movie screen of the sort on which his parents had likely watched hygiene films in junior high school. Jon settled in one and tried to make himself as comfortable as possible, which he found to be a difficult task since the chairs were clearly not designed for comfort. Eli took the seat beside him and spoke into the darkness.

"Alex, you ready with the reel?"

"Just threading it now, Boss. Be ready in just a sec," said a softly drawling female voice from somewhere behind them.

"Here, boy. Have some. It's buttered," Eli said, offering Jon a bag of popcorn that wasn't there before. He took a handful of the oily kernels as both of them crunched in silence.

The projector rattled to life and the beam pierced the darkness. On the screen appeared an image all too familiar: the edifice of the Church of the New Revelation's Seaside Cathedral. It was widely regarded as an architectural monstrosity that somehow fit well in a town that once featured a multi-story 1950s futurama-style junk shop called the Gay Dolphin. The overabundance of glass was deceptive, though. Passers-by could see in most of the time, but when services started, they went opaque to maintain some level of privacy for the "worshipers" inside.

"A lot of this isn't going to be anything you haven't heard before," Eli said. "I'm just trying to put some things in perspective for you. This, as you know, is the home church for the New Revelationists. Nothing wrong with them per se. Just another enterprising, self-styled mystic gathering a willing flock around him simply because he can. That's been going on almost since I can remember."

The image changed to that of a CNR service in progress. "Now, up in the pulpit there we have the Rev. Lawrence Whitaker, who you already know." Actually, he was as familiar to Jon as any of his agency's clients simply because his account was the most visible. Whitaker was handsome in a way that appealed to women without alienating the men – more like a feelie actor who was aging well than some of the super-androgynous boys showing up everywhere in popular culture. He was probably around forty even though the press releases Andre churned out for the church insisted he was in his mid-thirties. His hair, though still perfectly coiffured, was moist around the edges with perspiration in this clip, and his face was creased with the concentration he was putting into a prayer. It was obvious he had reached the crescendo of the service. The band behind him had begun a slow, sensuous rhythm. The choir – all of whom wore near transparent approximations of traditional choir robes – accompanied the band with almost sub-audible vocalizing, all of it coming together as a throbbing hum. Couples of every conceivable combination held each other and swayed to the pulsating sound, some already exiting toward the meditation chambers looking fiery-eyed with the spirit of Whitaker's lusty God.

"Whitaker still amazes me. He managed to use his small ministry to turn the widespread elimination of most of the nasty STDs into a major new religion. He's going to be your contact."

"My contact?" Jon asked around a mouthful of popcorn.

"Just be patient. All will be revealed," Eli said as he munched.

The image changed again, this time to that of Veronica Whitaker, a stunning woman with an equally stunning mane of red hair. She was wearing a very formal bit of nothing and gyrating against Whitaker in much the same manner as the people in the congregation were against each other. She was one of those women it was impossible not to recognize. Not only was she gorgeous, but she was everywhere. Jon would see her during the brief stops he would make on the church's shopping channel, usually hawking some new line of cosmetics or risqué "worshipwear." She would also make appearances on the morning and late-night talk shows and the celebrity gossip roundups. She graced magazine covers everywhere. Editors, particularly of the fluffy "features" sections, loved her like the goddess she thought she was because she was a one-woman story generator. Fashion story? Women followed her choices of dress obsessively. Religion? She could spout any of a number of Bible verses to back up the foundation of the CNR's "sanctified sin" theory. Sex? She claimed to be an expert in not only several Eastern sexual philosophies, but was a renowned collector of erotic art and artifacts.

Jon had never, however, seen her in quite as provocative a situation as the one he was watching. As the image of her grew larger, he noticed a classic Veronica Whitaker touch: what ordinarily would have been sequins were actually tiny crucifixes dangling from the borders of what there was of her outfit.

"You know the story behind her?"

"Back when Andre was reporting he kept trying to find out. We all knew the party line that they had met while Whitaker was an adjunct professor teaching a comparative religion class at Carolina, but nobody bought it," Jon said. "Seems like all the evidence to the contrary had been wiped away."

Eli grinned. "Wiped away is right. Whitaker originally met her, if that's what you want to call it, on an interactive porn site for redhead fetishists."

"A what?"

"Yeah, they manage to leave that out of the official church history. Seems the good reverend always had a weakness for the scarlet-haired women and vigorous self-gratification. She was doing feelie-casts from her dorm room to earn money for college originally, but then Whitaker barged into her chat room one night and started laying it on."

"Laying it on how?"

"Oh, the usual self-righteous preacher business, talking about how what she was doing was a sin against God and nature, and defiling the temple of her body. Of course, during this entire discussion he was strapped into a feelie rig with Veronica administering a virtual hand job. They kept up the online relationship until Veronica knew him well enough to meet him in person. It was quite a romantic little encounter. He read to her from the Gideon Bible in a $60-a-room rat-hole motel while she did things to him they don't teach in Sunday school." Then there, up on the screen where Eli was pointing, was a visual record of the entire event. Jon swallowed his popcorn hard and tried not to choke. Then he tried to concentrate on not getting an obvious erection.

"By now, of course, she knows she's got the guy hooked and has begun to grow somewhat attached herself. Must be the preacher charisma that drives these girls nuts. After that, he convinced her to become his personal assistant with lots of fringe benefits just so he could have himself a little plaything. It didn't take long for the folks at his church to realize something was wrong, though. Too many 'private' conferences with Miss Veronica when he should have been making his visitation rounds. The church leaders found out and quietly asked him to resign. He did some tent revival stuff around the state that summer and they lived for a while on what was left of Veronica's feelie-cast money. It didn't take long before he realized his plaything had bigger things in mind. She's where the whole idea for the Church of

58

the New Revelation came about."

"So he didn't even think of the idea himself? It was Veronica?" Jon said around more popcorn.

"For the most part. One day after they announced the AIDS vaccine had been perfected and would be available soon, she was thinking out loud about how there would be a lot less evil in the world if people didn't have to hide the things most religious faiths considered sins. That one comment led to the creation of the entire New Revelation philosophy and the two getting married. The rest is in the official history. They started the ministry from an abandoned arcade in Myrtle Beach, buying up abandoned motels a few streets inland to house their growing out-of-town congregation. When Hurricane Abner hit and washed his temple out to sea, he took it as a sign to build an even bigger operation. He moved back a street and started again, still buying up motels and abandoned property. Two more hurricanes and about three blocks later, he'd gone through three progressively larger locations and owned a six-block swath of property that stretched from the beach back about a half a mile. Veronica suggested he start selling off some of the property to finance construction of a massive home church, which he did. The result is the Oceanside Cathedral." Again the image of the huge complex. A two-block line of scantily clad worshipers crowded the sidewalk of Ocean Boulevard. Then the picture changed to that of the CNR Shopping Channel, which combined feelie technology with home shopping to give viewers the impression that they were being personally waited on by Sister Veronica herself.

"Now Veronica runs the entire commercial end of the ministry, designing new products that reflect the church's beliefs and marketing them to members. She also adds the glamour to the whole movement. The girls worship her and the boys lust after her, so when you think about it you couldn't ask for a better spokesperson for your relatively new religion. She takes special pleasure in personally initiating the members of the church's youth group lucky enough to be invited to the private compound outside Myrtle Beach."

The image changed again, this time to that of a man of indeterminate age wearing what Jon imagined was an expensive white suit. He was malevolently good-looking, all angles with his high cheekbones and sharp jaw. Even his hair, blond streaked with gray, seemed mean, sweeping back as it did from an immaculate widows peak. He stood behind a technician in what Jon assumed to be the control room of Whitaker's vast studio complex and stared intently ahead. Though he was probably watching one of the control room monitors, the perspective made Jon feel as if the man was using his bottomless gray eyes to peer directly into his consciousness.

"Ah, here we go. This is the focus of the little story you're going to investigate for us. He's known as Lucas Schaefer and he works as special advisor to Whitaker. Not a crime in itself, of course, but it does lend itself to a certain access to power. Also not a crime, but it gave us reason to start examining his actions a little bit more closely than we would the assistant manager at a Cleaver's.

"When we ran an initial background check on Schaefer based on the available earthly information, everything came up green. According to his birth records, school documentation, past work records, credit reports and all the usual avenues used to prove somebody's existence, he really was Lucas Schaefer. We have him down as being born in Reading, England, graduating second in his class at Oxford and working as a PR rep and all-around idol-maker for a variety of political and religious organizations after that. But when we checked into our own records, know what we found?"

Jon shrugged. "Enlighten me."

Eli held his thumb and forefinger up to form a circle. "Zip. No records on him on our end whatsoever. Not in the master files, not in the Holy City files and not in those of any other major or minor deities."

"You have files?"

Eli paused, a little aggravated. "Think of it more as a collective consciousness, like a universal computer memory. We even checked at the home for aging deities over on Olympus. Nothing. After we checked with everyone around here I tried to get some help from our counterparts in the Underworld, but as usual they weren't very cooperative at all."

"So, basically the only problem with this guy is that you don't know anything about who he is or where he came from, right?"

"Jeez, boy. Ain't that enough? No wait, I'm sorry. I keep forgetting I'm talking to the famous ex-newspaper man. Everything has to be confirmed by at least two sources, right?"

Eli was hitting him in a weak spot and Jon knew it. But he wasn't going to bite. "Most of the time, yeah. But I'm still having trouble believing you're who you are and I'm even here, wherever here is. Don't you think you could give me something a little better?"

Eli sat back in his chair and crossed his arms, his eyes narrowing. "All right, boy. Try this on for size. Your man Andre, from your firm? Well, the two of you now have more in common than being newspaper expatriates. He washed up dead today on the beach south of his resort."

Andre dead? That couldn't have happened. The guy was on vacation with his *wife*, for crying out loud.

"His wife reported him missing this morning. Luckily he hadn't been in the water long and the crabs hadn't gotten to him so he was easy to identify."

Jon tried to absorb it. Andre's death was almost hitting him harder than his own.

Eli easily surmised Jon's feelings. "Yeah, I know. That's a bad sign. Worse, he's not the first. An executive at Nikura International who died in a car bombing the other day, he's connected to this, too," Eli said.

Jon tried not to think about Andre's wife sobbing over his bloated corpse at some dirtwater island morgue. "Whoever this Schaefer guy is, he must be onto you," Jon said.

"I doubt he's onto me, but he's sure onto somebody," Eli said. "Now you can see where my concern lies. These individual lives – even yours, I'm sorry to say – don't mean much in the cosmic scheme of things. But as an all-knowing, all-seeing sort of being, I have a tendency to pretty much have an idea of what's happening in my sphere of influence, which is everywhere. That's why the fact that someone I know little to nothing about has risen to this level of power concerns me. Schaefer's nearly at the top of the fastest growing religion in America."

"He's the guy behind the guy," Jon said, staring at a point in space as his mind worked. There was always a guy behind the guy. He and his newspaper pals called them the puppet masters. They were the ones who convinced reluctant candidates to run, who used the ego and ambition of another to further their own, usually more far-reaching, goals.

"Exactly," Eli said. "Which puts him in a position to influence those in government, business and the beliefs of a good portion of the public. And from past experience that ability has proved very handy when someone wants to affect the judgment of your run-of-the-mill human. But that's the least of my concerns. What really bothers me is how someone with the power to elude me happened to just appear out of nowhere then manufacture an entire life history. The last thing I need in this universe is a coup by some joker who's managed to just sneak up on me."

"Now other than Scheaffer, Veronica is the one you're going to have to watch out for," Eli said. "She was just a free-spirit college party girl when Whitaker found her, but as you can see, her ambition gets the best of her. Now she considers herself on par with Mary Magdalene herself, if you buy that story about her and the Kid having a little something going on."

"Did they?" Jon interjected. He'd always wondered, so he figured he might as well ask.

"Not in the way filthy-minded humans think. But anyone who knew them will tell you there was a connection between them that probably transcended physical love. But there were a few other obligations involved. The shitty part about being a trinity is that majority rules, and the little baby who landed dirtside was definitely in the minority."

"True."

"Anyway, back to the topic at hand, the benediction of each service involves Veronica and Whitaker heading off to their meditation chamber as Jesus and his faithful disciple to consummate the supposed earthly lust between the two. It's some pretty hot stuff for church, especially for around your parts. Since you're going in as a non-member, she'll certainly invite you to a service if she doesn't try some...um, more personal testimony first."

"So I imagine you expect me to use the same resolve I used to get away from Ashley to put her off?" Jon said, feeling simultaneously proud at his ability to resist and sad about the unexpected outcome.

"Don't be so sure, loverboy," came Alex's voice from behind them, prompting Eli to turn and scold her for apparently letting the cat out of the bag.

"What she means, boy, is that we expect you to do whatever is necessary to complete this assignment for us. If that happens to involve granting Veronica's more carnal requests, so be it."

Eli then stood and called to the back of the tent. "Thanks Alex. That's going to be it for today. I'm going to turn Jon over to you so he can get the rest of the details."

The light faded as Jon heard the projector being switched off.

Then, from the blackness, emerged his wife, Linda, dressed exactly as he had seen her last and looking more beautiful than he could have imagined.

He cleared his mind, reminded himself of where he was and what he was doing there and promptly passed out cold.

The hot wind whipped off the highway like it was blowing straight off the face of the July sun, forcing Krista Rogers to squint to keep her eyes from drying out. Not that there was any danger of that happening, since she was sure the humidity had to be in excess of 300 percent. But each time a truck passed she felt as if the breeze it left in its wake would wick every bit of moisture in her eyes right out of the tear ducts.

She'd been on the move since before dawn and decided she would have to stop soon. Her hastily prepared backpack had begun digging into the bruise on her right shoulder, and the sweat running down her face had formed several tiny rivulets which seemed to run straight into the small cut on her lip, producing a constant, throbbing sting.

After a few more minutes and a few more shuffling steps, she decided to cut her losses and rest. The backpack fell to the asphalt and Krista followed it, sitting roughly against the aluminum guardrail that probably couldn't keep a bicycle, not to mention an eighteen-wheeler, from barreling over the edge.

She felt like an old towel someone was still trying to get one last use out of — wet, limp, threadbare and dirty. Her hopes of finding a ride out of Philly by this route were fading fast, and she kicked herself for being too cheap and scared to even invest in a maglev ride south into Chester or Wilmington. As it was, she'd been walking the shoulder of I-95 all morning and hadn't gotten anything more promising than a couple of appreciative honks from the truckers.

Someone had to pick her up, she thought, out of a sense of convenience, if anything. Please, give me a ride. Have your way with me. Just get me out of this goddamn heat. After all, she'd done worse for less than having her life saved. Might as well make it count this time.

She unzipped an outside pocket on the backpack, a leftover from high school back in Erie, and pulled out a half-empty bottle of water she'd salvaged from the fridge on her way out of the apartment. The water was warm, but it felt good as she swished it around in her sticky mouth. She swallowed, took another sip and returned the bottle to the bag.

She thought she might be able to sit there until she finally succumbed to dehydration and passed out, but decided that with her luck someone would finally stop and get her to a hospital. Inevitably they'd check her belongings, find her ID and address and call Val to come get her. He'd be concerned and sympathetic — if he wasn't too stoned. He'd thank the doctors and take her home. Then he'd kill her.

Except by then Val should have been in jail, trying to

T
E
N

make friends with his cellmate in that aggravating, affected street pose he put on when he was sober. She hoped it got him cut up or sodomized for all his trouble, if not for nearly beating her senseless, at least for waking her from the most pleasant dream she'd had in months.

It was about home – the one that seemed a hundred years and a million miles away now. The lake effect snow was drifting in hand-sized flakes across the yard of her parents' tiny house. She and a friend were making snow angels, the moist whiteness caking in the wide knit of their mittens and their toboggan hats. Hearing a door slam, she hoped it was her parents – they were still together then – coming out to help her build a snowman or an igloo. But on the edge of consciousness she realized it was the door to the apartment. She felt the mattress sag under Val's weight, and then his trembling hand brushing away the hair from her face.

"Babe, wake up for a sec. I need you to loan me some money," he whispered, his voice raspy from a night of partying. Shit. He was crashing now and she knew what he wanted.

She made an annoyed noise and rolled over. She'd gotten to bed late after work and his hand tickled her face.

"I don't have any money," she said, still half asleep. "I don't get paid again until next week, and I bought some groceries today."

"You did what?"

She recognized his tone of voice and was suddenly fully awake. She rolled over to face him. "I bought food, Val. You know, so we could eat? Or have you started getting all your nutrition some other way?" she said, grabbing the right wrist and pointing to the string of 'dermals bearing tiny images of yin-yangs and the Incredible Hulk. She remembered there on the highway that she should've recognized that as a particularly dangerous combination. One brought on an overwhelming sense of inner peace, while the other could turn the tiniest, most meek pacifist into a vessel of pure rage and adrenaline-fueled strength. What resulted from the combination was a person very calm about the idea of hurting someone for no particular reason, and all the pharmaceutically powered muscle to do it with frightening ease. In her bleary anger, however, she didn't take precautions like she should have.

Strengthened and quickened by the Hulk 'dermals, he broke away from her halfhearted grasp and pushed her roughly down on the bed, his knee pressed in the crook of her right arm.

"I know you have some money in here somewhere, Krista," he said with almost psychotic politeness. "Now please tell me where it is before I have to *break your fucking arm!*"

She was already screaming. If felt like his knee was dislocating her shoulder from its socket. "I told you I don't have any! Get off me! You're breaking my shoulder!"

He stood and looked at her, laughing. "You lying ass bitch. You don't think I can find it myself?" With that he began striking at any vessel that might hide cash, moving to the kitchen and sending bottles and jars flying to the floor from the cabinets, their contents exploding on the grimy vinyl.

She got up and grabbed his arm. That just made him angrier. He pulled back and powerfully backhanded her across the face, sending her flying backwards into the stove and leaving her stunned on the kitchen floor. When she tried to get up he hit her again, this time with his fist balled up, the death's head ring he wore splitting her lip.

She lay on the floor again, feeling like she'd been slammed by an iron strapped to the front of a moving train. She tried to stanch the flow of blood and not think about how much it hurt. Most of all, she did every thing she could to not cry. Not now. That would make him think he'd won. After he had made his way through the kitchen to the other tiny room, she slowly rose. She turned and leaned against the stove. There, looking into the dull, greasy metal of the range hood, she saw her own reflection, her lip bleeding profusely and her eye beginning to swell in colors she didn't know the human body could create.

She realized then, looking at the pathetic, weak little girl she saw staring back at her, that the only way she would ever get out of this alive was to make him think he'd won.

"I know where we can get some money," she said as she turned to face him. She enjoyed his look of desperate glee.

She dressed quickly and led him up three blocks to South Street, then over two blocks to 5th, where Raul's Pizza sat in a space about as narrow as a walk-in closet. Krista was relieved to see all the lights were off, since she sometimes forgot that. Along the sidewalk only a few strung-out stragglers remained from the evening's loitering. The leader knelt and stroked the head of his chimera – this one a hybridized tiger – as it yawned and revealed teeth like daggers. They nodded in recognition to Val, but he didn't acknowledge them. On the way there, the hallucinations from the dermal combination had set in. When they finally arrived at the door of the heavily secured pizza parlor, Val was convinced he was being followed by a neo-Nazi cartoon duck wielding a huge dental drill and an oversized syringe marked "Pain Enhancer."

He was growing impatient to get away from the psycho poultry as she pressed her thumb against the pad next to the now dim neon Italian chef, which normally displayed a red disk of dough alternately flashing to give the impression of it being thrown. When they finally heard the solid metal click of the bolts sliding back, she opened the door quickly and motioned for him to go ahead. He rushed to the cash register and, like the idiot he was, began randomly punching numbers trying to get the drawer to open.

Her boss, Raul, put all his money into two things: custom tailored clothes and security precautions to keep out the roving bands of late-night marauders. As such, he never bothered to install a cash register newer than the old manual model the store had used since long before Krista's time. Val, who didn't have much experience holding down jobs of any kind, obviously didn't realize all he had to do was hit "No Sale" to get his wish.

By the time he got frustrated enough to look to Krista for help, she had already closed the door behind her on the way out, automatically reactivating the store's complex system of motion detectors, silent alarms and security cameras. Somewhere at the local precinct a tiny red light was flashing and Philadelphia's finest were being dispatched to the scene. Krista just smiled and waved to Val, who looked almost as helpless as she thought she must have earlier. In desperation, he went back to the cash register, and when he looked up again, she was gone.

Krista almost skipped back to the apartment, wondering if anyone would tell Val that any idiot knows a good businessman always puts his day's receipts in the bank's night deposit box. No doubt some armed robbery suspects in his new digs would be happy to enlighten him.

There was, however, cash back at the apartment. She reached into her drawers and scooped out what clothes she thought she might need. She then opened her battered paperback copy of "Catcher in the Rye" and ripped out the envelope taped there. Of all the places Val might look, she knew there was never any danger of him touching her small collection of books. Other than the memories, they were about all she had left of her dad. She considered taking them all, but decided to throw only "Catcher" into the bag. The digital clock radio changed to 5:23 a.m. She didn't look back as she walked out the door for the last time.

Now, as she sat under the blazing haze of the sun, the image of a sickly and strung-out Val sitting in a cell with someone who could use his rap sheet as wallpaper made her laugh. Still, the thought of facing him again prompted her to get up and move on.

She hefted the bag over her aching shoulder and touched the bruise around her left eye, immediately wishing she hadn't. It was still tender, and she knew the left half of her face probably looked like a ripe eggplant. All the more reason to keep moving as fast as she could.

A semi blew past, its wheels roaring against the pavement and the huge cell whining away under its hood, as she turned to face the Philadelphia skyline. There, the Nikura tower rose above it all like an art-deco dildo, its dome sitting proudly over the rest of the less endowed skyscrapers. Probably a conscious design decision by the management, considering all the people they'd screwed.

She then, slowly and deliberately, raised her right hand and extended her middle finger.

"Fuck you," she said to the skyline in a hard, even voice. It was to Val and all the other parasites like him. It was for the illusion that anything really resembled brotherly love in this shithole town.

The sound of air brakes behind her made her jump, but she wasn't too shocked to realize what was going on. Apparently some psychic trucker had picked up her pleading vibes, or was at least impressed by her boldness in flipping off an entire city from an interstate full of high-speed truck traffic. She wheeled around as a sudden burst of energy pushed her feet forward towards the eighteen-wheeler, which sat idling on the narrow shoulder. She pulled herself up in one powerful step with a strength that surprised her. The passenger door swung open easily and she slid into the high cab.

The coolness came as a shock, turning her sweaty epidermis into what felt like one big goose bump. She pulled the door shut and promptly lifted her shirt to just below her breasts and let the icy air from the vents blow against her bare, drenched torso.

"Thanks for stopping, mister," she said. If heaven didn't feel this good, she never wanted to go.

Something banged against the underside of the dashboard. "Ow! Goddamn it. How did you get in here?" Sticking up from under the driver's side of the dashboard was a pair of long legs and slender bare feet. She followed them down with her eyes to where she saw a pair of arms frantically tugging at something under the dash.

"You didn't stop to give me a ride?" She pulled down her shirt and held it there. She was prepared to bolt if she had to.

The driver shifted so he could get a look at her. It wasn't clear if he was successful. "You were hitchhiking on I-95." He said it as a matter of fact. "I hope you're not really that crazy."

She started to answer but was cut off. "Since you're in, can you give me a hand under here?"

"What the fuck is that supposed to mean?" she said, immediately on the defensive. It sounded just a little bit too much like a proposition she wasn't interested in. A pair of needlenose pliers lay on the dashboard. She grabbed them and aimed the pointed end at the driver.

"Sunrise two five nine, satellite tracking has listed you as disabled. Can you confirm? If so, we'll have an emergency crew on the way shortly," said a female computer voice from an overhead speaker.

"Could you please give me a hand *now*?" the driver said impatiently.

"What do you need?" He didn't want what she thought he had wanted, which made her feel better. Krista tried to get a glimpse of her anonymous rescuer's face.

"Pair of needlenose pliers lying up there on the dash. Hand them to me, please."

She was reluctant to give up her only weapon, but finally complied with his request. She placed the pliers, handle first like she'd been taught by her father, into his outstretched hand, then saw it disappear under the dash. The next thing she heard was a solid click from the pliers followed by a screaming alarm, prompting the driver to scramble back into an upright position and type something into a small computer console to the right of the driver's seat. The alarm immediately stopped.

"Control, this is Sunrise two five nine," the fellow said after pressing a small button on the steering wheel. "No need to send the crew, but my transponder's down. I'll be on manual from here on out. If I have any more problems, I'll let you know. Sunrise two five nine out." He then released the button. "And thanks for caring," he mumbled to himself.

After gunning the accelerator and waiting for a gap in traffic, he pulled the truck through three lanes and set the cruise control on seventy-five.

"What did you just do under there?" she asked after he seemed to relax at the wheel, still staring straight ahead and watching the road.

"Disconnected the transponder. Everything on the highway has them. They put out an identification signal so Highway Control can follow us on satellite tracking and keep everyone from crashing into each other. Now they can still see the truck from the satellite, but I'm not sending out an ID signal. As long as I don't cause any thirty-car collisions they probably won't care." He stretched his back to get the kinks out from the awkward position he held under the dash.

She couldn't figure him out. He was barefoot, but wore the shirt and trousers to what looked like an expensive business suit. The jet-black hair, the high cheekbones, the almond eyes and the dark skin made her think maybe American Indian. There was something not quite right about that assessment, though.

"So what landed you out there on the highway on a day like. ... Holy shit! What the hell happened to you?"

He'd turned briefly to make the first eye contact the two had experienced since he took her on. He looked at her with something between revulsion and sympathy, quickly turning his gaze back to the road to keep from unexpectedly crossing lanes. Krista just felt like she wanted to crawl under a rock and die.

She started to answer, but he cut her off, holding up an open hand.

"Never mind. I should know better than to ask stuff like that. It's really none of my business." He sneaked another glance at her. "Check back in the sleeper. There should be a first-aid kit or something. It might have a cold pack you can put on that bruise. You look like you might need stitches in your lip, too."

"It looks worse than it is, but it feels as bad as it looks," she said with a weak grin, the best she could muster with the damage to her face. She wanted to cover all the bruises, but there were too many and they were too large.

"Believe me, I know the feeling. The lav is all the way in the back if you want to get cleaned up. I think there might be some clean clothes back there somewhere. Bunks, too, if you want to crash."

She got up and moved to the rear of the spacious cab. The damn thing was *huge*. Past two single bunks that could fold up into the wall much like those in the train compartments she saw in old movies was the tiny lavatory. The floor was made of slats of dark wood, and she noticed there was even a hand-held showerhead attached to the faucet. She found the compartment marked with the unmistakable red cross and sat on the plastic toilet lid, pillaging around until she found the cold pack and a tube of antibiotic cream.

"So, you mind telling me your name?" Mako shouted from the front of the cab.

"It's Krista. No 'L,' just an 'A' at the end."

"Nice to meet you, Krista Noel. I'm Mako."

She laughed quietly. Japanese, maybe? That had to be it. He seemed kind of tall to be Japanese, though. And the name seemed to ring a bell from somewhere.

More searching in the kit revealed a bar of hotel soap, which she used to begin scrubbing the road grime and sweat from her face. She didn't realize how dirty she'd been until she saw her skin emerging in clean spots swirled with lather and dirt. This was also the first chance she'd had to gauge how badly Val had actually hurt her, and she didn't like what she saw.

Her left eye was nearly swollen shut, the flesh around it puffy and purple. Her lip looked much the same, only with the extra added bonus of what seemed like pint of blood caked around the quarter-inch gash in her lip. Once the blood was washed away, though, it didn't look nearly as bad. The soap, however, also served to add a painful sting to her lip's already persistent throb. She applied the antibiotic and a small bandage to her lip and examined the bruise on her shoulder. That could probably wait for attention. She was more concerned about what people might be able to see, so the eye won out in getting the cold pack.

Otherwise, she was simply a more sweaty and sunburned version of her usual self. Her normally spiky blonde hair was matted by half a night's sleep and a morning of sweat. Her entire body could use a wash, but that would have to wait. Her eyes — at least the one that was still open — looked tired, and she realized she should probably get some sleep. Her one concern was whether to trust her driver. She's heard of girls ending up dead in ditches hundreds of miles away from their points of origin after hitching rides with psychotic truckers, not to mention the "favors" many drivers expected in exchange for providing rides. Still, forced sex with this guy would probably be better than the consensual sex she'd had with Val.

The thought brought on a wry smile, the crooked one her dad always teased her about, before she checked herself. What was she thinking? She'd exchanged maybe four sentences with the guy and already she was making him out to be Mr. Wonderful. Great start to a long trip, Krista. But she needed sleep in the worst way, and those bunks looked more inviting with each passing moment. She moved back up to the passenger seat and settled in. The cold pack felt blissful against her eye.

"How far are you going?" she asked. She faced forward, but kept her eyes on him.

"That's a good question," he said with a smirk. "So far, to visit a relative in Delaware. Where are you going?"

She thought for a moment. She had no idea, really. Her primary goal had been just to get away from Val and get out of town. She'd make arrangements to have her paycheck from Raul's transferred to her wherever she landed. So far that was all the planning she'd done.

"Anywhere south," she offered. She arranged the cold pack on her eye and tried to stifle a yawn.

"Great. I'll wake you up when we get to Key West."

She laughed, but his tone was serious.

"Look, I'll drop you off after I make my visit. Does Wilmington work?"

"Are you going farther?"

He brushed back the hair that hung long over his right eye, giving her a better view of his profile. "Don't know. Depends on what happens next. But I don't think it would be the best idea for you to stay with me. I'm kinda in the middle of some shit."

"Yeah, I think that's going around," she said. "I guess that would be fine. Anything that gets me away from Philly is a step in the right direction."

She tried and failed to suppress another long yawn. "Sorry. It's been a long night."

"No doubt," Mako said. There was a long pause. "Listen, if you want to crash on one of those beds back there, you're welcome to. But if you don't, I'll understand."

She studied him, her eyes narrowing as if that would make it easier for her to detect some hint of psychosis, some small shred of sexual deviance.

"You understand I don't trust you, right."

"Oh, absolutely," he said. He strung the word out, sounding almost like one of the South Street stoners. The two of them probably had more in common than they imagined. "All I'm saying is, you're dead tired and I'm going to be busy up here driving. The beds are back there, and as far as I know the sheets are clean."

He had no idea how sweet those two words – "clean sheets" – sounded to her. She'd slept so long enveloped in Val's junkie stink that Mako might as well have said the bed included a full-body massage and pancake breakfast.

"You'll be up here driving, huh?"

"Yep."

"And how long is the trip?"

"Twenty minutes if we were still under guidance, but a bit more with us on manual. Time enough for a nice little lay-down."

She said nothing and moved back into the sleeping cabin.

Her clothes were still moist with perspiration, but the institutional white sheets were indeed clean and pulled taut over the thin mattress. She yanked back the top sheet, slipped under up to her waist, and was asleep as her head hit the pillow.

Krista woke with a jolt when she felt the truck stop suddenly, then back up, then stop hard again. Finally she heard the sound of creaking metal and crumbling stone, then felt the truck roll over something that seemed entirely too large for it to be rolling over. After they came to an abrupt stop, she heard the cab door open and close, then the sound of footsteps walking away on some sort of gravel.

She needed clean clothes. It seemed like days since she'd showered, but there was no time to bathe. Anyway, she was too curious about what the truck had hit. A rummage through her backpack produced only a pair of jeans and two turtleneck shirts. Damn – scooped clothes from the wrong drawer on the way out of the apartment. Then she remembered Mako had said something about clothes. After some searching, she popped open a compartment built into the cab's wall and found a pair of khaki pants small enough for a slim adult man and a white work shirt with an embroidered Sunrise Moving patch above the left breast pocket.

The shirt wasn't going to be a problem, but the pants presented a fashion challenge. The inside tag said the waist was 32 inches, which she immediately assumed would be too large for her narrow hips. And the length was simply ridiculous. After feeling around in the bottom of her bag, she also found the Swiss army knife she knew had to be down there somewhere.

It didn't take as long as she expected to cut off the legs of the pants, and the Sunrise patch ripped off cleanly once she snipped a couple of the stitches. Looking closer at the patch, she noticed that what she thought was a solid line under the Sunrise logo was actually tiny print. It read "A Division of Nikura International."

She cursed herself for being so stupid not to realize it before. She knew the name rang a bell. He was Mako Nikura. She'd heard somewhere that the company's head had been blown up in a car bomb explosion and that the son was due to take it over, but nobody could find him to do it.

And if someone who stood to inherit a gazillion-dollar company didn't want to be found, it would only natural for him to try to escape once they did find him. Which meant she was probably in even more trouble with this guy than she was getting kicked around by Val. Mako was right. He *was* in the middle of some shit.

She slid into the cut-offs and cinched them around the waist with the belt she was wearing when Mako picked her up. She tied the shirt at the bottom and rolled up the sleeves to de-emphasize the fact that the clothes were designed for a man and peeked into the front of the cab.

Ahead of the truck loomed the largest, most palatial home

E
L
E
V
E
N

71

Krista had ever seen. It was three stories, brick and stone and seemed to go on for a half-mile in either direction. The truck sat in the home's wide half-moon driveway, an elaborate bed of flowers and shrubs at its center. She checked the mirrors, passenger side first. In it she was struck by the sight of a gate — or what used to be a gate — lying in the driveway in two heavy wrought iron sections. She could see gouges in the surrounding wall where each side had obviously been ripped out of their brick posts.

Motion in the driver's side mirror caught her eye, and she changed position to see what was going on. Standing next to the trailer were Mako and a fellow who looked more like Krista's image of the typical Japanese corporate mogul: middle aged, short, fat, balding and sweating profusely in the hot sun. From the motions of their hands and their facial expressions, she could tell the two were arguing about something, but the idling engine prevented her from hearing anything outside the cab. Behind them, she saw what looked like two miniature tanks, one aimed out of the gate and the other aimed in the direction of the two arguing men. Security drones. Since the destruction of the gate, the two devices were no doubt there to make sure no one got in or out. The older man kept glancing in their direction, and that made her nervous for her and Mako's well being.

She needed to do something, if not to save Mako's skin so he could drive her out of here, at least to save her own and avoid getting caught up another lousy situation. She was pretty sure Mako was unarmed, and all she had at her disposal was a dull pocketknife and some sweaty underwear. Slightly dangerous, but she had no idea what those little armored toys out there were packing.

She looked around the cab, and seeing no compartments obviously marked "Weapons," she checked the glove box and under the dashboard and came up with nothing. Nothing hidden in the sleeping bay or the lav, either. In desperation, she moved to the front of the cab again and touched the small computer screen on the dashboard.

"You have accessed the Sunrise Moving Corporation's onboard computer system," said a sultry computerized female voice. Jeez, she thought. Knowing some of these truckers, the thing probably also made coffee and offered dirty feelies to go along with the porn-girl voice. "Please make your choice from the items on the screen."

She touched the Manifest icon, represented by a clipboard superimposed over a Sunrise truck, and was immediately reading off the personal possessions of the Brabbage family, formerly of Hackensack.

She read down the list quickly, seeing nothing that could help her unless she planned to sneak up on the tanks and drop a couch on them. Finally, near the bottom of the list, she found Mr. Brabbage's gun collection, which seemed to be as good as it was going to get as far as weapons went. It would just have to do, she thought as she eased out the passenger side door.

^^^

"You are meddling in affairs you have no business with, Mako," Hiroshi Nikura said as he dabbed sweat from his forehead with an already saturated handkerchief. "These accusations are an insult to the memory of your father and the honor of this family."

"Uncle, I know you had something to do with this. I've seen the evidence. I know what you're doing. What I want to know is why you had to kill father."

Hiroshi's lips tightened over his small teeth, a vein in his head growing more defined with each tense moment. "I did not kill your father!" he shouted, suddenly turning and walking back towards the house.

"Then who did? The car sure didn't blow up by itself, did it?" Mako said, holding his ground.

The older man turned back towards Mako, having seemingly calmed himself. "Mako, you are upset over the death of your father, I know. I am saddened, also. He was my brother, after all. But the whole situation has obviously affected your judgement if you think that I might have had something to do with his death. What I can believe even less is that you would make these accusations on the word of a gaijin slut like … "

"Like Andrea? Or like mother? Is that what you mean, Uncle?" Mako was trying to remain calm, but subconsciously he felt his teeth beginning to clench, his hands balling into fists that sought only to turn the fat little man's face into a grotesque, bloody mess. "I know you hated mother, but I still don't know why. Do you think gaijin women are only good as mistresses?"

His uncle just stood there looking ridiculous sweating through his suit, but Mako knew he'd struck a nerve. "Fine. If that's how you feel, I suppose there's no reasoning with you. But I'm sure the cops would be pretty interested in Nikura's illegal weapons shipments. After all, it is kinda suspicious that a moving van would be carrying enough weapons to stock an armory."

"Lies! All lies!" Hiroshi shouted, becoming even shriller.

Mako spread his arms in resignation. "Well then, let's just go have a look at my cargo and you can decide."

His uncle's eye twitched almost imperceptibly and a thin smile curled up on one side of his mouth. His jaw muscles clenched wildly and the vein in his forehead became even more pronounced, but it was the motion of his left hand in his pants pocket that put Mako on alert.

The metallic locking noise and the whir of the small servo motors on the security drones were all he heard before the firing started. Mako was already running back toward the cab when the first rounds hit the driveway about a foot away from his uncle's Italian wingtips, and dirt and stones erupted from the driveway in a tight line following Mako all the way to the closed door of the truck.

The bullets were coming at what seemed like a million rounds per second, but the slow tracking drones did allow him enough time to open the door and dive into the cab before the door's entire interior was shredded by gunfire. He had just enough time to cover his head before the next few rounds sent shards of glass from the shattered windshield flying around the compartment.

"Krista? You all right?" he shouted into the cab when the firing stopped.

As if to answer his question, he suddenly heard a heavy thump and a loud hissing from the roof of the cab and, looking over his shoulder back out the ruined door, spotted a slender trail of white smoke emerging from the same spot. The

73

stream ended in an ear-bursting thud and a plume of black and orange flame where the two security drones previously sat. Krista's bruised face then appeared upside down in the driver's side doorway.

"You okay in there?"

Mako checked himself quickly, finding only a few nicks from the broken glass, and began gingerly brushing himself off. Krista disappeared for a moment, then reappeared right side up on the truck's snub-nosed hood. "Fine. What are you doing up there?"

"Tell you in a sec," she said as she pulled from the waistband of her cut-off shorts what appeared in her hands to be a ridiculously huge automatic pistol, then aimed it and squeezed off several rounds at Mako's uncle, her eyes closing tightly with each shot.

Once he saw the explosion, Hiroshi Nikura had turned on his heels and run towards the front door of his mansion, sure he would make it until he saw the masonry around the antique oak doors explode in a flurry of smoke and stone chips. In a delayed act of self preservation, he threw his sweaty bulk to the ground and waited for the fatal bullet to reach him, that he might be through with the nasty business which had led up to all this violence.

But the bullet did not come.

"On your feet, fat boy. You're gonna give us the fifty-cent tour," Krista growled as she placed the muzzle of the gun in Hiroshi's left ear. It was the same voice she used when she was forced to toss junkies out of the pizza shop when they started to hallucinate on the neon holograms of Italy that hung at each booth. She hoped it worked better on this guy than it did on South Street.

"Please! Don't shoot!" Hiroshi whimpered.

Mako grabbed Andrea's packet and leaped from the truck cab. "No such luck, Uncle," Mako said as he kneeled at the prostrate man's side. "Seems to me that by trying to kill me with your little remote-control toys over there, you might have implicated yourself in Father's killing a bit more than you would have liked."

"Mako, I beg of you, please don't pursue this. You have no idea what you are tampering with," Hiroshi said, sounding more pathetic by the moment.

"I might not know now, Uncle, but I will when you tell me. Or else my friend here will be forced to use the gun she's holding in your ear. And if that one doesn't work, there are plenty more where that one came from, right? Now get up and take us to your office."

The older man struggled to his feet, his clothing now completely drenched in perspiration, and led them through the impressive front doors into the front foyer, Krista holding the pistol steadily aimed at his eardrum and whatever might lie behind it the entire time.

Servants were clustered around the huge entryway looking frightened. One fellow was already on the telephone.

"Hey, Jeeves! Drop the phone or I plug the boss!" Krista shouted at the man, who regarded her carefully, then placed the phone gently back in its cradle and switched off the video monitor. Hiroshi just whimpered. "Nice crib, fat boy. Who'd you have to knock off to get this? *Your* father?" she asked as they passed the mismatched displays of early American paintings paired with delicate Japanese sculpture and ceramics. Mako's uncle didn't respond, continuing to shuffle along quietly under their encouragement, but the comment didn't go unnoticed. Mako knew she had overheard the conversation and that she now knew far more than she should.

"Mind if I ask you how you know how to fire a rocket launcher?" Mako whispered to Krista.

"What's to know?" she said. "The instructions are printed on the side in, like, fifth-grade language and little pictures. Any idiot could shoot one of those things."

They arrived at a tall, heavily paneled door. At Mako's prompting, his uncle allowed his eye and fingerprint to be scanned. The bolts in the lock slid back and they entered, Krista urging Hiroshi ahead with a slight push into his neck with the pistol.

Mako immediately headed for his uncle's desk, a huge, wrap-around monolith made of dark wood. "Sit in the chair, Uncle. Then show us the computer. You're going to give us some information." The man was crying now, sobbing and muttering incomprehensible statements about regret and forgiveness. Mako grabbed his face with both hands and looked into his eyes.

"Uncle! You have a chance to do something right, now. Do it for Father! He will forgive you!"

"No ... I can't do it. He'll kill me. I know he will," Hiroshi said, blubbering like a child.

"Who will kill you, Uncle? Father is dead, he won't kill you."

"Not Akiro ... I didn't know they would kill him, either. But he doesn't care. He won't stop ... I can't do it," Hiroshi said, placing his head on his arms on the desktop, his body heaving with his deep sobs.

"This isn't getting us shit," Krista said. She was growing impatient with the unexpected drama. Lord knows she hadn't signed on for any of this.

Hiroshi Nikura's sobs subsided for a moment. He wiped his eyes and face with the sweaty handkerchief. "There is a stick. Everything I know is there. But I think someone stole it from me. It has been missing for a week."

"A stick? There was a stick in ..." He remembered the packet Andrea had given him. The stick was the one thing he hadn't looked at. "I think I know where it is, Uncle. I think I might already have it."

Hiroshi reached into his pocket and extracted a delicate, expensive looking box. His demeanor seemed to have changed. "I am sorry, Mako. With the upset, I fear my heart is affected. I must take my medicine."

The pill was tiny and there was only one in the box. Hiroshi placed it in his mouth and held it there. His jaw muscles clenched as he bit down hard. Then, without warning Hiroshi's body convulsed, his eyes fixed and staring straight ahead. His breath came in short, raspy heaves. He drooped forward onto the desk and, just as quickly as it had all begun, it stopped.

Krista still held the gun on the older man, but now looked around nervously. "Mako? What the hell's going on? Is he okay?"

Mako grabbed the hair on the back of his uncle's head and raised it. His eyes were frozen in a grotesque grimace, a trickle of oddly colored saliva running from the corner of his mouth. Mako lowered the head, pressed two fingers to his uncle's neck and felt for a pulse. Nothing.

"Fucking shit!" he said, kicking the leather upholstered swivel chair. "He's dead!"

Krista again holstered the gun back in the waistband of her shorts. "This is a big problem, isn't it?"

"Other than another person in my family being dead, not really. He told us what we need to know." Mako pulled the silvery packet from his waistband and looked inside. There the stick was. He handed it to Krista.

"Whatever you do, don't lose that."

"Safe as in the arms of Jesus," she said as she handed to Mako the old fashioned Glock 9mm pistol she'd been carrying. "You might want to take this. Since I don't think we'll be going back to the truck, you won't have a chance to go shopping in that gun shop you were towing."

"Sorry, I don't do guns. Scare the hell out of me."

"Great. Fine. You're the one getting shot at, and *you* want to be a pacifist. Well buddy, my pacifist days are over," she said as she expertly released the clip to check the number of rounds, then firmly popped it back into place with the heel of her hand. "But I'm only going to back up your skinny ass for so long if this keeps up. This is simply not my scene."

"Fine, fine. We'll talk about it later. Right now, we've got to find a way out of here. Any ideas?"

"Yeah," she said. They both heard the sounds of voices approaching from down the hall. "This dump have a garage?"

Mako grinned and shook his head. "You have no idea."

Andrea Turner tried to find something to do besides cry, but it wasn't working. She even found herself asking around to the other assistants in the outer offices to see if they had some extra work they might need help with.

She was trying to occupy herself by paging through a fashion magazine on her screen, but it was all just words and pictures and pixels scrolling by. Nothing congealed into meaning. How appropriate.

Seeing Akiro's son earlier that morning hadn't made the meaning of the last few days any clearer. She found herself thinking of Akiro even more, which just threw her deeper and deeper into a depression she had to hide. To look upset because your boss died is one thing, but to look like you're lamenting the death of a lover is quite another, and she didn't want anyone in the office to suspect the latter even though there was nothing anyone could really do to her about it now.

Other than the diluted genes which gave Mako his vaguely Japanese hair and eyes, he seemed nothing like his father when she first looked at him. He was tall and skinny, yet athletic in comparison to his father's paunch. Akiro had tried to eliminate his belly with daily workouts and a diet that avoided the overindulgence he was often subject to — an attempt to make himself more desirable to her. Mako, on the other hand, struck her as looking more like a pure-bred American Indian than the son of a wealthy Japanese corporate magnate.

When she watched him skillfully elude Yoshi and Spivey she knew exactly whose son he was. There was the glimmer in his eyes when he used her intercom to inform them they were trapped. His gait (though that of a slimmer, younger man) and the deeply sympathetic way he looked at her when she implored him to find his father's killer — all told her that Mako's genetic path led right to Akiro Nikura's doorstep. It was the glimmer that made her tremble simultaneously with recognition and deep sadness. It was such a glimmer that had originally attracted her to Mako's father, and it was such a look that often remained with Akiro as he followed her into the tiny bedroom of her Rittenhouse Square apartment, where his enthusiasm would spark inspired innovations in their lovemaking. As a surprise for his most recent birthday, Andrea even studied the traditions of the Geisha, hoping to stoke the enthusiasm even more. Akiro was delighted, and teased her that she was naturally blessed with the porcelain-white skin Japanese women could only achieve through heavy applications of powder and make up. That, combined with her Nordic crystal blue eyes and blonde hair, made him quite aroused.

The irony was that she could have very well ended up

T
W
E
L
V
E

working for Mako in the same capacity as she did for his father. She never thought of herself as the type to sexually engage both a father and a son, but she could see herself becoming attracted to the younger Nikura just from their brief meeting earlier.

She only hoped Mako's youthful rebelliousness and disdain for what his father did wouldn't prevent him from seeking out his father's killers, even if it was only at her pleading request that he do so.

Frustrated with the magazine and her helplessness in the terrible situation, she turned away from the screen and looked around the immaculate office suite, its sterility broken only by large pieces of modern art (which she had helped pick out) and carefully maintained tropical plants. There was total stillness. She was essentially serving as the assistant to a dead man, which left her with precious little to do other than sulk over that man's death. No calls had come in, and all that did were being routed to the assistants of Akiro's subordinates in the outer offices. Since there was no one offering her any work, she decided it would be a good time to take a break, if only for a change of scenery.

She had made coffee as usual that morning out of habit, but she and Spivey had been the only ones drinking it. What was left in the squat decanter was rapidly turning to tar, so she bypassed it and went straight to the ladies room to touch up the lipstick she had unconsciously chewed off fretting over everything that had transpired during the past forty-eight hours.

On her way back to her desk she noticed someone waiting there. The fellow didn't look threatening with his powder blue polo shirt, khakis and leather loafers, but since the troubles with terrorist groups using random civilians to bomb highrises in New York, no one was being too careful. Besides, all of Akiro's appointments had been canceled after the accident, and security was hyper-vigilant about alerting her to anyone from the lobby coming up without the visit being pre-arranged. She tapped the phone in her ear and spoke "lobby security" into the tiny microphone. The officer on duty said the fellow was an associate of Mr. Nikura's and had level five security clearance that seemed to check out, so he'd sent him on up.

Andrea thanked him and disconnected. She put on her cheeriest business face that said "I'll be as polite as I can be, but if you piss me off I'll have you thrown out on your ass," and rounded the corner back to her desk.

He was older, but in some ways it was hard to tell. Everything about him seemed a little off, from the artificially brown head of neatly coifed hair to his smooth, almost baby-like skin. "Can I help you, sir?" she said.

He said nothing, but held up a small package that she could see was addressed to Akiro. When she approached to accept it, she noticed something else was off. His face, which seemed strangely youthful, didn't match the age-spotted crepe of the skin on his hands. She then saw the tiny black cylinder partially hidden beneath it the package, but before she could speak she felt two quick thumps. A wisp of smoke rose from the dark circle, and as Andrea fell, she looked down to where her hands had unconsciously risen to shield herself and saw they were covered with her own blood, streaming from the two neat holes in her stomach. She saw the man's feet turn and take him out of the office. The lights faded and she dreamed, drifting off to thoughts of Akiro, Mako and geishas.

^ ^ ^

Linda Templeton looked at the telephone receiver as if there was something it knew but wasn't telling her. She was positive Jon had headed for the beach cottage, and she was trying to convince herself he had arrived safely and was simply out sulking on the beach.

She hung up, disgusted with herself.

Why should she be calling him back? He was the one that had done everything wrong. He was the liar. She had every reason to send him away.

But that still didn't explain why. Jon Templeton was no rapist, and he certainly wasn't stupid. He wasn't even the type of man to go after a cheap piece of ass. She shook her head and clenched her eyes shut. Yes, yes, she told her conscience, which was busy reciting all the things she'd learned in her college self-defense class. She knew one was about power and the other was about sex, but still she found them hard to separate in her mind. Besides, if he were to put a price on a piece of ass, hers was much more expensive, what with requiring monogamy, support, understanding and love, and was, she was sure she could say, worth every bit of work he put into getting it. As far as she knew there were no problems with their relationship, either underlying or overt. If there were, Jon would have said something.

Well, that's not really true. She knew he was miserable at his new job. Everything about it was the polar opposite of what he had worked for his entire career. At the newspaper, his job was revealing truth. Now it was hiding it, spinning it, making sure that if the truth did come out, it was the officially sanitized version – the one that would allow the firm's clients to emerge shiny and bright from a shithole. Three months of lying to former colleagues for a living had taken its toll on him. His attitude had changed. Every time she asked him how things were going at work there was the pause while he steeled himself to say everything was fine.

She had told him again and again not to take the job on her account. They had money saved. Despite the ugly way Jon and the newspaper had parted, they allowed him to be "laid off" and collect unemployment. And God bless this old house they inherited from Jon's Aunt Lil. Aside from work to update the plumbing and electricity and the usual taxes and such, they'd never had to pay one cent on the place. They were in good shape financially and there was no danger of bill collectors showing up at the door. He should have felt no pressure to take the next job to come along.

But obviously he did. She imagined the pressure was more subtle, not coming from her necessarily, but from their situation. They wanted to have a child, and Jon wanted to spend time with that child. They both knew reporters' hours weren't conducive to that. He also knew that as an investigative reporter, there was no telling who he might piss off next, and the thought of somehow endangering his family because of his work was unacceptable. Why would it lead him to this, though? Could it have been me?

She looked up to catch her reflection in the vanity mirror. Her eyes were red from crying, the dark circles underneath eyes betraying her lack of sleep during the last few days. She could see in her own face a map of her husband's personality, the features of each tied together by his love of the details of her body. She had never thought herself gorgeous — still didn't, really, she thought — but her husband, through his looks at her, his fingers grazing across her skin, told her every day how beautiful he thought she was. She recalled the tenderness of his touch as he would caress her face as he kissed her, the way his thumb, when she smiled, would find the cavernous dimple in her cheek and stroke it as if...well, as if he was trying to transmit the sensation elsewhere.

The face she saw there was the face of the woman who had married Jon Templeton, and yet different. He said better, but occasionally she thought not. She preferred not to consider the need for wrinkle cream any time in the future, but still she occasionally found a deepened crease or a gray hair in her otherwise deep brown mane, random strands now bleached a lighter shade from their last week at the beach together. And unlike many women her age, Linda had avoided the seemingly inevitable arrival of extra pounds, in part because they remained childless, but also thanks to genetics and both of them working to stay trim. After all, neither of their lifestyles lent themselves to any strenuous activity, so they had to do something.

In short, Linda felt as if the two of them were both still deeply in love, and as a novelty few of their contemporaries could boast of, it was still each other they were in love with.

So what was the problem?

As if to answer her question, the telephone chirped. She answered quickly, immediately flipping on the video display. She was disappointed to see the face of a woman she could only assume was Ashley DuBose. She reminded Linda of the Barbie dolls she played with as a child after she'd given them a permanent haircut. She seemed too made-up, and her pixie-length hair was certainly bleached something other than its natural color. Certainly her boobs were fake. Probably has feet molded into the high-heel position, too. Although if the rumors about her were true, she was very anatomically correct. But that doesn't justify what Jon did to her, does it?

"Hello, um ... Mrs. Templeton?" the image said softly. Linda felt her mouth tighten with anger. At whom she wasn't sure.

"What can I do for you, Ashley?" Why was this happening? Shouldn't the police or a lawyer have advised her against this?

"I have a confession to make, Mrs. Templeton. May I call you Linda?"

"Ashley, I hate to say this because we're talking about my husband, here, but should you really be calling me now? I'd think it would be a bad idea for your case or lawsuit or whatever you're going to bring against Jon."

Without warning the screen split, with Ashley's face moving off to the right and another appearing right beside it.

"Linda, this is Aubrey DuBose, Jon's boss," said the second face.

"I recognized you, Dub. And I guess that would actually be former boss."

"Whatever. Linda, I didn't call to split hairs with you. I just wanted to get down to the truth of this whole ugly matter." He went to light a cigarette and was having some difficulty. She noticed then that his right hand was bandaged and splinted. "Now, I don't know what Jon might have told you yesterday, but I'm sure you two have discussed his not working here any more and the reasons why."

"Yes, the subject did come up," she said. She knew she was looking at Dub like he was an idiot.

Ashley broke in. "Mrs. Templeton, I just wanted to say that what I told Dub yesterday about Jon assaulting me wasn't true. Jon has never come onto me at all. I trapped him in the newspaper library and tried to ... um, I made some improper advances toward him."

"I see," Linda said, trying not to give away her immense relief at the truth finally being revealed. "What *did* he do?"

"Well, not much, which is kind of unusual for a guy." Linda was mortified that Ashley looked as if this actually bothered her. "He didn't lay a hand on me. It really didn't seem like he wanted anything to do with me. I was sort of surprised. But I pushed it, and he still wouldn't budge. I'm not used to that, I guess, and decided to get back at him. I really didn't mean for him to feel like he had to quit. I'm sorry," she said, weeping quietly.

Linda couldn't take it any more. "You conniving little slut. What gave you the right to screw with my husband's life just because he had the good sense not to screw you?"

"Now, Linda. I don't think such language is necessary," Dub said. He was obviously thrown off by her outburst and was likely reviewing in his head what legal action he could be subject to. "I'm sure we can settle this like civilized people."

"Civilized behavior obviously doesn't run in your family, Dub. Thank you for your honesty, Ashley. Now all I have to do is find Jon and tell him the heat is off from both of us." And apologize.

"He's missing?" Dub asked, managing to sound genuinely concerned. Probably worried about some kind of liabilities claim if Jon ran off and hanged himself, she thought.

"Not officially. I have a good idea of where he is, but I'm having some trouble getting in touch with him. Silly me, I kicked him out of the house when I thought he was a rapist, Ashley." She hoped the sarcasm in her voice burned through the telephone lines and resonated in Ashley's ears.

"Well, when you find him, please give him our deepest apologies and tell him he's welcome to come back to the firm. We already miss ..."

"Thank you, Dub. If he's interested, I'm sure he'll call. In the meantime, our lawyer will be in touch. Goodbye."

Linda hung up. The image of her husband strung up by a belt lingered far longer than she preferred.

She immediately scribbled out and transmitted an e-mail message to Jon's mother saying they both would be out of town for a few days.

Then she grabbed her purse and headed for the maglev station.

Jon awoke with a start, thinking he must have just had the most disturbingly realistic dream — no, make that nightmare — he'd ever experienced. The sky was a clear azure and the bright sun shined its warmth down on him. He decided he must have fallen asleep on the beach while bemoaning the life that seemed to be crashing down around him thanks to an inappropriately placed pair of peach silk panties.

Beneath him, however, there was grass instead of sand and a beach chair. And as difficult as it was to look at directly, the sun seemed to shimmer in a way that Jon thought was highly unusual. With his eyes shielded, he was sure he could make out some faint sort of structure inside the intense light.

"Annoying, isn't it?" said a vaguely familiar female voice.

He wasn't on the beach at all, but in the idyllic park-like surroundings of his dream, which he was quickly realizing was firmly grounded in his present reality. The speaker was sitting in the shade of a huge oak tree, the branches of which hung long and low from its immense trunk. Jon could see that she leaned against it, her hands clasped behind her head and her legs outstretched. He was sure he'd heard her voice before, but he couldn't place the face, which was partially hidden by the shadows of the tree's foliage.

"Pardon me?" he said, still trying to get a fix on who he was addressing.

"I said it's annoying, isn't it? The city that never sleeps up there," she said, pointing above her. "The boss has always thought it was a little gaudy."

"That's a city up there?"

"Come on, Jon. Use your head. You had to be doing something in Sunday school besides flirting with the girls next to you. That's the Holy City, New Jerusalem, final destination of all good and righteous Christians," she said with a hint of sarcasm. "You do remember where you are, don't you?"

Jon breathed a sigh of resignation. "Still dead?"

"Yeah, still extremely dead. But not as dead as you could be. For some reason you keep demonstrating the characteristics of being flesh and blood. Even the boss said he'd never seen anything like it, especially that little fainting spell you threw."

The voice in the tent! That's where he recognized it. And Linda! He had seen her walk out of the darkness looking like his fondest memory of her, and he remembered his head immediately swimming with the impossibility of the scene.

"What about my wife? I remember I saw her just before I fainted. She's not dead, too, is she?"

The woman under the tree suddenly seemed uncomfortable, pulling her knees up to her chin and wrapping her arms around her legs.

"Well, that's kind of why I'm here. The boss told me to apologize to you once you woke up. When you thought you saw your wife, that was me. It's a little shape-shifting trick one of the folks over in the Native American zone taught me and I haven't quite learned how to control it yet."

"Great. I'm dead and will never see my wife again, and you decide to impersonate her. Thank you so much ... what was your name?"

"Alexandria Chaumont. Alex, to my friends."

She stood and moved into the sun in front of Jon and extended a delicately shaped hand. Even when she wasn't trying to impersonate his wife, she was quite beautiful. Like everyone here, she was dressed casually — barefoot with only a plain white T-shirt and a pair of cut-off blue jeans. Her full auburn hair as straight as a horse's tail hung over her shoulders, and her aristocratic features — especially her high cheekbones and eyes like onyx — held in them a hint of something more exotic. She looked to be about 25, but Jon imagined age had no real meaning here.

"I'm sort of a special assistant to the boss when he needs me. That's why he had me running the projector for him in there. He prefers to let me handle the technical stuff."

Jon ignored the hand, stood up and looked around as if there was something far more interesting going on elsewhere.

"Well, it was nice to meet you face-to-face when you weren't trying to spook the hell out of me. Apology accepted. Now you can go tell Eli your mission was accomplished."

Jon turned away and began walking in a randomly chosen direction, then stopped and looked around.

"How, exactly, would I go about finding Eli, by the way."

"Why?" she said, standing with her arms crossed and looking at Jon with thinly veiled amusement. "Do you want to file a complaint?"

"It's not out of the realm of possibility, but no. I wanted to get back before I was late for something."

"Please. The guy sits with his fingers on the dials of time and space and you're worrying about being late? Trust me, when he wants you he'll find you. I think he'd prefer you let some of this soak in, anyway. Now could we please call a truce? I'm not used to dealing with this much hostility. Most people are glad to be here. And if they're male and worth a damn, they're usually glad to be with me, too."

Jon smiled and agreed with those anonymous dead men, admiring the totality of her form from the short distance.

"A truce ... All right. But no more impersonations," he said as he approached her and extended his hand. "Deal?"

"Deal." They shook, and Jon suddenly felt a quick hum of energy from her hand, followed by what felt like a light tranquilizer taking effect.

"Whoa!" he murmured as he sat back down on the thick lawn and held his head. "What was that?"

"Oops. Sorry," she said as she sat beside him and giggled. "I forgot to warn you about that. It's empathy. I can't help it."

"If that was another attempt to be funny, I'm rescinding my truce." He let his brain return to normal. "Did you say empathy?"

"Yeah. Raw, distilled, unfiltered empathy. That's one of the great things about this place. When you come here, your spiritual essence is focused and you're able to use it even more effectively than you were during life. Mine was empathy. I'm sure yours will be creativity of some sort. Maybe you'll publish a novel here. We love reading new books."

"If it can manage to drag a book out of me, then this really is heaven. I couldn't even get one started when I was alive. And by the way, I didn't mean to imply earlier that I wasn't happy about being here. Considering the alternative, it's great. I just feel like I had so much other business to take care of while I was alive. No one ever feels like they've accomplished all they wanted to, right? I guess I've accomplished even less than that, especially in the last few days. And then there's the whole Linda thing. What is she going to do when she finds out what happened to me? What will she think?"

"Shut up and turn around," Alex said matter-of-factly.

"What?"

"Close your mouth and turn around. I'm going to rub your shoulders. Don't tell me you don't need it," she said as she cracked her knuckles loudly. He complied, but not without some reservation. When her strong hands grasped his shoulders he felt the calming hum penetrating his body. They moved in long, powerful strokes across the muscles, tensed like steel bands, across his back. He found himself groaning and his head lolling forward as she applied the perfect amount of pressure at each tense point.

"You know, the boss told me it's amazing how we humans can hold on to so much tension even after we've been relieved of our flesh-and-blood bodies. I think that's why people like me are so popular with him. I imagine he figures humans are more empathetic to each other. I'm the most empathetic one he knows of."

Jon's eyes were closed as he was momentarily lost in the expert manipulations of Alex's hands on his neck and shoulders.

"Two questions. How did you get here, and what qualifies you to be so very — oh, yeah, right there — empathetic?"

"Answer to question one: three-quarter-inch musket ball through the chest. Answer to question two: I was a prostitute."

"Ah, well then. That pretty much covers it." Now where to go with this line of questioning? "Mind if I ask the circumstances of these two events?"

"End of June, 1862, outside Richmond. Business at the establishment where I worked had dried up because of the fighting, so a couple of the other girls and I headed for the battle lines. With all the wounded, though, there weren't many fellas interested in what we had to offer, so the other girls went back. I decided to stay."

"That doesn't seem too bright. You just said …"

"Don't let the name fool you. My daddy was one of the Charleston Chaumonts, but when he came home from what was supposed to be a sales trip to Tennessee with a little Cherokee girl, nobody back home was too pleased. Then they had me without the benefit of a good Huguenot wedding. It wasn't too long before he left us in Richmond and took off to Savannah to marry some debutante his mother picked out for him. Anyway, Momma taught me some of her herb medicine before she died and I thought I might be able to use it in the field hospitals. Only problem was, everything I would try to heal the doctors would just end up cutting off. I lasted about two weeks before one of those little balls came by with my name on it. It must've been ugly. I'd seen what those things could do."

"Excuse me if this sounds ignorant, but it was always my impression that the gates of heaven didn't exactly swing wide for ladies in your line of work," Jon said as he rolled his neck, trying to further relieve the tension her hands had soothed.

"For some, it might not have. There are just as many supposedly good people doing bad things down there as there are supposedly bad people doing good things. The trick is sorting them out. Personally, my upbringing didn't prompt me to depend on some white-haired god in a bathrobe any more than it did to depend on men in general. I guess it all had to do with having my heart in the right place. My customers went away from me like they'd just left confession, only a little more satisfied. Their bodies were happy, and their minds were clear. More than one time I ended up just sitting on a bed with a young fella whose daddy had brought him in for his first tumble, just showing him all the places on a woman we liked to be touched. Nothing worse than a man who's got the initiative but doesn't have the basic practical knowledge. There's no end to the damage he can do. But after one of my lessons, it was guaranteed he'd make some woman real happy some day."

"So why here and not walking on the streets of gold up there?"

"Simple. Up there is Christians only. You've got to be a card-carrying member of that club to get into Caesar's Palace. Then once you get there, you end up bored stiff because it's so damn dull. Who wants an eternity of dull? Down here we get the thinkers, the ones who would stand up and say what they believed in, even though it might have gone against the prevailing sentiment. We get the doers. There's always a debate or a concert or a reading. It's like a non-stop cultural and scientific festival. No jealous angels to push you around. No self-righteous people you thought you'd leave behind on earth. Just beauty and life. No stagnation allowed here."

"You know," Jon said, his head hanging forward in sheer bliss, "Linda is really good at this. Sometimes, she'll even use a little baby oil that she's warmed up and that feels really good."

"Don't you mean it felt really good, Jon?"

Damn it. "Yeah. I suppose so. Am I having an unusual amount of time getting used to this, or does everyone go through the same thing?"

She continued her ministrations, but was silent for a few moments. "You miss your wife very much, don't you?" she asked, seemingly ignoring his question.

"Were you ever in love, Alex? Did you ever have someone who became the center of your universe and gave everything you did deeper meaning than it had before? Well, that's what it was like for me with Linda. Once I saw her I knew I had to know her, and once I knew her I knew I couldn't live without her. And it's been like that the whole time. Even when we fought over money or her job or my job, I knew that everything would be okay in the end. And now it's not going to be okay. I've reached the end, and she's not here with me and I feel like I got short-changed on the time I could spend with her before I left. And what's worse is she probably still thinks I'm a really awful person. She'll think I was too much of a coward to admit how awful I was so I drank myself to death. And I know she's somewhere wondering what led to all this, and I just want to be able to hold her and tell her the truth and say I'm sorry and I love her."

The motion of her hands stopped. "You're a really good man, Jon. And all of us that were human know what you're going through right now. But you have to realize you're special. You've been chosen to do something very important now that you're dead because of what you were best at when you were alive."

"But Linda ..."

She put a hand on each shoulder and turned him around toward her. "Think of it this way: If you don't do what the boss is asking you to do, there might not be a Linda. Can you imagine that? A creature or being that can elude the boss can do so much damage to the whole universe that we can't even begin to conceive of it. So while you may have been important to Linda in life, in death you're important to everyone, everywhere."

Jon just stared. Alex's intensity showed on her face, driving home the significance of what he'd been asked to do. He could see now why Eli insisted Alex be his guide. She provided a perspective on things Eli never could, because he was above it all. At the same time, she was the one who made him realize how desperately he wanted to be reunited with Linda. But if he did his job and performed to Eli's satisfaction, maybe they could work something out.

He was staring off into the distance as he thought, and Alex moved her eyes into his line of sight and placed a tender hand on his cheek. "You all right in there?"

He breathed in deeply and pulled himself together. He was dead. There was nothing he could do about that. But it seemed he still had plenty of work ahead of him.

"I think I'm ready to get started."

The two of them walked for what seemed to be miles, but as Jon quickly found, there was almost no way to judge either time or distance here. Landmarks shifted at will, and regardless of the perceived distance he never grew tired.

Eventually they arrived at a large building, which looked to Jon's eyes — untrained as they were in ancient architecture — like some government building or temple from the classic Greek or Roman eras. They spotted Eli sitting at a small cafe table on the building's huge stone patio. He was dressed in light cotton walking shorts and a short-sleeved silk shirt the color of key lime pie, his dredlocks pulled back and tied together at his neck.

"Hello, children. Have a seat," he said just before sipping on a tiny cup of what Jon guessed was espresso. "Anybody want anything? No, wait. Let me guess. Jon, for you," he said as he extracted from an ice bucket a Coke, melting ice running down the sides of the curvaceous green bottle.

"And for your lovely companion," he said, placing a tall glass of lemonade in front of Alex.

The two drank while Eli took a sip from his dainty cup. All three were silent for a moment, enjoying Eli's refreshments and the warm breeze blowing across the courtyard of the building. Finally, Eli broke the quiet.

"So Alex, why don't you give our new agent his full assignment. I know the suspense is killing him."

Jon cut his eyes at Eli. "Is that supposed to be some kind of joke?"

"Ha. Right. You've got to have a pretty good sense of humor to run the universe, boy, but you're giving me way too much credit. Just listen to the lady," he said before taking another sip from his cup.

From somewhere Alex had produced an official-looking manila envelope dossier. She unwrapped the red string from the tiny cardboard disk and slid out the contents. They included photos of the Whitakers and Scheafer, as well as several forms of identification bearing an image of someone who looked like a 50-year-old version of Jon.

"We're going to send you back," Alex said, and Jon's heart leapt. Her empathy obviously working overtime, she immediately clarified what that meant. "You will be in disguise and won't be allowed to contact anyone you associated with in your life as Jon Templeton."

Jon tried not to look as disappointed as he was. *Suppose I should have known better,* he thought.

"Your cover is going to be as Johnny Temple, a sales representative for the aerospace firm OrbiTek. They design and build

F
O
U
R
T
E
E
N

communication satellites for a number of firms and small countries."

"You expect me to just waltz into CNR headquarters and start selling them a satellite like it was a box of Girl Scout cookies?"

"Not exactly. Schaefer did all the footwork and presented the Whitakers with packages from five companies. A representative of each company has been personally invited to meet with the Whitakers and be run through their personal approval process."

"Personal?"

"Very personal," Eli said, sitting back and obviously enjoying the look on Jon's face.

Alex touched Jon's hand to draw his attention back to her. "Four of the reps have already met with them. You're the last."

"That still doesn't change the fact that I know nothing about satellites – or selling things, for that matter," Jon said.

"Trust us, you'll know. Think of it as us downloading all the information into your brain. When you need it, it will be there. Otherwise, we just need you to be your usual charming self."

"Great. And what am I supposed to accomplish while I'm busy being so charming?"

"At some point you'll meet with Schaefer. He handles all the dry business for the Whitakers. We need you to find out as much as possible about him."

"Think he'll submit to an impromptu interview from his friendly satellite salesman?" Jon's voice dripped with sarcasm.

"Of course not. But you won't be able to spend time with the Whitakers without dealing with him, either. Use some of those well-honed investigative skills we've heard so much about. The Reverend is notoriously chatty, so it shouldn't be hard to get him started on the subject. And if all else fails and you realize you're not getting what we need you to get, give Veronica a tumble."

Jon laughed. That was ridiculous. After all, the reason he was here in the first place was the result of simply looking like he was fooling around. To actually do it was beyond his comprehension.

"Laugh now, boy, but she's not kidding. Veronica Whitaker's got a voracious sexual appetite, and it's unlikely she'll let you leave without giving you a test drive. If some tidbits about Schaefer happen to come out in the midst of some pillow talk, so much the better."

They were serious. Deadly serious, from the looks on their faces.

"The key," Alex said, placing a hand on Jon's, "isn't finding out *who* he is. We already know all about that and it hasn't told us a thing. You're going to have to find out *what* he is."

"That doesn't make any sense. I saw in the tent – he's a severe looking Englishman with distinctive fashion sense," Jon said. "Are you saying I should expect something else?"

"It's a big universe, boy. You never know what you'll run into," Eli said, a little too cryptically for Jon's taste.

Alex interjected. "Think of it this way, Jon. So far, Schaefer has set up a false identity for himself – a false existence, really – and has eluded any attempts by the Boss to find out any more about him. That sends up some pretty big warning flags around here specifically because it's not the type of thing humans – or any other species, for that matter – are capable of."

"So the scale of this isn't just global …" Jon said, half to himself.

"It's universal," Eli said, leaning forward and emphasizing his point with a sharp poke on Jon's chest. "There are no editors. No fact-checkers. No retractions or corrections. You screw up on this story, boy, and chances are all this will be gone. And it's likely that it won't go in a very nice way."

Jon mulled this for a moment, then spoke, trying not to sound too hesitant. "I still want to do this for you Eli, because I know how important it is to you," he stammered. Damn. Why am I so nervous? Then he answered his own question: Because he's going to say no, that's why.

"And everything in existence." Eli interjected.

"Right, that too. But … "

"A 'but?' I'm about to send you off on probably the most difficult, meaningful thing you've ever done in your life and you're giving me a 'but?'"

"Just hear me out. I want to know what will happen to me after I'm finished with the mission."

"You'll come back here, of course. Don't forget, as far as I'm concerned you're still dead. What's sparked all this sudden concern, anyway? You getting cold feet?"

"Not cold feet really, I'm just concerned about what's going to happen afterwards."

Eli's face softened. Jon kept forgetting the old man was omniscient and realized he knew exactly what was wrong. "Look, boy. We here at Almighty Amalgamated have an excellent retirement plan. You can pop over to Muslim Heaven and get the full virgins and rivers of milk and honey treatment any time you like, or we can set up some time for you over in Valhalla. You get to hack some Viking's brains out and join him for mead afterward. Or you can just spend your time here with us and work on that novel you said you could never get started. After all, you do seem to get along well with the locals," he said, flashing a quick smile at Alex, who actually blushed, "and we think you'd be a good addition around here. You're already something of a celebrity, anyway."

"But there's my wife. I miss her, Eli."

Eli flashed another look at Alex, this time of concern. "Now come on, boy. I thought we were clear on this. You're dead. People who die leave behind other people they love. That's the way it works. There's no going back for good. The only way we're getting you back for this assignment is to temporarily send you as someone else."

"And I understand that." He was growing a bit more confident now. "But I figured that with you being who you are, we could work something out."

"There's no working things out, boy. I don't meddle. It's been my rule from the beginning and I'm not likely to change now. Why do you think I grabbed you when I did? You're my man. My investigative reporter. My bulldog. I couldn't let those stiffs up there have you." He gave Jon a fraternal pat on the shoulder. "Look, you're doing fine and she will do fine. Your job is to make sure she and everyone else is around to do fine."

"But…"

"No more buts. Now quit your worrying and come inside to get a look at the brand new you."

The three of them rose, Eli leading them through the huge doorway of the building and into a dimly lit entryway. He was distracted from Eli's comment by his own failure to bring him over to his side. Damn, I really screwed that one, Jon thought. He felt like the same darkness that filled the building was engulfing him. Now he was positive his eternal reward, however shiny and bright on the surface, would be less of a reward without Linda. But that couldn't be the end. He knew he had to be able to strike a deal somehow.

"Hey, boy. What do you think of the place? Look familiar?"

Broken from his introspection, Jon responded quietly. "I've seen buildings like it in books. It looks Greek."

"Ever heard of the Alexandria library? Repository of all the world's greatest knowledge at the time it was built. This is an exact replica, including the original scrolls and texts, of course. We managed to get copies of the good stuff just before it was destroyed." As they walked, Eli gazed around like a tourist from the boonies visiting on a package tour. "I'll tell you, if there's anything humans can do that I can't, it's architecture. I managed to create the entire universe from what amounts to cosmic Pla-Doh, but that was just me thinking real hard when I was too young to really know what I was doing. You folks actually sit down and dream this stuff up. Amazing."

The three of them entered a blindingly white room behind an ornately decorated doorway. The primary piece of furniture inside was a long pedestal with a draped body lying on it. Several people wearing equally white t-shirts and pants were scattered around the room conferring with each other, occasionally glancing at the white clipboards they held.

I've obviously been thrust inside some heavenly bleach commercial, he thought. He half expected the woman walking towards them to begin chirpily rattling on about whitest whites and brightest brights. That is, until he realized who she was.

"Aunt Lil?" He recognized her only from ancient pictures he'd seen scattered around her home – now his and Linda's. Gone was the woman he remembered as being bent and frail for most of his life. This Lil stood straight — and unexpectedly tall, he noticed — and had apparently chosen to freeze her age at somewhere around her late thirties. Strands of her chestnut hair were just beginning to turn silver, but her face remained untouched by the signs of age. Rather, she carried herself with the maturity and self-confidence that could only come from living a life as complete as she had.

To her immediate family, Lil often seemed more of an eccentric embarrassment than a family matriarch. As a young woman, Lil often rejected the accepted standards of her time. She smoked, she drank, she swore around children

and adults and made it a point to eschew underwear to fight the oppressive summers before air conditioning. Worst of all for small town South Carolina, she held
opinions that deviated from the conventional wisdom of the day. She ignored her
mother's insistence that she join one of her high school's sororities. During World
War II, she bypassed home front "Rosie the Riveter" jobs and the USO and went
straight for the chance to be a nurse in the thick of things in the South Pacific. After
supposedly breaking a string of U.S. Navy hearts (up until their deaths Jon would
still hear Lil's contemporaries whisper about her being "loose"), she returned to
the quiet complacency of Carlton. There, she worked as a midwife for both black
and white patients and proceeded to raise hell by challenging the entrenched
racism of the time. This, of course, mortified and alienated many of the town's powerful and influential and embarrassed her kin, many of whom had vested business
interests in segregation remaining the status quo.

In spite of all that, the final straw for her family was her living as a single
woman until she was 35 – officially qualifying as an "old maid" – when she did
the unthinkable and took up with a young accountant of 25. It was his maturity
that originally attracted her, she told Jon, but she admitted to Jon that as time went
on she realized there were other, more private advantages to having a younger
man.

Jon held a fondness for Lil since he was a child, mostly because she was
the rowdy, subversive antithesis of everything one's elders were supposed to be.
She was the one who, ignoring her age, would get down on the floor with the children for a game of cards or to play video games. And, perhaps most meaningfully,
she always invited him to join the adult conversations and always solicited his
opinion on subjects that seemed far too important for a child's opinion to matter.

As he grew older he learned to tap her vast experience. When his well-
meaning parents gave twelve-year-old Jon "the talk" and superficially and uncomfortably ran through matters of human reproduction, he turned to Lil to get
the real scoop. She later returned from the Carlton Piggly Wiggly with a quart of
milk, a bag of Quaker Quick Grits, a brick of liver mush, a bunch of bananas and a
box of Trojans. The milk, grits and liver mush – which she sliced and fried up like
patty sausage – were for her breakfast. With the rest she showed Jon first how to
protect himself using the condoms and a banana as a stand-in for a phallus, then
opened the magazine to a page featuring the most beautiful – and most naked –
woman he'd ever seen.

"Honey, I'm going to tell you something that you'll find out for yourself
later. There's a big difference between men and women. Men are like a 747. Y'all got
more little buttons to push than you know what to do with. Women, now, are more
like a fancy grandfather clock – they're all about finesse. First you got to wind 'em
up just right, then listen to their rhythms, then make adjustments as needed." Her
advice was so valuable, he found himself later turning to her for her own opinions
on decisions he had to make in his adult life. She was not a religious woman, but
had a deep spirituality that extended beyond the edicts of individual holy books to
encompass the universe and life as a whole. New age before new age was cool, Jon
thought.

"God or whoever has a purpose for everything and everybody, and your little life is just part of another bigger scheme," she said to him after he lost his first high school job, a gig mowing lawns and planting azaleas with a local landscape contractor. She didn't make him feel much better about getting the boot for "lack of initiative" in mowing and planting, but did assure him that the world would not end with his unemployment.

Towards the end of her life, she had taken to nipping on Kahlua in her Sanka, sniffing on a tiny bottle of drug store camphor to "give her a lift" and napping more than anything, but she always seemed to have time and energy to spare for Jon. Her once broad and somewhat cavalier attitude about her fate after death began to get more serious and focused. A week before she died, Jon visited her again and found a woman who had adopted the faith of one who knew her death was imminent. She seemed to have shrunk visibly since he last saw her just a week before, but the sparkle in her crystal blue eyes remained.

"Whatever happens to you Jon, trust in the Lord. It might look mighty dark, but you've just got to believe He's got a plan to make it all better," she said, her tiny, withered hand gripping his with surprising strength. Then, breaking into a smile, said, "And if it turns out He doesn't, then screw Him." That was the Lil he loved.

He nodded his head and strained back tears, knowing she was still very unsure of what her eternal destiny would be or whether there was even one to worry about.

"Don't you worry, Lil," he said, patting her hand. "When I get there I'll look you up, unless you've got a date or something."

She smiled sweetly. "Take your time, sugar. It'll take a while for me to find someone up there with a mind as dirty as mine."

That woman, the tiny and bent 101-year-old, was little more than a shadow of the vibrant, beautiful one standing before him now. "Jonathan, sweetheart!" she said, hugging him tightly. "It's about time you got around to seeing me. You know I'm not the type to forget a promise." She sneaked a look around him to see Alex standing just behind. "But I see you've been busy getting oriented. I hope our dear Alex has taken good care of you."

"I'm sorry, Lil. I'm still trying to get used to the idea of being here in the first place. But you're right. Alex has made it a lot easier to bear." Alex smiled at the comment.

She held his hand and patted it firmly, a familiar gesture, but one that felt odd coming from a woman not far from his own age. "Then you're excused from not having come to see me first thing. Anyhow, if you had you would have spoiled the surprise."

"Surprise?"

"Surely the Boss told you about the refit we've been working on?"

Eli interrupted. "Actually, I did mention it. But considering your history with Jon, I thought it might be best for you to handle this, Lil. I wanted to make sure we tread lightly, and since I tend to be a bit more blunt, I hope you don't mind if I leave you to the demonstration. Call me if you need me," he said as he walked out.

Alex gave Jon a little kiss on the cheek. It was startling, but gave him just the right little buzz of comfort he needed. "I'll leave you two to catch up before we get started," she said as she walked over to another white-clad worker and began examining the body.

When they were alone, Lil hugged him again, then leaned back to softly pat his cheek. "You're such a sweet boy, Jonathan. I'm so sorry we had to see you here so soon, but I'm glad things have been going well so far. I had a feeling you'd end up here, too, when the time came. Thank goodness we both managed to avoid that gaudy casino up there. But don't you know," she said, laughing, "if they made the mistake of letting me in up there I would've just gotten booted right back out. Mercy, they're a pompous bunch! But enough about me. What's your excuse for not coming to see me like you promised? What have you been up to?"

"Not a whole lot," Jon said. "Sightseeing, mostly."

"Pshaw! I know what kind of sights you've been seeing. I think our Alex might have a little crush on you. She's glowing like I was when I met your Uncle Theodore." The thought had crossed Jon's mind, but he felt it would be safer to change the subject.

"Is Uncle Ted here? I thought surely you two would be together."

"No, honey. The marriage vows end when that line goes flat." Jon wondered if she'd been coached to say that, then mentally scolded himself for his paranoia. "Besides, you know what a church-going man Theodore was, in spite of being married to me. Those busybodies snatched him up to New Jerusalem as quick as you please. Got him working in that unholy bureaucracy in Saint Peter's office now, I hear. Still bean counting, too. Once an accountant, always an accountant, I suppose. He wouldn't be happy here, anyway. He'd have too much free time. He'd always want to mow the lawn or something."

Jon caught a glimpse of Alex, who was meticulously examining the body on the pedestal.

"Well, Lil, you certainly do look good for a 101-year-old. Not that I had any doubts that you weren't ... "

"As ugly as that beat-up skin sack they buried? Trust me, Jonathan. You have no idea how glad I was to ditch that worn out bag of bones. It wasn't even worth the trouble the worms took to eat it. I decided since I was in my prime in my thirties, I might as well go back to that period. I find a lot of the men like a more mature look, anyway," she said with a wry wink.

"Speaking of mature looks, you might want to come take a look at this, Jon," Alex said, still examining the body.

Lil led him to the pedestal, where he found himself looking down upon himself, aged just enough to make him suspect he was looking at his sleeping father at around the age of forty-five. His hair, which had been in need of a trim before his untimely departure, was neatly cropped and styled into the latest executive coiffure, with distinguished touches of gray added at the temples. The lines around his eyes and mouth were more distinct, and some of his sparse chest hair had even begun to turn a light silver.

"Jonathan Templeton, meet Jonathan Templeton, alias Jonnie Temple, satellite salesman extraordinaire," Lil said with a flourish. "And a mighty fine specimen of middle-aged manhood, if I do say so myself. We've already got your wardrobe and kit bag together, and all the arrangements back on terra firma have been made, so all we have to do is get you back in the meat machine and you'll be ready to go."

Jon stared into his own body lying motionless on the slab, then looked at Alex, who regarded him with a smile that betrayed a hint of sadness.

"You look good, Jon. Almost too good. Nice job on the refit, Lil," she said, Lil acknowledging her compliment with a gracious nod. Alex then walked over to him, took his face in her hands and gave him a long, tender kiss.

"Good luck, satellite man," she said with downturned eyes.

PART

TWO

ACTS

Linda Templeton was expecting to discover any number of things inside the family cottage in Surfside Beach, which she found with both the back door and screened porch wide open. A "Dear Linda" letter, perhaps, or even her husband sprawled in the bed with another woman who, in his despair, he had trawled from the sea of female flesh to be found in bars up and down the strand. She even halfway expected to find him dialing the phone, frantic because he wanted to try to explain the situation to her and couldn't find her at home.

What she did not expect was to find nothing.

And not even a little nothing. There was an immense, gaping maw of nothingness. Save the open doors, there were no indications anyone had been here any time since the last trip they took here together during Fourth of July week. Everything was in its place. Nothing had been moved and nothing obvious had been stolen.

She began to grow genuinely concerned about what might have happened to her husband, since so far he had done nothing she might have otherwise expected him to.

As if to make him suddenly appear from whatever crevice in which he might be hiding, Linda stood in the center of the living room, her hands on her hips much like her mother when she was frustrated, and said with a hint of worry in her voice, "Jon Templeton, where could you have gotten to?"

"Beats me, but the last time I saw him he was heading this way," said a female voice. It was Regina, speaking from the screened porch, startling Linda with her unannounced appearance. She was leaning against the doorjamb, her arms crossed over a modest bikini top. "Smelled a bit like he'd been drinking, too."

"Sorry Regina. You gave me a scare," Linda said. "Yes, I imagine he was drinking. How long ago did you see him?"

"Oh, it was around 3:30 yesterday afternoon. He was walking from the pier up here. Said you were doing some business or something this weekend and he had come down by himself."

"Well, it doesn't look like anyone's been here. Any idea where else he might have gone?" Linda asked, knowing she was betraying more worry to the girl than she wanted to.

"He didn't say anything, but in his condition yesterday he couldn't have gone far," she said. Then Linda knew Regina was catching on to her concern. "Is everything okay with you two? You seem upset."

Linda tried to speak, but the trembling of her lip and the tears welling in her eyes came so fast she couldn't control them.

"No, things really aren't okay," she said as her eyes filled up. "I accused him of raping a coworker and threw him out of the house before I gave him the chance to explain why he had another woman's panties in his trouser pocket, but then I found out one of the women at his office had tried to seduce him and he turned her down so she tried to get him fired and instead he quit, and I was sure he'd come here but he didn't, and now I don't know what I'll do because I can't find him to tell him I'm sorry and I still love him."

When she finally broke down, it was into the arms of the younger girl, who held her gently. Linda just sobbed, the relief of letting out her worry transcending her embarrassment.

"Is there anything you have to do at home in the next couple of days, Linda?" Regina asked after a few silent moments of consoling and back-patting.

"No, why?" Linda asked, composing herself a little as she sniffed into Regina's shoulder. God, what a joke I am, going on like this. She stood and wiped her eyes with the back of her hand. It was then that she noticed the change in Regina. The girl had gone from being the mousy neighbor girl to a self-confident beauty in the course of a season.

"I just thought you might want to stay with me rather than hanging around the house waiting for Jon to come back. I mean, I'm sure he will, but there's no reason for you to make it worse on yourself by being alone, right?"

"I suppose. Are you sure you won't mind?"

"Don't worry about it. Just leave a new message on your v-mail at home so he'll know where to get in touch with you. In the meantime, it'll just be us girls."

"Okay," Linda said, wiping her red and swollen eyes again. "But I don't have any clothes."

"Relax. I keep tons of clothes here in the summer, and I'm sure some of my skinny clothes will fit you," she said.

Linda smiled weakly. "Are you kidding? Look at you. You look great. What's different?"

"Don't worry. I'll fill you in." She guided Linda out the door and pulled it closed behind her. "Come on. Lock this place up and let's go."

Mako waved his cash card in front of the drink machine scanner for the fifth time, the disused contraption finally submitting and charging him for the two cans of Coke that subsequently fell with a thunk into the catcher below.

Riding in the super-cooled truck cab, Mako hadn't really realized how hot it had gotten. Of course, if they'd been thinking about such things, they probably wouldn't have made it this far. Among the fifteen in his uncle's garage, there had probably been a higher percentage of cars with air conditioning than without. But when Mako laid eyes on the lemon-yellow 1971 Mustang Mach 1, it was love at first sight. He plucked the keys from the small cabinet where they hung next to those for turn-of-the-century Lamborghinis and Ferraris and slid in over the smooth vinyl. When the engine turned over, the roar that filled the cavernous garage sounded like the end of the world. Hell, even in this godawful heat he got goosebumps just thinking about it.

Once they hit the road, though, Mako was rudely reminded of what life was like without artificial climate control. Rolling the windows down did little more than create a hot breeze, but they made do. Krista faded in and out of sleep until a little before the Virginia-North Carolina line, so she didn't seem as troubled by the heat until she awoke. Then all she requested was a restroom, a shady parking spot and a cold drink. Thankfully, he had managed to find some cover at the rest station, even if it did happen to be in the shadow of a tractor-trailer rig similar to the one destroyed in his uncle's front driveway.

He walked back to the car, holding one of the cans to his forehead and letting the cool condensation run down his face. Krista had taken off the cheap, oversized sunglasses he had bought her at the last truck stop and was once again examining her bruises in the rearview mirror. She was the one who originally pointed out the Mustang, partly because she'd never actually been in an internal combustion car, he thought, but also because the four-inch square collector's license in the front left corner of the windshield gave them virtual immunity from transponder requirements. They could be tracked by satellite visually as just another vehicle on the road, but obtaining any other information about the car would be very tedious – and often not worth the trouble – for whoever was manning the Highway Patrol monitor station.

As someone who made it his business to think quickly on his feet, Mako was impressed by Krista's seemingly natural talent for it. Fifteen years of soft living had made it necessary for him to train himself to work the streets, but for Krista, who he guessed was not a child of any privilege, knowing the right thing to do seemed to be just a matter of course. He was starting to be glad he had her along.

"Your drink, ma'am," he said as he slid into the seat and handed her the sweaty can.

"Do you think this eye looks really bad?" she said, still examining the tender swollen flesh. "I'm thinking about trying to cover it up with some make-up or something."

"You mean that's not the newest style?" he said with mock horror. "Hell, I've seen lots of folks going for the smacked around look. People showing up at the salon just to get popped a couple of times."

She looked at him and frowned at the joke. "Could you be straight for just one minute, please? I mean, if I'm riding with you, I don't want people to think you did this to me."

Mako could see why she wouldn't want to go around looking like a boxer's practice bag, but wondered why she worded it as if for his benefit.

"So, who did do this to you?" he asked, before finally opening the can and taking a long swig. He knew he was taking a chance at prying, but figured it was unlikely she would volunteer the information without some prompting.

She sighed and went back to fiddling with the eye, pressing around the perimeter of the bruise to test its tenderness. "A character from a two-year-long bad dream is about all you need to know, I think. Anyway, didn't you say something about knowing better than to ask questions like that?"

"Call it a lapse of good judgment." He paused, considering his next question. "Was it over sex, drugs or money?"

She was quiet for a moment. "A little of each, I guess. It was my live-in. He was looking for a fix and was convinced I had some money stashed away, so he tried to beat it out of me."

"Did you?"

"Of course, just in case this sort of thing came up. Never can tell when a girl's going to need to make a break from some prick with legs."

Mako wondered how many times some girl had said the same about him.

"And where would Mr. Prick be now?"

"He would be slapping some brand new dermals up and down his arm with me lying bleeding on the floor if he had anything to do with it. But he didn't, so he's probably sitting in a tiny cell while some axe-murderer tries to make him his boyfriend. It would serve him right."

"How'd you manage that?"

She recounted the story. At first Mako tried to decide if she was exaggerating to make her boyfriend sound as stupid as he did. Clearly, she wasn't.

He whistled in awe when she finished. "Jeez. Remind me to never get on your bad side."

She popped open the can and took a long swig. "You're doing pretty well so far," she said, wiping her mouth with the back of her hand. "No drugs that I've noticed, you haven't tried to rape me..."

"Always a plus," he interjected.

"Yeah, and I've only had to save your life once today. Very few points in the negative column so far."

"Oh yeah? What is in the negative column?"

She took on a look of mock seriousness. "Definite family issues."

He laughed hard. "Yeah, I guess you could say that."

"Still," she said, flashing a crooked grin in spite of the swollen lip, "It's not every day a girl gets picked up by the heir to a major multi-national corporation."

He took a long drink. It felt incredible to have something cold inside him. The heat seemed to have penetrated to his core. "Make that reluctant heir," he said, once again placing the cool can against his face. "You'll notice we are traveling in the direction exactly opposite from company headquarters."

"Which brings up the question 'Why?'" she said. "Seems like unlimited wealth and power might be somewhat appealing."

"Wealth and power are overrated," he said before taking another sip. "Well, maybe not the wealth, but it's not like I've been living off my father all this time. I was doing my best to make my own life before he got killed."

"I think I heard about that," Krista said. "What happened again?"

"Car bomb, right in the middle of Philadelphia."

"The one in Rittenhouse Square? Oh my God … I walked right past that spot that night. That was your dad?"

He nodded and drank, trying not to think about what it must feel like to have your body torn apart by flying bolts and reinforced aluminum. "How about you? Any folks?"

"Not anymore. Mom took off with some guy she met in a feelie chat room back when I was ten and my dad raised me. When the job market tanked he crossed the line into New York to try to earn some money fighting for the Empire State Irregulars. He got shot in an ambush near Niagara Falls."

"How old were you?"

"Sixteen. All my other relatives were gone and I had no interest in catching up with my mom, so I hit the road. I was in New York City waiting tables for a while, but came down to Philly just before the martial law took effect. Seems like since my dad died my life has pretty much been a series of really bad jobs and even worse boyfriends."

"I know exactly what you mean," Mako said. Krista looked at him and arched an eyebrow. "I mean, without the boyfriends, of course."

"Okay, so your masculinity is intact," she said in a consoling tone, laughing and patting him on his forearm. It was a sweet gesture, one that he hadn't experienced in a while. "So, what about that little thing with your uncle trying to blow the living shit out of you? Somebody might think you two didn't get along."

"Uncle Hiroshi's always been the bigger weasel between he and my dad, but that's not saying a lot. I never thought he'd sell out my father like he did, though. Uncle's reaction pretty much confirms that he had something to do with my father's death. I just don't know what it is. If I'm right, that stick you're carrying has all the evidence I'd need to connect him to the bombing. It's just too bad I've got to lose my good help."

Krista took another long gulp and looked directly at him. Mako was struck by his own bluntness. "Yeah, too bad," she said.

"Decided where you want me to drop you off yet?"

Her manner turned cold. "Not really. I'm gonna go pee and see if I can boost a map, and when we get back I guess we should go. No use putting it off, right?" Mako could tell she was angry now, but there was nothing he could do. He'd put her in too much danger already.

"Hey, about that boosting. Take this instead," he said as he handed her the cash card. "No use starting any more trouble than we've already had, right?"

She turned it over between her fingers. "I guess not. Be back in a sec."

She closed the car door, and Mako watched her as she headed for the restrooms. She looked out of place in her cut-off trousers and the oversized Sunrise Moving shirt, but not unattractive, even with the bruises. Just looking at those made him angry at the guy who did that to her. He'd seen it happen too many times himself when he was first on the streets. Especially on the girls who worked the corners in some of the seedier parts of Canaveral and Cocoa Beach. For them a bruise was nothing. Part of the job. If it wasn't the john that did it, it was probably her pimp. He'd even seen one woman they pulled out of a hourly rate motel — the ones that looked like coffins stacked together — who had bites on her face so bad it looked like she'd been attacked by some kind of wild animal. He never did find out if she lived, but when he saw her it looked like there wasn't much of a chance.

Krista seemed smart enough to have avoided pulling that gig, but she still had that look – the one that made you think that at 20 or so she'd seen enough shit for three 80-year-olds. Good thing she managed to keep real jobs, even if she never could find a real boyfriend.

He tried not to think about how he was going to be sorry to see her go. She'd gotten him out of a bad spot he really didn't expect to get out of. If he thought all this was over, he might even ask her to stay. But he knew it wasn't. There was someone who had wielded such a strong influence over his uncle that Hiroshi would rather kill himself than face the consequences of his cowardice. Was it blackmail? Unlikely, since Hiroshi had never married and was the notoriously focused one of the two brothers. As executives at Nikura, the two men held influence over elected officials and military commanders, so he imagined some sort of threat could have come from either group. But what?

Mako was sweating profusely thanks to the heat building up inside the car and its sticky vinyl seats. He got out and leaned against the side of the car, wiping his face on the upstretched front of his shirt. He held the material to his eyes and closed them, enjoying the brief interval of dryness before the tiny glands began pumping again.

"'Scuse me, neighbor," said a thickly drawling male voice from behind.

"Yeah," he said without looking up. "Whatcha need, buddy?"

Then there was the pain in his back, just above his waist and off to the side, like his insides were going to explode, and he was doubled over by the side of the car, its door still wide open.

"I think you know, surfer boy. Got something that don't belong to you, and we'd like it back."

Mako managed to open his eyes despite the pain that still throbbed in his lower back. The first thing he saw was the guy's shoes. Brown leather loafers, a shiny penny stuck in a slot on each of their tongues, then tanned, hairy ankles.

"Don't know what you're talking about, man," Mako said through the pain.

The loafered foot came up and connected with Mako's solar plexus, just the right spot to knock the air out of him despite the strong abs he'd developed in the water.

"Don't bullshit us, kid. You know what we're talkin' about. Belonged to your uncle. You got it from the blonde bitch at your daddy's office. Now start remembering."

Krista. She still had the stick. Jesus. She's probably on the way back from the restroom now. Hopefully she'll have enough sense to take off before she gets herself hurt.

"I don't have it. You can search me. Check the car, man," Mako said between heaving gasps of air.

"What'd he do with the girl?" asked a female voice, raspy from what must have been a few centuries of liquor and cigarettes.

"Gone," Mako said, choking.

"Says she's gone, Monique."

"He's shittin' us. I'll go check the little girls' room. You stay here and search him, boys. I'll call if I need you."

A hand at his collar and another on his waistband and he was being dragged up. Standing up made the breathing harder. All he really wanted to do was curl up in a ball and die. Whoever had him slammed him hard up against the hot steel of the car's roof. A hand inside his right pants pocket found the keys. Mako heard them being tossed away.

"We find anything in here, we're gonna be real upset that you lied, boy."

Mako's head was turned towards the front of the car, so he couldn't see how many others there were. Someone had opened the trunk and was looking inside. Mako felt like telling him not to waste his time. He hadn't bothered to open the trunk himself.

"Nothin' here, H.," said a new voice.

"Check the glove box and under the seats. Got to make sure we don't miss anything … Hold on, there. Got Monique comin' in." Mako worried how much longer his face could remain on the car's roof without sustaining severe burns.

"Says we can leave him. Dwight's bringing the van around," his personal tormenter said to the assistant. Mako then felt the man's breath, hot and moist and smelling of halitosis, stale cigarettes and bourbon, close to his ear.

"Good thing you didn't lie to us, boy. Nothing I would've liked better than turning your little Jap ass into sushi."

A hand grabbed Mako's hair, and with a quick-wristed motion slammed his forehead into the roof, sending him sliding down the car's side in loose-limbed unconsciousness.

The music was the first thing to penetrate the haze Krista found her mind swimming through. At first she thought it was a dream, something sparked in her subconscious by the motion of the car and a station Mako was flipping past on the radio. When the pain kicked in, though, she knew that were she stupid enough to call out for him, he definitely would not be there.

In her incapacitated state, she tried to place the song. It sounded old. Real old. More like the stuff she vaguely remembered her grandparents listening to than the '90s rock her dad loved. It was soulful and pleading, the singer's voice seeming to beg from the bottom of his heart. The beat, however, was that of a dance song, bouncy. In her delirium, she almost thought she felt her head pounding to the same beat. Beneath it was something else. A low, droning sound. They were in some sort of vehicle, the tires humming along asphalt to produce a painful accompaniment to the throbbing of her head, the murmur of female and male voices barely filtering through the other noise.

"Heads up, y'all. I think she's comin' around," a thickly drawling woman's voice said.

Krista detected through her eyelids what seemed like a camera flash. Then another. She coughed and opened her eyes, trying to get away from the constant stream of the cigarette smoke issuing from the woman's mouth, and couldn't help but blurt out a repulsed noise when she felt her grow closer.

"Harlan! Turn down that damn music. We're trying to work back here!" the woman shouted without warning. The volume went down and she was sweetness itself. "All right, sugar. That's more like it. How's your head feel?"

"Like shit. Who the hell are you?" Krista said, trying to escape the woman's breath. She had to fight to keep from making a frightened noise once she got a good look at her. She was obviously a regular patient of a sub-par plastic surgeon. The woman was older than Krista expected, probably in her mid-seventies or eighties, but with every square centimeter of skin either stretched to its limit or artificially plumped. Her unsettling visage was accentuated with badly streaked hair and flashy jewelry, each piece bearing some gaudy variation on a crucifix.

"We're friends, darlin'. Trust me on that one. Lord knows you've gotten yourself into enough trouble with that little Jap fella already. We just thought we might be able to help out," she said, taking another drag and leaning back into the swivel captain's chair..

At the reference to Mako, Krista immediately felt the pocket where she had placed the computer stick he had given her to safeguard. It was gone.

"Don't you worry about that little item there, darlin'. It's in the right hands now. You just see if you can sit up and take a sip of Coke. Dwight," she snapped at the little man sitting in the seat next to her, "get up and get the girl a Coke."

Dwight didn't look much like a kidnapper. He was short and dumpy in his Madras shirt and khaki pants, his tanned, age-spotted ankles showing beneath the high-water hem, and looked like another patient of whoever had done the woman's face. He reached into a small refrigerator and pulled out a red can, popped it open and gave it to her. She took a few small sips and sat up slowly, trying to avoid making the pounding in her head worse.

"We sure were pleased you had that little stick on you," the woman continued. "We'd planned on just using you as a hostage to get him to us so we could get it then, but we sure do hate to go that route when we don't have to, know what I mean, sugar? Sometimes violence just ain't the most productive way to accomplish things."

She regarded Krista with a friendly smile but inquiring eyes, as if searching her face for some hidden secret. "So, honey, tell us about how you happened to get attached to our little half-breed? What'd he use? A little hypnotic in your Co-Cola? Some heavy-duty 'dermals? He promise you money for a little poon?"

Krista came to the final realization that these people actually thought Mako had somehow kidnapped her to be part of whatever plot they believed him to be involved in. For the moment, she decided to play along.

"I don't really know," she said, looking like it was hurting her to think. "He picked me up outside Philadelphia and then we went to his uncle's place. That was in Delaware, I think."

An intense look crossed the woman's face. That is, that part of her face that wasn't pulled too tight to register emotion. "Oh, lord. It's worse than we thought. He didn't make you watch, did he darlin'?"

"Watch what?"

"Watch what, she says," the woman said, shaking her head at the other occupants of the van. "She's trying to deal with it by blocking out all the terrible things she's seen. Saw a show about the same thing on the TV just last week."

"Trying to block out what?" Krista interjected. "What are you talking about?"

"Why, that little Jap fella puttin' three bullets in his uncle's skull, that's what. He didn't make you watch, did he?" she said, taking a long drag on her cigarette and looking as if she hoped Mako had.

Krista, suddenly on the defensive, sat up quickly, only to receive a stream of regurgitated cigarette smoke in her face.

"Mako didn't kill anybody," she said, coughing. "His uncle poisoned himself somehow. Mako didn't even touch the gun."

"Then maybe you want to tell us why the household help found the old man slumped over his desk with his head leakin' all over the mahogany?" The woman shook her head again and looked around at her cohorts. "Then there's that secretary he shot at his daddy's big office building up in Philadelphia. That boy's a regular one-man hit squad, honey. I'm surprised you lasted this long."

She again looked around at her respectfully attentive companions. "Child's gonna need more deprogramming than we thought, boys. Little nip must've put the hoodoo on you with some of that ninja hypnosis or something," she said, holding her hands, fingers out, in front of her eyes and wiggling them to represent what Krista imagined were Mako-produced hypno-rays.

"Lucky for you Harlan's trained in getting past all that stuff real quick." She pointed her cigarette at the van's cab. The scrawny man driving turned around and smiled, revealing another unnaturally smooth stretch-face. His teeth were so white they were almost blue, and he bore a crucifix tattoo on his left cheek, making him look like the department store mannequin of holy redemption.

Before Krista could even muster a vocal expression of her revulsion, Harlan was mercifully distracted by the electronic chirp of the phone bud in his ear. He accepted the call and stiffened visibly after the caller had time to identify him or herself. He mumbled a few words back, disconnected and relaxed.

"Monique, that was him. He said to bring her right in so he could see her tonight."

When he said Monique, it came out Mown-ache, and Krista thought to herself that here before her sat the living incarnation of every backwoods redneck ever impersonated by a California TV actor. All these years she thought no one could live up that such an exaggerated stereotype, and here it turned out that the very person who did would be the one responsible for what Monique called her deprogramming, whatever grisly practices that might involve.

"Damn him," Monique said. "The man knows we're just doing this as a favor. We got other business to take care of." She took another thoughtful drag from her cigarette and exhaled decisively. "Well, Mr. Big Hoss can go screw himself, is all I got to say. We had an itinerary all set up for tonight and he's fixin' to blow it. We ain't gettin' paid enough for this shit. He can wait 'till tomorrow."

"I don't know, Monique. He sounded pretty intense to me. Might not be a good time to piss him off," Harlan said, sounding nervous.

"Harlan, the man always sounds intense. All that pussy around him all day and you'd think the man would get laid once in a while, but no. He just gets all pent up – internalized emotions, they call it. Saw it on a TV show. Now how about take your balls out of your shirt pocket and put 'em back where they belong for a change, would you please? I got no time for your whiny-ass shit today."

The man was clearly hurt by the jab and turned to face the road again. "And don't sit there poutin' like a whipped dog, either! Did you send him the picture like he asked us to?" she shouted as she crushed her cigarette into an ashtray in the chair's arm. Harlan grunted "Yeah" and Monique seemed satisfied.

She then turned to Krista and smiled artificially. "Well, darlin', looks like you're in luck. Instead of Harlan, you get to meet with the big man himself. He'll be real happy when he sees your sweet little ass roll in, even though I don't imagine he'd know what to do with it. But in the meantime he's got a real nice picture of you to let him know what to expect."

Monique reached into a small purse and nodded to Dwight. "Dwight, honey, how 'bout do me a little favor and grab our little toy out of the case there."

She pulled a compact from her bag and used the mirror to apply another heavy coat of lipstick to her already over-painted mouth. Krista saw the man turn and remove something from a small plastic box, then heard the sound of glass against plastic. She didn't at all like the sudden feeling of tension she was getting from her captors and began slowly inching toward the front of the van, hoping she could somehow overtake Harlan and escape out a side door.

Without smearing her lipstick, Monique snapped at her other companion, who had been dozing noisily in the other captain's chair.

"Earl, how about you get off your lazy ass and hold her down before she causes some trouble. Shit! One day you're gonna realize ain't everybody in the world as stupid as you." Earl moved quickly and placed a tight grasp on her right arm and shoulder, turning it painfully behind her back. "Now sugar, we got a ways to go yet, so I'm gonna ask you to do me a favor and take a little nap," she said sweetly. "We've got a little social engagement once we get to where we're going, but I'll be sure to wake you up in time for the festivities."

As a period to the sentence, Krista felt a sudden sharp pain in her shoulder and then the hiss of the pneumatic hypodermic gun wielded by Earl, and then darkness.

Mako tasted blood. It was crusted down his nose and across his lips and cracked as he sat up from the pavement and tried to realign his muddled thoughts. There had been other people here after Krista went to the restroom, but he couldn't remember seeing them, just pieces of them. A shoe, an ankle, the cuff of a pants leg. Nothing else.

The sun had moved from its place directly overhead to behind the tall pines surrounding the rest stop, leaving Mako in the shade as he gingerly touched his forehead and sat against the side of the car. Still, the heat was oppressive, and sweat trickled down his face and neck until it was absorbed in the neck of his shirt. He was sure it made a pretty picture with the dissolved blood flowing along with it.

He reviewed again what happened leading up to his unconsciousness. Something had obviously gone very wrong. Krista was gone with the stick. He hurt everywhere, particularly around the nasty bump on his forehead, which kept him out for at least two hours, if his gauge of the sun's position was right. The people who had attacked him were prepared to handle a fighter, sneaking up on him and catching him off guard. They were probably specifically prepared to handle him.

He slid up the side of the car, his head still swimming slightly, and made his way to the bank of phones next to the computerized tourist information console. Inside was a pair of children playing with the controls, randomly hitting buttons until they received an answer they found appropriately amusing. They left quickly when they caught sight of Mako's injured face and bloodied shirt. He reached for his cash card before remembering Krista had it. Damn. He'd have to call collect. They'd know where he was, but at least he'd have a half-day's lead on them. To further conceal his whereabouts, he made sure to switch off the video link before dialing collect to the switchboard of the Nikura Tower.

When the electronic operator answered and he stated "executive suite," there was a bit of confusion as to why the new head of the company was calling collect. Eventually he got the chirpy, computerized "thank you, one moment please" he sought. He tapped impatiently on the console as the line switched over and buzzed several times before being answered by a raspy male voice.

"Yeah?"

He was caught off guard.

"Uh, Andrea Turner, please."

"Who's calling?"

"A friend," he said, suddenly nervous.

"You got a name?"

"Who is this? Where's Andrea?"

E
I
G
H
T
E
E
N

"This is Detective Dipolito with Philadelphia Homicide. Who did you say you were again?"

Mako hung up and dialed collect to his uncle's number. Another unfamiliar male voice answered with a brusque hello and agreed to accept the charges. Upon hearing his name, the guy at the other end was suddenly his best friend. Another cop.

"Mako, my man! Boy, have we been looking for you. Listen, kid. There's been a real bad accident with your uncle, and we could use your help."

If only it had been an accident, Mako thought. Still, rather than implicate himself immediately, he decided to feign innocence.

"Accident? What kind of accident? Is he okay?"

"Not really, kid. Listen, why don't you just come in and let us talk to you. I really think..."

He hung up again and dialed a number with a Florida area code, leaving the video on this time. The accidents were getting far too frequent, and he feared Krista had somehow become the unwitting victim of another one of them.

The phone seemed to ring forever. Finally, someone answered and the fleshy form of Eddie Swift came into view in front of a rack of firearms.

"Who the fuck is calling me collect?" he said before registering who it was on the screen. "Mako? Is that you?"

"How's the pawn business, Eddie?"

Eddie accepted the charges. "Bro, we heard you'd been kidnapped by the Yakuza or some shit. You okay?"

"Yeah, for the time being, but you're not too far from the truth. What's the word coming down on me from your associates? Heard anything odd?"

"My associates? Hmph. My associates aren't worth shit anymore. Everyone's either working the black market up on the lines in New York or turning into a legit businessman. Renaldo, guy used to deal down on the beach? Dude's opening a Cleaver's franchise, if you can believe it. As if the drugs didn't get him enough ass."

"Yeah, great," Mako said, trying not to sound too impatient. "Anything else about me?"

"Hearing nothing but rumors, man. Something about a bounty, but I got no numbers on what you're worth. Couldn't be much if you're healthy enough to call me."

"A bounty. Fucking beautiful. You know where this is coming from? Who's paying? It looks like I had some candidates to collect, but I don't think they were looking for me as much as something I had."

"No clue, brother. I see what you mean, though. Your head looks like a pound of raw hamburger. This is all some very shady shit if you asked me," Eddie said, leaning close to the phone. "What the hell are you into, anyway?"

"Beats me, but I'm in deep," Mako said as he looked around outside the booth. "Tell me something. You know anything about something called the shag?"

"Which one, the dance or the terrorists?"

"Um ... Both," Mako said, trying not to let his confusion show.

"Well, the dance, my folks used to do it. They do it old Motown and blues, mostly. Black folks up north call it the bop. Kinda like the jitterbug on 'ludes."

"The what?"

"The jitterbug, kid. It's kinda...no, nevermind. It'd take too long to explain. Real popular up in South Carolina, though. Why? You lookin' to take some dance lessons?" he asked, chuckling so his double chins undulated under his face.

"No, but I think it might have something to do with my recent difficulties. How about the terrorists?"

"Saving Humanity, Affirming God. Some whacked out shag geezers who got Jesus when Whitaker decided screwing in the name of the Lord was okay. Low on tolerance, though. Run around pointing guns at people if they don't like the way they dance and whatnot. Also do some small-scale domestic and Central American arms stuff to finance their youth fixation. Very weird shit – lots of plastic surgery and fiddling with DNA – but sounds strictly small-time to me."

"You know where they operate out of?"

"South Carolina, mainly Myrtle Beach and Florence. Florence is the coastal mag-lev hub. Real big concentration of shag fanatics around there, so that's probably your best bet."

"Thanks, Eddie. You've been a big help. Can you do me one more favor?"

"Name it, dude."

"Forget this call."

"What call? Hey, you must have the wrong number. I don't accept collect-fucking-calls," the huge man said just before switching off.

"Thanks, man," he said to the fading screen.

On impulse Mako began driving south again. After what Eddie told him about the radical shaggers, he was positive they were the ones who had grabbed Krista and probably the ones responsible for his father's death. Their connection to his uncle, however, remained a mystery.

He also figured he wasn't dealing with a pack of brain surgeons, since whichever fellow had checked the trunk had left the keys in the lock, not even bothering to toss them into the woods or down a sewer grate like any clear-thinking criminal would have.

He was averaging about 90 miles an hour as he barreled down the concrete slab of I-95, the hot wind whipping his hair and the intense sun burning down on his left arm, which was propped in the window in a deceptively casual fashion. He had already cruised up and down the dial of the aging radio looking for some grain of information, something some persistent reporter might have dug up on the death of his father, but there was nothing. Either music or totally unrelated news reports – primarily about celebrity sex lives – blared from the grainy speakers. Apparently his father's death had been filed away as yet another suspicious death of yet another Japanese corporate magnate, and the press, each outlet owned by another rival corporate magnate, was believing everything it was being fed.

Finally, he switched it off in disgust and concentrated on figuring out what might have happened to Krista. He had headed south again because that was where it seemed like he needed to be, and also because that's where he strongly suspected

Krista was being taken, either as bait for him to follow or because whoever her captors were thought she was somehow involved in Mako's nasty business.

Well, in a sense she was. She had fired the rocket launcher and pistol at his uncle's house, but more out of a sense of self-preservation than out of concern for his safety, he was sure. He knew he shouldn't have even let her stay in the truck. The guilty feelings for letting her get in as deep as she had welled up inside him, and he decided that before he could pursue his own goals, he would have to make sure she was safe and no longer endangered by what he wanted to accomplish.

So here he was, driving to her rescue, an inadequate white knight riding an internal combustion steed. Other than the names of two cities, he had no idea where to look for her. What he did know was that he had to save her, if only in exchange for her saving him. But there was a deeper concern.

There it was again. God, it sickened him. He'd managed to avoid feelings through countless "girlfriends" and one-night-stands he'd picked up at competitions. Now, though, he felt himself becoming weak and pliable over someone he had known barely a day and who might very well look on him as a new disease she couldn't be rid of soon enough. Even so, he didn't seem to mind. His brain was already shifting from thoughts of revenge on behalf of his father to saving her from whatever unpleasant fate she was bound to meet at the hands of her kidnappers.

He couldn't keep driving forever, though. He had to decide what he was going to do and exactly how he was going to do it. He had to think of it like a scam or a surfing competition. Clear your mind, stand back, look at the ocean and read the waves. Where can you catch the best one and where is it going to take you?

He decided his first objective was definitely to help Krista, no matter what that took, and at the same time liberate the stick that would reveal his father's killers. A far second now was actually finding his father's killers. That was long term, since his father was already dead and there was very little he could do to change that. Krista was in danger now, and the longer he waited, the more the opportunities for something bad to happen to her multiplied. He didn't know her captors and had no way to know what they might be capable of, so he considered the worst. She had the memory stick and he was sure there were several ways they could dispose of Krista's body very discreetly after they got what they wanted. The possibilities were endless and each one made his stomach turn and his foot press that much harder on the accelerator.

There was the little he knew of the SHAG organization from talking to Eddie, which told him little to nothing about what to expect if they were the ones who took Krista. Militant groups forming around religious organizations were a dime a dozen. But they sounded like brain-fry victims of the extra-crispy variety.

He was familiar with the New Revelationists and thought he might have even had some girlfriends who attended the ribald Saturday night services. It was easy to peg the CNR girls. In spite of what initially seemed like modesty, they still were the most alluring on the beach. He decided it was because they put such reverence into their hedonism. They didn't screw you just to get you to like them. They were on a mission from God.

The Revelationists did a lot of dancing at their services, but that was just one element for them rather than the focus of the whole production. Where the dance fit in for SHAG he just couldn't guess. From what Eddie told him he figured it had kind of faded out among the young people, since Eddie's parents did it and were way into their seventies. That would make these terrorists elderly by most standards, but apparently no less a threat than any other group. So rather than take Eddie's mention of the group with a grain of salt, Mako took it with the utmost respect. Eddie mentioned Florence and Myrtle Beach as possible home bases for the group. Since Mako's only experience traveling up and down the east coast was by air, he pulled off the interstate and found a prehistoric looking gas station. The place was staffed by an elderly woman who seemed delighted to see him – he imagined these places didn't get a lot of visitors anymore – until she realized the stain on his shirt was blood. She just pointed him to the restroom without saying a word.

He leaned toward the mirror and got his first good look at the damage his attackers had done. Thankfully the restroom was relatively clean and the soap dispenser full. It took him ten minutes and what seemed like an entire dispenser of cheap paper towels to get cleaned up. Once he was finished, though, the result wasn't bad. All that remained was an inch-long gash surrounded by the beginning of a bad bruise on his forehead.

When he emerged from the restroom, the woman – her hair tinted blue and her scent reminiscent of moth balls – treated him like a different person. He chatted her up, listening to the exploits of her brilliant grandchildren in Raleigh, while he scanned the shop for maps and clean shirts. There were no maps, but there was a Web terminal he could use to plot a route and extend himself another cash card from the Swiss account. The transaction would tag him again, but the cash card would render him semi-anonymous once more.

The map showed that if he continued south, he would eventually run straight into Florence, then be able to take another route from there almost directly to Myrtle Beach. If it was any easier and if he believed in that sort of thing, he'd think it was divinely ordained.

Once he got there it would be harder, he thought. His face had been on TV for at least 48 hours and he didn't expect to just walk in and ask if anyone knew any renegade shagging New Revelationists, but that might be exactly what he would have to do.

The computer calculated his ETA for Florence at about 10 p.m. A few more screens later he got a Chamber of Commerce list of nightspots there, which he winnowed down to those playing exclusively to shag crowds, printing the extensive list for use again when he arrived. Cash card and map information in hand, he bought a Snickers, a Coke, some cold-pack bandage strips, headache powders and a fresh T-shirt that read "Myrtle Beach" using his shiny new cash card. When he left the lonely gas station lady, he felt like he was abandoning his grandmother.

The sign behind the bar at the Final Frontier read "Maximum Occupancy: 100. Exceeding this number is a violation of the fire codes of Florence County and the state of South Carolina."

Eustace stopped to tighten the rubber band that held his ponytail and caught a glimpse of the sign for the first time since he'd started tending bar there a week earlier. It was a tiny but official looking document in a simple metal frame, placed conveniently out of view behind the rows of import and domestic beer bottles.

He laughed when he read it as he reached into the cooler to pull out another two beers for the guys at the end of the bar. He turned and laid out a white paper napkin – bevnaps, the kids who worked here called them – then popped off the bottle caps and placed them down beside two clean beer glasses before adding the charges to their tab.

He looked out at the bright pulses and swirls of color and light on the dance floor, oversized holograms of the singer bobbing and weaving sickeningly over the crowd. At least 200 people were jammed onto the brightly lit platform, not to mention the 70 or so people hovering in limbo between the bar and dancers. They were all moving, the incessant beat of the music pumping out of the huge bass-driven speakers suspended from the ceiling. They looked more like a single amorphous organism rather than a few hundred male and female bodies.

Two women walked up to the bar holding hands. Both were attractive and provocatively dressed, and Eustace made a special effort to make sure his eyes met theirs as they waved hello. The blonde he didn't know, but her brunette friend was Frankie, a variation on Frances or Francine, he assumed.

"Hey, Eu," Frankie said with a grin over the noise.

"Hey to you, too, pretty ladies," he said after leaning in toward them. "What can I get you?"

"Amaretto sours all around," Frankie said.

He nodded and set upon his work.

"Nice to see you decided to come back this weekend," Frankie said as Eustace poured their drinks.

He had spoken to Frankie the previous weekend and found her intelligent and funny, and he'd thought for a moment about asking her out. Then he remembered where they all were and quickly came to his senses. She, meanwhile, had immediately pegged him as straight and was amused by his attention.

"What can I say? I like it here. The money's good, the clientele isn't nearly as prone to violence as the crowd in the biker bar I left, and it's a hell of a lot easier for me to turn down an ugly man at the end of a night than an ugly woman. All I got to say is, if y'all can stand an old ex-military breeder like me, then the world's a better place for it, right?"

"Amen," Frankie said as she slapped down a cash card blinking $100. "Keep those drinks coming, and whatever's left over is for you." She winked and leaned forward while the other woman surveyed the crowd. "I'm doing my best to get lucky tonight."

"And I'm here to help you, sister," he said as he went to get orders from his newest arrivals.

The club was crowded and hot tonight despite the relentless effort of the air conditioning. Those coming off the dance floor were bathed in sweat, which meant they would be heading to Eustace soon enough.

His long sleeves didn't help keep him cool. He often wished he could safely wear short sleeves here, but couldn't take the chance of flashing the Special Forces tattoo on his right forearm. Ex-military didn't faze anyone here. Hell, half the younger guys probably had to change out of uniform before they came out tonight. Special Forces were different, though. The implication that he had been involved in some of the Army's less respectable actions was too much to deal with, even if those implications were accurate. He liked his customers, and he knew that with the time these guys spent at the gym, a lot of them could easily kick a fag-basher's ass with one hand and while keeping the other around his boyfriend's waist. He didn't want to start anything that couldn't be finished without someone ending up dead, especially when there was a pretty good chance that someone would be him.

As Eustace finished topping of a guy's Captain Morgan with a spritz of Coke from the bar gun, he felt a light tap on his shoulder. He turned to find his boss, Roth, towering over his five-foot-10 frame.

"Any problems tonight, hon?"

"Nice and quiet, boss. Everyone having a great time, it looks like."

He made a dissatisfied noise. "Looks are deceiving, darling. I know better than anyone." Eustace silently agreed. On the street Roth looked like professional boxer out for a stroll, but every third Thursday of the month he hosted the club's standing-room-only drag show as Formica Dinette, looming over the audience in a series of sequined gowns and blonde wigs that tacked six inches onto his six-foot-four presence. "The scuttlebutt is those crazy geezers with the shag music are at it again, and I don't want any disturbances. Damn if they don't have enough of those tacky little holes of their own in this pit stop of a town."

"Well, whatever comes up, I'm sure I can handle it. That's one of the reasons you hired me to begin with, right?"

"You're right, but I wouldn't hear of forcing you to crack skulls with your bare hands. Because they're rather nice hands, and I'm sure they've seen their share of skull cracking already." He turned his back to Eustace, watched himself apply a fresh coat of lipstick using a tiny hand mirror, and calmly said in his fey baritone, "No, honey. You remember that little chat we had about our friend under the bar. Anyone who tries to take out this club or anyone in it, I want them blown the fuck away."

Roth snapped the compact shut and cut his eyes back toward the crowd as if to prove his point. An older woman who had obviously spent a lot of time on the table trying to look much younger was leading another, younger woman dressed in a dirty work shirt and khaki shorts and looking like someone had very recently kicked the shit out of her.

The grandma leaned in. "Little girls' room?"

He pointed the way, then leaned forward, a glass in one hand and the bar gun – the non-lethal one – in the other. "You need some ice for that eye?" he shouted across as they walked away.

The girl looked back for a moment, flashing him what he thought was a look of panic, but quickly turned forward again after a rough nudge from the older woman.

"Some girls never learn, do they, dear?" Roth said with a dramatic sigh. "I'm going home now, Eustace. You keep an eye on those two. My woman's intuition lit up as soon as they came in."

"Sure thing, boss." He reminded himself to send one of the waitresses in to check on them in a few minutes when Frankie motioned for refills on their drinks, which he mixed and didn't think any more about it.

^^^

Harlan sat behind the wheel of the van smoking edgily and listening to the beach music CD he always put on when he was nervous. Dwight and Earl sat at the van's rear, the back doors open just enough to allow them to make a quick exit. Both of them impatiently fingered the triggers of their aging AKs and alternately dabbed the perspiration from their faces and necks with soiled handkerchiefs. Harlan's door was ajar as well, and the ping of the seatbelt warning repeated annoyingly beneath the soulful 4/4 beat of "Stagger Lee."

Harlan was outfitted with only a sidearm, since it was his job to come in after Monique and the boys secured the place so he could initiate the evening's entertainment. Across his chest were strapped two bandaleros specially designed to hold CDs.

"Damn it, I always get nervous before we do this," he muttered in between drags.

"C'mon, H. You know these things always run like clockwork. Room full of fags and dykes – they can't help but run screamin'," Dwight said.

Harlan chuckled at the thought. Dwight was right, or at least had been so far, he agreed silently. "Couldn't do it without her, that's for sure. That girl knows her shit."

"Yeah, bo," Earl chimed in. "But has she got to be so damn mean about it? I mean, damn, sometimes she treats us all like we're lower 'n dog vomit."

Earl was right, too. Harlan hated the way she pushed him around and treated him like he was an idiot, but sometimes, when they watched the New Revelationist services on the church's pay cable channel, she'd get all worked up and let him be her meditation partner. He'd slap on a couple of Turgidex patches and in five minutes be harder than Chinese calculus. It didn't happen that often, but when it did it made everything else worthwhile.

By his count, this would be the fifth nightclub they had hit in that many months. Each visit was another step in stomping out that heathen noise they called music, that spastic jerking they thought was dancing. None of them knew what real music sounded like, so it was their job to save their eternal souls by showing them, whether they liked it or not.

They had the sheriff on their side. Harlan knew that. If he hadn't agreed with what they were doing in the first place, they would've paid him off. If that hadn't worked, they would've showed him the video of him and a 15-year-old prostitute doing things at a whorehouse out in the county that would make the slimiest feelie king blush. Luckily, they didn't have to go that far. So, whenever the Feds would roll into town to investigate rumors of some old shaggers running guns to revolutionaries in Central America or Quebec, the sheriff would laugh and give them fatherly slaps on the back and ask them where they heard such nonsense. Then he'd send them back to Columbia or Atlanta or Washington full of barbecue and bourbon, but without any more information than they had when they arrived.

He caught himself staring into space and realized he had almost smoked his cigarette down to the filter. He crushed it out in the ashtray, looked at his watch and his attention was immediately focused again.

"You boys ready? It's almost time."

Both nodded their heads and simultaneously knocked the weapons' clips in with the butts of their hands then chambered their first rounds.

Harlan breathed deep and exhaled slowly. "Tick tock, Monique. Tick tock, darlin'," he said to the air.

^^^

Monique was trying to work the explosive putty onto the stall's toilet paper dispenser with her left hand as she held her pistol on Krista with her right hand. Krista imagined it was nearly impossible for the older woman to see, since the entire room was painted black and lit by only a few ultraviolet bulbs buzzing and flickering overhead. Krista was doing as she was told, sitting quietly on the edge of the toilet seat. Two male voices murmured from the next stall, and Krista recognized the sounds that followed and tried not to listen.

"How much longer is this going to take?" she said, worried that if the noises didn't drive her crazy, the cramped quarters would. The stalls, despite the obvious signs they were frequently used otherwise, were not designed for two.

"I told you to shut up," Monique hissed, trying to work a timed detonator into the putty. "I only brought you in here to keep you safe from Dr. Octopus out there in the van, so act like you're grateful. Sweet young thing like you, Harlan would've been on you like white on rice and I would've been stuck in here with no back up. Besides, I've got to get you to the man in good condition."

After embedding the detonator and setting the digital timer, Monique motioned for Krista to stand up and move toward the stall door. Once outside, Krista was placed in the bathroom's back corner as Monique knocked on the door of the adjoining stall.

"Ollie, ollie oxen free, boys. Better leave now if you want to get out with

115

all your parts still connected."

The door opened with one of the men zipping his red vinyl pants and the other looking highly agitated until he saw the pistol.

"You boys better scoot on outta here if you don't want to get your pretty little asses blown off, so shake it," Monique said as she waved the weapon toward the door. Though they were noticeably concerned about their own welfare, both shot Krista a glance that said they knew she was probably there against her will. Both were tall and well built, each sporting a closely cropped crew cut and the barest hint of eyeliner and looked quite able to take out the elderly, fragile, chain-smoking Monique. Neither one moved.

Krista looked for anything that could help her take the older woman down from behind, but aside from a plastic trash can and an aging condom dispenser firmly attached to the wall, she was unarmed.

"That's a pretty serious weapon you've got there, ma'am," said the taller one, his pierced nipples clearly visible through his black mesh tank top. "Did you happen to have any military training back when you were young? I suppose that would've been in the Civil War."

The shorter one snickered, the wrinkles in his silk shirt shimmering with each movement of his shoulders.

"It's a damn shame when ugly old redneck bitches have to bring pistols to queer bars to try to get laid," he said as he nudged his companion, both of them seeming more relaxed as they better assessed the situation.

Monique, becoming more infuriated with the two men with each passing moment, began haphazardly waving the pistol between the two men.

"Now, I'm not playin' with you fellas. You better scoot before this whole place blows."

"Sorry, ma'am, but there was already some blowing going on and you interrupted it, and that really upset us…"

Without finishing his thought, the taller one moved one step toward Monique, his arms a blur of motion. The next sound Krista heard was the metallic clank of the pistol against the toilet bowl and the sound of it hitting water, followed by Monique screaming and holding her arm as she fell to her knees.

As Krista stared in horror at the bone of the older woman's forearm protruding from the skin, both men grabbed her solidly, lifted her up and carried her out the door.

"Was there really a bomb in there?" the taller one asked as they lifted her down the narrow corridor.

"Yeah. That putty stuff, I think," she said after struggling to remember the real word. "C4, is that right?"

"Shit. Do you know how much?"

Krista made a fist. "About this much."

"Do you know what the timer was set on?"

She shook her head no, but made sure to tell them there were men waiting outside for the explosion to signal them to come in.

In the club both men dropped her to her feet and ordered her under the heavy wooden bar as they went to Eustace, yelling at him over the pounding music. She saw the ponytailed bartender curse and rip a huge gun from under the bar, his feet then running out of view as her two rescuers hit the floor.

Pushing past the dancers and drinkers, Eustace climbed the narrow stairway to the control booth and pushed the confused DJ out of the way. After trying in vain to turn off the music, he succeeded in switching on the PA he grabbed the microphone.

"May I have your attention everyone? We have an emergency. Would everyone please move in a calm and orderly fashion to the rear of the building and lie flat on the floor."

Nobody moved. Too late to argue, Eustace thought.

"Thank you for your cooperation, folks," he said.

The charge went up, sending pieces of tile, wall and plumbing flying across the dance floor from the opposite wall. He ducked and covered his head just in time for the glass panel to shatter above him. Damn it. He knew this was going to happen sooner or later. He had no idea of how many weapons he might encounter or what kind of enemy might be wielding them, but he was ready to take out as many as he could before he would let them have this club.

The screaming from the crowd as it ran toward the farthest corner from the restrooms and huddled together almost made Eustace sick. Fighting the insurgents in Cuba after the Second Revolution, he learned nothing was more universal than the sound of bombs and human screams.

The music played on and the dance floor effects were still operating, the brightly colored lights and video holograms making eerie specters leap and duck in darkness through the dust and smoke of the explosion. Finally Eustace found the kill switch for the music, and for one moment there was silence broken only by the whimpers and voices of the club's patrons crowded together on the floor. It was shattered by the unmistakable sound of AK-47 fire ringing through the room. Pieces of foam ceiling panels drifted to the floor and made bizarre shadows as they floated through the precise beams of laser light.

Squatting, Eustace gently pulled back the hammer of the pistol and looked over the edge of the sound booth. He aimed at the figures moving into the smoky doorway. He imagined they were professionals, but he detected a hint of hesitation in their entrance. At first he saw only two until another one, apparently unarmed, walked in between them and placed his arms on his hips as if he already owned the place. That's the boss, Eustace thought. The pistol's sight fell on his upper chest and Eustace held it there as he regulated his breathing to cut his movement to a minimum.

"Hey, everybody," the man shouted like a redneck master of ceremonies. "Y'all ready to do some real dancing?"

Dancing? The question was so outrageous Eustace actually let his concentration slip. Who the hell were these yahoos and why were they shooting up his club?

Then he remembered what Roth said about the gun-toting shaggers raiding dance clubs. He had been positive they were nothing more than tall tales designed to cover for insurance scams, but suddenly he wasn't so sure. As such scams went, he much preferred a fire started from the friction of two insurance policies rubbing together to the ricochet of automatic weapons fire.

"If Mr. DJ would kindly allow my colleague to join him, we'll show you why God loves shaggers and how he can love even heathen sodomites like you," the leader said as he slipped out of his CD bandalero. He passed it to a shorter companion, who took the belt, gripped his weapon and began walking toward the sound booth. The DJ's face contorted into an expression of terror, and Eustace was concerned he might wet himself right there in the chair. He was visibly shaking and looking to Eustace as if he might know what to do.

He didn't, but he wasn't going to let the DJ know that. The gunman was at the base of the sound booth stairs now, and Eustace thought quickly and motioned for the DJ to stay put, which obviously didn't thrill him judging from the way the vein in his forehead was bulging and the sweat pouring down his face. Holding his breath, Eustace moved quietly back into the shadows.

When he mounted the last few stairs, Eustace could tell the interloper was glad to see the terror-stricken look on the DJ's face. The little man, wearing a Madras shirt and khaki pants, of all things, slung the CD bandalero off his shoulder and threw it at the DJ.

"CD number two, track seven, nancy boy. 'Give Me Just a Little More Time' by the Chairmen of the Board," he said as if quoting scripture. "Time for some real music around here."

The guy was still chuckling to himself, marveling over his own encyclopedic musical knowledge, Eustace imagined, when the muzzle of Eustace's gun flashed and blew him back down the stairs, his face still wearing a shocked and confused expression when his body hit the floor below.

Through the ringing in his ears Eustace heard the other two men yelling, trying to figure out what happened. He looked over the edge of the broken-out window to see both of them moving out of the doorway and down onto the dance floor among the sprawled bodies of the club's patrons. The muzzles of both of their weapons – the one Eustace thought was unarmed now carried what looked to be an old Glock 9 – were aimed down at a dangerous angle, and he knew even a direct hit on either of them could still result in a jerking muscle pulling the trigger and letting a few deadly rounds loose on an unsuspecting customer.

They kept moving, backing and turning, checking all sides while stepping among the prostrate and prone bodies, an occasional whimper rising up from one of the people on the floor. As they drew closer to the bar, Eustace spotted the two men from the restroom sprawled among the other customers. They knew enough to get the girl out of the can before the bomb blew, and Eustace figured their decidedly military look was more than just a fashion statement.

He reset his aim to the breaker box directly behind the bar. It was easy to spot, covered as it was with an American flag with the pink triangle-and-fist emblem embroidered where the star field should have been. He slowed his breathing, took aim and waited, his left hand cupping his right to steady the pistol. The men kept moving towards the bar, right where he wanted them.

Two shots rang out and made their mark on the circuit panel directly behind the clenched fist, sending up a shower of white sparks and throwing the entire room into darkness.

Both men immediately shouted out for each other in panic, but their screams of concern quickly turned to screams of pain accompanied by the wet cracking sound Eustace knew all too well from back when death and destruction were part of his job description.

He was listening to their legs being broken, which was, as much as it disgusted him now, exactly what he'd hoped to hear.

Eustace reached under the control panel and found the heavy-duty flashlight, kept there so the DJ could find his way out in case the power went dead, and shined it in the direction of the bar. It was easy to find them. He just aimed toward the screaming. There he saw both of the crew-cut men standing holding the gunmen's weapons on them as they lay on the floor holding their legs and writhing.

Eustace hurried down the stairs and to the front door, checking for other gunmen.

"Anything you want us to do with these guys?" the taller one shouted.

"Just hold them there while I get these folks out and call 911," he shouted, then checking outside a final time. "Okay, everybody who can walk, let's get you out into the parking lot."

The comment prompted a smile from his two new comrades, who assured frightened and bloodied customers that it was all right to get up and move around. Meanwhile, Eustace funneled the patrons into the parking lot, sorting the injured as he went and asking them to stay around since the police might need to ask them questions. He knew that gesture was futile, since many of them didn't want their names on police reports as having even been there anyway.

Still, he felt it was necessary to give everyone the benefit of the doubt. If the smoke coming from the restroom area was any indication, one of the club's neighbors would be calling the fire department any moment now, anyway.

"Where the hell did you guys learn to do that?" Eustace asked them. He was surprised he wasn't the only one in the club who knew such bloodcurdling tricks.

"Marines. Three tours in Afghanistan along the Pakistani border. The old guys showed us how they used to bury themselves in the sand and use that trick on the Soviet ground troops. Never thought it would come in handy here," the shorter one said.

"No shit? Well, Semper fi, boys. Semper fuckin' fi."

When the last person left, he went to the bar phone and dialed 911, getting the bored face of the police dispatcher on the tiny screen. He told them only that there had been an explosion and shots had been fired at the address and the gunmen had been subdued,

He wanted them to be sure everyone was already safe in case they decided to send in an overzealous SWAT team before the fire engines showed up. The last thing he wanted to hear tonight was more guns.

A random sweep of the flashlight beam found the young girl with the banged up face curled up in a ball behind the bar with her hands covering her ears. Eustace kneeled and gently pulled her hands from her head.

"Hey, kid. How're you doing?" he asked softly.

"Is it over?" she whispered, sounding like a tiny girl rather than the grown woman he saw that she was.

"Yeah, honey. It's over. My bet is those people were not your friends."

"And I'd say you'd win that bet," she said.

The scent of warm tar hung in the air as Mako drove into Florence and past the strips of gaudily lit motels and fast food places. Smells like a railroad town, he thought, remembering the brief history provided in the Chamber of Commerce profile that accompanied his printed directions. The maglev hub was built over the city's old rail yard, which used to serve the same purpose when the heavy freight trains still ran through here. The trains were less frequent, but the unmistakable creosote odor of tar-soaked railroad ties cooking in the July heat still lingered all over the city.

He followed the instructions and turned right at the next light. He was headed for a shag club called McLean's, simply because it was close to the interstate exit and comfortably in the middle of the alphabetical list the computer gave him. It was a hell of a system to decide with, but since he knew nothing about where he was going or what he was getting into, it seemed appropriate to blindly pick one of the nightspots on the list.

The night air was thick and moist, the stillness making it feel even closer and stickier in the Mustang's vinyl driver's seat. Nobody was on the street save a few drunks wheeling their way from a fortress-like convenience store, occasionally lifting their paper bag-wrapped bottles for another sip.

A city police car whined toward him at the next light. Every muscle in his body temporarily seized up as he hoped the locals would be too ill-informed to recognize him. The cop simply raised two fingers from the steering wheel in a casual wave and drove past. Mako exhaled and allowed his ass to unclench.

Up ahead he saw a sign beaming into the night. A giant pair of loafers similar to the ones worn by his assailants alternately flashed on and off in brilliant blue and red neon above the name "McLean's" and, in smaller script, the words "cash welcomed." He pulled into the parking lot and cut the lights and engine. Lots of antique steel sitting in this lot. If he were more inclined toward the criminal, he could make a mint here in one night, if not from the cars themselves just from their antique status stickers. He eyed a group walking to the door after stopping at the other antique – an old fashioned ATM that actually dispensed paper money. A bunch of khaki-clad geezers, from what he could tell. Given his own odd attire, he was sure he wasn't dressed appropriately for the place.

Mako peeled himself off the seat and stepped out of the car, the doorman sitting on a wooden stool outside the club already eyeing him suspiciously as he crossed the parking lot. Assuming the posture he used at surfing competitions — the one that said I know I belong here, how about you? — he casually strolled up to the ATM and withdrew $500 off the balance of his card. Without putting the money in his pocket, he approached the doorman.

"What can I do for you, son," he asked through his mustache, already signaling that he had no intention of letting Mako in.

"Heard a lot about your club. Thought I'd come check it out," Mako said as he looked the place over from the outside, trying to remember where the emergency exits were. "What's the cover?"

"No cover, but it's a private club. You don't look familiar. You got a membership card? Or maybe you're on the guest list?" he said sarcastically as he pretended to consult his clipboard without ever breaking eye contact.

"Now come to think of it, I do believe I have mine with me tonight," Mako said as he peeled off three one hundred-dollar bills.

"All right, my man," he said as he slapped down each bill on the clipboard one at a time. "There's my membership card, there's my I.D. and that should cover next year's dues so we don't have to go through this little dance next time I roll through town."

The bouncer sat stunned for a moment, looking at the money as if it was a tarantula ready to sink its fangs into his hand if he got too close. He shot Mako a penetrating gaze, trying to figure out his motives, but Mako simply smiled back.

"My friends call me Ben," he said, meeting the man's gaze directly and tapping a finger on the face of the long-dead statesman adorning the top bill.

Though it took a few seconds for the bouncer to realize what was happening, once he got on track with what Mako was suggesting the money quickly disappeared from the clipboard.

"If anyone asks, I didn't see you and I sure as hell didn't let you in, okay?"

"I can dig it, man. I was never here, you were never here. Everybody's happy," he said as he opened the door and slipped into the club.

The air inside was about thirty percent oxygen and seventy percent cigarette smoke, the stinging forcing Mako to narrow his eyes to little more than slits. I guess this place has to be private. Any public place would be shut down for allowing this much cigarette smoke without a few dozen drones working the room. He pressed through the crowd, made up mostly of elderly people trying to look about forty years younger – some of them obviously having partially succeeded through surgery – and ignored their strange looks. He kept his eyes forward the whole way, considering whether the stares were because he was so young, because he wasn't entirely "white" or because they recognized him from the news.

The music blaring over the sound system was old — real old from what Mako could tell. So old he barely recognized it. Some of the club's patrons were on the small dance floor doing something that involved about a thousand variations on a four-step, the man and woman occasionally holding hands or performing a spin, all while looking like they were floating about an inch above the floor. He assumed that was shagging. Sure doesn't look like the kind of thing that would turn folks toward a life of terror, he thought. Then again, to see people in church or temple or kneeling toward Mecca, you wouldn't think religion would drive them to killing each other, either. Above the dance floor, a large-gauge model train chugged along a shelf that looked as if it had been built especially for it. A brass plate on the second car said, "Leroy Wooten: 1941-1998." So the coal car was a fucking urn.

Mako wondered if ol' Leroy had just loved this place so much he wanted to stay for eternity or if he'd actually dropped dead on the dance floor. Given the look of the clientele, he was surprised the funeral train wasn't towing more engraved cars.

Mako leaned up against the bar and casually held another hundred between two fingers, waiting to catch the bartender's eye. The old fellow finally came Mako's way and cocked a fleshy, hairy ear toward him. Mako leaned close and stuffed the bill in the breast pocket of the man's sweaty shirt.

"I'm looking for someone named Monique," he shouted. "You wouldn't know where I could find her, would you?"

The old man pulled the pocket open and looked inside to confirm the denomination, his chin pressing into his neck and forming about 13 brethren. Seeming to find what he saw satisfactory, he motioned for Mako to follow him and walked through a doorway beside the bar. Mako checked behind him, saw the crowd was still focusing on the dancers or each other, and followed the bartender's lead.

The last thing he saw clearly as he walked out the establishment's back door was a poster with his picture on it and the word "Wanted" underneath. After that, everything was projected against a blurry background of deep, throbbing pain.

Whatever hit him the moment he stepped out of the door was big, and the person wielding it not too small, either. Mako felt the impact across the side of his head and the sound of his skull taking the full force of the blow. Then feet, seemingly hundreds of them repeatedly flying towards him, each one similarly shod in brown leather loafers. Any attempt to shield his body from the kicks only resulted in more severe attention to an unexposed portion of his body, and finally, through the fog of his pain, he decided it would be in his best interest to convince his attackers they had either killed him or knocked him out. He stopped fighting and just lay there, trying to think like a dead man. At that point, it was relatively easy.

He heard nothing. These fellows were smarter than his earlier assailants were in that they didn't give themselves away by gabbing and tossing around each other's names. They at least got points for professionalism, as well as a bonus for brutality. Mako wished he had at least gotten a chance to get over the day's earlier beating before he had to submit to another.

He lay there listening to the sound of his own breathing, coming now in raspy, hollow, irregular heaves. He was sure that at least a few of his ribs were broken. Actually, only a few would be a convenience at this point, he thought.

The silence was unexpectedly broken by surprised sounds of pain that were not his, of which he was certainly grateful but still curious. He kept his face well hidden, listening with satisfaction but some apprehension to his tormenters falling, the noises of their agony masked from the bar's patrons by the music thumping through the walls. Mako allowed himself a brief peek over his arm to see what was happening, only to be rewarded by the sight of an unconscious, stretch-faced old man falling directly in front of him, his nose a red meal of bone and cartilage and his blue Oxford button-down splattered with blood. Mako decided he'd better keep playing dead.

The fellow he saw fall must have been the last, because after he landed there was silence again, which again stoked Mako's apprehension about who exactly had come to his rescue. For all he knew, having seen physical evidence of the bounty Eddie had spoken of, his savior might just turn out to be a competitor for the undoubtedly substantial sum someone was offering for his capture. At least, he hoped only for his capture.

His questions, however, were not answered. The next thing Mako felt was a delicate prick in his upper arm, and he didn't have to pretend to be unconscious any longer.

"Yoshi, you scared the living shit out of me! What the hell did you think you were doing?"

"Saving your life, it would seem," the huge man said as he repacked the hypodermic gun he had used to revive his young employer, who at the moment was groggily lying in the back seat of a very ordinary looking early-model cell automobile and rubbing the back of his head. The blows he took at the club only added to the symphony of pain that his body was already experiencing. This throb, he decided, would have to be a cello. It was low and resonant, but powerful enough to be detectable along with the piccolos and violas of agony in various parts of his anatomy. He felt his side and found Yoshi had wrapped his damaged ribs before waking him up.

"As you grow older you will find it is rarely wise to go into establishments displaying a wanted poster with your picture on it," Yoshi said without expression. Almost everything the man did, now that Mako thought about it, he did without expression. It was one of his most annoying characteristics, right behind showing up in the middle of the night to steal him back to his father's corporate nightmare. "I had the advantage of several law enforcement sources to provide information on the terrorists' possible whereabouts, but I was not aware you were so resourceful. It was fortunate that we tracked your father's killers to the same place."

"I don't know if you'd call it tracking. I just sort of read a list of shag clubs and guessed. This one was right in the middle, so I thought it would be a good place to start," Mako said as he slowly sat up, his eyes squinting with the pain. He looked around and saw that they sat in the middle of the empty parking lot to a long-abandoned strip mall. Most of the stores were either burned out or had front windows broken, the letters MART dangling at odd angles from the largest building's façade. The flicker from a single street light cast an eerie green glow on Yoshi's hair and skin as he stood outside the car's open back door.

"Ah, then you are simply lucky. Those people would have killed you. Although, from the appearance of your head, it seems someone has already tried to do that today. Fortunately, you have a very hard head."

"Yeah, very funny. So far people have tried to kill me three times today, if you count Uncle Hiroshi unloading his toy machine guns on me in his driveway. And that was all before 10 a.m. This," he said pointing to his forehead, "is from some of those lovely SHAG folks I met earlier in the day. They're not very bright, but damn, are they mean."

"But not very efficient. I don't believe your most recent assailants were interested in anything other than the bounty, however, which leaves us to find the ones from earlier today. Do you know what they wanted?"

"Andrea Turner gave me a memory stick that I think might've had some information on who was really behind all this," Mako said. He slid across the seat and dangled his long legs out of the door, pausing to smack a mosquito having a bloody little late-night snack. "But Krista had the stick, so they took her and left me."

"Krista?"

"Oh, sorry. She's this girl I picked up on the way out of Philadelphia. I gave her the stick for safe keeping after Uncle killed himself. She saved my life, too, if it's any consolation."

"You are putting yourself in entirely too many situations where it is necessary for someone else to save your life. I expect you to be more thoughtful about putting yourself in jeopardy now, if only to spare me the trouble of having to save your life again," Yoshi said as he crossed his arms over his chest. "She is most certainly dead, but we still need to find that stick."

Mako had considered the possibility, but didn't dwell on it enough to actually accept such a theory. He decided if Yoshi wanted to operate under the assumption, that was fine. Mako was sure she was alive and was determined to find her and the stick.

"What do you know about SHAG, Yoshi? I got some basic information, but nothing concrete. Mostly small-time arms dealers and musical terrorists from what I heard."

"My sources told me the same thing. That is how I ended up here. The arms dealing is not a surprise, but I do not understand the purpose in bombing nightclubs. What can be so important about a dance that an entire organization would be built around it?"

"And not even a very interesting dance. Beats the hell out of me why they'd want to shoot people over the damn thing." Mako rolled his shoulders to try to alleviate the pain in his back, finally coming to the conclusion that whatever Yoshi had used to wake him had no pain-killing properties. His whole body throbbed, and it's likely that's just the way Yoshi wanted it.

"What do you suspect was on this stick?"

"I don't know, but Uncle Hiroshi wasn't very happy about the fact that we had it. He took some kind of poison right after we told him about it. That's when we left."

"Hmm. According to the police, Hiroshi-san was found with multiple bullet wounds to his head. They suspected that you had shot him. You did not?"

"No, I didn't," Mako said, not trying to hide his indignation. "And neither did Krista. Although she certainly had the opportunity. Not a bad shot, really."

"The time for worrying about this girl has passed. We must recover the stick if it will help us find your father's killers. Fortunately, our task is being made easier by this SHAG group's determination in seeing you dead. Do you have any idea where else your assailants might be?"

"No clue. There are at least a dozen clubs like this around town, and something tells me we might expect the same reception at each one if the person hanging up those posters has been as busy as I think he's been."

"You are probably right. You had better stay out of sight for the remainder of the journey."

Mako laughed in a quick burst, stopping as soon as he realized how much it hurt. "Oh, right. Like you're not going to stand out like a sore thumb there, big boy. Something tells me the population of oversized Japanese bodyguards isn't as large around here as it might be up north. What's Plan B?"

As if to answer his question, the horizon lit up in a blaze of fiery orange smoke. Both of them winced and covered their eyes against the blast, waiting until the explosion had turned into a low burn before looking again. They watched for a moment, then simultaneously turned to look at each other.

"Suppose that might have been a nightclub over there Yoshi?" Mako said hopefully.

"I prefer to know rather than suppose. Get in the car."

^^^

There wasn't much left of the building when Mako and Yoshi arrived – only a burnt husk and a few smoldering piles of debris to indicate it had once been there. Mako and Yoshi drove up slowly outside the strips of yellow tape the fire department had strung up around the block. Chips in the tape cast life-size holo images of firefighters in full turnout gear repeating, "This is a dangerous area. For your own protection, please stay back." Combined with the flashing of red and blue lights, the crackle of police radios and the feathery arcs of water from fire hoses, it all made the disaster scene eerily beautiful.

Yoshi didn't have to try to look inconspicuous, at least where his ride was concerned. The car he had rented or liberated or whatever was terminally inconspicuous. Mako wasn't sure if he could remember what it looked like if someone asked him. It was also one of a number of vehicles slowing down to gawk. Many had already parked their cars and set up digital video gear to record the scene in the hopes of selling some cheap and easy shots to the local TV stations, who rarely risked the safety of their talent by actually sending them out on assignment, or the Webcasters who depended on freelancers to fill bandwidth. Mako had friends back in Florida who had friends who knew arsonists who made a tidy living selling on-the-spot video of their own torchings. Others would simply upload it onto the computer networks for snuff enthusiasts to add to their collections. If someone happened to die in the blaze, its value would increase ten-fold.

He scanned the scene for a sign of anything familiar. He saw nothing that he even remotely recognized. Only the carnage of burning wood and scorched brick and pavement surrounded by the debris of the building's destruction. Small pockets of men and women dressed for clubbing stood around the perimeter, either looking shaken or simply staring blankly at the flames licking at the already brightly lit sky.

In the charred ruin that was formerly the building's face, Mako saw the remainder of a sign, The Final Frontier, and a marquee that declared tonight "'90s NITE!!!" He finally turned to scan to his right through a grassy field that must have been the building's overflow parking lot. It was mostly empty, but what cars were left — the sheer fact that there were cars at all — indicated the clientele of whatever had been there didn't hurt for money. Along with an assortment of internal-combustion collector models, there were a few of the swanky new aircars and a number of high-end cell rigs.

Then he saw it. A large blue I-C conversion van, definitely not a collector model, probably early '90s vintage, with an airbrushed license plate on the front that read "Shag Mama" over a similarly rendered beach sunrise.

"Yoshi, stop the car," he said, grabbing the huge man's arm. "Stop it now."

"What do you see?"

"I think it's their van. Jeez, they're more stupid than I thought. The bitch has 'Shag Mama' right there on the front of her van. What kind of people are these?"

"No doubt very overpaid people, if this is any indication of their professionalism," Yoshi said dryly as he pulled over and parked with the rest of the cars in the grass lot.

Mako was out of the car and across the street as soon as they stopped. He stepped gingerly over the fire hoses and ducked under the yellow tape while the firefighters and police were otherwise occupied. Yoshi was not far behind.

Mako didn't see any sign of Krista, and became even more worried something might have happened to her inside the club when he saw two soot-stained firefighters emerge from the wreckage shaking their heads and talking into their headsets. The first one to appear finished his transmission, then turned to face the line of ambulances lined up just inside the yellow tape and gave a two-handed wave back in his own direction. Jon turned to follow his gaze and watched one of the technicians grab a folded black bag — a body bag, he quickly realized — and run toward the fireman. Well, then. That's it, he decided. No need to hang around and confirm what I already know.

With that, he turned to walk slowly back to the van, head hanging, trying not to think about that lovely, battered face damaged further by the ravages of fire. Still, something made him take one last glance over his shoulder back at the ambulance from where the EMT had bolted. There stood a tall man wearing a mesh shirt, his hair high-and-tight like the military guys who came and went through Canaveral on a regular basis. As Mako turned, the fellow spoke to someone sitting on the open rear bay of the ambulance, moving to reveal just enough of the other person's face for Mako to see her bruised, swollen eye.

He shouted her name as he ran full speed toward the ambulance, watching her look around trying to pinpoint where his voice was coming from.

He shouted again and finally she saw him, rising from her perch and running towards him. The crewcut guy and a shorter carbon copy bolted after her.

Mako and Krista converged were in each other's arms before either realized what was happening.

"You're okay?" Mako asked quietly, holding her tight, her head resting in the center of his lean chest.

"Yeah. I'm okay. God, I'm glad to see you. I thought you were dead," she said, gripping him equally as tight, making him groan with the pain in his ribs.

"Had a couple of pretty good chances today, but nobody was up to the job," he said, laughing, then grimacing with the pain it caused him. "Watch the ribs. They were the worst casualties."

"Sorry," she said, embarrassed that she was holding him so tightly. Mako was relieved to be free of the excruciating pain but still didn't want her far away again. His fingers trailed down from her shoulders to her hands, which he held tenderly. Stepping back, she got her first good look at him and gasped.

"Jesus, what happened to your head?"

"Another casualty of the day, compliments of the folks who nabbed you. See what happens when you're not around to save my life? I get into all sorts of trouble."

The two crewcut guys were standing a respectful distance away until Mako and Krista parted, then approached them, casting protective glances at Krista.

"Guys, this is my friend I was telling you about. Mako, this is Barry," she said, pointing to the tall one, "and Lewis," she said, putting her arm around the shorter one. "They saved my life."

"Seems to be a lot of that going around today," Mako said, shaking both men's hands. "What happened here?"

"All we know is that some redneck bitch was holding Krista at gunpoint in the men's room while she tried to set some explosives," Barry said. "We got Krista out in time, but after the explosion went off these three nut cases with CD bandaleros and some high firepower broke in and tried to take the place over."

"CD bandaleros? Did you ever get a listen to the music?" Mako asked.

"God, no. Eustace took care of the guy trying to get into the DJ booth and we took care of the other two. They were strictly amateurs. Those Kalashnakovs they were using still had sand in the chambers from Afghanistan. I was surprised they even fired."

"I'm glad they didn't for long," said an older man in a long sleeve T-shirt. After pocketing a telephone, he came up behind Lewis and put both hands on his shoulders. "If the Marines hadn't been there, we all would've been in trouble. You must be Mako. You really Akiro Nikura's kid?"

"Yeah, but don't spread it around. That fact hasn't made me too popular today."

He wasn't as tall as Mako, but had the lean, powerful build one gets after hardcore military training. Though he wore his long, salt-and-pepper hair in a ponytail, Mako could tell from his bearing that Eustace was once called upon to risk life and limb on a regular basis. When the two shook hands, Mako felt like he was gripping a steel coil wrapped in weathered flesh.

"You're Eustace?"

"Yep. Your lady friend is mighty lucky she managed to make it out of there without a scratch. Anybody who'd been in that toilet would've been in a couple dozen pieces. Whoever those people were, they meant business," Eustace said.

"Tell me about it. Nobody seems to be too happy about me trying to find out who killed my father."

"Oh, so that's what this is all about. Well, if these folks had anything to do with it, I don't think they're going to tell you much. The old lady died in the explosion. I took out one in the club and the other two have matched sets of broken legs thanks to my boys, here. Right now the medics are trying to keep them from going into shock. Personally I think they're fighting a losing battle."

"Jeez. You guys are nothing if not efficient," Mako said as he noticed Yoshi approaching from across the road. "Speaking of efficiency, here comes my...er, associate, Yoshi. Yosh, I was just telling the folks here how efficient you were."

"Unfortunately for our adversaries, the same can not be said for them. Does this stick look familiar?" he said as he held up the flat reflective plastic, the flames further distorting the rainbow image dancing across its surface like on an old CD. The label read: "Dance lessons."

"That's the one, my man. Where did you find it?"

"As a further indication of their expertise, your attackers took it upon themselves to hide it safely in the glove compartment of their van. So far they have failed to impress me."

"Find anything else interesting?"

"Only a few more weapons, mostly of a Soviet-era vintage, some explosives not very safely stored and this," he said, holding up a matchbook bearing the gaudy logo of the Church of the New Revelation. The huge man then turned to Krista. "Pardon my employer's rudeness, but his social skills are lacking. I am Yoshi. You are Krista, I presume?"

"Yes," she said, somewhat in awe of his immense size and genteel nature. "Nice to meet you."

"A pleasure," Yoshi said, bowing in the traditional manner. He then addressed the others. "Is there anything else you might have discovered that would help us find out who these people are?"

Eustace stepped forward. "Just this," he said, handing over a phone bud. "Got it off the leader before the cops got here."

Yoshi then turned to Krista. "Please tell me, Miss Krista, did anyone make any calls on this phone that you can remember?"

"There was one that came in. They never said who the caller was, but he was a man and he seemed to make everyone kind of nervous. He said something about bringing me in tonight. Monique, the woman in the van, was upset because she wanted to come here tonight."

"Did you ever hear where this man wanted you brought?"

"No, they didn't say. I'm sure if they had said I would've remembered. Everything seemed to get very tense after he called."

"That was no doubt whoever had hired them to retrieve this stick," he said, then turning to the other men in the group. "Gentlemen, I appreciate very much your efforts in assisting my employer's young friend. You have been most helpful, and I would like to impose on you once more."

"Name it, dude," said Eustace.

"Thank you. ... If it is not too inconvenient, I require the use of a computer."

TWENTY TWO

Jon Templeton stood naked in front of the full-length mirror and ran his hand down the length of his left arm, then down the center of his chest. Everything felt the same, maybe better, he thought. He certainly had aged well, if this was, in fact, what he would look like at around 50. He looked more like a well-traveled 40, the years of experience showing around his eyes and in his carriage, but a spark of youthful vibrancy still alive inside. He was certainly in better shape than when he died, not that he was in any danger of atrophying then, but everything seemed somehow better defined. Turning around, he marveled at the view from behind.

"Damn. That is the tightest ass I have ever seen," he found himself muttering to the image.

"Your Aunt Lil does fine work, but I wouldn't be surprised if she put a little more effort into your refit, boy," he heard Eli's vice say in its island lilt. "She wanted you to look good."

Jon looked in the mirror and saw the old man sitting on the edge of the bed wearing a white band collar shirt and a jacket with no lapels, the deep taupe color matching the pants and brown hurrache sandals blending with his chestnut skin.

"Don't bother to knock," Jon said, ceasing the inspection and moving to the closet, which had been well stocked prior to his arrival.

"Don't need to. Seen everything you got and a couple of interesting variations. Besides, we're not operating on my time any more."

"So I noticed," Jon said, picking out a shirt the color of orange soda and a suit the color of lime sherbet. He'd seen the same outfit in a magazine and knew the shirt alone probably cost more than his entire wardrobe. Socks. He needed socks. "Speaking of which, should I bother asking how I managed to spend a week or two in the hereafter and only a day passed here?"

"I won't bore you with technicalities, boy. Suffice it to say, some things just work differently there than here. Time and space happen to be two of the biggies."

"So what's on the agenda?" he yelled from the cavernous walk-in closet. The hotel suite they had put him in was three times bigger than his first apartment out of college. The closet itself was about as big as his freshman dorm room had been. His kitchen had been about as big as the shower in this suite, but wasn't nearly as comfortable. He didn't think it was possible to fit that much seating and that many showerheads into one stall. A freaking baseball team could have showered together in there. He couldn't wait to see the rest of the place since Eli had just sort of zapped him naked into the shower. That would prove difficult to explain to the front desk staff if it wasn't possible for the old man to somehow plant the memory of him having already checked in. Lil assured him that his arrival was accompanied with much style and flirting with desk clerks and generous tipping. He hadn't met these people yet, and already they were ready to kiss his ass. Not a bad way to make an entrance.

"First, I had down for you to give your scruffy new body a flea dip and shave, which you've already taken care of. Don't know how you people handle the maintenance. It's no wonder you don't take care of your cars," Eli said, getting up from his perch on the bed's corner and gazing out the window at the ocean.

"Check. What's next?"

"Next, I've got someone that you need to visit before we can really get started. He'll be our final elimination of sources about Schaefer's background."

"I thought you'd already checked all that out," Jon said, walking out of the closet. He then threw down a pair of Argentine vented wingtips that looked like they were made of rattan and stepped into them, then kneeled to lace them up.

"Well, not exactly. Remember how I told you we had a little trouble with our underworld sources?"

"Ah, yes. I was wondering when we'd get around to this explanation. You're not telling me I'm getting all dressed up to go to Hell, are you?"

"Nope. Might be seeing some of the same faces, though. Here's the address," Eli said, handing Jon a business card from the pocket inside his jacket. "Better get a move on, because your first meeting with Whitaker is for lunch at his estate at 12:30, so don't spend your whole morning sightseeing.

"Oh, and don't be surprised if you get invited to the New Revelationist service tomorrow night. Remember, we're trying to finalize this satellite deal, so it might be a good idea to say you'll go. Plus, it'll give you a better chance to get close to Schaefer. Later, mon."

And he was gone. Jon hated how he did that. It was so unassuming. No smoke, no fade out, no flash of light. Nothing. Just there and then not there. It gave him the willies.

He checked himself one last time in the mirror in preparation for his appointment, then pulled out the card Eli had given him.

It was an old-style paper business card. Jon didn't see many of those any more, but he liked the feel of it – like holding onto a valuable antique that was at one time purely disposable. It read:

Musical Instruments | Electronics
William Z. Robert
PAWNBROKER
Pre-owned Items Bought-Sold
1800 New Ocean Blvd.
Myrtle Beach, S.C.
Jewelry | Souls

It was 9 a.m. when Jon walked out of his hotel room and into the plush gaudiness of the elevator. A screen set flush into the wall showed fit, beautiful couples cavorting in the sea while telling captive riders of all the fabulous attractions they could find along the Grand Strand. Meanwhile, a pop-up appeared next to him. It was a different fit young couple, both exceptionally attractive and generic at the same time. The man was shirtless and toned and the woman was fit, gorgeous and wearing a tasteful bikini. They were discussing with each other in blatantly commercial language which restaurants they planned to patronize.

"Where should we go for dinner tonight, sweetheart?" asked the man.

The woman replied, "I hear Cleaver's Restaurant at 423 Ocean Boulevard has world-class burgers and the largest selection of beers in Myrtle Beach, honey."

"Yes," he said, giving the woman a nudge. "And I hear the view's not bad, either." False, insincere laughter followed. In some ways it was like watching a 3-D version of a poorly dubbed movie. The acting was awful, and as with older holo-projectors like this one, occasionally the audio and the video were a second or two off.

He and Linda had been on many vacations here, but with the cottage had never been subjected to the constant commercial onslaught that guests of the hotels were always hearing and seeing. A few more floors of this and he'd be clawing at the walls to get out.

The video and pop-up ran on for the duration of the ride. They discussed Calabash sim-seafood. Then the woman departed – eerily exiting the scene through the wall – and the man was joined by a male buddy. They discussed in the same stilted fashion the wide selection of "gentleman's clubs" in Myrtle Beach. There, Jon knew from personal experience, the lovely, surgically enhanced trailer park runaways of the region would be glad to give you a complete anatomical rundown of the female figure to the throbbing beat of the latest dance music. For a little personal attention, all you had to do was offer your donation of a hundred-dollar chip to the Temple of the Velcro G-String.

Then, of course, there was the Church. In every conversation, it was said as if the word was capitalized, and everyone knew what you meant when you said it. Bigger than the virtual reality music palaces where you could feel like you were onstage with whoever the hot country ticket was at the moment. Bigger than the piers of the Catawba casinos that glowed a mile out into the ocean. Even bigger than the annual spring break bacchanals jointly sponsored by the video music networks, the booze companies, the adult feelie industry and the universities.

It had to be big. It was all those things rolled together, concentrated into a giant, super-modern complex looking out into the Atlantic, wrapped tight and tied with the bow that was the blessing of the Almighty Father.

It was God, but it wasn't Michelangelo's severe, bearded and nightgowned God reaching out to give life to Adam. It was God as he would be in a beer commercial. Here He was buffed and toned, wearing the latest style swimsuit, splashing seawater on a curvy pair of appropriately multicultural and surgically enhanced sprites, each holding a can of the beer that could make you popular like this guy, too.

It was Jesus, but it wasn't the scrawny, starved and beaten Jesus hanging from the cross in simultaneous defeat as a human and triumph as a savior. It was a big-haired, rock-star Jesus with a huge erection, leering down from the cross at a wild-eyed Mary Magdalene, brazenly caressing herself in front of him.

It was exactly the opposite of what everyone who had ever gone to church up until the CNR's explosion had ever been taught. It went against all the ideas of sin in the traditional moral sense. It suddenly gave license to the ribald, pagan impulses that Christianity had forced the Celts and the Normans and the Romans and the Watusi and the Polynesians to suppress. It said eat, drink, screw and be merry, but be kind and treat each other well and the world will be a better place. Oh, and by the way, the sacramental drugs are on us.

And the people ate it up. Church membership grew exponentially by the day. And even the ones who didn't become members at least showed up at one service, sitting in the special balcony reserved for those who didn't wish to participate in the fanfare down below. Sort of a religious voyeurism, Jon thought. We don't want to join in with your heathen display, but we'll be glad to sit back and watch.

He arrived gently at the lobby and stepped jauntily out of the elevator, feeling powerful in this body and in these clothes. He found it was easy to project self-confidence when he knew he looked damn good and could honestly say, without any hesitation, that the Lord was on his side. Or Eli, at least, and wasn't that even better?

He could already detect the desk staff and valets snapping to attention and putting on big smiles for his benefit. As he stepped out of the hotel lobby he saw the black '15 Corvette rumble slowly up to the curb. The valet was being extra delicate because the collector sticker clearly designated it as an expensive vehicle, probably worth what the kid would make in a few lifetimes at his current rate. The internal combustion engine probably had the kid spooked, too, now that Jon thought about it. At 17 or so, the young fellow was probably about five when they started phasing out the I-C cars and replacing them with cell vehicles, so the only thing he was used to hearing from a car was an electric hum.

Jon pulled a ten dollar chip from his pocket and gave it to the kid who held the door for him. As he slid into the seat, he felt it mold around him like a living organism. The wheel was wrapped in supple leather, the kind you couldn't buy legally anymore, and his fingers grasped it gently, as if he was taking hold of a baby's arm, enjoying the softness but not wanting to damage it. He pressed his foot down a quarter inch on the accelerator and created a noise he hadn't heard in many years. He saw the valets start at the sudden roar from under the hood, turning their noses at the exhaust that resulted. He knew the smell from long ago and relished what they must be experiencing. A little more pressure on the gas and he let go of the clutch, the wide tires grabbing and squealing before he headed on his noisy way out of the parking lot.

The territory was familiar to him as he made the turn onto New Ocean Boulevard, so the GPS screen did little more than track his progress, all the while glowing with eager anticipation of someone making a wrong turn.

The automotive traffic was light save for a few huge RVs with Canadian plates. A child raised in Myrtle Beach could grow up thinking such lumbering houseboats were the only thing Canadians drove if no one told him differently, he thought. Even the recent border hostilities hadn't changed the popularity of the destination for the U.S.'s northern neighbors. They might be shooting at each other across the Ontario-Quebec border, but they were still headed through enemy territory to Myrtle Beach for vacation, dammit. Because of the large numbers of Canadian refugees who'd bolted for the U.S. as things flared up, portions of the Grand Strand had come to be called Little Montreal. Suddenly all those Canadian flags that had flown along I-95 and throughout Myrtle Beach as courtesies to tourists became symbols of a divided nation.

Jon was tempted to roll the window down as he rode and looked for the address listed on the card, but he knew he should stay neat and that meant staying cool. Even this early in the morning, the heat and humidity were already building to the crescendo of oppressiveness they would reach by mid-afternoon, and he knew it was important to look good at Whitaker's, if only to impress his wife. From what Eli said, though, he'd gotten the distinct impression that Veronica Whitaker was not hard to please.

He drove through the intersection before the address and spotted his destination on the right, an empty spot in front of the nondescript pawnshop looking as if it was being reserved just for him. He wheeled into the space and stepped out of the low-riding car, remembering to arm the security system. If he remembered correctly, this model carried a static generator that could discharge 40,000 volts along the car's exterior after being charged during a five-minute ride. The more malicious modified them with manual switches from inside the car and used the jolt to discourage street people from trying to sell them flowers from off the curb or wipe their windows for tips.

One of his former clients bragged about sending a man into another lane of swiftly moving traffic with the charge after tempting him to the car with a twenty. The client had been reelected to the Legislature four times. As a reporter, Jon had harbored a suspicion that the fellow was a raving sociopath. When he arrived at Hampton, DuBose and Associates, that suspicion was confirmed after their first meeting as vendor and client. Jon thought now that it might be better to be dead than still working for people like that.

The place was one of the few on the boulevard that had avoided being overtaken by the neon pinks and blues of the hotels and beach shops. It looked like a typically seedy pawn shop in any city other than the Fun Mecca of the Southeast. Then again, this commercial row was just about all that was left after the hurricanes ground up the Grand Strand.

The pawn shop's brass door knob was unpolished, and the door itself even stuck a little when he tried to open it, suggesting that no one might have used it in a while. When he did finally get it open he heard the jingle of tiny chimes, which caused corresponding chills to creep down his spine.

The place was a museum of obsolescence. Each wall was stacked from floor to ceiling with an unbelievable array of old stereo equipment. Guitars of all shapes hung from the ceiling, a testament to an eternity of failed rock-god aspirations. Televisions going back to the days of the huge floor units with manual tuners lined the walls, with antique 8-track and cassette tape players and yellowing computers that looked like they could snap a desk in two stacked on top. Hangers placed too close together up and down the back wall held an impressive variety of rifles, shotguns and other large weapons. Above it all, a single, slowly rotating ceiling fan was the only thing that seemed to be working, but not well enough to even stir the dust. The store smelled of mold and hundred-year-old cigarette smoke, and was, from what he could tell, completely unstaffed.

He called out to the emptiness, a single "Hello," which he tried to say with as much authority as he could muster. There was no reply, so he stepped farther into the store, drawing his finger lightly along the top of an ancient video game unit and creating a clean gash in the midst of a thick layer of filth. He walked up to the glass case at the rear of the store, peering through the dingy pane at the items on display. Mostly class rings, wedding bands, a few engagement rings and lots of gold chains of every shape and size, all lying together in a thick bundle that he decided would be impossible to untangle if anyone should ever want to buy one.

On top of the case there was a rusty old-fashioned desk clerk's bell. He tapped it, hoping for some service, but it made only a dull thud against the tarnished metal. Still nothing from anyone resembling an employee of the establishment. There seemed to be some noise coming from a room behind the case, so he leaned over as far as he could without getting the grime from the glass on his suit. He was mildly surprised to see, propped up on a battered wooden desk, a pair of nicely shaped female legs ending in impossibly high stiletto heels.

"Excuse me. Could I get some help up here, please?" he said to the legs.

"Sorry, we're closed. Come back later," a thickly drawling voice answered.

"The sign on the front door says you're open."

"The sign's wrong, sweetie. I say we're closed. Have a nice day."

He listened closely and could barely make out the sound of the GNN morning show. The anchor was leading in to a story about the growing tensions between the U.S. and China. After years of China buying up U.S. debt, the nation suddenly decided to call in its loans after some Taiwanese nationalists allegedly backed by private U.S. interests decided to detonate a bomb in Tiananmen Square.

"Look, I don't need to buy anything. I just need to talk to someone," he said. He was beginning to get uncomfortable in the leaning position.

"Sweetie, people never come in here to buy anything. And there's no one here to talk to you. We're closed."

"Well, I'm sorry. The sign says you're open and I need to speak to Mr. Robert." Eli had filled him in on the French pronunciation – Ro-bear. "Is he your boss?"

At the mention of the name Jon heard the scrape of chair legs against the floor and saw the legs disappear as the person connected to them toppled backwards. Almost immediately she was there in the doorway, dusting herself off and trying to fix the towering beehive hairdo that had partially collapsed. She was pretty in an overly made-up, trailer park sort of way. Her face bore a drawn-on beauty mark he imagined was designed to attract male attention like the glowing extremities that luminescent fish used to lure unwary sea creatures as food. She was packed tightly into a too-small pink cotton playsuit with the words "Can't Touch This" written across the left bosom in cheap iron-on letters.

"Did you say you needed to talk to Mr. Robert? I'm so sorry, mister...?"

"Temple. Johnny Temple." Damn it, it almost hurt Jon to tell another human his name was Johnny. "Is he in? I'm in a bit of a hurry."

"Do you have an appointment?"

"Sorry, I don't. But I do have this," he said, showing her the card Eli had given him.

Her eyes grew exponentially, seeming to fill half her face in surprise and awe. She stammered a moment and immediately picked up the receiver of an ancient beige office phone, the row of chunky plastic buttons along the bottom of its keypad dim except for one red one, which she pressed with a trembling finger. She turned away from him and spoke in low tones that he couldn't quite make out. By her hand gestures, however, he could tell she was getting flustered over something being said on the other end. After a few moments, she turned back to him and hung up the phone.

"He'll be with you in just a few minutes," she said with a forced smile. The woman nervously eyed a door behind her. It was ancient with a dirty frosted window, the word "Office" stenciled on it in simple silver block letters. Jon tried to act patient and cool, but the looming presence of fifty years of electronic refuse seemed to be gradually closing in on him. Some of it was stacked precariously anyway, and for some reason he seemed to be getting an increasing sense of impending doom, as if all of it could suddenly come crashing down on him, leaving him trapped beneath a hundred long-obsolete turntables and dozens of disused Ataris, X-Boxes and VCRs. An ignoble tomb if there ever was one.

The silence was broken only by the tinny sound coming from the television in the other room and the squeaks from the slowly turning ceiling fan. Jon then detected a low, almost subsonic, rumble. It started in his bones, the way the bass from speakers at rock concerts used to thump against his sternum and resonate through his ribs like he was a human xylophone. When the sound finally became loud enough to be heard, it rattled the store windows, filling the air with dust and making Jon worried that some of the stacked items would be knocked from their perches.

The woman was becoming more agitated as well, wide-eyed and quickly tapping her outrageously long acrylic nails – complete with butterfly appliqués – on the display case. Her attention was focused only on the door. It was as if Jon wasn't even there anymore. She then made a slight noise, almost a squeak, and he saw a red glow had appeared behind the glass of the door, steadily growing brighter. He almost asked her if she shouldn't go get a fire extinguisher, but it just didn't seem appropriate considering her state. Fires spur people to action of some sort. They don't petrify people with fear.

The rumble grew and the glow increased until it simply stopped. A moment passed during which both Jon and the woman stared intently at the door, waiting for something deserving of the intense buildup to happen. They were finally rewarded with nothing more ominous than the creak of the door as it opened under its own power and revealed nothing more impressive than a man sitting behind a desk.

The woman placed a hand on her ample chest and looked as if she was about to have a heart attack, closed her eyes and breathed deeply.

"Mr. Robert will see you now," she said, then fainted into a hair-sprayed and blue eye-shadowed heap. Jon vaulted the counter to rush to her aid, even though part of his brain was telling him she had enough Aqua-Net on her hair to shield her against armor-piercing bullets, so she probably wasn't in any danger of a concussion or cerebral hemorrhage or the like.

"Aren't you the fuckin' white knight to the rescue?" the man said without getting up.

This just made Jon angry. "She's fainted. Don't you think we ought to get her to a doctor?"

"Leave her. She pulls the same shit every time I show up," said Robert, who hadn't moved a millimeter to render assistance to the woman. "It's my fault for hiring the local yokels. Been working here since nineteen-fucking-eighty-nine and she's still not used to that. Come on inside, Mr. Temple. You can close the door behind you. She'll be back in front of the TV in no time."

Jon reluctantly got up from where he was kneeling over the woman and walked into the office as Robert produced a gold pack of Benson and Hedges cigarettes and unceremoniously lit one, silently offering the pack to Jon. It felt like it had been years since his last cigarette. Since he'd died – boy, it still felt strange to say that – he hadn't had a single craving. Now the desire to breathe the smoke deep into his lungs came upon him like a primal urge. He immediately assessed his possessions and confirmed what he already knew. He had no NicaChew on him, no fall back. No crutch, except, of course, that he was already dead, so what harm could another smoke do him? Still, he was determined to be strong in the face of temptation. Jon stared at the pack, breathed deeply and waved it off. "No thanks."

Robert sniffed, seemingly surprised that Jon refused, and replaced the pack on the desk. He was not what Jon expected, especially after Eli's briefing. He seemed of indeterminate ethnicity – maybe Italian somewhere – with thick dark hair trailing down the back of his neck in what his dad used to call a mullet. Jon imagined the length in back was to compensate for the thinning of the hair that remained on top. On his face was a full beard that was in need of a trim, and the droopy lids and the dark half-moon circles under his eyes suggested it had been a while since he had slept well. He wore a white tank T-shirt and, on his legs crossed at the ankles under the desk, Jon saw khaki chinos and black high-top Chuck Taylor sneakers. His ancient metal office chair creaked as he leaned back and pulled on his cigarette while tapping out a quick rhythm on his thigh with the other hand.

Jon never did quite figure out how he lit the cigarette, since he never saw Robert use a lighter or a match.

"So, Temple, what brings a sharp dressed guy like yourself to my establishment? Run short on cash at the casinos? Gotta watch out for those Indians.

138

Those guys are ball-busters. Or maybe you met a stripper and want to head up to Dillon to get hitched. You'd need to hock that flash car you've got parked outside for that one. Or maybe you've got something more valuable in mind?"

"None of the above," Jon said. "I'm interested in information. I believe your clerk mentioned something to you about a calling card I showed her at the desk."

"Mentioned it? She was fuckin' apoplectic about it. Could I see it?"
Jon handed the card over as Robert leaned on his elbows and took another drag. The man took it, looked it over for a moment, turned it over between his fingers two times and held it up, the lettering facing Jon.

"Mind if I ask where the fuck you got this? This represents a very ... exclusive recommendation."

"A mutual acquaintance. I know him as Eli. I've been retained as an employee of his and I was told you could provide us with some information we needed."

Robert made a distasteful face and suddenly the card was aflame in his fingers. All that remained was a tiny speck of ash on the green desk blotter, which Robert flicked away. He tapped his cigarette into a heavy glass ashtray and took another drag.

"Information on who? If you're working for who you say you are, the problem shouldn't be lack of information. You should be in information up to your fuckin' eyeballs. After all, being omniscient has to have its advantages, right Temple?"

Jon leaned back and casually inspected his cuticles. He was playing this as cool as possible, especially since he imagined Robert expected him to be slightly freaked out. "Information or not, Mr. Robert? That's all I'm asking you to tell me. Otherwise I think our business here is done."

"Well, aren't we the smooth operator?" Robert said as he got up and stepped around his desk. He was shorter than Jon first expected, with a slight gut that accentuated his stooped shoulders. "What manifestation did you get, Temple? The Goddess Diana lookalike, all tits and ass and charisma?" He regarded the ceiling as he thought about it, then waved the thought away with his cigarette. "Hmm, no. Too obvious. Maybe the kindly old British gentleman?" This time he squinted at Jon. "No, not your type. The traditional, flowing white beard and robe and all that shit? That's a classic, but you're too cool a customer to buy that one."

He turned away for a moment, then whipped around and pointed the cigarette directly at Jon's nose.

"Got it! The old Rasta guy with the surfboard, right?"

Jon's surprise must have unconsciously registered on his face, because Robert was then positive of his guess.

"I knew it," he said, triumphantly taking another drag off the cigarette. "You got lucky, bud. When I get paid a visit, my company looks like somebody's nightmare of an eighth grade geometry teacher with a case of thermonuclear PMS. Hard to deal rationally with that one, let me tell you. Especially when she starts tapping on the chalk board with those long fingernails." Robert cringed slightly at the thought, then composed himself and returned to the matter at hand.

"But you didn't come here to talk about my troubles, did you? You want the skinny on someone, I know. That's always how I end up getting referrals like this. She doesn't like dealing with me any more than she has to. And hey, who can blame her. The place is a dump, it smells funny and there's no air conditioning to speak of. I wouldn't stay here if I didn't have to."

"What we're looking for is some information on Lucas Scheafer, the advisor for the Rev. Lawrence Whitaker. Eli seemed to think Mr. Scheafer might be in your employ."

"In other words, your boss Eli couldn't come up with any information on Scheafer through the usual omniscience channels, as ridiculous as it sounds. I think you're being yanked around, my friend. Eli — that's what it's calling itself? – might not keep tabs on everything going on all the time, but there's very little that gets away from him if he really wants to find out."

"I don't really think the extent of Eli's knowledge is the question here. It's the extent of yours. We simply need to know if Scheafer is working for you and whether we should continue wasting our time. If you're not inclined to tell us, I'm sure Eli will be glad to assume his geometry teacher manifestation and pay you a visit himself."

Jon caught him in mid-drag. Robert's eyes widened and he coughed slightly.

"Alright, Temple. There's no reason for you to resort to threats. I'll be glad to give you what you need, just because it's going to be so easy. But first I want to know what you're getting out of this."

"What do you mean?"

"Exactly what I said. What's in it for you?" he said as he met Jon's gaze and crushed the cigarette in the ashtray. "We're not completely ignorant of your situation around here." To illustrate his point, he opened a desk drawer and pulled out a heavy manila file folder, opening it to reveal a thick sheaf of typed pages, then reading from the top page.

"Jonathan Evan Templeton, born August 20, 1995, to Irving and Ellen Templeton. Attended public schools in Carleton County, South Carolina, and graduated from Carleton High School. Went on to the University of South Carolina, where you earned a bachelor's degree in journalism. Graduated to work as a bureau chief for the Grand Strand Reporter in Myrtle Beach, where you stayed for two years. Eventually moved to The Charleston Gazette where you started as local government reporter. Initiated an office affair with Linda Barton, whom you eventually married. Named lead investigative reporter two years later. Went on to write a series exposing politicians who were using their influence to buy up cheap ocean-front real estate then resell it to development companies." He took another drag and looked up at Jon, exhaling before he spoke "This is my favorite part. Unfortunately, one of the politicians exposed was Sen. Dick Garland, who happened to share sauna time with the publisher of the Gazette. A few intimate chats between two naked and sweaty men, and you're out on your ass for supposedly letting personal issues get in the way of the story. Turns out your mom has been offered a hefty price on her beach house by – you guessed it – the same company Garland was in cahoots with. After a month of unemployment and depression, you accept a job at Hampton, DuBose and Associates as media liaison, where one of your clients is – you guessed it again – Sen. Garland. You stay there for three miserable months until two days ago, when you quit amidst a question of your behavior towards a female co-worker. And I know your boy Eli was impressed by this: She hit on you, and you, like a big pussy, said no. The she accuses you of raping her." Robert then took a drag from his smoke and looked at Jon with a smirk. "Bitches, man. Last seen by your wife at your home in Carleton. Listed as dead according to afterlife reports one day later. Cause: drowning.

"Specifically," he said, looking back at Jon as his finger marked his spot on the page, "you ended up face down in the toilet bowl after downing a stomach full of cheap duty-free rum, slipping on a bath mat and whacking your head on the rim of the shitter. Pretty fuckin' embarrassing, if you ask me."

"Trust me, you have no idea," Jon said.

"And now, Mr. Templeton, you are here to see me, newly dead, using an assumed name and presumably a reworked face and body, trying to find out information on one of the most powerful organizations in the nation, and you expect me to believe you're not getting anything out of it?"

"I know it's probably hard for someone in your position to understand, but it's the truth," Jon said with a touch of indignation. Then he checked himself. Temper, temper. Mustn't let this guy get the best of you.

"My position? Temple or Templeton or whatever you want to be called, my position has nothing to do with it. I'm a businessman in a complex global organization, and all I ask is to be allowed to conduct my business in an efficient and organized fashion without too much interference from the regulators. That's the reason for the lousy digs," he said, waving his hand around the room. "They find my work necessary but distasteful, since without me they wouldn't look nearly as good.

"And because of that," he said, closing the folder and shoving it back in the drawer, "I am in a position to offer you something Eli was not. Namely, some compensation for all your hard work."

Jon was momentarily caught off guard. "What kind of compensation," he asked with a not too hidden measure of suspicion.

"My employer has authorized whatever you like. You're talking to a Class A, licensed and bonded tempter, my friend. You want it, we can get it," Robert said, leaning back in his chair, which let out an impassioned, rusty squeak that told of its age, and lighting another cigarette from the air.

"Mr. Robert, if you don't have anything to share with me I think it would be just as well that I turn down your offer. Somehow I don't think Eli would appreciate me striking a deal with you while I'm working for him," Jon said as he rose, brushed the wrinkles out of his suit and turned to leave. He then heard a drawer open and something drop on the desktop.

"You know anything about a video of the weekend that might be floating around, Jon? We keep hearing rumblings about one."

It was the voice of Paul Godfrey from the Columbia paper, exactly as he had asked it on the phone with Jon just days before. Jon turned and looked, but there was only Robert, still reclining, still smoking, but now with a tiny envelope resting on the stained blotter.

"Figured this might be something you'd be interested in, Templeton. No point in making a deal if we're not both honest with each other."

"Is that what I think it is?"

"It's the only copy of what you think it is. Not the best work of old-school porn I've ever seen, but then I don't think anyone's going to be watching this for the erotic content."

What Jon would have done to get his hands on that two days ago. Yes, it would have meant leaving Hampton DuBose, but he would have been leaving it with the story of a lifetime and a first-class ticket back into journalism. Now, though, there was no incentive to take the bait. There wouldn't be much reporting he'd be doing from the grave.

"Sorry. No deal."

Just as Jon was about to walk out the door, Robert spoke again.

"Oh, just one more thing. You miss your wife, Templeton?"

Jon turned slowly and met Robert's relaxed but level gaze. He had placed his legs up on the battered desk and was blowing smoke rings, each with a barely noticeable set of horns.

"What's that supposed to mean?"

"Just what it sounds like, my man. Do you miss Linda?"

"Of course I do. You think I enjoyed having Eli tell me I'd never be able to see her again?" Jon said, suddenly angry that Robert would even ask a question he obviously knew the answer to.

"Is that what the old man told you? Hmm. That's very interesting."

Jon closed the door and walked back into the room to lean over Robert's desk, his knuckles hard against the desktop. "Interesting how?"

"Well, like I said, I am in a position to offer you some form of compensation for your work, and the scope of my influence tends to reach into realms folks don't even consider most of the time."

"Explain."

"Shit, man. Do I have to spell it out for you? You could get to be with your wife again. You could get to be alive again, for cryin' out loud. Nobody's found a body yet, so technically your wife doesn't even know you're dead, just missing in action. How's that for convenient? Let's say I throw in the video of your pal Senator Garland putting it to those stripper friends of his daughter. That way, you get to live again and quite possibly get a chance of getting your professional life back, too. How nice would that be, huh?"

Jon paused, then sat heavily back in the hard wooden chair, unable to speak or even think very clearly. Too much weirdness. Too many decisions. Just too much right now. He wasn't sure he could handle any more and felt himself suddenly willing to pack the whole thing in. And those cigarettes were looking better and better by the moment.

The video he could have passed on. It was of no use to him if he was still dead. But if Robert just hadn't brought up Linda Jon decided he would've been fine. But after all, Robert being who he was, knew how to push all the right buttons, at what time and with the proper intensity. Jon decided it would be safer just to keep ignoring him.

"And speaking of convenience, I also happen to know Linda is here in town looking for you," Robert continued, still reclined and taking intermittent drags on his cigarette. "You're not going to get an offer like this one anywhere else, Templeton. Certainly not from your pal, Eli. He's not into making deals. He just expects you to be compelled to do something because he's who he says he is, then be satisfied flitting around his little hippie version of Central Park up there. I don't work that way, man. My way, you'll at least get something for all your effort besides what you should have expected anyway."

Still reeling from Robert's offer, Jon found himself actually forming the words to ask exactly what he'd have to do as part of the bargain. It was wrong, he knew, but he had to have an idea of what he would be passing up.

"Look, I know what you're thinking, but don't start getting those ideas about an eternity of torment and damnation. I'm after a much bigger fish, here. And we get enough biz in the souls department just lining up Top 40 groups to hit number one for a few weeks. That's almost too easy. Nah, I need something from you you've almost already got."

"What?"

"Scheafer. I want him too, because I don't know where he came from either. And frankly, it scares the living shit out of me."

TWENTY~THREE

Linda Templeton jerked awake. She quickly realized she was at the beach, which was usually a good thing, but was not in her bed or with her husband as she should have been. Not good. After painfully reminding herself of the previous few days' events and lying staring at the ceiling, resigned to a lifetime of confusion and unhappiness, she was reassured as to the state of the rest of the universe only by the smell of brewing coffee wafting in from the kitchen.

Her room in Regina's grandmother's cottage was much the same as the three bedrooms at her own. There was the requisite knotty pine paneling, a few poorly framed pieces of bad art and an eclectic mixture of furniture that had been banned to a life of enduring margarita spills, sand in its crevices and wet, salty bathing suit bottoms.

I shouldn't be here, Linda thought. I should be waking up next to my warm husband in our bed in our cottage, not having to depend on the hospitality of this girl who obviously thinks I'm the most pathetic creature she's ever seen.

She was wearing what she normally would to bed at home — a pair of panties and a T-shirt — the only problem being she didn't have any clean panties and the T-shirt wasn't even hers. That was going to be one of the first errands of the day. She didn't mind borrowing someone else's clothes, but she drew the line at sharing underwear, regardless of how clean they might be.

Nope, scratch that, she thought. She remembered that she would regularly borrow a pair of Jon's boxers to run out and get the paper or pad around the kitchen on Sunday morning after the two of them had made love the night before and slept naked, their bodies pressed against each other all night. But somehow that was different. Not only did it serve the practical purpose of letting her scoot around the house without causing scandal, it also often served to re-ignite her husband's interests from the previous night's play. She had lost count of the times their coffee and English muffins had grown cold while Jon's hand delicately made its way beneath the cotton material of the loose legs, pressing, caressing and opening with the practiced expertise one can only get from knowing one's partner.

But this was all wrong. Here she was in a strange bed thinking thoughts that did nothing but get her excited with no outlet for the quickly developing arousal. As soon as she realized the tips of her fingers were unconsciously trailing up her thigh towards the elastic of her panties, she quickly shook off any more recollections of anything remotely erotic. Besides, she told herself after a few moments, fantasizing about her husband wasn't going to help her find him or suddenly prompt him to show up. She was being self-indulgent at best, lazy at the worst.

She slid her legs from under the sheet and sat on the edge of the bed, pondering her reflection in the opposite mirror. The edges of the glass were pitted from salt exposure and her image was presented back to her through a saline haze, somewhat obscuring what she decided was her worst looking morning in a long time. She and Jon fought — it was impossible to be married without the occasional tiff. But she rarely found herself reduced to tears over anything her husband did. In this case, however, it was over something he didn't do. He didn't spend hours at the back door begging him to let her in. He didn't sleep on the porch. He didn't even try that hard to fight with her when she ordered him to stay away from their house lest she activate the burglar alarm.

She tried to decide what all that meant. Did it mean he had resigned himself to the futility of the situation, or was it an indication of his overwhelming guilt? Guilty or not, Linda had decided that while Jon might not have been blameless in whatever chain of events led to Ashley's panties ending up in his pocket, he didn't let a bad situation get any worse by falling victim to the woman's advances. Of that she had to be proud.

She gazed in the mirror again and brushed a curled brown lock of hair from her face, tucking it behind her left ear. Her eyes were still swollen from the night before and she hadn't really gotten much useful sleep in the meantime. She found it hard enough to sleep without Jon next to her under the best of circumstances. In this situation, though, there was even less comfort in sleeping alone. Though she was sure it would be just as easy to crawl back into bed and go on weeping, she forced herself up. She went into the bathroom and brushed her teeth using one of the many spare toothbrushes Regina's grandmother kept on hand for unexpected overnight visitors, then padded into the kitchen where the younger woman sat sipping a cup of coffee and nibbling on a jam-smeared piece of toast.

"Morning. How'd you sleep? Or is that a stupid question?" Regina asked around her mouthful of breakfast. She was already wearing her bathing suit with a white cotton tank top thrown over so she would look appropriate at the breakfast table. The girl's grandmother was no despot, but the rules she set down in her house she expected to be followed whether she was in residence or not. A shirt at the table for men and women was one of the biggies.

"Not stupid, really. I slept a little in between weeping uncontrollably and staring at the ceiling counting the stucco bumps," Linda said as she poured herself some coffee and proceeded to add sugar — the real stuff — and milk, stirring it to a warm brown. "I know I just look charming this morning regardless. I was hoping the swelling in my eyes would at least go down."

"Aw, don't worry. You look fine. Nobody but us girls here, anyway." Regina realized what she'd said and immediately apologized. "Man, that was stupid. I really didn't mean it that way, Linda."

"Relax, I know," Linda said, placing her hand on Regina's. "There's no need to walk on tiptoe around the whole thing. All I'm worried about now is where he is and if he's okay. I would've bet my life he would be at the cottage."

"I would have guessed the same thing. You want anything to eat? Grandmama keeps some of those little boxes of cereal here if you don't want toast."

"No thanks. My stomach's still not handling the whole thing very well and I don't think eating right now would help it," Linda said, patting her tummy in a vain effort to calm the nervous rumblings. "I just wish I had some idea about where to start looking for him."

"So you didn't see anything at all yesterday to indicate he might have been there?"

"Nothing. The only thing unusual was that the door from the porch was open. That's a little weird, but the last renters or the housekeepers could've left it unlocked the last time they were down here. Other than that, nothing looked touched."

"Linda, I don't want to be the devil's advocate, but are you positive there was no one else he could have run off with? You wouldn't believe some of the stuff I hear working the church's telephone support line."

Linda sighed and looked into her coffee mug — an ancient piece with a bleary-eyed orange and black cartoon cat on the side — pondering her husband's potential for infidelity. Aside from this situation with Ashley, she had never had any reason to suspect he had been anything other than faithful. The whole Ashley affair had been a misunderstanding over one screwed-up woman's efforts to bed her husband.

"There's no one, Regina. If there had been someone else I would have known. That's why this whole thing took me so by surprise. I didn't see it coming, which is what makes me believe there was nothing there in the first place."

"Okay. So we've eliminated another woman, and I guess another man."

Linda shot her a look, shocked she would even consider such an option.

"Okay, how about money trouble? Any financial problems?"

"Nope. Everything's dandy. That's my job, anyway. I do the books and he gets his allowance to buy lunches and pay for dry-cleaning, plus a little left over to play with. If something was wrong there, I'd know it for sure. No, it has to be something related to this Ashley thing. I know he was upset when he left the house, but I never thought he'd disappear on me."

"So, what do we do now? You don't know where he might have gone or why and he hasn't left any indication that he wants to be found. Should we start calling hospitals between here and Carlton? He might have been in an accident trying to get back after I saw him."

"If something had happened on the maglev we surely would've heard it on the news, but it's a thought. I just hope he wasn't mugged or anything. Sometimes that Florence station can get a little rough. Though from what he was wearing when he left, he probably looked more like a mugger than a muggee," Linda said, then took another sip from her rapidly cooling coffee. "You said you thought he'd been drinking. How bad was it?"

"Well, he was a little wobbly and I could smell it pretty strongly on his breath, but it seemed like he was handling it fine. If he drank more after I saw him, though, there could have been some trouble. There's no telling how much he'd had already."

Jon was no stiff when it came to drinking, but then neither was she. It was almost a rite of passage in the news biz that you get ripped with your coworkers. Linda remembered him on several occasions back when they both worked together being a bit inclined to overindulge if the situation allowed it. In all honesty, that was the way she ended up bedding him the first time. The two of them had both had weeks worthy of the worst journalistic nightmares. Stories had tanked, facts were wrong in the stories that did run and they were each at the ends of their respective ropes over relationships that had ended for each of them within a two-week span. To relieve the stress, Linda declared an unofficial holiday that Friday night during which the two of them would go out with the sole intention of getting torn up. Little did Jon know that all along she planned to lower his resolve enough that her overt flirtations would have their desired effect and lure him into her soft, sweet trap.

This time, though, she was concerned. The possibility of Jon having passed out between Regina's house and their cottage wasn't too remote considering his condition at the time the younger woman saw him. It was at that moment she decided to end any speculation and move on to some meaningful action.

"I think it's too early to call the police, but we'll leave that open as an option. First off, we have to go out and look for him. Maybe he's sitting in our spot down at the beach bar waiting for me to show up. For all we know, he could be lying dead between a couple of sand dunes or under some cottage that no one's rented this week."

"You really don't think he'd be that careless, do you?"

"Regina, this is my husband. This is the one man in the world that I ever wanted to spend the rest of my life with. The only man who I've ever thought is even remotely worth this much trouble. Can you understand that? If something's happened to him and I don't do anything to help him — especially after the little scene I put on the other day — I'll never be able to live with myself. So finish that toast while I put on some sunscreen. The first order of business is to get me some underwear of my own, then you and I are going hunting for my man."

Yoshi had no concept of what time it was until the gold of the morning sun peeked through the closed Venetian blinds of Eustace's living room and cast its glare on the computer screen. Only then did he realize he had been awake all night trying to connect the information on the stick with what Andrea Turner had given Mako.

The two-bedroom bungalow smelled of Old Spice and gun oil and seemed like a shrine to every military conflict since Hannibal crossed the Alps. There were pikes, spears, arrows, swords, rifles and pistols from every period of human warfare. Posters, newspaper clippings, miniature dioramas and medals documented seemingly every skirmish from the Trojan War to the Civil War and all the ones between and after. And it was obvious where Eustace's support lay in the latter conflict. There seemed to be every manner of Confederate memorabilia imaginable scattered around the house. "Don't get the wrong idea, now," he'd said to them when they entered for the first time. "The Confederacy per se makes me kinda ill. I just got a thing for lost causes, I guess."

They had left Barry and Lewis, Krista's saviors, at the bar to talk to the police and try to explain why, after a planned attack on a dance club by a group of well-armed and highly motivated terrorists, the only fatalities were the terrorists themselves.

Despite their exhaustion upon arrival, Yoshi spent a long time examining a print of a samurai in full regalia hung over a pristine set of 19th century katana swords. Krista was given the spare bedroom where she slept within ten feet of three cabinets containing firearms from the American Revolution to the ongoing fight for Quebecois independence. After making up the bed for her, Eustace bid them all goodnight and went into his room to sleep off the evening's anxieties. He had apparently spoken to the club's owner on the telephone just before Mako and Yoshi arrived and said later he hadn't had that severe a dressing down since his days in the service. In spite of the entire bar going up in flames, Eustace did say he'd won kudos for "making at least one of the fascist fuckers pay for their little stunt." "Hell hath no fury like a capitalist drag queen scorned," Eustace told them in all seriousness.

Yoshi stood, rubbed his eyes and performed a long stretch, drawing his breath deeply in through his diaphragm, holding it for a moment, then exhaling slowly. He performed the same motion, lifting his arms above his head until both hands touched, then drawing them down together before him as if he were praying, each upward reach coinciding with an inward breath and each descent followed by the hissing of air being expelled.

Mako, who had fallen asleep sprawled across a loveseat in Eustace's den, stirred and peeled an eye, recoiling at the shaft of sunlight piercing through the blinds directly at his face. He groaned and began to turn away until he caught sight of Yoshi, pausing to watch the slow progression of his morning ritual.

"Good morning, Mako," Yoshi said without stopping or looking in the younger man's direction.

"Is it? My back's all in knots. Why did you let me fall asleep on this midget couch? I'm used to sleeping on the floor."

Another long breath and stretch. "That is where you fell asleep, so that is where I assumed you wanted to be. Had I known you would have preferred the floor I would have woken you and suggested it." Another slow exhale, making him sound as if he was very methodically commanding Mako to be quiet.

"I can't believe you still buy into all that shit they taught us back home," Mako said as he sat up and tried to work the soreness out of his spine. Unfortunately, turning his body as he did only served to aggravate the rib injuries from the previous day. After a brief appraisal, he realized everything on his body ached, an unremarkable discovery considering what the several groups of people had tried to do to him in the course of that 24-hour period.

"You should try it," Yoshi said. "It brings focus and energy. The deep breathing stimulates the mind with oxygen, while the stretches allow the blood to be more effectively carried to the extremities. But I imagine you have such a ritual of your own."

"Yeah, it's called a 20-ounce Mountain Dew and a breakfast burrito. The Dew stimulates the mind with caffeine, while the cholesterol from the burrito activates the body's fight-or-flight reflex to avoid the arteries clogging. If that doesn't get you moving, nothing will."

"An interesting notion, but not one that will serve you very well in the long run," he said, stretching and inhaling once more. "But then again, you have never been one to look very hard at what will serve you in the long run."

Mako stared up at the huge man's back and immediately covered his face with his hands, groaning and drawing the fingers down over his eyes, pulling the bottom lids away, creating a gruesome, agonized picture.

"Jesus Christ, Yoshi. What are we, married or something? There's no reason for you to start this shit this early in the morning."

"Very well. Consider the subject closed — for the moment."

"Great. Lovely to have something to look forward to. Do you think this guy has any coffee lying around?" Mako asked as he shuffled to the kitchen and began to randomly open cabinet doors.

"One would imagine so, but I would not be surprised if whatever he had was World War I military issue," Yoshi said with eyes closed as he finished his last movement.

Mako laughed and shook his head in amazement. "Yosh, my friend, I had no idea you were such a funny guy. Why didn't I know this earlier?"

"Because the last time I saw you, you were 15 and preparing to escape from the school you were attending, shattering your father's plans for you and doing your best to frustrate me at every turn. Our dispositions at the time were conducive to many things, but humor was not one of them."

"I guess not," Mako said sheepishly as he pulled a can of coffee and a box of filters from one of the shelves. "Still, it's nice to see you loosening up a little. But I gotta tell you, man. You practically scared the hell out of me when you showed up at my place the other night. I knew someone would be coming, but I had no idea it would be you. And poor … um, Dina. She was petrified. The girl was shivering, for Christ sake."

"Indeed. And I thought it was because she was wearing only her underwear. What a shame that you had so much trouble remembering her first name, not to mention her last, which seems to have completely escaped you."

"Well, you can't give the boy too much credit for anything if he was dumb enough to shack up with some surfer groupie he hardly knew," said a yawning Krista as she padded barefoot into the kitchen from the guest bedroom. She was wearing a gray Army T-shirt that would have been a normal fit for Eustace, but on the small girl covered her completely from her neck to the middle of her thighs. Her previously spiky hair was matted outrageously and the bruises had begun to turn from their previous eggplant purple to more of a bluish-yellow tint. "Don't tell me. On your first date you tried to get her shot, too? Darn. I'd thought I was the first."

Mako stopped filling the coffee decanter in mid-stream. "What, did you guys get together while I was asleep and plan to give me a hard time this morning? And who said you and I ever had a date, anyway?"

Yoshi smirked. "It would seem your young friend and I are of a like mind concerning your decisions in life."

"Glad that brought a smile to your face, there Yosh. Tell you what. Sit down and listen to her tale of woe and then tell me if she's qualified to judge anything about my life. At least I had sense enough to leave the ones that turned out to be crazy. She moves in with them and sets up housekeeping, for Christ sake."

"I think everyone's had quite enough woe for the time being," the three heard Eustace shout from his bedroom, his head finally poking out from the partially opened door and staring back and forth between Mako and Krista.

"And if you two don't stop arguing, I'm going to have to put you in separate rooms. So everyone just stay civil and I'll make us some breakfast in a minute. The bathroom's open, for anyone who's interested."

Mako glared at Krista and finished filling the coffeepot, sneaking a glance at her as she walked quickly to the bathroom doing her best not to look at him, then noisily closing and locking the door behind her.

"Your defensiveness does not suit you, Mako. Perhaps you have grown a bit sensitive about the lifestyle you have led?"

"Listen, big guy. I'll tell you what's sensitive. My head is sensitive from being bashed on a car roof and smacked with a two-by-four. My ribs are sensitive because some assholes in penny loafers tried to kick the shit out of me. I'm a little shaken because my closest living relative tried to shoot me and then committed suicide in front of me. And I'm in an all-around pissy mood because my father is dead and instead of going to the funeral like I should have, I got dragged off by you

150

to that lame excuse for a city, forced into clothes that nearly suffocated me and told I would be responsible for running a company that, as far as I can tell, has never done anything other than make it easier for people to blow the living shit out of each other. And now, thanks to you, I have also succeeded in royally pissing off the only person that had even remotely begun to make any of this crap worthwhile," he said, pointing to the bathroom. "So aside from helping me out of a bad spot yesterday, I can't see that you've done a whole lot to give me a reason to be anything but sensitive."

In the middle of Mako's tirade, Eustace had entered the room wearing jeans and a white undershirt and simply stood and watched. He leaned casually against the tile countertop, his tattoos now fully exposed along the ripples of his sculpted arms. Yoshi, meanwhile, had maintained his usual placid calm, infuriating Mako even more because the man simply refused to get angry. Once Mako finished, still breathing heavily from shouting, Eustace broke his silence.

"Kid, I've got some lousy news for you," he said, stepping up to face Mako and raising a spatula to make his point. "Life sucks. People die. You're going to get hurt a lot along the way. The person you're in love with more than you ever thought you could be will either run off with someone who isn't you or die before you can tell them how you feel. That's something you're just going to have to get a grip on. You start making plans and God laughs good and hard before he turns the tables on you, so don't act like you're somehow being picked on.

"And here's another flash for you. We all had a bad day yesterday, my friend. Your man Yoshi and me? We've seen some shit, trust me, and I'm sure we'd both agree we'd rather be stuck in the eye with a sharp stick than go through yesterday again. God knows the last thing I expected to be doing was trying to save an entire nightclub from a busload of redneck shaggers. And your lady friend in there, something tells me she didn't get smacked around like that playing hopscotch. Your dad and that other guy are dead for whatever reason, which you can't do a damn thing about. And yeah, you hurt, but you'll get better. I'm out of a job and almost got shot up by some goon with an antique rifle. And I think our friend Krista might already realize she's better off even with you bozos than she was with the guy that beat her up.

"And you," he said, turning to Yoshi, "stop with the guilt-tripping. You sound like my goddamn mother and it's not making anything better for anyone."

He paused a moment to catch his breath and compose himself, taking a quick visual survey of his audience to make sure he'd made his point. He then breathed deeply, did two slow head rolls eliciting gruesome popping noises from his neck and returned his attention to Mako and Yoshi. "Now, how do you like your eggs?"

Both Mako and Yoshi were frozen with shock, struggling momentarily with the question and finally responding with their individual orders: scrambled for Mako and over medium for Yoshi. Eustace then went to the bathroom door to ask Krista the same question, leaving Mako and Yoshi alone in an uncomfortable silence while they considered their individual scoldings. It was a contest to see who would be the first to pierce the deafening absence of sound.

"Mako, in response to your question of my progress, I think I might have found a tenuous connection from which we can work," Yoshi finally said after Mako brooded for a few moments while scooping coffee into the filter. On the outside, the man seemed relatively unfazed by either outburst, but Mako knew his pride was wounded and the statement was one of reconciliation, however well disguised.

"That right? Let's see," he said, moving to pull up a chair next to Yoshi as the coffee maker began to burble and hiss.

"Throughout the series of orders and deliveries listed on this stick, there seems to be very little consistency. From an initial glance at the information, it would seem Hiroshi was secretly supplying any number of weapons to a variety of different organizations, which at their best could only be said to have questionable motives. SHAG is one of those, although the illegal weapons shipments are by no means limited to them.

"It would seem Hiroshi used a system involving something similar to skimming money. After an order from a customer for a certain number of goods came in, Hiroshi would quote them an inflated price, then add to that order whatever was requested from a particular group to whom he was selling on the side. While the requested goods would still be delivered to and paid for by the legitimate customers, a shipment of the illegal goods would go out under the guise of some fictitious family's personal household possessions and end up supposedly hijacked along the way. While the company ran the risk of losing customers because of Hiroshi's high pricing, many of those customers, especially the smaller Eastern European and Central American republics, had nowhere else to turn. The payments for the illegal shipments, meanwhile, were apparently wired to an offshore account your uncle kept for that express purpose."

"Great. So we know how Uncle pulled it off. But what was he talking about right before he died when he seemed so worried about what one person would end up doing to him?"

"I had the same question. It would seem, from Hiroshi's reaction, that instead of selling to a number of separate groups, he was in fact selling to one person or group. That theory was upheld when I did some research on the other groups besides SHAG listed as customers. None of them, according to my sources, actually exist. Almost all closely resemble existing groups, such as this one called the Quebec Freedom Front. There is no such group, but there is one which has claimed responsibility for a number of bombings around other Canadian provinces called the Quebec Liberation Front. Another, Cubana Libre, was disbanded two years ago when the surviving Communist Party leaders were rounded up and shot and the U.S. resumed diplomatic relations with the new democratic government in Havana. And now that Cuba is on the verge of statehood, the group would have no motive for existence. Yet it is listed here as being one of Hiroshi's customers as recently as six months ago. From what this information says, the only active group with which your uncle dealt was SHAG."

"Which must mean all the others were just set up as fronts for even more weapons that were going to SHAG. Do you think Uncle knew that?" Eustace had come back into the kitchen and Mako soon smelled the mouth watering fragrance of sausage being fried mingling with that of the brewing coffee. His stomach churned enthusiastically.

"At the beginning, perhaps not, but it would seem from a number of e-mails Miss Turner acquired that toward the end he strongly suspected that was the case. He e-mailed to someone with the initials L.S. on a number of occasions, questioning the person about the destinations of shipments allegedly ordered by other groups and how soon he will be able to discontinue the relationship with SHAG. Hiroshi seems frequently dissatisfied with this person's answers."

"Dissatisfied enough to worry about this person trying to kill him if he disagreed," Mako asked.

"Yes, at the very least. Hiroshi indicates on a number of occasions that he is no longer in control of his own life, having instead relinquished it to this mysterious L.S.," Yoshi said. "Within the past few weeks, the messages became particularly desperate, which I believe occurred in conjunction with this individual's latest purchase order." Yoshi then scrolled down the computer screen to a highlighted item on the spreadsheet. Under the Item category, Mako saw only a string of meaningless letters and numbers.

"Okay, so what's a Series 4 OPPA and why the hell would it cost $7.5 billion?" he asked, leaning closer to decipher what he was reading.

"Perhaps if you had paid any attention to the material on the company you were asked to read..."

"Hey!" came Eustace's voice from the kitchen. "Don't start that again."

"My apologies," Yoshi said. "OPPA stands for orbital platform particle accelerator, a focused energy weapon Nikura International was developing very secretly for the U.S. Department of Defense. The Series 4 model was the latest design to evolve from the original technology developed for defense against intercontinental ballistic missiles, with the difference being the new models were designed as offensive, rather than defensive, weapons. Its advantages include the ability to be concealed on something as small as an ordinary communications satellite without interrupting that satellite's operation."

"Jeez, no wonder Uncle was stressed. So now all we have to do is find out who this L.S. is, right?"

"Correct, but we have few leads as far as that goes, unfortunately."

"Few leads? What are you talking about?" Eustace said from the kitchen as he plucked sausage links from the frying pan and placed them on a paper towel-covered plate. "You've got someone supposedly at the top of this pyramid, with SHAG somewhere below him, right? Now didn't Krista say she heard the guy in the van talking to someone on the phone, someone that really put the fear of God into him? And I seem to remember you pulled a Church of the New Revelation matchbook out of that van, too. And everyone knows SHAG is full of nut-job CNR members, so it seems to me that just from that we can trace this L.S. character right up Ocean Boulevard to the church's doorstep. Not to mention that I know just where your mystery bad guy might be planning to stick his ray gun. The church has been running a pledge drive to buy a new satellite to beam into the Pacific Rim for the last year. You can hardly turn on the TV without seeing something about it. Now think about what sort of damage someone could do with a weapon like that aimed right at China or some other hotspot. Hell, as if things with China aren't freaky enough right now, all they need to start nuking us into the stone age is an excuse like that."

"That seems to be a reasonable assumption, but I fear it would be presumptuous to arrive at a place of worship accusing the leadership of involvement in such a plot without more basis in fact," Yoshi said. "I would prefer more assurance before we begin pointing fingers."

"Assurance? I'll get your assurance. Where'd y'all put that phone?" Yoshi rooted under the stack of papers from the information Mako's father compiled and found the slender plastic unit, handing it to Eustace. "If these people are as stupid as you guys say they are, this should solve all our problems."

Eustace placed the phone in his ear and instructed it to display the a list of the most recent incoming calls. From his vantage point a slender holographic list scrolled into view. None of the numbers identified the caller, so each time a number connected and someone picked up, he would ask to whom he was speaking. When he reached the seventh number, he listened again and after a moment gave a light chuckle.

"Okay, Yoshi," he said after hanging up. "Ask for a redial and see if I haven't just made your day."

Yoshi did as he was instructed and listened. After about three rings, a sultry female computer voice spoke. "Thank you for calling the Church of the New Revelation. The person you have called, Lucas Scheafer, is not available. Press one to leave a message with video, press two to leave a message without video, or press zero to speak to an operator."

Yoshi immediately hung up, looking completely dumbstruck. Eustace simply looked at him and grinned.

"Well, Yoshi, my man. You were right," he said as he slapped Nikura International's chief of security on the shoulder and sauntered back to the kitchen. "Dumbest fuckin' terrorists I've ever seen."

^^^

Mako hoped getting clean after two days of unusual dirtiness would help Krista's mood. It didn't. Everyone certainly looked and felt a bit fresher after taking turns in Eustace's Spartan bathroom, but Mako found himself being treated with the same degree of icy distraction he'd witnessed before Krista took her shower. The worst part was, if he had to guess, he would say her mood was even worse than it was before.

Over breakfast there was little small talk, most of it aimed in Eustace's direction, usually in the form of some compliment about his eggs. Eustace accepted each one gracefully, getting up intermittently to get more coffee for someone or remove the plate of sausage links from the oven where they were being kept warm. Otherwise, there was only the sound of chewing, the sipping of coffee and the clinking of silverware against plates.

Though Mako was encouraged by what Yoshi had found, the two hadn't had time to discuss their next move before Krista emerged from the shower. She had laundered her makeshift outfit from the previous day and augmented it with selections from Eustace's closet, which apparently contained a variety of Army surplus fatigues. The ensemble she had thrown together, one of Eustace's tank T-shirts pared with the now-clean Sunrise Moving shirt and olive green cargo shorts — the waist again cinched to fit her petite figure — was actually quite in keeping with current fashion.

Watching her as she ate, Mako found himself longing for a moment to take her aside and be the one to offer her the opportunity to stay. He was sure, now that she had adopted such a cold and distant demeanor, that she wouldn't be interested in seeing him any more this morning, let alone for the duration of a trip to Myrtle Beach. Not only had he likely become something of a jinx in her eyes, she was now under the impression that he was some sort of beach combing gigolo intent on screwing any pretty face that happened to flash a smile in his direction.

And what evidence was there, really, to discount that impression? That was the big problem; he couldn't think of any. He looked back on the years since he bolted from school and saw only the most shallow and superficial relationships with women with few redeeming qualities other than allowing him to sexually gratify himself and then dispose of them. The problem, he had long told himself, was not his attitude but those of the girls. They would sleep with anyone with a surfboard under his arm, so he was fully within his rights to let them go to pursue further adventures. There was rarely any consideration for their feelings or the ramifications of his actions. Those courtesies were more often extended to his surfing acquaintances, many of whom were also female, but with whom he'd never considered having any sort of sexual or romantic relationship. He imagined a number of TV psychologists would say his behavior resulted somehow from his mother's death at an early age combined with the fact that most of his education about life came from men who really didn't have a clue about the sticky issue of gender relations. After all, what the hell can you learn about women from a bunch of bald monks living celibate lives in the mountains of Japan?

Then he remembered something. Before his speedy departure from the monastery, the thing that struck his hormone-stoked adolescent brain the most was the ridiculous behavior of the monks at their morning prayers. Each day, they asked forgiveness for the deaths of the insects they might kill as they trod the stone paths in their robes and sandals. It seemed excessive and pointless to him at the time, especially in view of the fact that his mother had recently met the same fate as those unfortunate ants. To him it seemed to trivialize the deaths of people and things that really mattered. But that was not so, said one of the monks when Mako voiced his reservations about the practice. Rather than trivializing death, the prayers each day emphasized the monks' respect for life and all living things of the world. Such respect, he said, should cross all boundaries.

And there was his problem, staring him right in the face. The one lesson the monks had the time to teach him had been the one he most effectively ignored. Rather than possessing an all-consuming respect for women as a whole, he had selectively divided them into two groups: women he respected and women he was attracted to sexually. In the course of his life, the two had never crossed or merged in his mind. That is, until he met Krista.

At first, he was reluctant to even allow her along. Eventually, he became sympathetic to her plight and wanted to help her get out of what was an obviously dangerous situation. But she managed to handle herself like a pro, going as far as risking her own skin to save Mako's life.

He decided the defining moment was when he saw her head upside down in the shattered window of the Sunrise Moving truck after she had the presence of mind to use the shoulder-launched rocket she found in the trailer. "This," he remembered jokingly saying to himself, "is a woman I could love."

And so it happened that beneath the bruises, the road grime, the makeshift clothing and the slightly hostile attitude he saw the strong, determined young woman who lurked not far below the surface. He saw someone who refused to allow herself to stay in a bad situation because she didn't think she had any alternatives. He saw someone who was not afraid to tell him what she thought, regardless of what he might think in return. And most of all, he saw someone who probably would not let him get away with the majority of shit he had always gotten away with.

So it was with almost painful resignation that he admitted to himself that there was nothing more he wanted to do at that moment than kiss her delicate, wounded lips and promise her that as long as she was with him, no harm would come to her again. Of course he knew he could do neither. He would be lucky at this point to get her to speak to him, let alone allow him to kiss her.

Mako was the last to finish, pondering his situation as the rest of the group scooped up the final smears of yolk with the last pieces of toast, eventually leaving the table with their plates and leaving him to his thoughts. Eustace retired to his bedroom to speak again with his boss, who would have spoken to the insurance company and the police by then, while Krista sat in the front porch swing of the colonial blue concrete porch. Finding himself alone with a plate of cold eggs, he also got up after a few sulking moments and handed it to Yoshi, who had just walked over and started doing the dishes.

"Mako, have you considered your options?" he asked after dunking a plate.

"Not as much as I should have, I guess," he said as he backed into the counter so the two of them could face each other. "Based on what you found out, I guess we should at least head to Myrtle Beach and go to one of the CNR services to see if we can find out who this Lucas Schaefer guy is. Other than that, I have no clue."

"Are you sure that was the topic I asked you to consider the options of?" Yoshi scraped egg off the plate with his fingernail without looking up. "You have many things to consider before we continue this journey. I would like to believe you have them sorted in your mind before we move on."

Mako didn't have to answer. He knew exactly what Yoshi was talking about, wordlessly turning away and walking to the porch to find Krista visually dissecting the sprawling oak tree in Eustace's tiny front yard as the chains holding the swing gave a perturbed squeak with each pass. Mako couldn't remember ever feeling quite as invisible as he did when the screen door closed gently behind him and she didn't even stir. This was going to be much tougher than he thought.

"Krista, can I talk to you for a second?" he asked, lofting the question into the air like a clay pigeon awaiting a shotgun round.

"Talk all you want. No guarantee anyone will be listening, though," she said without turning toward him.

Accepting that as begrudging permission to sit down, he did so, his lanky legs sprawling out in front of him and stopping the motion of the swing until he made a conscious effort to lift them and allow her short, sunburned ones to resume their casual pumping motion.

"I don't know if you heard or not, but Yoshi thinks he might have figured out where we can find the people who killed my father. He's pretty sure they're in Myrtle Beach, so we're planning to leave for there today and go to the CNR service tonight. What I need to know is whether or not you'd like to go with us."

There was only silence in response. Mako was sure she was hearing what he said, but she seemed only to concentrate on using her eyes to bore holes in the ancient oak. Mako could only stare at his fingers fidgeting nervously in his lap and continue.

"Look, I know you had no idea you'd be getting into this much trouble when you climbed into my truck, but you have to remember I never had any intention of getting anyone else involved. Honestly, when you showed up all I could think about was how soon I could drop you off, so getting you into all this was never what I had in mind."

He paused, trying to gauge her reaction. Still, he saw only the back of her head. "What I'm trying to say is that if you wanted to stay here, I'd totally understand. Hell, Eustace seems to have enough connections in this town, I'm sure he could find you a good job." Her legs stopped pumping and the swing grew still. "But if you don't want to stay here, which I would understand, too, Yoshi and I would be willing to guarantee we would get you to Myrtle Beach safely and then you could do whatever you want. We don't know what's going to happen once we get there, so I wouldn't blame you if you never wanted to see us after we got into the city limits. And if you don't want to come with us and you don't want to stay here, I'd be glad to help you get wherever you want to go."

Mako waited patiently for any reply. The chirping of the birds outside were the only things breaking the agonizing silence. Still looking away from him, Krista finally spoke.

"Can you give me three good reasons why I should come with you guys? That's all I want is three." Mako began to reply but was interrupted. "Because right now, I can't even think of one. It seems like ever since I climbed in that goddamn truck with you I've been in worse trouble than I would've been in at home. Val might have beaten the living shit out of me, but he never fired a machine gun at me. And he never got me kidnapped or tried to blow me up, either. So what is there to realistically stop me from getting you to give me some money and taking a ride on a maglev to somewhere far away rather than taking a chance on all that happening again?"

Mako knew what he wanted to say as he looked up at her, tracing the contours of the left side of her face with his eyes. From that angle she looked entirely undamaged by any wounds. There was only the delicate sunburned pink of her cheek, the graceful line of her jaw leading to the neck he would sell his soul to kiss. But as much as he wanted to give her the only reason he could think of — that he wanted more than anything for her to be with him forever — he couldn't bring himself to lay that on her.

"Why are you being so quiet all of a sudden?" she said, finally turning to him. "You were the one that wanted to talk."

"I'm still trying to think of a good reason," Mako said, his gaze downturned once more. "And the worst part is the lamest reason is the only one that's true."

She turned her body toward him and tucked her legs up into the seat of the swing, leaning forward to move away the long hair that draped in front of his right eye.

"If you really meant what you said in there to Yoshi while I was in the bathroom, I think that would be a pretty good reason," she said tenderly.

"You heard that?"

"How could I not?" she said, laughing a little. "You were yelling at the top of your lungs and I wasn't even in the shower yet. That was the first time during all this you seemed to lose your cool. And I never would have guessed it would be over me."

"I just suddenly got a look at what a shitty life I'd led where women were concerned and Yoshi made me realize I was about to screw it up with you, too. And that was the last thing I wanted to do. It's not every day a beautiful woman ends up saving my life."

"And I can honestly say I've never had anyone care for me as much as I knew you did when you showed up at the club last night. That's when I knew I loved you."

Her finger brushed the strand of hair over his ear as her hand moved to his neck, pulling him gently toward her, their lips meeting in a careful, hesitant passion tempered by Mako's consideration for her hurt and aching lips.

Yoshi, discretely peering at the two from Eustace's living room window, mournfully shook his head at the sight.

"I coulda told you that was going to happen sooner or later," a chuckling Eustace said from behind Yoshi as he dried a plate with a dishtowel.

"I agree," Yoshi said. "I had only hoped that it would have been later."

The air conditioning blasted from the Corvette's vents but did little to offset the increasing heat of the day. Or perhaps, Jon thought, it was just lingering concern for the state of his immortal soul that was making him feel the flames of damnation licking at his feet.

But apparently there was no danger of that, at least based on the contract he and Robert drew up concerning Jon's sharing of information about Schaefer. Robert kept insisting the contract would be their little secret, but just how does one keep secrets from an omniscient being, Jon wondered. He was sure somewhere, somehow, Eli was sitting back shaking his head over how the supposedly righteous had fallen.

But at this point he didn't care. Somehow, the thought of an eternity of torment didn't faze him much when he knew he would once again have the opportunity to be with his beloved Linda for what would amount to a normal life span for each of them. Of course, Robert was quick to point out, that didn't mean either one of them couldn't be hit by a bus or die in a plane crash immediately after the agreement went into effect. Such was the unfairness of the universe and he couldn't do a damn thing about that without some more tangible collateral. But as far as artificially altered circumstances such as the ones he was in went, Robert said he was essentially free to set things right back into motion with Jon firmly back on the mortal plane.

So it was with an air of perhaps misplaced excitement and not-so-misplaced trepidation that Jon crawled through traffic on his way to Highway 17, which would lead him directly to the front door of the Whitaker home and the cradle of the Church of the New Revelation. Were it not for the traffic, he could have already been on the highway, but the streams of RVs were again impeding his progress. He dared not honk his horn to encourage them to move a bit faster. The gun slits installed all around the huge rigs made them a bit more intimidating than they would be otherwise. Good sense dictated that anyone on the road south of the U.S.-Canada border regard a rig with Quebec plates as a busload of armed revolutionaries, even if they were likely on their way to Disney World.

While he waited at the last stoplight before he could turn off New Ocean Boulevard, he pressed the memory key on the GPS. A pleasant blue dot flashed patiently over the spot where the Whitaker residence was located and a red arrow tracked his car's progress. He finally got the light and was allowed to turn right off the main drag, freeing himself from the midday cruisers and tourists and heading away from the coastline towards the highway.

Jon really didn't have any idea what to expect when he arrived on Whitaker's doorstep. All he knew was that, according to the GPS, he was getting closer. Of course, that would have been obvious anyway. The derelict stores from the old commercial strip had disappeared and the only signs of life along the highway were dense coastal forest and the camouflaged support pylons of the maglev. Even the number of other vehicles on the road had thinned from their already pitiful ranks. There was only one bus full of what looked like Japanese tourists barreling down the road in the satellite-controlled lane to his left. It soon turned off heading towards Murrells Inlet, no doubt to mount a lunchtime assault on one of the ubiquitous sim-seafood Calabash buffet restaurants tucked among the oaks and marshes.

The entrance to the Whitaker estate was marked by two immense palmetto trees sitting off from the highway, each flanking a high wall fashioned from the oyster-shell-and-mortar concoction unique to the state's colonial era forts and sea walls. He turned in to face a huge wrought-iron gate, noticing that beyond each oyster shell balustrade he could see 15-foot-tall chain link fencing topped with razor wire set back into the trees and extending along the highway. To his left, a wooden post rose discreetly from the ground, a button marked "Call" the only feature. He reached out and pressed it, prompting the holographic face of a lovely young woman to appear.

"Good afternoon. May I help you?" she said, smiling cheerfully. She reminded him a bit of Regina, particularly because it seemed from the head-and-shoulders shot of the camera that she was wearing little more than a bikini top.

"Yes. Jonnie Temple…" — God, how it hurt him to say that — "to see the Reverend Whitaker. I have an appointment."

"Hello, Mister Temple. We've been expecting you. Please drive through to the main house at the end of the driveway. We'll have someone there to meet you."

I'm sure you will, he thought. Can't have the heathens strolling around the grounds by themselves. No telling what they might see. He thanked her and drove through, closing the window to salvage what little cool air was left in the car as the wide tires kicked up a wake of gravel on the loose surface. In his rearview mirror, he saw the gates closing through a cloud of dust.

The place so far was typical of the few former plantations that survived the 19th century carnage and the subsequent 20th century onslaught of residential development. A long, one-lane dirt road lead through stands of huge palmetto trees and sprawling live oaks draped with Spanish moss, accentuated, he was sure, with the latest high-tech security offerings cleverly hidden among the native flora. After about a half-mile more signs of life appeared in the form of paddocks occupied by a few languidly munching horses. Where those ended, there was again a space of semi-wilderness, after which Jon saw the first signs of true human occupation.

To his right appeared a broad clearing of perfectly manicured lawn populated with what seemed to be at least 50 stunningly attractive people of both genders, all in their late teens or early 20s and all dressed in relatively the same fashion. The girls wore either one-piece bathing suits or bikini tops with a sarong sort of garment tied around their waists. The boys wore garments similar to the sarongs, but shorter. The were all engaged in either playing volleyball or croquet on the broad expanse of lawn, some pausing from their games to wave to him as he passed. Given their ages, they had probably never seen such a car in person, Jon thought. Then again, given the beliefs of Whitaker's church, being friendly to strangers probably came as second nature to them. Of course, given Regina's friendliness once under the influence of The Church, Jon thought better of waving back at the risk of encouraging Whitaker's nubile young disciples.

Soon Jon spotted the pristine face of the main house peeking out from beneath the oak canopy, projecting all the grace and power its designers originally meant it to. The driveway ended in a circle around a huge statue and fountain featuring an image familiar to anyone who had even stepped near Sunday school. It was Jesus inviting the children to visit with Him against the wishes of their parents, who thought them too young to be in the presence of the Messiah. As he pulled up in front of the regal front staircase, however, Jon noticed that instead of little children coming unto Him, those surrounding Jesus were youths similar to those he had just driven past. They were all in various states of undress gazing at the Son of God with something that could only be described as lust.

Then, as if one of the statue's figures had somehow come to life, one of the youths appeared at Jon's door as he climbed out of the low automobile.

"Mr. Temple? I'm Josh. I'll be showing you to the Reverend and Mrs. Whitaker," he said, smiling broadly. If I had a body like that at 17 or however old this young man is, Jon thought, I'd be smiling too.

"Nice to meet you, Josh," Jon said as he lifted his briefcase out. "This is quite a place the Whitakers have here."

"Yes sir. I hope you'll excuse us, though. It's a bit crowded this week because of the youth retreat. Please follow me," he said as he led Jon up the curving front stairs. The home was a perfect example of pre-Civil War architecture, the clean lines and columns in clear tribute to the Greeks and in so many ways more extravagant than the frilly conservatism of his own Victorian-era abode. But unlike his home, it seemed as if nothing here had gone unrepaired. Everything on the outside, from the paint on the clapboards to the slats in the shutters, seemed as pristine as it would have been the first day the house was opened to its original owners.

Josh led him through the opened double doors into the foyer. From what he could see, the home was just as immaculate on the inside as it was outside. Everywhere he noticed what seemed to be valuable antiques from all parts of the world, somehow combined to preserve the overall style of the home itself. Jon was so struck that while walking through the hall he stopped to get a closer look at a vase with a design he took to be Greek, probably original, he thought. Linda would have salivated at the thought of a home and design story on the place, and it's likely a number of magazines would have been thrilled to have the story.

Upon closer inspection, though, he realized what he thought was simply a festive scene adorning the vase was in fact a full blown orgy, the crowd of classical figures performing any number of carnal acts, most of which until the last fifty years were illegal in some southern states. Having stopped, Jon then realized everything within reach, from the colonial-era sideboard to the area rug he was standing on, featured some sort of artistically rendered erotica.

"I'm quite intrigued by the artifacts you have here. Who's responsible for this fabulous decorating job?" Jon said, purging his voice of any sarcasm that might come through to the lad. It was a trick he'd had to perfect as a reporter. Interview subjects were unlikely to reveal much if they thought you were mocking them.

"Sister Veronica personally chose every item in the house, Mr. Temple. She says there's nothing she likes better than shopping in the name of the Lord," Josh said as he continued down the hall.

"Well, we all serve Him in our own special way, don't we?" Jon said as he replaced the vase to its spot, looking up to find Josh gazing back at him as if he'd just spoken a divine truth whispered in his ear by the angels themselves.

The two emerged from the interior onto a broad veranda that apparently ran the length of the back of the house, ending to his right in a large, circular area that had already been prepared for lunch. Josh asked him to wait and excused himself to go down to the crucifix-shaped pool, which lay down a flight of stairs. Beyond it lay a large garden and the marshy fringes of the inlet in the distance. The flagstone deck of the pool was populated by youths similar to those he saw on the front lawn, except several of the girls lay beside or played in the water, unabashedly naked, the midday sun glistening off their oiled bodies. Not necessarily out of embarrassment but more out of concern for the legal status of the young ladies, Jon did his best to subtly avert his gaze.

"An impressive sight, eh, Mr. Temple?" said a voice from behind him. Jon turned to find a tall, nattily dressed man he immediately recognized, both by his appearance and his powerful aura of menace, as Lucas Schaefer. He was about as tall as Jon, not more than six feet, but through his manner and bearing seemed much taller.

"Indeed, mister?"

"Lucas Scheafer, at your service," he said with courtly bow and a clipped British accent. "I assume you're being made to feel at home?"

"Very much so, thank you. I believe young Josh is fetching the Whitakers as we speak."

"Very good. While the Whitakers are certainly responsible for deciding if they will be able to come to an agreement with you and your company for this project, many of the business particulars will fall to me. I wanted to be sure to introduce myself and also invite you to tonight's service. This satellite project is quite an undertaking, as you might imagine, but we're all very excited at the prospect of finally being able to broadcast into the Pacific and Asia. We feel there's a very real need for the word of God in those parts of the world."

Especially if it's delivered with a healthy dose of Western fire-and-brimstone poontang, Jon thought to himself. The Chinese will absolutely not know what hit them.

"And it's my pleasure to be considered to provide that opportunity, Mr. Schaefer. Our company is anxious to get on board with what certainly seems to be a growing venture."

"Growth is all we can expect. I look upon the Holy Spirit as being the same as entropy, constantly expanding as sin diminishes," Schaefer said.

"Well, it sounds as if the Whitakers couldn't ask for better help in achieving their goals," he said.

"I look forward to dealing with you again soon," Jon said, extending his hand. Schaefer, after a moment of hesitation, took it and gave it a firm, businesslike squeeze, and suddenly Jon found himself having to suppress the urge to yank it away in revulsion. While Jon had shaken hands with clients whose grips could best be described as clammy, Schaefer's was ice cold and downright slimy, despite its dry appearance.

After Schaefer excused himself, Jon felt the overwhelming need to wash his hands. He rubbed them together as he scanned the pool and found Josh, who was bent over to talk to someone sitting under an umbrella. That was Whitaker, Jon assumed. His assumption was confirmed when a good-looking, 40-ish man rose and wrapped his naked form in a slightly longer version of the sarongs the other men were wearing, then offered his hand to someone lying in the chaise lounge beside him.

A pair of long, shapely and startlingly pale female legs appeared, toes elegantly pointed until they found the stone deck as the rest of who Jon assumed to be Veronica Whitaker emerged from under the umbrella. He had seen her before, but only on television as he used the remote control to flip past the Saturday night services on his way to something else. On television she seemed far more glamorous than she did walking toward him, but no less beautiful. She wore a simple black one-piece bathing suit adorning her long, lithe frame. The alabaster paleness of her skin was in stark contrast to the tan body of her husband and the other sun-bathers around the pool, but it gave her an almost angelic radiance in the intense sun. Her red hair, the kind that probably would have gotten her hanged as a witch in Puritan New England, burned into his consciousness as the crowning glory of her beauty, flowing over her shoulders and framing her china-doll face, distinguished by lips that formed a perfect valentine. Jon had to remind himself not to stare as she approached.

It was as if one of the delicate creatures from a pre-Raphaelite painting had emerged from the canvas and decided to walk among humans. Her beauty was so stunning that Jon suddenly found himself surprised he even remembered anything about the pre-Raphs, as the college girlfriend who had introduced the style to him called the works of that particular movement. The names of the artists escaped him, but he never had a problem remembering they all seemed to share a fondness for redheaded women.

This particular woman, however, would have put all the ones he knew from art books and museums to pitiful shame. With the self-confidence that so often comes with women very aware of their effect on men also came an overwhelming and blatant awareness of her sexuality. She moved with enough grace for several ballet dancers, delicately placing each sandal-clad foot on each step with the poise of a finishing school graduate, but the exaggerated sway of her hips hinted at something more sensual lurking beneath the icy cool she tried to project. And if that happened to be a bit too subtle, there was always the four-inch crucifix cut out of the bust of her suit, revealing a smattering of freckles across the interior curves of her breasts, to remind one that she was indeed a carnal creature.

Her husband, on the other hand, was exactly what Jon had expected. Tan, handsome, older but not too old, with just a tasteful touch of gray at his temples. While not in optimum shape, Whitaker was no slouch, the muscles in his arms and chest still retaining their definition beneath a smattering of body hair. He moved the same way towards the veranda as Jon would expect him to in a suit as he approached the pulpit — self-assured and powerful in a non-threatening way, the kind of walk that inspires confidence.

Whitaker extended his hand before he reached the top step, a classic move they taught in classes on how to work rooms full of potential business contacts. Jon held his position and waited for the Reverend to come to him. The subtleties of power politics weren't lost on him and had seemed to become even more enhanced with his divinely granted physical upgrade.

"Mr. Temple, welcome to our home," Whitaker said as she firmly gripped Jon's hand and gave it a single squeeze.

"A pleasure, Reverend. And I presume this lovely woman is Mrs. Whitaker?" Jon said, turning to Veronica, who presented a graceful hand.

"Please, Veronica. It's a pleasure to finally meet you, Mr. Temple. We've heard quite a lot about you and your company." Jon noticed she held his hand just a moment longer than he would have liked. She let her manicured fingers stroke along the inside of his palm as she slowly released his hand, all the time looking at him as if she were gazing out from a porno feelie — or one of the church's promotional brochures.

"Well, I hope to at least reinforce the good things you heard," he said with his best businessman's smile and a self-deprecating chuckle. That was easy enough, but his next statement physically pained him. "And please, both of you call me Jonnie. With as much at stake in the course of this deal as there already is, I don't think there's any reason for us to rest on formality."

"I have to agree, Jonnie," Whitaker said. "I hope you're hungry. We've taken the liberty of preparing a lovely little lunchtime spread for you before we get down to business."

Whitaker gestured toward the table and they moved to sit. "And then we'll see what kind of spread we can find you for dessert," Veronica whispered in Jon's ear before she placed herself in the seat between him and the Reverend.

As Jon steadied himself from Veronica's unexpected comment, their tiny group was assaulted by a whirlwind of hospitality as kitchen help brought out an array of Lowcountry cuisine. Plates piled high with various shrimp dishes, cold fried chicken, sliced cold ham, potato salad, coleslaw and crab salad drifted by as Jon inhaled the scents he thought he had lost forever to his past with his ascension into the eternal sensory doldrums of heaven.

Very little at the Whitaker household seemed to rest on formality. Where Jon had expected a lavish production for his benefit, he found himself in a situation very much like one that might have been set in his mother's house if she were entertaining a bridge club or hosting a pre-nuptial luncheon for the daughter of a friend. He was served perfect sweet tea from pitchers running with condensation. Meanwhile the trio passed around bowls and platters of dishes that ran through his memory like blood ran through his body.

"Jonnie, do try some of Louise's shrimp and grits. We have the grits brought down from an old mill upstate and the shrimp were raised right here on the property."

Jon spooned the rich grits out of an iron serving cauldron into a shallow soup bowl, then ladled out shrimp and dark sauce from another, gathering both on his fork and tasting.

"Absolutely delicious, Reverend. It seems that with your own seafood farm and, I imagine, a vegetable garden somewhere on the property, the two of you are nearly self-sufficient out this way," he said.

"Nearly, but not completely, Jonnie. We're still subject to the whims of the Lord whenever he sees fit to bring storms to the area. But otherwise, we find we can get along very well here with very little contact from outside."

"Personally, it's the contact from inside I prefer," Veronica purred to Jon before delicately wrapping her lips around a forkful of tomato, slices of which had also been served with lunch. Jon felt his palms beginning to sweat.

"Still," the Reverend continued without acknowledging his wife's comment, "we find it necessary to spread the word about what we consider to be the new destiny for Christianity. Over the last 2,000 years, so many faiths have come and gone under the auspices of being the true word of God and all seem to have failed. They left people feeling unfulfilled and woefully out of contact with the Lord. Tell me, Jonnie, are you a churchgoing man?"

"Unfortunately, my job keeps me on the road quite a bit and I'm unable to be a member of a single church," he improvised. "But I was raised Methodist."

"Admirable. I was ordained in the Baptist church, trying to find time out from being righteously indignant about dancing, drinking and card playing to actually study the scriptures." Jon chuckled politely. The Baptists he'd known through his life were notorious for secretly breaking all three of those prohibitions. "You'll find that many men of God are little more than ventriloquist dummies parroting the words of the Bible without ever really understanding them. What I wanted to do was become a scholar of the Word. And it was in the midst of my personal studies that I met my lovely Veronica," he said, reaching out to take his wife's right hand.

Knowing the truth about Whitaker's "personal studies," Jon had to again struggle to maintain a polite demeanor. He felt compelled to mentally insert creative references to self-gratification at strategic points in the conversation.

As Jon suppressed the urge to smirk, Veronica's left hand found its way to Jon's leg under the pretense of straightening her napkin across her lap. As her husband continued and her right hand was again free to scoop more of the tiny servings she had allowed herself, the left hand remained gently placed on his thigh.

"You see, Jonnie, my wife was an undiscovered genius when it came to the human relationship with God. She discovered me studying the Scriptures one night," — *while beating the bishop* — "wrestling with the contradictions inherent in the Bible. I looked up from my work and before me was the vision of an angel sent down to tell me what I wanted to know."

"Sweetheart, you always exaggerate that part," Veronica said, doing her best to seem embarrassed as her hand trailed farther up Jon's thigh. It finally came to rest along the growing hardness at his crotch. "I was just impressed with someone who would put so much effort into something so many people take for granted, sweetheart. After all, anything important to you is always worth doing slowly and methodically and with great conviction, don't you think, Jonnie?" Her fingernails then lightly grazed his now fully engorged member, distracting him from the fact that he should probably answer her question before her husband grew suspicious. Having the busy hand of such a beautiful stranger in one's lap, however, is conducive to many things besides concentration, he thought. Worst of all, he found himself thinking that they both were taking quite a risk engaging in such behavior right in front of her husband and his potential client.

"Veronica, darling, I don't mean to interrupt what you're doing, but do get your hand out of Mr. Temple's lap. We're trying to talk business," the Reverend said as if he had asked her to refill his tea glass. Jon, meanwhile, was so taken with surprise that he flicked the meat from a crab leg he had been struggling with over the railing of the veranda and into the azalea bushes.

"Oh, honey. You're always talking about business when I want to play," she said, her lip protruding in an exaggerated pout. "You're so mean to me."

"Sweetheart, do behave for our guest. He's unfamiliar with our style of doing things here and I don't want to scare him away." Jon couldn't help but glance back and forth at them as they engaged in a playful repartee about his wife trying to feel him up. "Please accept my apologies, Jonnie, but my wife is anxious to finalize this arrangement, and she's been partial to your firm since we began receiving bids. Unfortunately she's getting a little ahead of herself."

"As opposed to later," she whispered in Jon's ear, "when I'll just be giving a little head."

Jon nearly inhaled a bite of half-chewed shrimp, but he managed to maintain his composure, finding himself still curious over what exactly finalization of the deal would entail.

"So Reverend," he said as he recovered, "just how was your wife responsible for your revelation?" *While polishing the pulpit.*

"Ah, yes. Well, we crossed paths originally in a computer chat room," — *while thumping the Bible* — "and after a bit of conversation, I began to minister to her. 'Are you a preacher or something?' she asked me. I told her that I was and that I was researching alternative forms of Christianity with the intention of bringing that additional knowledge back to my work in the pulpit.

"During the course of the discussion that ensued, Veronica revealed to me that she had never been to a church in her life. Her parents had been products of the secularism that was the norm in the later part of the last century and had never seen it necessary to give their child a religious education. So I took it upon myself to evangelize to this lovely lost woman. The strange thing was – and it took me years to realize this – but it was actually Veronica who was evangelizing me. After weeks of meeting occasionally online where we discussed elements of different religions while concentrating on Christianity, we agreed to meet. It was there that I truly saw Veronica's power as a messenger from God. There alone with her, a feeling of immense joy and peace mysteriously enveloped me. We talked and talked into the evening and time seemed to lose all meaning to me. I seemed to spiral downward into an unconscious state, during which I dreamed of many things I had never dreamed of before. I saw Christ coming to me, looking strong and sturdy like a carpenter should, his muscles powerful and his face determined, and the two of us became one."

Whitaker had, by this point, begun staring at some fixed point in midair, his eyes growing wider as he seemed to have his prophetic vision all over again for Jon's benefit.

"Then I saw Veronica standing beside Mary Magdalene, both of them so extraordinarily beautiful that I felt myself gasp. I then saw the two of them become one in the image of Veronica, and suddenly she was naked and so was I. Above us I saw another woman, this time it was Christ's mother, Mary, and she was motioning for Veronica and I to come together in the flesh, to merge the holy power of earthly sin and heavenly grace. It was at that moment that I awoke to find Veronica atop me, naked, our bodies wrapped together in an embrace that had been ordained by God himself, both of us climaxing with the power of all heaven behind us and flowing through us, destined to share in the creation of the one true religion, the most powerful force the world has ever seen and to tell everyone about it."

The impromptu trance apparently broken, the Reverend once again met Jon's eyes with his intense gaze. "And that, Mr. Temple, is why I need you."

Jon couldn't decide if he was appalled, aroused or terrified by what he'd just heard. After a moment of consideration, he decided he was all three. During the story, Veronica's hand had again found its way to Jon's lap and was gently stroking the length of his shaft along the inside of his thigh, obviously as aroused as her husband by the tale of the church's creation. The Reverend, meanwhile, had broken into a sweat and had the fiery glow of a man who had just finished telling followers they shouldn't worry about drinking the cyanide-laced Kool-Aid, because everything would be just fine once they got where they were going.

"You, Jonnie, are the last piece of the puzzle of the Church of the New Revelation. You hold the key to unlock the global message of our ministry. As I'm sure you're aware, the church has been conducting a fundraising drive over the last year to finance the launch of the final satellite in our global network. This satellite will orbit over the Pacific and enable us to broadcast our network into China and the surrounding nations, finally giving us global coverage and the ability to spread our message throughout all cultures and to anyone who owns a television."

"And we can help you with just that, Reverend," Jon said as he extracted from his briefcase a heavy sheath of papers, on the top of which lay a glossy promotional packet for the fictional company he represented. He was still doing his best to ignore his obvious arousal at the hands of Veronica Whitaker. "According to what you've already discussed with my superiors, just say the word and your satellite will begin construction at the Nikura International Aerospace facility in Charleston. Assuming you're agreeable to the terms you discussed with them, we will take delivery of the satellite there, after which it is set for a September launch date from our site in Kazhakstan. Assuming everything goes according to schedule, you should be ready to beam broadcasts off that unit within 24 hours after launch."

"Fine, Jonnie. That's exactly what was described in your company's bid and it seems that everything is going right along just fine. Now put all those papers away. We can save all the nasty business of signing and notarizing and check writing for Lucas. After all, that's what we keep him around for, isn't it? But before we put our final seal of approval on the whole shebang, I just want to emphasize how important it is and how much it would mean to us if you would join us as our special guest at our service tonight. You can't quite have a complete grasp of what our ministry is all about until you attend a service up close and personal," the Reverend said as he placed his napkin on the table and rose.

As Jon was deciding what to do about his prominent erection once he stood up, Veronica leaned in close, her lips against his ear and her hand at his crotch. "And he does mean up close and personal."

"So, now we're going to see the police, right?" Regina asked as she trudged along the boardwalk behind Linda. If it weren't that the two of them were trying to track down Jon, she would have considered the whole day a waste. Not one minute on the beach was spent doing anything other than looking for Jon or anyone who might have seen him. They had stopped at all the regular spots around the beach house first. There was the surf shop with the really cute blond guy behind the counter. Then the convenience store and even the little beachfront bar with the deck looking out over the ocean. No one had seen Jon or anyone fitting his description since the last time he and Linda had visited.

"Linda? The police, right?"

Linda was silent as she edged past the throngs making their way from one attraction to the other or simply cruising the wooden planks for the entertainment of others watching.

Frustrated at the older woman's failure to respond, Regina rushed to catch up with her, nearly plowing into a high school kid in his full '90s retro regalia of ripped flannel shirt and black combat boots. "Linda, we've got to go to the police. This isn't working."

Linda kept walking, seeming not to notice that Regina was even there. In desperation, the younger woman finally took Linda's arm and roughly dragged her into the open front of an arcade.

"Linda, look at me," she said over the noise of the VR games and the ancient skeeball machine at the entrance. "We've been looking all morning. He wasn't anywhere near the beach house and we haven't seen him anywhere downtown. It's been at least 24 hours. Don't you think we ought to go ahead and file a missing person report on him?"

"We called them this morning, Regina. They said they'd keep an eye out for someone fitting his description," she said, her face expressionless as she continued to search the crowd while at the same time avoiding her companion's gaze. They had called the police – at Regina's insistence – but had gotten a response just short of a brush-off. Apparently it wasn't unusual for husbands to go missing for days at a time in Myrtle Beach. The officer they spoke to suggested she start by searching the golf courses and titty bars.

"But it's not the same. Looking for him is one thing, but a missing person report forces them to do more. It will make them check other places and let other police departments know to look for him."

"No," Linda said absently. "We'll keep looking around here. Maybe he came to play a game."

"For God's sake, Linda, get a grip!" Regina said quietly but firmly, shaking her gently. "You're not even thinking straight anymore."

TWENTY SIX

When Linda finally did meet her young friend's gaze, it was as her lip trembled and her eyes welled up, the edges of her eyes growing moist with tears. "But he's got to be somewhere. I know he wouldn't just disappear like this." Her voice cracked with her last words and Regina suddenly found Linda weeping softly into her bare shoulder. While people continued to stroll by, Regina ignored them and their curious stares as she simply held her friend, gently rocking her and trying to console her above the noise of the games.

"Everything all right here, ladies?" a heavyset man with a sweat-stained T-shirt and a change belt asked, probably anxious to have them take their display out of his establishment.

"Not really," Regina said. "Could you tell us where the nearest police station is?"

"Sure thing. Just built us a substation right across the street so they could keep an eye on the boulevard traffic. I'm sure they'll be able to help you out over there, Miss."

Regina smiled her most pleasant smile as she led Linda, still weeping quietly, through the arcade and out to the street.

The foot traffic seemed to increase exponentially once they made it to the New Ocean Boulevard side of the arcade. Regina didn't think she'd seen that many freaks and freak-watchers since a church trip to South Beach in Miami, where they ministered to those that were still using their bodies outside the sanctity of the church. But since she was standing in the middle of the Church of the New Revelation's home city, she imagined a good portion of the unusual folks walking by could have ministered to her just as well as she could to them.

Linda, however, saw little more than the sidewalk and the palm of her hand as she continued crying while the two of them wove through the crowd, eventually finding a path through the gridlocked traffic of tour busses, RVs and meticulously maintained IC cars.

The Myrtle Beach police department, with the constant flow of tax money the city collected from tourism, could certainly have afforded something better than what seemed to be the substation the arcade owner spoke of, Regina thought. It seemed little more than an ancient store set amidst the glass and neon and holograms that made the boulevard look like a narrower version of the Vegas strip before the earthquake swallowed the whole place into the desert. The only thing that distinguished it from a building that might have been abandoned was "Myrtle Beach Police Department" painted on the window and that the adjoining building — a pawnshop — seemed in even a worse state of neglect.

Inside the nearly empty lobby, Regina sat Linda in one of the ancient wooden chairs, which had all been decorated with various carved profanities and representations of the female anatomy, and approached what amounted to the reception desk. It was staffed by an obscenely over made-up woman with a towering beehive hairdo, her eyes watching a pocket TV tuned to something that sounded like a raucous talk show while she faced a small electric fan.

"Excuse me …"

"Oh, hey sweetheart. I didn't even see you standin' there. What can I do for you?" the woman said, finally acknowledging her after a few moments.

"I'd like to file a missing person report, please."

"All right, hon," she said, turning to her computer, managing to type quickly despite her exceptionally long fingernails. "Has the person been missing for at least 24 hours."

"Yes, ma'am. And we alerted the police earlier today to be on the lookout for him."

"Okay, I'll just need his name and address."

"His name is Jonathan Templeton," she said, prompting the woman to pause and register what Regina thought might be recognition. She then turned to Linda, who had stopped crying and was now staring out the dingy plate glass window, her hand covering her mouth and her eyes looking as she were staring into the abyss of loneliness. Regina hated to disturb her further, but she didn't know their address in Carlton.

"Linda ..."

"Are you the next of kin, darlin'?" the woman asked, acknowledging Linda for the first time since they walked in.

"I'm his wife," Linda said with surprising calm. "'Next of kin' makes him sound like he's dead."

"That's what we're here to find out, honey. Can I have your home address, please?"

Linda, her eyes blank and fixed on a point in space Regina couldn't determine, rattled off the requested information with emotionless efficiency. She seemed to Regina to be getting her second wind, to have hardened her resolve to find Jon. Or perhaps she'd just given up and wasn't ready to admit it to herself.

"I'm gonna need a description, too, hon. Not much good trying to find him if we don't know what he looks like."

Regina saw a small grin curl Linda's lips, lips that Regina had always been a little jealous of for their shape, like the silhouette of a graceful bird in flight.

"He's beautiful and he doesn't know it," Linda said as if he had stepped into the spot on which she had fixed, filling her field of vision. "His eyes are calm, almost like tranquilizers, sometimes, like the floor of the forest after it rains, brown but flecked with green." Her voice trailed off and she was gone again, her eyes focused on the mental image of someone she was deciding she might never see again.

"That's all real sweet, honey, but we need something a little more concrete than that. Hair and eye color, height, weight, that sort of thing," the woman said a little impatiently.

"White male, mid-thirties, about six feet tall, 175, brown hair and eyes, fair complexion, clean shaven, no distinguishing marks or tattoos that I know of. Last seen in khaki shorts and a concert T-shirt. I forget what band," Regina said, trying to get the interview over with.

"Know any reason why he might have decided to run off? Any problems at work or at home?"

"Um ... yeah. He quit his job yesterday because of some problems and may have been drinking as a result."

"All right, hon," she said, her nails rapidly tapping the ancient keyboard. "I'll make a special note of that and put out an alert with all the other departments in the state. I'm gonna need a phone number where…"

She was interrupted by the blinking of a red light on her telephone console, an older model not fitted with a video screen, and an accompanying light chirping sound. The woman's mood changed immediately, a look of veiled dread suddenly betraying the true age she was trying to hide beneath the layers of makeup.

She kept typing.

"Did you say you had a phone number where you can …"

Again the phone. Blinking and chirping.

Regina began to rattle off the number at her grandmother's cottage, but it was obvious the woman wasn't paying attention. Before she had uttered her second syllable, she was stopped by the receptionist's upheld hand. Her smile was forced, unable to hide the unease she felt.

"I'm sorry, sugar, but I've got to get this," she said as she picked up the receiver and, with the slightest hesitation, pressed the blinking button. "Yes sir? Mmm hmm … Yes, it's her. No, sir, no sign. All right, I'll let them know."

She hung up the telephone and breathed deeply, trying to calm herself. "Detective Robert would like to speak with you ladies. He thinks he might have some information that will help you out."

"Oh, great," Regina said, surprised by the good news. "Should we just go on back?"

"No!" The woman nearly leapt over the desk to block her way. "I mean, no. He'll be with you in just a moment."

A minute passed. Regina knew it was a minute because she saw the antique digital clock — the kind with the numbers that tumbled over instead of actually changing shape — go from 1:34 to 1:35, the time between passing at the speed of a slug. She took the occasion to move back to comfort Linda, who sat perfectly still and strangely emotionless.

Some sort of heavy truck passed outside, rattling the plate glass window and sending an almost undetectable hum of vibration through the building. But after the truck passed it continued. When Regina saw the receptionist grin something that was more like a grimace, she noticed the sorry excuse for a smile was meant to distract them from her long-nailed fingers gripping the edge of the desk in anticipation of something likely to shift her from her spot.

The humming continued, growing more intense and now visibly shaking the walls and furniture of the dingy office. Dust moved from where it had been settled, raising small undulating clouds in corners all around the room. Chips of plaster began to fall from the ceiling as the woman finally gave up her charade and emitted a tiny, terrified squeak, her face squeezed into a grotesque mask of someone who expected her doom sometime in the very near future.

Then came the light. Regina had been nervous from the start, but the red glow that she noticed slowly brightening from under a door behind the receptionist made her genuinely worried. She rose and bolted to the front door grasping the knob and found the door would not give. She wrestled with it, feeling the knob turn but the door refusing to open. She looked behind her again, the glow growing brighter as the shaking continued, rising to the point where the ceiling was raining dust and plaster, the floor covered with a then dusty white film.

And then it stopped. All movement ceased. The only noise that remained was the sound of traffic and pedestrians passing by outside and the tinny drone from the woman's portable TV.

That is, until the door from under which had shone the ominous red glow slowly creaked open on hinges that sounded as if they were manufactured during the Bronze Age and hadn't seen a drop of oil since.

"Detective Robert will see you now," the woman behind the desk said, her eyes still closed as Regina led Linda past her and through the open door and into a small windowless office.

"Afternoon, ladies," said a stooped, bearded man who leaned against a wooden desk, one thigh hitched up on its edge. He took a long drag on a cigarette and tapped the ash onto the floor. "I'm Robert. I understand the two of you are looking for someone?"

"Would you mind telling me where all that shaking ..." Regina began, holding Linda tightly against her.

"Water pipes."

"What?" she said, not quite grasping his answer.

"Water pipes. Always had a problem with them here. That little episode you witnessed happens every time someone flushes the can. A pain in the ass, if you'll pardon me, but that's what you get when you're working with taxpayer money. Now, have a seat and tell me about this missing husband of yours, Mrs. Templeton."

Regina looked behind them and saw two chairs identical to the ones in the lobby, chairs that hadn't been there before. She sat, nonetheless, if only for Linda's sake.

"The last time I saw him was Thursday when I threw him out of the house because I thought he had raped a woman at his office," Linda said, her voice flat and hollow.

"Mmm hmm. And what makes you think he might have come here afterwards?" Robert said after pulling on his cigarette, tiny puffs of smoke exiting his mouth before the remainder was forced out through his nostrils.

"We have a cottage here, over in Surfside, that was empty. I know how much he loves it there, so I assumed that would be the first place he would go."

"You also assumed he'd go there because he wanted to make it easy for you to find him, right?"

"Well, I suppose that had something to do with it, too. But I called him there yesterday and there was no answer. And there was no answer on his mobile. That's when I decided to come down. Other than the back door being open, it didn't look like anyone had been there."

"Mrs. Templeton, I hate asking these kinds of questions, but they are necessary. Can you think of anyone else he might have gone to stay with? Maybe the woman at his office?"

Had Regina known that question was coming, she would have warned him to ask it in a more diplomatic way. Not that it would have done any good in the long run, but it might have kept Linda from doing what she did.

And what she did was this. As soon as Robert had clipped off the end of his sentence, Linda was up and in his face, grabbing the cigarette he'd just replaced between his lips and violently crushing it out in the heavy glass ashtray on the desk.

"Listen, I don't know why everyone around me is intent on making my husband some lecherous adulterous bastard, but I am sick and fucking tired of it. My husband is missing. MISSING, understand? He's not shacked up in Tahiti with some blonde cupcake from his office. He's injured or in trouble or kidnapped or..." She stopped, unable to say it, even though Regina knew what it was that had stuck in her throat.

Robert, meanwhile, looked as if nothing had happened, tapping another cigarette from the pack that lay on his desk and placing it between his lips, ignoring Linda's proximity to him, which would have made anyone else scramble to regain his personal space. "It's not unusual for the spouse to be as upset as you are in a situation like this, Mrs. Templeton, but we've got to explore all the possibilities. You'd be surprised what some married couples don't know about each other. Now please, sit back down and let's help each other out."

Regina took her hand as she sat again and Robert exhaled a cloud of tobacco smoke towards the ceiling. She couldn't recall seeing him light it. "So you're sure there's nowhere else he might have gone? Another relative, maybe?" Robert continued.

"No. I spoke to his mother and he wasn't there and all his friends in town said they hadn't seen him. No charges had been made on any of his credit cards, and no money was taken out of any of our bank accounts. The only thing I found was a one-way charge to Surfside on his maglev card."

"You narrowed that down pretty well. Mind if I ask what you do?"

"My husband and I were both newspaper reporters. Now he works in PR and I'm a freelance writer."

"Ah. If had to guess, I would have said you were a cop," he said, a wry smile crossing his lips. "But even though you seem to be doing pretty well with your own investigative work, I'd like to suggest you leave this to the professionals. We've got the information you gave us and we'll distribute that to the other departments in the state. But in the meantime, I'd like to suggest you get some rest. I know it's been a hard couple of days for you. Maybe take in a movie or go somewhere nice to eat. Take your mind off things a bit until we find your husband."

Regina was suddenly struck with an idea and squeezed Linda's hand excitedly. "I know what we can do! The big church service is tonight. I was supposed to go but I was planning to stay with you instead. But that might be the best thing for you."

"Regina, I don't know. I've never been really interested in..."

"Oh, come on. You can sit up in the gallery while I go downstairs for the

174

service. It'll be fun."

"Never been to a New Revelationist service in person, Mrs. Templeton?" Robert asked, his eyebrow cocked in a way Regina wasn't sure she like the implications of.

"No, so far I've missed that little life experience," Linda said, trying to be polite for Regina's sake.

"Hey, might not be a bad idea," he said. "It'll certainly take your mind off things, and from what folks tell me, you never know who or what you'll see there."

"I know," Linda said. "I think that's what I'm worried about."

"All right ladies, you'll have to sort this one out yourselves," Robert said. "But in the meantime, Mrs. Templeton, I can assure you we'll do everything in our power to find your husband. And if you ask me, I think we'll end up seeing him before the weekend is over."

"Thank you, Detective Robert. I'm glad we decided to come see you," Regina said as she and Linda rose to leave.

"It's my pleasure, ladies," he said, guiding them both toward the door. "And if you do decide to attend the service tonight, you might want to just say a little prayer for your husband. The possibility of a little divine guidance never hurt anything, know what I mean?"

"I hope to hear from you real soon," Linda said just before they exited onto the street.

"Oh, don't worry. I'm sure we'll be seeing each other again before you know it."

Robert saw the white button on his telephone blinking. He pulled the last drag from his cigarette and stubbed it out in the ashtray as the door closed behind the two women, taking his time before pressing the button and picking up the dingy beige receiver.

"Yeah?"

"I've got to admit it. Your work is smooth. You almost made it look like the whole thing was their idea," said the female voice. It rang with echoes of pi, parallelograms and calculations of the circumference of a circle.

"That's the trick. It was their idea. I just encouraged it and put a little personal spin on it. Now, is there anything I can do for you besides graciously accept your shallow praise? I'm kinda busy. Got a busload of cash-poor Canadians showing up today looking for some firepower to cart back up north."

"You're sure she's going to show up at the service tonight?" the voice said.

"Listen, you and I made a deal, right?" Robert said, extracting another cigarette, which was lit by the time it touched his lips.

"Sure, but I know about your deals. That's why I'm calling."

Robert paused and took a deep drag. "Good point," he said, exhaling. "But you've got me a bit over the barrel, don't you think? I mean, it's not like I can run off and hide."

"True. Just focus on that line of thinking and we'll all get through this just fine."

"My end of this isn't what I'm worried about. Is your man up to the job?

I mean, he's dealing with some serious shit and I don't think he has any concept of just how deep it is."

"You let me worry about that. You just make sure we see her at that service tonight."

"Right," he said before hanging up and taking a thoughtful drag from the cigarette. "Accepting orders to send people to church," he muttered to himself, shaking his head. "What has my fucking life become?"

It was nearly 2 p.m. before Barry and Lewis knocked on Eustace's back door, each one carrying a suspiciously heavy canvas duffel bag. The three men shook hands, reacquainting themselves after the previous night's meeting under the less than normal circumstances.

Though Eustace didn't expect to be fighting his way through any enemy lines of defense once they reached Myrtle Beach, his boss considered having the two men along more insurance than he could hope for. And Eustace was thankful Roth managed to track them down, not a small trick in itself.

When he'd mentioned their names to his boss while discussing options for rebuilding and whether Eustace even still had a place to work, Roth's voice brightened noticeably.

"You mean those two buff Marines? Huuuney, let me make some phone calls. I think I might be able to find out where you can get in touch with those sisters," Roth said.

"What for?" Eustace asked. "Those guys have done enough just keeping anyone in the club from getting killed."

"Eustace, baby, you know I love you, but sometimes that cute Army skull of yours is just so thick. You're going down there with your little rag-tag assault team. ..."

"No, no. There's not an assault team. I'm just trying to help these folks out before they leave," he said, a little confused about what Roth was getting at.

"But baby, it is an assault team, because you know how Mama Roth feels about her club. That club was like my child. And all those poor babies that were there for a good time and got so scared last night, those were Mama's grandchildren. And when somebody goes after your children and your grandchildren ... well, there's just nothing you won't do to make them pay, am I right, sugar? And Mama just wouldn't feel right letting you go on this little trip unprepared. Lord knows if you're gonna go, Mama Roth wants you to take care of business, understand honey?"

Eustace had cut short his protests at that point, knowing that further argument was futile. Without his knowledge or consent, he'd been volunteered by his boss for a mission of revenge against what amounted to a big, fat speculation. Neither he nor Yoshi was perfectly sure the CNR was behind this business of his dead employer. At this point it was nothing but a guess. And Eustace, not being a betting man, wasn't particularly interested in laying odds on anything that might involve his death or dismemberment at the hands of domestic religious terrorists in CD bandoliers. The best he hoped for, he suspected, was that they would arrive in Myrtle Beach and somehow discover that the CNR had nothing to do with this mess, what was supposed to be a terrorist group was in fact an isolated group of geriatric nut jobs and all of them could spend the evening in one of the Indian casinos wagering on something other than their lives.

But Roth, damn his nancy ass, was just so fucking convincing. Somehow he could look deep into Eustace's soul and see that, despite his bartender's general distaste for things homosexual, he liked his job and he liked his customers and didn't have much of a chance of getting a job anywhere else in the private sector that didn't involve blowing things up, serving as a bodyguard for someone he would never want to protect otherwise or acting as a security "consultant" for some company that was more interested in protecting proprietary information that its employees. Roth — figuratively speaking, of course — had him by the balls and knew exactly when to squeeze.

An hour later, Roth called back to say he had tracked the two down through several mutual friends, one of whom was a drill instructor at Parris Island who was emphatic about his sexual preferences being kept under wraps. Not that Roth ever indulged in blackmail, of course. Just a little "motivational speaking," as he called it.

An hour after that, both men showed up wearing white T-shirts, khaki fatigue pants and spit-polish black boots. Outside was parked a Humvee mottled with gray and black urban camouflage that the men had "requisitioned" from the local National Guard armory by conning the 19-year-old PFC into thinking they had direct orders from his superior.

Eustace led the two into his living room and repeated the introductions from the night before, then placed one of the bags on the kitchen table.

"All right, boys. Let's see what kind of goodies you've brought your favorite bartender," he said, unzipping the bag and pulling the canvas to the side to reveal an arsenal. "Well, will ya look at that, boys and girls? Must be Christmas in July at Eustace's house."

"Mind if I ask what the hell we're going to need this stuff for?" Mako said, arms crossed, regarding the bag with concern and not a little awe at the firepower it contained.

"Just a few items to cover unexpected contingencies, kid," Eustace said as he pulled a pistol from the bag, checked the chamber and sighted down the barrel. "It seems to me, considering that you were so worked up about your day yesterday, that you'd be a little more enthusiastic about having some support on this trip. But since you're so squeamish about the realities of doing something like this, you need to think about what you're really after on this little adventure, because my boss is interested in me kicking some shagger ass."

Mako sniffed, prompting Krista to jab him in the arm and scowl. "I'm just glad you guys came prepared," she said. "Unlike some people around here, I'm way too familiar with what these jokers will be using to shoot at us."

"If it comes to that," Yoshi chimed in. That didn't surprise Eustace. The big man seemed like just the type to avoid violence when possible, then open up a big can of industrial-strength whup-ass when it was necessary. "Executed correctly, this should be nothing more than a reconnaissance mission and the danger should be minimal."

For the first time since their introductions, one of the newcomers — Barry — spoke up. "Folks, we're here as a favor to Roth and in our own interests, considering what went down at the club last night. But it would help us quite a bit if we knew what the hell all this was about before there was any danger of people shooting at each other."

"And for starters, could someone please tell us who those freaks were who tried to pop us last night?" Lewis asked.

"You want the unabridged or Reader's Digest condensed version?" Eustace asked as he tucked the pistol in the back waistband of his jeans. "Personally, I'm still trying to get the whole drama worked out, myself. You want to fill the fellas in on this one, Mako?"

The younger man seemed suddenly uncomfortable as all eyes turned to him. "Yeah, Mako. Please do explain to all of us why we're here," said Krista, looking amused by Mako being thrust into the role of public speaker.

"Um … Well, we think that my father's death may somehow be connected to the same folks that shot up the bar last night, apparently because they're somehow connected to someone who was trying to buy an orbital weapon — a particle accelerator — from my father's company. We're not positive who that is, but we think it's a guy working for the Church of the New Revelation named Lucas Scheafer, and that this particle accelerator will be launched on the church's new communications satellite."

"Aw, man," Lewis said, grimacing and running his hand along his flattop. "Any idea what they might want to do with it once they get it up there?"

"Beats us. Far as we know, the church hasn't got a grudge against anyone. Hell, maybe this Scheafer guy just wants to start World War III," Mako said.

"Wait a sec," Barry said, looking puzzled. "Weren't we in World War III?"

"That was Iraq III, buddy," Lewis whispered to him.

"I believe what Mako is referring to is the potential of a nuclear conflict between the United States and some other nation," Yoshi said. "Since this satellite will open the Church of the New Revelation's broadcasts up to China and the rest of east Asia, it's quite possible one of those nations could be the target of this weapon."

"But what the hell for?"

"That, my boys," Eustace said as he gathered up the bags, "is what I believe we're on our way to finding out."

The only time Jon could remember staying so consistently aroused was in junior high school when he shared three classes in a row with Jennifer Paris. She was an angelic blonde who was in the full bloom of adolescent womanhood before most of her peers had even considered the prospect of having cleavage. Her insistence upon always wearing tight, short T-shirts to school, even in the dead of winter, never helped his situation. The chilly temperatures of many of the older classrooms simply made her already prominent breasts more noticeable thanks to her perpetually hard nipples. As a result, he often found himself considering drastic measures to alleviate his erectile distress so that going to the head of the class wouldn't become an exercise in public humiliation.

With age, such sights tended to arouse him in a more psychic, rather than physical, fashion. His current situation, however, was a bit overwhelming for his already taxed psyche and physique.

It wasn't that there were so many naked or half-naked people roaming around the Whitaker compound. It wasn't even that some of them were obviously in the middle of advanced foreplay in full view of anyone who chose to walk by. No, the problem arose from the presence of Veronica Whitaker. Lithe, sensuous and scarlet-tressed Veronica. Mrs. Lawrence Whitaker. Queen and high priestess of the country's newest and largest religious movement. Living embodiment of Mary Magdalene. And on top of all that, an apparently insatiable sexual carnivore.

She stayed in close proximity to Jon through the entire tour, taking every opportunity to graze his crotch, run a finger along the crease of his butt, lick his earlobe or touch herself in the most blatant displays of public autoerotica he'd ever seen. All of this took place within feet and just out of the line of sight of her husband. Every move she made, it seemed, was designed to lead Jon up the narrow spiral staircase of arousal she had created. One misstep and he assumed it could be tragic for both of them. But as long as they both trod carefully, it seemed Veronica was confident they would both reach safely whatever pleasures waited at the top.

And that's exactly what Jon was worried about. He knew that climb upward would have to end somewhere with – dare he even think it? – a climax and the subsequent decent. Only the sweetly brutal Veronica knew where and when that would take place.

Their tour began with the pool and adjacent pool house, each accessorized with naked and semi-naked figures both living and artfully rendered on the inside walls, as if to give still more stimulation to the bubbling volcano of hormonal lust that populated the estate this weekend. Inside the shade of the pool house, the walls shimmered with the water's reflections of the blazing July sun. Several couples had retreated from the heat and instead were creating some of their own, busily kissing, caressing and fondling one another on pillows, cushions and chaise lounges placed around the room. As he and the Whitakers walked through, Jon caught sight of an oversized whirlpool tub in another room set in front of a huge bay window that gave an excellent view of the gardens. Inside the tub he counted at least five people — two male and three female and all likely underage — enjoying themselves at the hands or mouth or genitals of someone else.

It could have been the set of an elaborately produced bit of feelie porn, but it lacked the sleaze. There were no mustachioed and tattooed men swinging their oversized phalluses like Excalibur, and there were no jaded, glassy-eyed breast augmentation poster girls moaning in cinematically exaggerated pleasure. These were innocents exploring what in Jon's youth was completely forbidden — or at least inaccessible given the company he kept. He imagined that despite the amount of it going on here, someone from local law enforcement would also think it quite illegal. The minimum age for participants at this retreat seemed to be 16 years old, and Jon imagined the state of South Carolina, in prosecuting Whitaker for corruption of multiple minors, wouldn't be inclined to listen to any First Amendment "freedom of religion" arguments in his own defense.

"As you can see, Jonnie," the Reverend said as they walked out of the pool house, "we encourage our younger members to explore the sacred union between men and women to steer them away from self-destructive behaviors later in life. Veronica and I feel that so many problems in the world begin when men and women simply can't get along, and so much of that begins when we're young. If we can remove the jealousy, the competition and the stigma from young people when their sexuality is blossoming, we think it makes them better adults and better members of the church."

Jon would have replied with something more intelligible than nods and well-placed "Mmm hmms" if he didn't have a clear view over Whitaker's shoulder of his wife leaning down to administer deep, long kisses to both the boy and girl in one of the pool house couples. As if that wasn't striking enough, Veronica then allowed the boy to slide a hand under her sarong and momentarily fondle her before she followed them out, her eyes locked on Jon's, her hips swaying enticingly to each side as she readjusted her thin wrap.

Jon's distraction apparently went unnoticed by the Reverend, who was too caught up in describing every aspect of the estate, along with the church's positions on everything from birth control — they provided it for their young guests at no cost — to the impending broadcasts into China and the Pacific rim. Jon caught bits and pieces along the way, but if asked to repeat any of it, he could only describe what Veronica was doing to him or herself as her husband spoke.

Things only got worse from there. From the pool they went to a large garage and climbed aboard an electric golf cart. Whitaker drove with Jon beside him in the passenger seat. Veronica reclined in back with one leg propped on the seat, her thin skirt falling open to reveal the high cut of her bathing suit.

They drove along thin gravel paths that seemed to connect the entire estate, stopping first at the sculpture Jon had noticed when he arrived. Whitaker proceeded to describe the story on which the figure was based, noting that in the Bible it never exactly referred to the ages of the "little children" Jesus invited to his side against their parents' protests. "Given our active youth recruitment and emphasis on creating a holy atmosphere in which people can indulge their physical and spiritual desires, we thought the sculpture quite appropriate for the estate," Whitaker said. "And it's inspired some very interesting interpretations of the story in our youth organization's dramatic productions."

"Mmm hmm," Veronica said, not trying to hide the suggestive tone in her voice. "We have the boys almost fighting to play Jesus in that one. And they're all usually as hard as that granite sculpture during the show."

He imagined such a state of arousal wasn't uncommon on the Whitaker estate, but he still felt more than a bit self-conscious about his own noticeable state.

Again they climbed aboard the cart and whirred off down the pathway. The next stop was the stables, an impressive array of structures befitting the world-class steeplechase training center in his own town of Carlton. There were more adults around there, probably members of the full-time estate staff. Still, though, the equine area had its share of desirable young people roaming about performing a number of chores.

"This is quite impressive, Reverend," Jon said, noting that the young women working in the stables wore the usual jodhpurs and boots, but were all wearing sports bras, thin white tank T-shirts or bikini tops. The young men were dressed the same from the waist down and wore no shirts, a fact that was not lost on Veronica as they entered the shade of the stables.

Though those inside took notice of their entry, work continued until Veronica called to a young man using a pitchfork to heave hay into one of the stalls. He had the lean, fit build of a swimmer and a complexion darkened by either many hours in the sun or many applications of self-tan lotion. Sweat ran down his face and the center of his chest and matted his bleached-out hair against his forehead.

"Wade, this is Mr. Temple. He's going to help us get our satellite up and running." Jon shook the young man's hand and they exchanged pleasantries. "Wade is part of our youth missionary program that will travel to the East once we begin broadcasting."

"Very impressive, Wade. Congratulations on being chosen. It sounds like it should be an exciting trip." The young man could barely keep his eyes off Veronica as Jon spoke.

"It will be, Mr. Temple. I don't think anything is more exciting or motivating than being chosen to spread the word of Christ in other lands." As well as spreading the legs of a few dozen Asian converts, Jon thought.

"Well, good luck on your trip, Wade. If everything goes according to schedule you won't have to worry about my end of the bargain. We'll get that satellite up there for you to do your good work."

"We really appreciate it, Mr. Temple. Thanks for helping us out." Jon shook the young man's hand again and he returned to work, Veronica taking a moment to visually devour him as he resumed heaving hay over the stall door, biting her finger as she watched.

"Wade is one of our brightest young stars around here. His first youth retreat was last year after his parents joined the church. Since then he's taken particular interest in all of Veronica's pet projects, especially the missionary work."

Not to mention a turn or two in the missionary position, from the looks of things, Jon thought. He wondered if there was a young man on the estate that day that Veronica had not benefited with her own special brand of private evangelism. From the looks of things it seemed unlikely. And no doubt if there were any who had gone without sampling her charms, their turns would be up soon.

It was back in the golf cart and on to the gardens, elaborately designed and arranged to reflect the Antebellum style of the rest of the estate. While Whitaker led the way through one of several garden "sitting rooms" arranged with encircling hedgerows, marble benches and small statuary — erotic, of course — Jon found Veronica next to him sliding the left shoulder strap of her bathing suit down to reveal her freckled breast. The pale flesh exposed, she moistened a finger with her tongue and lightly stroked the hardening nipple, the dappled sunlight from between the sprawling live oaks overhead playing over her skin and hair. Whitaker was either oblivious or totally aware of what was going on and didn't care. He was rambling on about how the gardens were based on a design he found on a map of the original plantation and how the oaks had been around since before America had been colonized.

That led him into a soliloquy on how the founding fathers — as well as the area's indigenous population — would have approved of what he was doing. "The Indians, you know, Jonnie, were great fans of using mind-altering substances as part of their religious rites. They sought visions as guides for how they should live their lives, and by providing certain controlled substances to my congregation, I'm doing the same thing. I wish everyone could spontaneously have the same experience that moved me to create the church, but many folks need a little bit of help in that department," he said, still unaware of what his wife was doing behind his back.

"Lawrence, darling," Veronica said, covering herself again before her husband looked around. "I'd like to show Jonnie the grapevines. Do you mind?" She could hardly stand still with the excitement — feigned or genuine — of doing so, and Whitaker took notice, obviously enjoying her girlish glee.

"I suppose, dear, but be right back." He seemed disappointed that he would be momentarily deprived of his captive audience. "I'm sure he's got other things on his schedule this afternoon."

Veronica immediately took Jon's hand as she skipped back to the path and towards the vine, a long, dense, low structure at the edge of the garden which seemed to have walls made of wide leaves growing over lattice. Inside, it was dim and cool and smelled of earth and vegetation. It reminded him of his childhood in Carlton.

"Have you ever had a scuppernong grape, Jonnie?" she asked excitedly as she turned to him, seeming hopeful that he hadn't.

"Yes, but it's been a long while. My aunt used to have a vine like this."

"I love this place," she said, turning away from him and toeing the spotty grass beneath her. "Sometimes if I'm not feeling great, I come out here just to think and relax. It's always so cool, even when it's really hot outside like today."

"It does feel much better under here," he said, taking a moment to wipe the residual sweat from his forehead.

"Sometimes I like to come out here to pray, too. I do a special prayer when I'm out here. Would you like to see it?" she asked, her eyes wide in what he imagined to be feigned innocence.

Jon had never been invited to watch anyone pray before, but considering everything else he had watched her do that afternoon, observing a prayer would be the least of his worries. "Sure. I'd love to."

"You know what the great thing about scuppernongs is? The have really thick skins that you have to peel off before you can eat them. That makes them really firm," she said as she sat cross-legged against one of the vine's supporting posts, delicately arranging her sarong before reaching behind her and pulling two fat, reddish-green pieces of fruit from within the leaves. She placed both on the ground between her legs and assumed a meditative pose, breathing deeply in through her nose and exhaling through her mouth with her eyes closed. This went on for at least a minute, enough time for Jon to begin worrying that Whitaker would come looking for them. Somewhere in the back of his mind he also feared Linda would appear to find him in the middle of yet another reprehensible act.

Then Veronica's hands rose gracefully, the fingers of each hand touching an opposite shoulder, then tracing down slowly over her breasts, where they lingered momentarily, encircling her nipples through the material of the bathing suit long enough for them to stiffen again. Her fingers then continued their downward journey, delicately stroking beneath each breast and along the outside.

Veronica's breathing was becoming more rapid, a light flush developing on her chest and up to her throat. Her hands again inched downward over her stomach, then down between her legs where her fingers efficiently slipped beneath the bathing suit's fabric to pull it aside.

While Jon was reeling at the position she had put him in should they get caught, he was at the same time mesmerized by her "prayer." His body, too, was rebelling against him.

Her left hand held the fabric away from the skin and her right hand then began a slow stroking motion around the narrow, manicured length of fiery red curls, her hips responding to her own touch by slowly gyrating. Her finger then traveled farther down, tracing the lips he imagined had already become moist from her continuous displays, then pressed inside, her body stiffening then relaxing in a single moment.

Jon's discomfort had already reached the point where keeping the Whitakers happy — particularly Veronica — was the only thing forcing him to remain and witness this, hoping to himself that it would end soon and without the two of them being discovered.

Veronica reached for the grapes she had plucked from the vine. As her legs moved from crossed to spread, she held them both in her right hand. Suddenly she gasped and her back arched. Delicately, with almost surgical precision, she was pressing one of the grapes inside her, her middle finger guiding it in slowly after she nestled it against the parted inner lips. As it disappeared, he quickly remembered the other grape. It followed the first one. After the fruit had been completely inserted, Veronica paused to stroke with her middle fingertip the erect pearl partially hidden beneath her strawberry thatch. Her gyrations increased in intensity. Veronica bit her lip and whimpered, no doubt to avoid more excessive vocal expressions.

Each second now seemed like an eternity during which Whitaker would have plenty of time to rush in, discover the two of them and shoot them both dead, even if he was the type of guy who enjoyed knowing his wife was screwing other men. Jon's senses were giving him fits. Between Veronica's visuals and every noise outside the vineyard sounding like it was her husband approaching, he didn't know whether to begin pleasuring himself to relieve his distress or run.

Veronica's body tensed to come. The muscles in her stomach and legs tightened and her mouth opened in a delicious ruby circle, but the sound caught in her throat, ending in an almost childlike gasp as her body allowed her to breathe again.

Gradually she regained her composure, adjusting her bathing suit and returning to a cross-legged position. Her eyes still closed, she resumed the deep breathing with which she had begun the display. After about ten cycles of inhalation and exhalation, she took a final breath that seemed to be designed to fill her toes with air, then released the air slowly, with a small sigh.

"Amen," she said, a sly smile crossing her lips before she opened her eyes and looked straight at Jon. "So, Jonnie ... what did you think?"

Before he could answer he heard Whitaker calling across the garden. "Veronica, darling! I think Jonnie's seen enough of the grapevine, don't you?"

"I'll be right there, sweetheart," she called as she stood and made some final adjustments to her appearance. "I supposed we'd better go before my husband thinks we're up to something scandalous, don't you?" She stepped forward then, only a few inches separating the two of them, reaching down to stroke a finger up and down along the very obvious indicator of his excitement. "And Mr. Temple, I suggest you keep that pistol holstered until you're prepared to use it. Otherwise, you could hurt someone." And like that, Veronica passed him and skipped girlishly out from beneath the vine to meet her husband.

Throughout the rest of the tour of the garden and in the golf cart on the way back to the house, Jon felt as if Whitaker's eyes were on him, intently regarding him with the suspicion he deserved. But the Reverend chattered on as if there were nothing wrong, explaining the historical or religious significance of various sights as they passed. All the while, Veronica reclined in the back seat, giving him a contented smile whenever he happened to look in her direction.

By the time they arrived back at Jon's car it was nearly three o'clock. Having indulged the Whitakers' hospitality and endured Veronica's torture long enough, Jon thought it would be a good time to mention that the papers for the final step in the purchase process had still not been signed.

"Such preoccupation with business, Jonnie. Where's the focus on the spiritual? The mysteries of the universe?" the Reverend asked. "I tell you what. We'd still love to see you at the service tonight, and if I don't agree to sign the papers until after then you'd have a perfect excuse to join us and celebrate the power of the Lord. And considering your potential importance to the future of our ministry, I'd like you to be Veronica's and my special guest at the service tonight so we can introduce you to our church and television congregation."

"Please, Jonnie," Veronica, said, barely pouting, before he could object. "It would mean ever so much to all of us, and we really think you'll have a wonderful time. Then after the service, we can get together with Lucas and do all that nasty paperwork. What do you say?"

He had them in the bag, it seemed, and were he not destined to be won over by Veronica's deadly combination of girlish excitement and womanly sexuality, he admitted to himself that he had to give in for the good of Eli's mission. It seemed Scheafer was the one with whom he had been allowed the least amount of contact, even though finding out about him was the primary goal of the entire sordid enterprise. Besides, it would be interesting to see the orgiastic event live and in person rather than in edited snippets on late-night TV.

"You both have been so kind, there's no way I could refuse you invitation. What time should I arrive?" Jon found himself saying.

"Excellent," Whitaker said, rubbing his hands together with glee. "And forget any nonsense about getting yourself there. The service begins at nine, so we'll have a car pick you up at your hotel at seven. That way we'll have some time for some fellowship before the service. That sound all right?"

"That'll be fine. Is there any mode of dress that's most appropriate?"

"Just three words, my friend. Dress to impress. Of course, it's unlikely such a fine specimen as yourself would go unattended to even if you arrived in sackcloth and ashes," the Reverend said, giving Jon a friendly pat on the shoulder.

At that exact moment, Josh, the young butler, arrived with Jon's briefcase, which Jon took as a cue that it was time to leave. "Well, then. I look forward to seeing you both tonight," he said as he took the case and walked towards the car.

Just as he slid himself into the low seat and closed the door, Veronica broke away from her husband and skipped to his car. He lowered the window and she leaned forward, resting both arms on the car door. "Jonnie, I almost forgot something." She opened her right hand to reveal two plump, glistening scuppernong grapes, slightly crushed, the moist flesh erupting from the thick skin at several points along the surface of each. "I wanted to give you one of these before you left," she said, plucking one from her hand and placing it at Jon's mouth, which opened to accept it before the implications hit him.

He absorbed the distinctly sweet tangs as she leaned forward to kiss him, her tongue snaking along his lips and around the grape.

"Thank you for a lovely day," she said after breaking the kiss, her chin now resting on her hands. "And this," she said, holding up the other grape, "is just a taste of things to come."

PART THREE

REVELATION

"Larry, darling, it's clouding up a bit," Veronica Whitaker said as she lowered her oversized sunglasses, looked out from beneath the umbrella and examined the darkening sky. "Do you think it might storm?" She so disliked it when it rained on the nights of the church's services. But they had something to be thankful for, she supposed, since the day had been gorgeous and she'd had the chance to meet Jonnie. She particularly enjoyed that part of the day, especially when he got all cute and blushy while she was praying under the grapevine.

Larry was murmuring intently into the air as he watched his words transcribed on the hovering 3-D display of his FlexReader. She watched him as he sat forward to confirm her assessment of the weather, the way his chin was defined when he looked up, the way his sculpted chest shone in the afternoon light, his hair moist at the temples where it was beginning to gray. She loved seeing him like this, lost in the spirit as he dictated his sermon, knowing the effect his words would later have on the congregation of faithful gathered under the Ocean Cathedral's towering spires.

He muttered in agreement and returned to his dictation, but not before he caught Veronica looking at him and smiling. He smiled back and continued with his sermon as she adjusted her sunglasses and lay back in the chaise. She knew she shouldn't disturb him again, but she couldn't help wondering what his reaction to their lunch guest had been.

"Sweetheart, I think we made an excellent choice going with Jonnie on the satellite project, don't you?"

Still reclined, she turned again to look at her husband, who had already instructed the device to pause. "Absolutely, my love. He seemed to have everything in order and also seems to be an upstanding gentleman."

"And don't you think he was just the biggest cuddly doll? I thought I was going to just eat him up as soon as he sat down for lunch." She could feel herself getting all squiggly inside again just thinking about it.

"So I noticed," he said, chuckling. "For a moment I thought you were going to scare the poor fellow away."

"Oh no," she said, rolling over on her side to face him, her lavender-painted toes pointed and one knee drawn up in a pose she knew her husband would appreciate. "He was quite fearless. And he seemed to appreciate what he saw, too. He was very excited the entire time he was here. I can't wait to see him at the service tonight."

She had already done her best to restrain herself from thinking about Jonnie's impending presence after their interlude earlier, but now the thoughts came rushing up from her subconscious in better quality 3-D than on a FlexReader. Her sensitive nipples hardened beneath the material of her bathing suit and her hand unconsciously trailed down her torso.

"Gracious, darling," Larry said. "I think our friend Mr. Temple had more of an effect on you than I imagined." Veronica could tell in his voice that he was enjoying watching her, hoping she would proceed further. Her legs were already parted slightly, allowing her fingers to find their way beneath the high-cut bathing suit material – what Larry liked to call her Holy Cross. It was already more moist there than she expected it to be, her body issuing a familiar baptism, a sign that what she was doing was a good and righteous thing in God's eyes.

In the midst of her reverie, her eyes opened to slits and she saw Larry's hand moving, too. Once the feeling overook her she knew she had to act on it. She knew it wouldn't be long before he was just as aroused.

"Are you enjoying watching me, darling?" she asked, the narrow piece of material now pulled entirely to the left, her middle finger slowly slipping inside.

"The spirit is flowing through you today, isn't it Veronica?" He increased the rhythm of his strokes along his engorged shaft, now fully emerged from his sarong. He would be very close soon, and Veronica decided that she didn't want him to go any further without her.

In one fluid motion, she threw a folded towel on the pool deck between them and kneeled at her husband's side, feeling the heat from his body on her face as she leaned forward to delicately kiss his fingers as they moved slowly up and down his length. This, she thought, is a truly holy thing, a sanctified obelisk representing the power of the Lord flowing through him. For a moment she hovered over it, teasing him by looking into his eyes and licking her lips. As if suddenly picking up the psychic message she was trying to send, he released his grip, allowing Veronica to immediately take over, gently cradling his hardness in her loose palm and allowing her breath to play over the tip. At each moment she exhaled, she felt a slight shudder run through Larry's body. She enjoyed having him at her mercy like this, reminding him that she was the inspiration for his successful ministry, that she was the good woman behind this successful man.

"Whom do you worship?" she asked, accentuating the consonants to tease him even more.

"You, darling," he moaned, his head rolling back and his eyes closed. She smiled, knowing he enjoyed giving himself up to her as much as she enjoyed taking over.

"And who is your goddess?"

"You are," he sighed, barely audible.

The clouds parted and a warm shaft of sunlight broke through directly onto her back, like the hand of God himself pushing her forward to engulf him, which she did. She took him deep into her mouth as she felt his body rise and writhe in response, his hands gripping the armrests of the lounge chair so tightly that she heard the fittings groan and squeak.

Then, as suddenly as she'd felt the need to consume him, there was motion on the pool deck behind her husband. A figure, standing respectfully still, waiting.

"Ahem," it said without the slightest attempt at subtlety.

Her mood destroyed, Veronica released her husband and let her head fall to his lap in exasperation.

"What is it, Lucas?" she said, not hiding her aggravation.

"I'm terribly sorry to interrupt, Mrs. Whitaker, but we had an appointment at four o'clock. We're still having some trouble with our supplier for several of the catalog items."

She looked at her watch, confirming the time. "So we did. Why do you always have to be on time, Lucas? Didn't you see we were in the middle of something?"

"It's all right, dear," Larry said, emerging from the wave of sensory overload she had inflicted upon him – and inflicted well, damn it – to try and smooth her ruffled feathers. "Go and meet with Lucas. It's obviously important."

"I'm so sorry, darling," she said, patting him gently where he was already beginning to soften. "I promise I'll make it up to you at the service tonight."

"Of course you will, sweetheart. Now go have your meeting."

Lucas kept a respectful distance as Veronica rose and adjusted her bathing suit to make herself presentable again. Not that it mattered, of course. Despite the almost constant presence of young, attractive and often naked young people – not to mention herself – she had never seen Lucas express even a passing interest in sex or anything sexual. There was not even a lingering glance over the body of one of their many young disciples or any evidence that he was in any way excited by the goings on. He was all business all the time – some would say the perfect employee as a result. But it frustrated Veronica to no end, because whether she chose to admit it to herself or not, sex was one of her most powerful human relations tools. As such, she found him occasionally tedious and frequently frustrating.

She wrapped the sarong around her waist and bent down to kiss her husband as she adjusted it. "I'll be back as soon as I can, darling. Don't start anything without me."

"Don't worry, love," he said as he tucked himself back in. "I'm saving it all for you."

In a moment her face changed from the pleasant smile she kept for her husband to the more severe face she reserved for business. She knew Lucas noticed, because she saw him almost stand at attention as she approached.

"Again, Mrs. Whitaker, I do apologize. It wasn't my intention to interrupt." His voice betrayed no remorse. It sounded to Veronica like something being produced from an emotionless machine, a pretty accurate description of Lucas, now that she thought of it.

"Forget it, Lucas. Let's just go ahead and get this over with."

She followed him into the cool of the house, their steps echoing across the wooden floors until they reached the double doors of Lucas's office, where he opened the door for her and ushered her inside. She couldn't ever recall being invited to Lucas' office – most of their business was conducted poolside or in her and Larry's offices. She couldn't imagine what might be so serious that Lucas must violate the sanctity of his private space.

The room was dimly lit with all the shades closed and the curtains drawn over them, only thin beams of dusty light penetrating the room from outside. Veronica paused a moment when she noticed that not only was the room dark, but smelled slightly of mold. She wondered where it came from and made a note to have Lucas get the air-conditioning system fixed as she sat in a leather wingback chair facing his desk.

After Lucas closed the door and arranged himself behind the desk, they were ready to get down to business. "Now, Mrs. Whitaker, I must confess to you first that I might have misled you about some things."

"Misled me? Lucas, whatever for?"

"Suffice it to say that all the catalog goods have arrived and are in stock and no shipments will be delayed. That was merely a ruse to allow the two of us to speak privately."

She was on her way out of the chair. "Lucas, I'd much prefer Larry be here for this. You know that any concerns of yours should be shared with both of us."

"Mrs. Whitaker, please don't go. I chose to speak to you privately only because of a deep wish not to burden your husband with too much at this very intense time. My concerns, you see, have to do with our visitor this afternoon, Mr. Temple."

"Jonnie? What on earth could worry you about him?"

"It's difficult to explain," he said, leaning back in his chair and knitting his fingers together. "Of course we did an exhaustive background search on him before he arrived, as well as on his firm as soon as they presented us with a bid for the project. Naturally everything was in order, or he wouldn't have made it this far in the process."

"So far I don't see what might prompt your worries, Lucas." She was beginning to get impatient and wished he would get the point, for goodness' sake.

"Unfortunately, I can't really explain it effectively. It's more of what you might call a gut feeling. Frankly, Mrs. Whitaker, despite the fact that everything about Mr. Temple and his firm checked out fine, I've a feeling that everything is just a bit too perfect."

She laughed slightly and nervously adjusted her sarong. "Really, Lucas, it does seem now that you're wasting my time with this. I spent quite a lot of time with Jonnie today and I didn't get the impression that there was anything wrong with him at all." In fact, there were quite a few things very right with him, she thought.

Lucas became very serious then, leaning forward onto his desk and regarding her with a penetrating gaze. "Mrs. Whitaker, you know that I make it my first obligation at all times to protect the interests of the church and everything with which it is involved. And as a result, I occasionally have to use such crude methods as gut instinct and intuition to do my job. Unfortunately, the world outside this plantation is harsh and often unwilling to accept things that diverge from the status quo, and we are doing nothing here if not challenging the status quo. Our methods and beliefs are, despite our growing membership, strange to some and distasteful to many, which usually prompts concern from a variety of organizations and government agencies. So far, we have managed to maintain our organization as we like it without outside interference. But as our word spreads and others learn of us, it can be safely assumed that eventually members of those organizations or agencies will want to examine us more closely. Am I making myself clear, Mrs. Whitaker?"

She didn't like being lectured to, and that's exactly what Lucas was doing, making her feel like a little girl when it was she that should be wielding the power in that room. She had always wielded the power over the men in her life, and it was unlikely things were going to change now. "Are you saying you think Jonnie might not be who he says he is?"

"It is always a possibility, Mrs. Whitaker. We are reaching a level of visibility where it is only a matter of time before the government becomes interested in our activities. I think it's always safe to be on one's guard when such a situation exists, don't you?"

"Of course. But I have to ask you again why you're not including Larry in this discussion."

"It's very simple. I'm quite aware of the rapport you established with Mr. Temple today, and I believe we can use that to find out if my suspicions are correct. All I ask is that you continue your plans of staying as close to him as possible in the hopes of noticing anything suspicious. If you suspect something, I ask that you report it to me first so we might allow your husband to focus on more important matters."

It suddenly struck Veronica that this was a milestone. Never before had Lucas made such an obvious entreaty for her or her husband's assistance, which obviously meant that he was very much in need of it. It also meant that he was very much in a position to make a deal. But probably not the one Veronica had in mind.

Almost without realizing what she was doing, Veronica rose and moved, catlike and with sudden determination, to the opposite corner of the desk, resting against it so her leg showed through the high slit where the sarong wrapped around upon itself. "You know, Lucas, you're asking quite a large favor. It's not my usual practice to go around spying on the men I'm attracted to. I don't know if I can rationalize this sort of behavior, even if it is in the best interest of the church."

Lucas's face betrayed no reaction. "Please, Mrs. Whitaker," he said, his voice flat and emotionless.

"Veronica, Lucas," she said. Now it was a challenge, and one she refused to lose. How dare he be so blasé. She lifted herself to fully sit on his desk and propped her tiny feet up on the armrests of his chair. "There's no reason for such formality when we're on the verge of making such an important breakthrough."

"I'm not sure I understand." Again, flat. Was he a eunuch, for goodness sake?

"It's a simple exchange of services, Lucas," she said, unwrapping the sarong and leaning back on one arm, using the fingers of the other hand to stroke slowly up and down her thigh. "You ask a favor of me, and in return I ask a favor of you. Isn't that how it normally works?"

"Yes, but…"

"It's not like I'm asking you to make any more of a sacrifice than you're asking of me, is it Lucas? After all, there are worse things you could be asked to do than make your beloved employers happy." Her free hand was now making a path higher, over the material between her legs, then slipping beneath with practiced fluidity. "And I think you understand what would make me happiest right now."

"Mrs. Whitaker, I simply couldn't. It simply wouldn't be proper." She was moving from aggravated to furious. No man had ever been so nonchalant in her presence. At that moment she threw out all the accepted tenets about employer/employee relations – which she tended to ignore anyway – and wanted only for him to take her.

"Oh, proper, shmoper," she said, gently snapping at him and giving him a less than fierce scowl. "I'm surprised Larry's trusted you this long knowing you haven't slept with me. It just isn't done, don't you know that? C'mon, now. Don't be a scaredy cat."

With that she reached down to take his hand and place it on her thigh in the hopes it might make itself upward of its own accord. Instead, she found herself recoiling at the feel of his skin. It was cool and clammy, not like the cold sweats of a person who was nervous, but more like someone had made a gelatin mold of a human and set him up in front of her.

The phone next to her on the desk began to quietly chirp.

Lucas noticed the revulsion on her face and immediately tried to cover for it, still unfazed by the sexual energy she was doing her best to project. "I'm sorry, Mrs. Whitaker, but you must excuse me to take this call." Still he was all business.

Veronica regarded him for a moment more, then slid off the desktop and rearranged her sarong as Lucas led her back to the door, taking special pains, she noticed, not to make any further physical contact. Before he opened it for her, he again gave her a deeply serious look, the phone still chirping in the background. "I'm sorry to rush you out, but I'm assuming our arrangement is still in order?"

"Yes, I suppose," she said, still trying to get rid of the all-over creepy feeling. "If it's this important to the church, I'll be glad to let you know if I notice anything unusual."

"Thank you," he said, opening the door. "Now, if you'll excuse me?" She took the hint and stepped into the hallway, resolving to let herself forget the abortive attempt at seduction and be the good minister's wife. Her back to him, she turned and looked over her shoulder. "And as always, nice doing business with you, Lucas." He grinned weakly as he closed the door and she started back down the hall.

But as hard as she tried, she just couldn't get the awful sensation of his clammy skin out of her head. And what was so important about that phone call that he couldn't take it while she was in the room, anyway? After all, she was High Deaconess Veronica Whitaker, whole partner in all things having to do with the Church of the New Revelation. All decisions came down to her and Larry, didn't they? So there was no reason why she shouldn't know what was going on inside Lucas's office right now.

She stopped and removed her wooden sandals that had made such a racket coming in from the pool and tiptoed back to the double doors, trying to avoid creaking boards and making sure to place her ear against the door as gently as possible.

"I'm sure I don't know what you're talking about," she heard Lucas say, followed by a momentary silence. He didn't sound like he was talking to anyone about the church. In fact, it sounded more like a crank call.

"I'm sorry, did you say Nikura? I wish you had been more specific earlier, sir. Perhaps we can make an arrangement for the item's safe return? A reward would be in order, of course." There was a pause while the party on the other end spoke. Apparently whoever it was did not speak kindly.

"I assure you, sir, there is no reason to make threats. I'm quite capable of discussing this in a civilized fashion if you are," he said. Again a pause. Veronica was doing her best to control her breathing so there would be even less of a chance she would be detected.

"I'm afraid I must object to a meeting. Perhaps there is another way we can accomplish this? It would be most unfortunate for me to have to resort to other measures to ensure the item's safe return," Lucas said.

Other measures? Lucas was suddenly sounding less like the business director of a church and more like a mobster, Veronica though.

"I see," Lucas said. "I was beginning to wonder about their whereabouts. Fine then. A meeting it is." There was a lengthy pause as Veronica imagined Lucas was given the meeting location. She was not by nature a nosey person, but she wished at that moment she could hear what was being said on the other end and who in the world was saying it.

"Fine. I have the instructions."

Veronica heard him hang up the phone and as quietly as she could, turned and tiptoed back down the hall.

"How'd I do?" Mako said, folding up the tiny telephone and handing it to Yoshi, who kept one hand on the steering wheel and both eyes on the road.

"Given that I have little experience in either extortion or subterfuge, I am not the best judge. But under the circumstances I would have to say it was adequate," he said over the roar of the tires as they sped toward Myrtle Beach.

"Yoshi, guys who have no experience in subterfuge don't sneak into houses to kidnap their employers' sons in the dead of night," Mako said flatly.

"Point taken. It would seem my extensive qualifications for accompanying you continue to grow."

"Okay, kids. Let's cut it out up there. I don't want to have to turn this thing around. Some of us are trying to do some real work around here," Eustace said from the back seat as the wind from the open windows whipped strands of his ponytail across the slim black glasses he wore. His right hand, meanwhile, hovered a few inches over the surface of his computer, the fingers typing into the air, while he occasionally murmured voice commands into an unseen microphone.

"Whatcha working on?" Mako said from the passenger seat.

"Getting in touch with some people who can put me in touch with some people, my man. And calling in a few favors in the meantime. Our friend Roth has been busy, too. I already had some goodies waiting for me when I logged on," he said.

"Such as?"

"Such as the detailed floor plans of the Church of the New Revelation's complex in Myrtle Beach, rendered in lifelike 3-D, compliments of the Horry County Building Inspector's Office."

"How'd we manage to stumble on that?" Mako said.

"Wasn't any stumbling involved. Roth has been busy calling in his chips, too. Turns out one of the county building inspectors is one of The Final Frontier's regulars."

"So we managed to wrangle a personal favor?"

"Not really. All those times he was showing up at our club, his wife and three kids thought he was either at the Baptist Brotherhood meeting or the Masonic lodge."

"Ah, well. No wonder he was so willing to help. At least we know someone who has some extortion experience," Mako said as he smiled at Krista, wedged in the back seat between Barry and Lewis looking like a Pekingese sitting between two pit bulls.

"What I'm wondering," Krista said after her long silence, "is what exactly you guys are going to do with all this information. So far I've seen an assload of guns, a bunch of camouflage and this junk heap we're riding in. We've got a meeting with this guy Schaefer, but what I've yet to see is a detailed plan."

"Damn!" Barry said, looking across Krista at Lewis. "I knew we forgot something before we left. The plan!"

"What? You mean you didn't bring it?" Lewis replied, unsuccessfully trying to suppress a grin.

"No. I thought you brought it."

"You guys think you're funny, don't you?" Krista said, looking up at the two men. "I'm serious. I'm concerned we're just going to barge in there and not know what the hell is going on."

"Well, my dear, we appreciate your confidence," Eustace said, still staring into space like a blind man. "But I think between the Marines, the Special Forces, Nikura International's head of security and a surfer boy who barely skated past a breaking-and-entering conviction …"

"Hey!" Mako said, his head whipping around. "How'd you find that out?"

"Looked up your rap sheet, kid. You seem like a nice guy, but I still like to know about the people I'm working with," Eustace said, then turned again to Krista. "You don't think that between all that know-how we won't come up with something?"

"I suppose so, but so far I haven't seen anything that would indicate we had come up with something. And besides, how come I wasn't in the list of people qualified to help come up with a plan? I've got a little know-how myself."

"My mistake, mademoiselle," Eustace said. "Everyone in this merry band is welcome to offer whatever they think will help. And let's also remember that just because you haven't heard anyone actually describe a plan doesn't mean no one has one. But right now, I'm taking advantage of Roth's forward thinking and taking a little virtual tour of the target. Seems like they split the congregation up when you enter. Church members go into the main sanctuary on the ground floor, while all the gawking *touristas* get sent up to the balcony to watch the festivities from on high."

"Given that we are not members, the process presents something of a tactical problem," Yoshi said.

"It does, at that, but only if we plan to attend the service. If what I have in mind works, we won't need to set foot in that sanctuary. And even if we do, it's not like we can just stroll in the front door demanding to see Mr. Schaefer and threatening to shoot the place up, either. But as heavily guarded as that front door would be, I would imagine the other doors would be pretty well watched, as well, at least electronically." He paused for a moment, his head moving from side to side as he scanned his virtual surroundings. "Oh, man. Electronic is right. I just arrived in the security control room. This place is wired to the gills. Just looking around I'm seeing ten video monitors with about twenty channels apiece. Not much gets away from these folks."

"Another tactical issue?" Mako said.

"Yep. Plus I wouldn't be surprised if the church has some eyes set up all over that block and across the street."

"Um, not to throw too much of a wrench into things, but that might present a little problem," Krista said, sounding like she was concerned she was going to ruin the whole show. "I think when the folks from SHAG grabbed me they took my picture."

"Well, that does present a problem now, doesn't it," Eustace said, typing into the air again. "I think we can take it for granted that they immediately sent a copy of that shot to our friend Mr. Schaefer and that he immediately scanned it into the church's security system. You step too close to that building, sweetheart, and that console in there is going to light up like a Christmas tree. That will probably get the police there, and the last thing we need if there's shooting is the local yahoos joining in and using us for target practice. I just hope the meeting point will be safe from prying eyes."

"I suggest removing Miss Krista from the equation entirely," Yoshi said.

"Hey! What the hell is that supposed to mean? I've got as much right to be in on this thing as anyone. Let's remember who almost got blown up in your ladies room, Eustace," Krista said.

"And she can shoot," Mako added.

"Again, point taken. But you feeling left out is no reason for the rest of us to jeopardize this whole thing. How far away from the church is that meeting point we gave him, Barry?"

"Across the street and about half a block south. It's a Cleaver's, so the focus will be on the waitresses. Can't guarantee it's not under surveillance either, though," he said.

"Ah, hold on," he said after some more virtual typing. "Got an aerial view of the four blocks around the church. The Cleaver's is just dandy for the meeting, but I'm afraid I'm going to have to agree with our man Yoshi on keeping you off the scene, darlin'. That's just a little too close for comfort."

"Great," she said, crossing her arms and pouting. "So what am I supposed to do while you guys are running around doing all the cool stuff?"

"Cool stuff?" Mako interjected, not even trying to hide his indignation. "Weren't you the one ready to walk out the door if you had to deal with any more of this crap?"

"Yeah…" she said, suddenly meek as everyone turned to her and waited to hear her reasoning for changing her mind. "But it was just starting to sound fun."

"Fun? Have mercy, girl. Your mood swings are going to drive me to my grave," Eustace said. "Tell you what, since you're so worried about missing out on all the fun, I'll give you a special job to do. While the big boys are doing all their nasty cloak-and-dagger work, you get to take that fat cash card Mako's holding on to and go down to the Oceanside Hilton about five blocks away from the church to reserve us a nice, cushy suite for the night." Mako wondered how Eustace knew the money was there, but then realized the man had made it his business for a long time to know what was going on around him.

"You're not serious," Krista said, rolling her eyes. Eustace, since he was oblivious to her expressions, carried on as if everything was fine.

"Perfectly. And the best part is Mako will be going in there with you."

"What the hell are you talking about?" Mako said, his face stony.

"Didn't you tell me something about a wanted poster with Mako's picture on it, Yoshi?" Eustace said.

"Yes, very prominently displayed in the nightclub in which we encountered several people apparently seeking the bounty on Mako's head," Yoshi replied from the driver's seat.

"See, kid. Can't have you flashing that celebrity mug of yours around everywhere, either."

"This is so not fair. That asshole probably killed my father and my uncle. I should be going in there with you guys," Mako said, nearly on the verge of a pout himself.

"Kid, everyone here has an interest in seeing this guy get what he deserves. I'm just trying to keep us from getting killed. And if those security cameras around the church pick up a shot of you or Krista, all our good work and good intentions are going to go to waste. Got it?"

Mako paused and glared at Eustace, then realizing it was fruitless turned to his other comrades. None offered him the sympathy or support he sought. "Yeah, got it," he finally said.

"Good. Now, as for Barry, Lewis and Yoshi, you guys are going to be our advance team. I brought along a few toys I'm sure you guys will enjoy. One of you check in my bag there in the back and you'll find some subvocal communicators an associate of mine requisitioned from Ft. Bragg."

"An interesting term to use – requisitioned," Yoshi said. "Why not just say stolen?"

"Aw, now, Yoshi. Stolen is such a judgmental word. Maybe these little doodads wanted to be taken out of that dank old warehouse. Maybe a more appropriate word is 'liberated.' Regardless, we've got them now and I think they'll come in handy. I think I also have one for the glitter twins to share between them."

Barry had reached around and extracted the devices. They consisted of little more than a tiny earpiece and a plastic disk nestled in black foam inside a metal Army-green box.

"How does this work?" Mako said after opening his and examining the disk, which measured little more than a half-inch in diameter.

"You peel the film off the back of the disk and lick it. Once it gets tacky, you press it against the hollow of your throat. Then you take the earpiece and slide it in like a regular earplug. The disk at your throat will pick up and decipher the quietest and least distinct vocalizations in your throat, so you don't really even have to use your mouth. The earpiece, meanwhile, picks up transmissions on the same frequency from about three-quarters of a mile away."

Holding the tiny black disk on his finger, Mako watched as its surface suddenly rippled and changed color to precisely match that of his skin. "Nice little camouflage function on there, too," he said.

"Oh yeah, I forgot to mention that. That'll help keep you from looking like you've got some freaky new dermal slapped on your throat. Now, Yoshi, Barry and Lewis, I'm going to want all three of you to wait in line to get into tonight's service. When I give the signal, I want you to cause some sort of scene. Actually, it's probably best if Barry and Lewis pretend not to know you, Yoshi, all the better to pick a fight with you."

"I agree. And I assume that when the security personnel arrive to inquire, we will then use them to gain access to the building."

"Right you are, sir. Then you'll let me know as I'm meeting with Schaefer. Hopefully we'll be able to use the fact that you fellas are holding down a position inside the church to our benefit. I'm sure Schaefer will be much more reasonable knowing we can bring down the entire church on international TV."

"And meanwhile, Krista and I will be – what? – lounging in the whirlpool bath while we raid the mini-bar and watch a pay-per-view feelie?"

"VR porn really isn't my bag and they always gouge you on the liquor from those courtesy bars, but hey, whatever gets you kids through. Although I'd stop sounding like I was getting the shit end of the deal if I were you," Eustace said.

"That's the truth," Barry said. "Sounds like a pretty good set up to me if you want to trade places, Mako."

"Never fear, big guy," Lewis said as he grinned and winked. "We'll be taking advantage of the facilities soon enough."

Jon decided the thing he needed most was a drink. Something tall and frosty, not too heavy, with just enough of a kick to lay him out and let him forget about his troubles.

Unfortunately, that drink seemed to be as far away as ever. Human traffic clogged New Ocean Boulevard, making it nearly impossible for any sort of vehicle to move at any more than a few miles an hour, giving Jon ample time to mull over his predicament and his thirst. So far, he had struck a deal with a minion of the underworld, witnessed numerous acts of possibly illegal (but no less tittilating) sex, shook hands with a man whose body temperature didn't seem to be above that of a flounder and was partially seduced by an exhibitionist religious fanatic.

It had been a full day.

And in spite of all that, the thing that weighed most heavily on his mind was the thing he could do the least about: Find his wife and tell her what was going on, or at least that he loved her one last time before being banished to heavenly inaccessibility. She was here somewhere, he thought as he scanned the crowds on the sidewalk and milling among the crawling traffic. How hard would it be to find her? Not very, he imagined. He had a few ideas on where she might be, but considering that Eli was constantly monitoring him, there didn't seem to be much he could do beyond what he had already done. Striking his deal with Robert was dangerous enough, but it didn't interfere with the thrust of Jon's mission. In fact, it gave him extra incentive, since Robert seemed just as interested in Schaefer's background as Eli. Jon had never been the sort to play both sides of a dispute, and the last time he had it had been with day and night Metro editors who each had specific – and wildly differing – ideas about one of his stories. Under the circumstances, though, now seemed a better time than any.

Traffic inched ahead as the mid-afternoon sun seared down on the vehicles and throngs of tourists, finally coming to a halt for yet another interminable traffic signal, obviously designed with the pedestrians in mind. Before today it had been so long since Jon had actually driven along New Ocean Boulevard that he'd forgotten what it could be like. Of course, that was when cars and people were about even in number and equal in their disregard for each other. These days, the pedestrians held all the cards, and they constantly played them, stepping out in front of traffic without a thought about personal safety – their own or that of the vehicles' occupants.

Craning his neck to see over the car in front of him, he saw the problem. A gaggle of tourists had wandered into the street, apparently picking up on the fact that they weren't likely to get run over, and were busily snapping photos of the Ocean Cathedral, glimmering in the mid-afternoon sun like a ten-story diamond.

Just then, his eye caught movement close to the car. Jon slammed the brakes and the car jerked to a stop to avoid nudging – at this speed it could only be called a nudge – the attractive young woman in a bikini top and short wrap around her waist who had strolled in front of him. Jon hit the button to lower the window as she approached, hoping to scold her for walking in front of a moving car. He was cut off just as he was about to begin a surprisingly paternal "Young lady, you should be more careful" rant.

"Good afternoon, sir. Welcome to Myrtle Beach, where God's love lives and is waiting for you," she said, producing a slick, full-color tract featuring a prominent photo of the Ocean Cathedral and Lawrence and Veronica Whitaker. "I'd like to personally invite you to the service at the Church of the New Revelation tonight at 9 p.m. so that you may accept God's love into your heart."

"Thanks," he said, waving off the pamphlet and trying not to be too distracted by her adolescent breasts, which she draped over the door as she bent into his car window. "I'm already attending. But maybe I'll see you there."

"That would be a treat," she said, flashing a megawatt smile. "Have a blessed day." She then turned and sashayed back into traffic.

If there was ever any doubt in anyone's mind as to why the Church of the New Revelation was so popular, Jon decided he had only to present that young girl, equally stunning on approach as she was on departure, as evidence. Attractive, shapely, well-spoken, spiritual and scantily dressed, Whitaker's minions made up an insurmountable army of temptation and forbidden fruit. What heterosexual male wouldn't become a regular churchgoer if doing so offered the very realistic prospect of some enthusiastic rumpy-pumpy with a woman such as the one who had just visited him? Or with her and some of her friends, for that matter. Jon recalled having to be forced by his mother to attend his church's youth group as a teen-ager. He was thrilled to discover that the term "youth group" was church code for "spend a few hours pretending to be religious while you flirt with your contemporaries of the opposite sex." Whitaker, realizing that was the way many people felt, simply expanded on it and made it more appealing for grown-ups

Jon noticed other members of Whitaker's covert army traveling among the vehicles. They were all camouflaged in some sort of beachwear, which guaranteed they would fit in with the other bleached and sunburned tourists. They approached cars, RVs and commuter trams with equal impunity, always being welcomed because their sheer aesthetic appeal immediately broke down any wariness. "What harm could such an attractive young woman/man be?" the cars' occupants would think to themselves. Then they would find themselves mysteriously in possession of religious tracts full of testaments and confessionals and artfully posed tableaus of happy men, women and children going about their churchly duties, the pamphlets providing no hint as to the load-bearing beam of decadence that supported the entire organization.

The shutterbug tourists finally out of the street, things began moving again, allowing Jon's speedometer to once again go past 20 miles per hour. Five minutes of relatively unobstructed travel later, Jon pulled up to the curb in front of the hotel, where he watched as the valets argued among themselves about who would park the car. Finally, the manager arrived and seemed to declare, based on the pantomime Jon could make out through the car window, that he would bear the burden. As Jon got out, the valet manager was there at his front fender, standing absurdly at attention. It seemed at that moment that perhaps Eli had gone a bit too far in programming these folks to kiss his ass, but Jon wasn't complaining.

"I'll take care of that for you, sir," the fellow said a little too eagerly. He looked to be in his early twenties and could quite possibly been one of the young retreaters at the Whitaker plantation.

"Thanks. And could you make sure it gets a wash sometime today? I won't be taking it out again this afternoon and I want to get some of that salt off." Jon was pushing his luck with the VIP service, but what the hell.

"Very good, sir," he said, waiting until Jon had stepped inside the lobby to get behind the wheel and roar off into the parking garage.

Inside the lobby it was cool and fashionably sterile, the furniture's varying shades of beige contrasting against the gaudy clothes of most of the tourists milling around as they checked in for their holiday weeks.

Standing there, he couldn't help thinking that he had forgotten something he was planning to do. He then caught sight of the hotel patio on the opposite side of the lobby. The café tables and Pellegrino umbrellas reminded him – A drink! At that moment he realized again how thirsty he was and headed for the pool bar.

It wasn't as hot – or as busy – as he expected it to be. The sun was sitting at enough of an angle to cast the areas closest to the ocean side of the hotel in shadow. A dry-erase sign announced that tonight's happy hour began at 5 p.m., and it seemed most of the revelers were still on the beach sleeping off the festivities of the night before. He looked up at the sky at the developing squall line and imagined the threat of inclement weather might also be keeping them away. Around the pool he saw only an elderly couple lounging on the deck while a child – their grandson, he imagined – played in the water. Nearby, a hotel maintenance man clad in blue coveralls was busy sweeping sand from the stairs that led down to the beach.

Jon perched himself on a faux bamboo barstool and waited, hoping the bartender, who sat on her own stool with her back turned to him, would feel his presence without him having to interrupt her. She didn't, and he found himself growing impatient before he realized after a few moments that she was quietly sobbing. He immediately tried to decide if he should get up and leave her to her misery or inquire as to what was wrong. Before he had a chance, he heard her sigh heavily, apparently trying to compose herself. She wiped her eyes with the backs of her hands and ceremoniously closed a book, which Jon hadn't noticed she was reading. She moved to turn towards him, and trying not to embarrass her, he looked away, examining the way the high sun played on the waves until she addressed him.

When she caught sight of him, she gave a little start. Damn, he said to himself. He hadn't meant to scare her. Now she would think he was some sort of lurking fiend.

"Jon? Oh my goodness. You nearly scared the daylights out of me," she said in a familiar voice, prompting him to turn toward her.

It took Jon a moment. She looked like someone he should know, but there were slight differences that momentarily gave him pause. Finally it hit him.

"Alex? What are you doing here?" She looked even lovelier here than she did when they first met. Her auburn hair was pulled up into a loose approximation of a bun, and her bikini top, colored a light shade of lavender, only served to accentuate the splash of freckles over her chest, shoulders and upper arms.

"What do you think I'm doing here, silly," she said, still dabbing at her eyes. "I'm here to keep an eye on you. I was supposed to be in disguise, but we see how well that worked."

"Great. I should have known I'd get my very own babysitter. That was some pretty sorry undercover work, by the way. At least you weren't trying to look like my wife again. But what's got you so upset?"

"Oh, just this," she said, brandishing a worn paperback book. "Silly stuff, really. Someone suggested I read it."

Jon held out his hand so that he might take a look at it and found himself surprised at her choice. "'A Farewell to Arms'? Good book. I had to read that in high school then found myself reading it again when no one was making me and enjoyed it much more."

"But it's so sad," she said, nearly on the verge of bursting into tears again. "She dies at the end, Jon. Just like that, she gets sick and dies."

"Hemingway was a bit of a melancholy soul. You know how he died, don't you?"

"Well, he never would tell me, but Eli filled me in. When I told Papa I was working on this assignment, he said it might be a good idea for me to read this."

"Interesting choice," Jon said, impressed that Alex was picking her company so well. He wondered for a moment what the significance of that little bit of required reading might be, especially coming from the author himself. But just as quickly, his thoughts were back to his thirst. "So, since you're posing as a bartender these days, think I might have a beer?"

"Sure," she said, smiling sweetly through a few residual tears. "This is a strange experience, me crying over something like this. Usually it takes someone else's real pain to bring this on."

"That's what made Hemingway so great. He could convey so much emotion so effectively in so few words." Jon usually thought it pompous to talk about authors in such a way. It certainly creeped him out when someone else referred to one of his own stories in the same breathless, adoring fashion. Still, Hemingway held a special place in his cynical, bitter heart.

"I guess so," she said as pulled a chilled Asahi from the cooler and popped the cap. "But enough about that. How did your visit with the Whitakers go? I heard through the grapevine that you turned out to be quite popular with Sister Veronica." Her emphasis on the word grapevine revealed Eli had probably filled her in fully on what went on.

"Like you don't already know all the dirt, Miss Alex," he said, returning her knowing grin. "Let's just say she's one of those people who are easy to know," he said.

"Are we talking biblically, here? Because according to what I heard, that red-headed temptress put on quite a little show for you," she said, standing there looking like she was expecting him to downplay the events of which she already knew all the sordid details.

"Have you ever been over there?" he said, trying not to sound too defensive. "The place is an underage sexual fiesta. The entire plantation is overflowing with naked teenagers doing God-knows-what to each other right out in the light of day. Veronica and her little prayer session were just the cherry on top of that sundae, so to speak." He took another swig of the beer, if only to calm the nerve endings still left tingling by Veronica's teasing.

"So, let me get this straight. You were there on her turf, with her broadcasting her intentions with every step, with probably the full consent of her husband, and you didn't swoop in on her like Sherman on Atlanta?"

Jon gazed at her momentarily, then turned away, suddenly concentrating on tracing a line in the ice and condensation on the side of his beer bottle. Thunder rumbled off in the distance, the clouds making good on their threat to ruin the day for beachgoers. "I don't know. The time just didn't seem right. Besides, I figured it would be better to leave her wanting to guarantee I got an invitation to the service tonight."

Then she was in his face, her chin resting on top of her hands clasped on top of the bar. "Baby doll, you're a great actor but a pitiful poor liar. I know exactly what your problem is, and there's no reason for you to be thinking about her any more, okay?"

Then, from beside him, the hotel maintenance man who had been gradually sweeping his way towards them for the past few minutes spoke. "Listen to the señorita, my friend. She knows what she's talking about."

"Pardon me. Can we help you with something – Jesus?" Jon asked as he sat up straight, making sure to use the correct Spanish pronunciation of *hay-soos* after he noticed the man's name embroidered on the patch on the left breast of the hotel work shirt. "I was having a private conversation with the lady."

The fellow's features were those of indigenous America rather than European settlers, and Jon couldn't help wondering why the man's appearance seemed familiar. His brown skin was tanned even more deeply on his face and arms. His black hair he wore closely cropped all around, which only added more emphasis to the thick black mustache that drooped over the corners of his mouth. His eyes were his most striking feature. They seemed impossibly deep and wise for a hotel handyman, at the same time filled with some sort of overwhelming sadness that Jon couldn't identify.

"I overheard your private conversation, and I still say you should listen to the lady," he said. As he leaned on his broom, Jon noticed his huge hands, gnarled from what must have been years of manual labor. His English was impeccable, with only the slightest hint of a Spanish accent. "She knows what she's talking about, and so do I. That wife of yours is pretty and I'm sure you loved her, but you've got more important work to do now, *hombre*."

Jon looked at the maintenance man and then Alex, who obviously didn't know who he was either. "Mind explaining how you knew that, friend?"

"Oh, I'm sorry. Jesus Zabarra, at your service, Señor Templeton," he said as he extended a thick-fingered hand.

Zabarra? He knew he recognized that name, but couldn't remember from where. Then it came to him in a flash of mnemonic light. "Jesus Zabarra, the guy who was organizing the tobacco migrant workers?" It had taken a moment, but there it was. The first thing that flashed through Jon's mind was the slogan that was plastered across billboards in the state's prime tobacco-growing counties against the background of angry Latino agriculture workers in protest: "Big labor. A shot in the arm for workers, or a shot in the foot for South Carolina?"

"One in the same, *amigo*," he said, seemingly amused by the recognition.

Then it hit Jon. One of the items he had seen on the front page of the newspaper on his way to work the day all this began. It had been about Zabarra, and not a happy story, either. "But last time I heard, the word was you were ..."

"Dead. That's right, my friend. Three days ago, coincidentally. Bullet from a 30.06 caught me right about here," he said, pointing to the left side of his head. "Guess those tobacco farmers didn't like the prospect of having to pay their migrant workers more than a few dollars an hour or provide them with decent living conditions. So now I'm a martyr. That's okay, though. I'm used to it by now."

"Oh my gracious, it's him," Alex said, drawing her fingers up to her mouth in shock. This worried Jon more than anything, to see the heretofore unflappable Alex in states of distress twice in such a short span of time.

"Who?" Jon said, now growing frustrated that he was somehow being left out of the loop.

"The Kid. It's him. Damn, is Eli going to be pissed about this."

"You mean ..." Jon felt himself turning white. He turned back to Zabarra. "You're him?"

"Yeah, but you're going to have to trust me, man. The stigmata bit gets a little passe. Besides," he said, hooking a thumb over his shoulder at the family around the pool. "Don't want to gross out the tourists."

"But what are you doing back?" Jon said, almost angrily. Eli had assured him this mission had no apocalyptic implications, but he was growing less inclined to believe anything Eli had to say anymore.

"Relax, man," Zabarra said as he held up both hands to Jon. "This is an ongoing gig. Remember that verse about 'everything you do to them you do to me'? Well, that's what I've been doing for 2,000 years, man, coming back and giving you people another chance, hoping you'll get it right. And even if I wanted to quit, I'd still be outvoted two to one. Being the minority in a trinity is a bitch."

"But why come see me?"

"Just take it from me that there are a number of parties besides your employer interested in a successful outcome to your mission. And unfortunately, every time we look around, all we see is you mooning over your lost love."

"Well, pardon me, but you never had much experience with lost love, if I remember correctly," Jon said.

"Think again, *hombre*. I've got stories that would break your heart. But I'm not here to complain about my own predicament. I'm here to get your attention back where it needs to be."

Jon had had it. He just wanted to toss the whole business out the window and be left alone, but every time he rounded a corner it seemed as if he ran into another impatient deity. He knew what was important to him, and decided he couldn't care less about the problems of those on the astral plane.

"Well, what the hell do you expect?" Jon said, turning fully around on his stool to face Zabarra eye-to-eye. "I get stupid one time and drop dead. Then, instead of going to my eternal reward like I was supposed to, I get yanked to the side to help Eli fill in the blanks left from his divine oversight, then I'm told, 'We need you to save the universe, but by the way, you'll never get to see your wife again.' That's bullshit, my friend. This whole thing is bullshit. I haven't let one moment pass since I walked from my house without thinking about Linda."

Zabarra looked at him gravely. Jon could see his knuckles turn white as his huge hands tightened around the broom handle. "And so far it's done nothing but cloud your judgement. Take that scene over at Whitaker's. You could have had Veronica then and there if you'd shown a little initiative. But no, you had to be the good husband, doing nothing but watching her little show instead of getting in there and getting the information we need. The Boss is trying to be subtle by sending his little cupcake to keep you distracted…"

"Hey, who are you calling a cupcake, handyman?" Alex said, having warily stayed out of the discussion until then.

"… while you're in his employ, but I don't have those kind of tools at my disposal. All I can do is emphasize to you how important this is to everyone involved, yourself included."

"Fuck you." Jon muttered under his breath as he turned back towards Alex.

"What did you say?" Zabarra's hand had a firm grip on Jon's arm. Ready to whip me around to face him, Jon thought. So much for turning the other cheek.

Jon calmly turned toward him once more, this time standing and facing the maintenance man nose-to-nose. "I said fuck you. You and everyone in your celestial good ol' boy network. You all got me for free to do whatever the hell you needed. But you know they say you get what you pay for, so this is what you got as part of your little bargain. Lucky you. But since you folks have me over a barrel, I guess I've got to cooperate, right? Right. But while you and all your winged flunkies on high are flitting around fretting over keeping your heavenly houses in order, I made myself a little side bet."

"A what?"

"C'mon, Zabarra. You must be a gambling man to keep coming back again and again to try and save the human race's soul. We're a longshot. A losing bet. I know for a fact because I wrote about how screwed up we were every single day. But here you come, again and again. What will it be next time? Publicly drawn and quartered? Torn apart by an angry mob? What's the matter? Crucifixion wasn't good enough?" His volume was rising steadily with his level of agitation. And despite the threatening clouds, Jon imagined even the most brutal verbal assault wouldn't get him struck down by lightning.

"Well I'm not a martyr, pal. I'm just some schmuck trying to get through the day. And today I saw an opportunity and I rolled the dice," he said, removing his contract with Robert from his inside jacket pocket. "And you know what? Behind everyone's back I managed to get the thing no one wanted to let me have. So thanks to this, I'll finish the mission gladly. I'll do what it takes and find out what everyone seems to want so desperately to know. And you know what I'm going to do then, Zabarra? When I'm finished with you and Eli and your little club, I'm going to turn my back on all of you, flash this," he said, slapping the contract against Zabarra's chest, "and I am going to go back to my goddamn wife!"

By then he was yelling, feeling the muscles in his face tight and stretched into an angry mask. He looked over Zabarra's shoulder and saw the couple by the pool nervously coaxing the boy out of the water and herding him back inside the hotel leaving nothing but three sets of wet footprints.

He was breathing heavily, still grasping the contract in his hand tight enough to nearly crumple it, when Zabarra snatched it from him.

"Let me see that," he said, opening it from its half fold and reading quickly. His expression changed from one of angry annoyance to one almost of pity, then his lips pursed like Jon's dad's did when he saw something unsatisfactory on one of his report cards from school. "*Cabron*, I thought you were smarter than this."

"Jon, honey, what have you done?" Alex was chewing nervously on her index fingernail, tiny lines forming between her eyebrows.

"Well," Zabarra said, reading from the contract again, "it seems our friend took his meeting with Mr. Robert as an opportunity to make arrangements other than the ones he settled on with the Boss, specifically, to be allowed to return to his wife after the successful completion of the mission."

"Oh, Jon. I honestly thought we were beyond all this," she said.

Jon was concerned at Zabarra's reaction, but he vowed to himself not to let them know that. "Beyond what, Alex? You of all people should have known how I felt. You've known since the very beginning."

"True, dear, but I guess I just put too much faith in my own powers of persuasion."

"Looks like we both have that problem, eh, Alex?" Zabarra said. "But I'm afraid our friend Robert's powers of persuasion are still firmly intact. Tell me, Jon, did you read the fine print on this contract before you signed it?"

"Of course. It's not like I didn't know who I was dealing with. Robert specified a no-strings contract that wouldn't result in loss of my soul or anything resembling eternal damnation and torment."

"At least you knew that much. Can you show me the fine print you read?" he said as he handed Jon the contract.

"Sure," he said as he pointed to the tiny, almost illegible type at the very bottom of the parchment page.

"Mmm. That's what I thought," Zabarra said. "This could present more of a problem than we anticipated."

"Why? What's the matter now? Everything on there should be perfectly legal and binding based on the conditions of the contract," Jon said before he realized he was trying too hard to sound like he knew what he was talking about.

"The problem is that isn't the fine print. That," he said, pointing to what looked like three hairlines at the very bottom of the page, "is the fine print."

Jon felt the color drain from his face, his head swimming with the implications of whatever clauses Robert had chosen to hide. Still, he maintained his composure just as it seemed the people around him were losing theirs. Alex began quietly weeping behind him, while Zabarra simply regarded him with an expression that said he knew only too well what drove Jon to strike such a deal.

"Read it," Jon said, his own voice seeming to echo in his ears.

"Man, I really don't think we ought to dwell …"

"Read it!" He felt like he was shouting. He knew he should be shouting, only not at Zabarra. He should be shouting at himself in the mirror, asking himself how he could be so stupid, so determined to foil the superior forces aligned against him.

Zabarra broke his gaze and lowered his eyes to the parchment. "The signatory agrees that all conditions of this contract will be rendered null and void should contact be made by any means between him and Linda Templeton before the requirements of his primary assignment as outlined section one, paragraph one are executed and rendered complete by the assigning being."

"So, in other words…" Jon began. He didn't need it explained to him. He knew what it meant; he just wanted to hear someone else say it.

"In other words, you've gotten yourself in a bit of a bind, my friend," Zabarra said. He folded the contract and handed it back to Jon. "According to this, if you even catch sight of your wife, even overhear her in a crowd, you're stuck. Robert said she was in town, right? Well, it looks like he set you up to fail, just like he does with everyone else. Except this time, you got lucky. No fire and brimstone for you, but he gets everything he wants and you get to spend eternity with our lovely bartender. Not what you wanted, I know, but still not a bad deal. If you ask me, I think you wasted your time even thinking about cutting a deal with Robert, but I'm a bit biased."

Alex came around the bar, still sniffing and dabbing at her eyes but no longer crying. "Nobody did ask you. And if you were Jon under the same circumstances, you might have done the same thing." Her arm slid under Jon's, her hand gripping his tightly, her warmth coursing through him, relaxing him from the adrenaline rush of his anger. "Oh wait, I forgot about the eternal martyr. Well we're human beings, or at least used to be, and we're not built to sacrifice ourselves forever, no matter what it's for. And even though what Jon did may have been incredibly stupid, I respect him for it. I wish someone had loved me that way back when I was alive."

Jon gazed down at her. Her gaze was firm in the face of Zabarra's, despite the fact that he outranked her by a million links in the heavenly chain of command. He imagined her standing on the battlefields outside Richmond, resolute in her mission to heal in the face of so much death and carnage, refusing to back down against rifle and artillery fire or butcher surgeons. He wondered at once how much likelihood there was of him seeing Linda before the mission was accomplished, then how he would manage spending the rest of eternity with this woman who was so unlike his wife but who made him feel so good. She felt him looking at her and turned her gaze up to meet his, smiling sweetly, her moist, reddened eyes glistening in the light softened by the approaching storm clouds.

Thunder rumbled low and long, signaling that the heavy rain was still at some distance. Though a thousand things swirled through his addled brain, Alex's tender caress seemed to provide clarity to his thinking. He was suddenly able to prioritize again, and realized that no matter what happened to him or what he had mistakenly agreed to, he would somehow be with Linda again. But first he had to take care of the matter at hand, if only to get Zabarra off his back and reassure Alex that he wasn't going to botch the entire mission. He looked at her again and mentally thanked her. She smiled sweetly and squeezed his hand again as if she'd read that very thought, after which he turned his attention back to Zabarra.

"Well, Mr. Zabarra, thank you for the tip. And don't worry about finding out what you need to know. Everything will be taken care of," Jon said. "And as for the remainder of the mission, I don't think any more motivational visits will be necessary, do you?"

"I guess not," he said, stroking his thick mustache. "Still, I want you to promise to stay on target. Deal with Robert or no, you have to get through this and find out what we need to know. An awful lot is riding on it, *cabron*."

Linda Templeton held the black wisp of a dress in front of her, gazing at her reflection in the pitted full-length mirror bolted to the wall of her room. It just didn't seem like her. The neckline was cut ridiculously low and the hemline almost obscenely high, the material the type that, in the right light, could conceivably become transparent. Regina had pulled it from the back of her closet – where she kept all her conservative clothes, she said – and presented it to her as something appropriate for someone visiting a Church of the New Revelation service but not actually participating.

In fact, it was the last thing Linda would ever consider wearing even near a church, but as she was constantly being reminded, this was no ordinary church. She had seen the services broadcast on TV and knew that the decadence hinted at there only scratched the surface of what went on out of the camera's view. But she still felt odd, holding the dress up again and regarding its potential transparency. She lowered it and looked at herself – her normal self – in the mirror.

Two days of misery had taken their toll. Her eyes were still somewhat swollen and red and the two tiny worry lines between her eyebrows wouldn't seem to go away. But standing there, clad only in a newly purchased bra and panty set, she realized her reluctance to wear the dress came from her own hang-ups, certainly not from an inability to carry it off. Everything was still where it was supposed to be, without the sagging and drooping and expanding that so many women regarded as inevitable. It had taken constant work, but she had managed to maintain herself into her thirties without the cosmetic or surgical alterations so many of her contemporaries opted for. That made her feel better about how she would look tonight, but it would take some effort to make her feel better overall.

The last time she had worn a dress like this was when she and Jon took a rare two-week vacation to a resort in Costa Rica before the revolution. She had packed only bathing suits and sunwear, with the exception of one tiny and unusually revealing black dress. She wore it to the end-of-the-week party the resort hosted for its guests who would be departing. Her bare arms, back and legs glowed in the torchlight after an application of sesame oil, the material moving effortlessly against her skin the whole evening. Her favorite part was the response it elicited from Jon, who stood stunned when she appeared from the bedroom in the little bungalow they occupied. That had been her plan, because she never would have worn such a tiny fashion confection to anything back in Carlton, lest she be branded less than virtuous by the local gossips and subsequently hit on by their husbands.

Second to Jon's response was that from the other men at the party, nearly all of whom asked her to dance at one time or another, much to the consternation of their wives or significant others. That had been a good night, she thought, remembering the feel of Jon's assured hand at the small of her back, turning and twisting her along with the Latin music. He took well to the dance lessons they attended for three months before the vacation. She relished the control and precision he exerted on the dance floor, the way her breasts brushed against the material of the dress when he held her close, the way his hand would graze her bottom and he would smile at her as if she were the only woman in the world.

Regina's voice from the living room broke Linda from her reverie. "How's it going in there? The dress look okay?"

"It'll fit, if that's what you mean. I'm just wondering what you wear under it. I don't have a black bra or underwear to go with this."

The younger woman appeared in the doorway, only her head visible from behind a large chest of drawers. Almost magically, with nothing more than a modified hairstyle and the application of some makeup, she had transformed from a young girl just discovering her sexuality to a brazen woman of the world. "Underwear? You're not serious, are you? The less underwear the better. It takes too long to get out of," she said, grinning lasciviously.

Regina then walked all the way into the room and Linda was able to take in the extent of her preparations for the service. Or lack of preparation, as it were. Regina was barely clad in a diaphanous white creation that didn't even have enough substance to warrant being called a dress. In the front, the translucent white material covered her from her throat to her upper thigh, about where a daring miniskirt would normally fall. Except the front was all there was of it, and there wasn't much there. Regina's small breasts were partially obscured only by the horizontal "beam" of a large, gold sequined cross on its front. The wisp of material was totally open in back and tied together much like a fashionable surgical gown, revealing all of the girl's back and backside, covered only by satiny white panties flecked with gold to match the outfit's other component. Her two-inch heels completed the picture, forcing her muscles of her legs, from her ankles up to her bottom, into permanent tautness and reminding Linda of the sheer perfection of the 19-year-old female ass.

"What do you think?" Regina said, striking a comically severe model's expression and strutting from the door to the bed and back again.

Linda held the dress up to herself in the mirror once more and sighed. "I think I need to get over feeling scandalous for even considering wearing something like this. Next to you I'm going to look downright dowdy."

"Oh, come on. You'll look so good all the regular church members will be dying for you to come down into the main sanctuary – men and women. Besides, I don't think you could look dowdy if you tried. Dowdy women slouch. You've got great posture. You'd be surprised how much of a turn-on that is for some men, even if it is just because it makes your boobs jut out more."

They both laughed at the remark, but Linda couldn't help feeling a twinge of sadness. Jon had said after they had been dating a while that one of the things he first noticed about her was the way she carried herself: always determined, with long, proud strides and her head held high and her eyes forward. He said it looked like she knew precisely where she was going and it would take an army to stop her from getting there.

But it was one of a million such twinges she'd felt in the past few days. She began to wonder if she would ever again go through a day without those twinges, because the lingering possibility of never seeing Jon again was growing ever greater, despite the assurances of Detective Robert. She felt as if preparing for this service was in some way a prelude to less pleasant preparations, perhaps for Jon's funeral.

It hurt to say it to herself, but she decided she had to. He had been out of contact for days, and whether she was angry with him or vice versa, staying out of touch like this just wasn't like Jon. Had he been able, he would have tried at some point to track her down or get in touch with her again. Any phone calls to their house in Carlton were being forwarded here and her mobile hadn't left her person, so if he had tried to call she would have known. She had received no e-mails from him or anyone he knew. She had finally spoken to Jon's mother after they returned from the police department, a reckless move that proved to be much trickier than Linda expected. Linda had called from their beach cottage, giving Bonnie the impression that she and Jon were together and that everything was fine. In the course of conversation, though, Linda mentioned that Jon had meant to call her earlier that morning and asked if he had. She hadn't heard a word from him, and Linda said Jon must have gotten too busy fixing up around the house while she was out on the beach. The ruse seemed to work, and Jon's mom was none the wiser.

But Linda knew. And the knowledge of Jon's potential fate gnawed at her. The worst part was feeling so very helpless that all that remained now was to get dressed, put on her best "I'm a strong woman struggling happily through adversity" face and step into the Church of the New Revelation, in the hopes that all her fears might be unfounded.

Jon stood at the French doors leading out onto his hotel room balcony, gazing out to sea and estimating the time of arrival for the approaching storm. He was trying not to think about Robert and Zabarra and Eli and all the others who somehow seemed intent on sacrificing any chance at happiness he might have for their single-minded goals. The clouds boiled up, a break in the lowest layer revealing the anvil tower of condensation rising above the ocean and moving towards land. Occasionally, bright flashes of lightning would spark high above, illuminating the clouds from within, while on the distant horizon he saw streaks of electricity making their ethereal contact between the ocean and sky. He had the room's air conditioning set too high – he could tell by the developing condensation on the exterior side of the windows – but he didn't care, even if it was giving him goose bumps.

Then Alex was there behind him. He hadn't heard her come in, but her aura of warmth was detectable a split second before he felt her arms wrap around him from behind, her palms flat against his chest as he changed focus and caught her reflection in the glass.

"Hey, Mr. Templeton. Got something on your mind?" He felt the fullness of her breasts, the nipples taut from the cool air, pressing against his back through her thin dress as she caressed him. She was trying to seduce him again, trying to lead him to the bed to draw his attention away from his moral torment. He had to admit that were she still alive and still a practicing professional, she would surely have a legion of devoted clients and a very comfortable lifestyle. As fond of her as he was, though, he couldn't help seeing himself in that light. Without even sleeping with her, he saw himself as little more than a client who simply had a very resourceful benefactor willing to provide him with whatever he required to be happy.

The only problem was, as a benefactor Eli fell pitifully short. He had provided Jon with Alex not to keep him happy, but to keep him distracted. Eli knew what would make Jon truly happy, and kept that from him on purpose. And Jon felt himself beginning to chafe under the burden of Eli's misplaced generosity.

"Aren't you already on overtime?" Jon said, his focus again shifting to the rolling storm clouds.

Her caresses stopped. "Mind telling me what that's supposed to mean?"

"It's supposed to mean that I get the hint. Tell Eli he won't need to try any more tricks or send you to put me back on track or keep me distracted or whatever it is you're supposed to be doing."

She removed her hands from him as she stepped back, and again he saw her in the window. Her face was hard, her lips stretched tightly. "You think you know so much, don't you? Damn it, Jon. Are you blind? Can you not see what you're doing to me?"

"Keeping you from some other duty Eli has for you to perform, maybe?"

Now, Jon had been slapped in the head before, but only by his mother during one particularly intense bout of adolescent rebellion. Still, that swat from his mom didn't hurt him nearly as much as the open-handed blow Alex nailed him with. He immediately whipped around to face her. "What the hell was that for? That hurt!"

"You bet it did, mister. That was for calling me a whore." She followed that with another slap to his left cheek, knocking his head to the side with its force. "And that's for being such a narrow, self-centered jackass."

"I don't..."

She stopped him with her upheld palm and a stern look. "Let's get a few things perfectly clear. My working days are long over and the Boss is anything but my pimp, understand? And even if I have no problems with jokes about my former line of work, comments like that are completely uncalled for. And as for my reasons for being here, you get this straight. The Boss has nothing to do with it. I chose to come here on my own, not at his request, Jon Templeton. And I came here because I care about you, not because of any blind devotion to this quest we've put you on. I came because I missed you, because you seemed like you needed some support, not because I was worried you were going to stray. Don't you know that if the Boss ever thought you would seriously deviate from what he asked he wouldn't have hired you in the first place?"

She was crying again, standing there in all her pure beauty, hands on her hips now as tears streamed down her cheeks, breaking Jon's heart worse than before. This was the development he expected least and he imagined it was for exactly the same reason Alex had said. He was simply spending too much time worrying about himself to pay attention to what was going on around him.

The sky rumbled, throwing a low, dull vibration through the glass. Jon stood there, looking at her, the tears subsiding and Alex sniffing and wiping her runny nose. Time to focus, he decided. Linda or not, agreement or not, this business needed to be finished, and deliberately hurting Alex was no way to do it, especially after all she had done for him.

He stepped forward while she held her ground, still glaring at him through teary eyes. He extended his hands in a gesture of openness, of contrition. He tried to tell her with his own eyes that what he said had been said in anger, in the confusion of all the events whirling around him, and in recognition of his undeniable love for his wife. He approached closer still, now close enough to feel the breath from her quiet sobs, then held her, wrapping his arms around her and pulling her close. She buried her face in his shoulder.

"I'm not a whore, Jon. Not for Eli or anyone else," she said, barely above a whisper.

"I know," he said as he stroked her hair, feeling her still trembling.

"And I can't help it if I'm in love with you, either." He imagined that she expected him to turn away, but he held her tighter still, planting a kiss on her forehead as he leaned back to look her in the eye.

"So that's our only problem, then?"

"Problem?" She was upset again. "What the…"

He smiled at her, hoping it would calm her. Thankfully, it did. "You know what I mean, Alex. But as problems go, I'd say that's not a bad one to have. Besides," he said as he pulled her close again. "It's nice to have someone around who I know I can trust."

"Always, Jon. Forever and ever."

Thunder rumbled again in the distance as Jon caught a glimpse of the clock. "It's getting late," he said gently. "I need to get ready for the big night."

Alexandria Chaumont, once of Richmond, Virginia, most recently of some ethereal domain Jon knew only as Heaven, once a prostitute but never a whore, then stepped back and gazed at him for a long moment, her hand reaching up to caress the face that was still somewhat unfamiliar to him.

Then she smiled a different sort of smile than he'd seen before, one he couldn't read despite the time they had spent together. Her face was drying and her eyes were still red, but even inflamed blood vessels couldn't hide the mischievous gleam that had returned. "Okay, then. Since you won't let me scrub your back, I suppose I'll have to settle for picking out your clothes."

Even five blocks away from the Church of the New Revelation, the boulevard looked more like a pedestrian mall than a thoroughfare for cars. Gazing out the window of the Humvee as they crawled along with the other traffic, Mako decided the atmosphere was more like that of Miami's South Beach than a place that was supposed to be a spiritual center. But having had his share of experiences with CNR girls back in Florida, he knew this sort of spirituality went far beyond showing up for church and dropping some money in the collection plate. Those girls put their all into their worship, literally body and soul, willingly giving themselves to members of the congregation without so much as a "Hi, my name is…"

"Looks more like these folks are going to a nightclub than a church service," Krista said. "Most of these people would be more at home on South Street. Check out this guy," she said as they passed a fellow not far from his and Krista's age wearing assless black leather chaps and a matching codpiece, topped off with a cross-shaped breastplate it looked like he had fashioned together out of aluminum foil and a couple of pieces of twine.

"They are a colorful crowd, aren't they?" said Eustace, the VR glasses now removed. "And Whitaker gets 'em young, too. I once got invited to a service in Florence by a couple of girls – couldn't have been more than 14 – wearing less than that guy. Thought I was in the middle of some police sting on pedophiles. Worst part was they were so insistent. I about walked into traffic trying to keep them from touching me while they talked to me."

"I'm afraid there are many others whose treatment of the situation would not have been as ethical," Yoshi said from the driver's seat. "I'm surprised many of their practices have not drawn more attention from the authorities."

"I heard Whitaker keeps the wheels pretty well greased here in town," Eustace said. "Between the CNR and the Catawba casinos, I'm sure the local police don't want for much. I bet if you asked them if they'd investigated underage sex at the church, they'd tell you they couldn't do it until they got a complaint. And I can guarantee none of the people in that service is going to complain about anything. They're all having way too much fun."

And as if conjured forth from Eustace's words, one of the prettiest girls Mako had ever seen suddenly appeared beside their vehicle, easily keeping pace on foot with the slow-moving traffic. He was startled when he saw her not because of her mysterious appearance, but because she was wearing only purple bikini bottoms and a matching – but highly transparent – half-shirt that barely covered her breasts. Her short, blonde hair gave her a look that was probably a little sophisticated for her age, and the misty droplets of rain that had begun to fall sat like morning dew on her nose. The sight was impressive, and had he still been in Florida by himself, he might have chosen to strike up a conversation with her. But he was careful to remember Krista was in the back seat and acted as nonchalant as he could.

"Hello, there," she said, removing a flyer from a stack she carried and handing it in to Mako. "I'd like to invite you to the Church of the New Revelation service tonight at nine o'clock to accept the word of the living, loving Lord into your hearts."

Mako noticed that, like all the CNR girls he'd known, she had a small cross tanned somewhere on her body, this one just visible beneath her top. "A little something to keep your mind on Jesus while we bask in the glories of the flesh," Miranda, one of the CNR followers in St. Augustine, had told him one night after a surfing competition. He had just wished she would shut up with the religious testimonials and get down to business. This time, however, he had to pretend he didn't see it out of respect for the woman he had decided he loved and who wouldn't hesitate to box his ears should she have any concerns that he was looking.

"Thanks," he said, taking the flyer and turning his eyes forward again as they pulled ahead of her.

"Nice bit of self-control, there, surfer boy," he heard Krista say.

"Yeah, well … I know the type. Ignoring them almost doesn't help. I'm just glad traffic started moving before she climbed in and just started humping me right here."

"Oh, that's a charming picture," she said, clearly more amused than upset by the prospect.

"We're here," Yoshi said, thankfully turning Mako's thoughts away from the young disciple. The Humvee stopped in the middle of a crowd of tourists and faithful.

"Okay, kids. You have everything you need?" Eustace said.

"Subvocal communicator, tracking device, cash," Mako said, counting them off on his fingers. Then to Krista: "We forgetting anything?"

"No," she said as she climbed over Barry's lap to the side door. "Now let's get out of here before it really starts raining and those nymphs swarm the truck with their little wet T-shirt party."

"Hey, and keep the communicators off unless there's an emergency," Eustace said. "The rest of us are going to be on the same frequency, and we don't need a lot of idle chatter from you two getting in the way."

"No problem," Mako said as he and Krista hit the pavement. "We won't wait up for you guys."

"Better not," Barry said as he dislodged his pistol and discreetly sighted down the barrel. "The party might run a little long."

∧∧∧

"What do you mean, you can't take a cash card? It's money just the same as anyone else's," Krista said, trying to sound businesslike and at the same time convey her annoyance with the desk clerk, who just stood there, his pursed mouth and patronizing eyes only infuriating her more.

"I'm sorry, ma'am. It's against the hotel's policy to accept any payment without a valid credit card," he said, sounding more like a politely scolding third-grade teacher with each moment. Valid credit card, my ass, she thought. She could tell as clear as day the skinny fuck just didn't like her looks. It wasn't like there weren't a few dozen women younger and sluttier-looking than her roaming around the lobby as they spoke, all the little hussies in town to "worship" in their see-through creations adorned with whatever random religious imagery their hormone-stoked little brains could come up with.

"I'm sorry, but apparently I didn't explain myself clearly enough," Krista said, keeping her voice calm and measured. "I represent one of the performers at tonight's CNR service, and we've had a reservation here for at least three weeks, confirmed by one of your employees two days ago."

It was lame, but it was the best she could think of with such short notice. Jeez, Eustace really dumped her into it. And Mako – what the hell was taking him so long in the restroom? She needed some back-up and it looked like she was going to have to wait for it longer than she would like.

"Do you have the confirmation number, ma'am?" he said, his disdain amplified even more.

"No, I don't have the confirmation number…" she squinted to see his name on his faux gold nametag. "And I'd appreciate it, Brian, if you'd just look in the computer and make sure the reservation is still there. It should be listed under Artists Management Associates." Where the hell was she coming up with this? And perhaps a better question, where was she expecting it to get her?

Brian consulted his records. "I'm sorry, ma'am. There doesn't seem to be a reservation under that name. Are you sure you have the correct hotel?"

"Goddammit!" she shouted loud enough for everyone in the lobby to hear. "I specifically request a suite for my clients and all I get is the runaround. What kind of place are you people running here? I bet you've even got fleas in the linens and cockroach cameras in the bathroom." Krista looked around to see several of the hotel's guests standing and staring, then whispering nervously between each other.

"Miss, please. There's absolutely no need to shout." Brian was suddenly gracious, smiling and trying to catch her eye as she surveyed the results of her tantrum. "I'm sure there's something we can work out."

"Not with you. You've worn out your welcome and you haven't done anything to help me. I want to speak to the hotel manager now," she said, crossing her arms and standing her ground like a stubborn child.

"Of course," the clerk said, the ends of his mouth turning down again as he reached for the telephone. Krista stood there, still wondering what had become of Mako. She was keeping a close eye on Brian, making sure he was taking care of her business, noticing he was still not happy about having to speak to the manager. In the middle of the conversation, a confused expression crossed his face, after which he switched to another line on the telephone console. Where his end of the conversation had previously been a highly subjective version of his conversation with Krista, he was now answering in single words. "Yes. No. I understand." That was pretty much the extent of it. She wondered what changed as she looked in the direction of the restrooms and wished Mako would reappear soon.

"I'm sorry for the delay, ma'am," Brian said after hanging up, suddenly smiling and rubbing his hands together a little too nervously. "Our manager is in a meeting at the moment, but he should be out in just a little while and will be glad to speak to you. If you don't mind, I'd like to have you wait in our hospitality lounge until he arrives," he said, motioning to a door behind the reception desk marked "Authorized Personnel Only."

Krista considered her options, and decided that if it took a short wait, it was worth it to at least have a place to stay tonight. "Fine, but I'm here with a colleague." Well, *that* was a word she'd never used before without joking. "He'll be looking for me at the reception desk. Please tell him where I am."

"Most certainly ma'am," Brian said as he opened the door for her and ushered her through. "We'll tell him as soon as he arrives."

Mako rounded the corner outside the opulent restroom expecting to see Krista standing at the reception desk waiting for him. Instead, he saw only the typical bustle of a busy hotel lobby, but without Krista's face present in the crowd.

"Hey, man," he said to the swishy-looking desk clerk. "I was supposed to meet a girl here. Short – probably about five-two – with blonde, spiky hair."

The clerk looked confused. "I'm sorry, sir. I haven't seen anyone fitting that description. Perhaps she's waiting for you elsewhere?"

Mako regarded the clerk, who maintained an expression of distant helpfulness. "Yeah, that might be it. I'll check in the hotel bar, if you don't mind."

"Not at all, sir. It's through those glass double doors at the rear of the lobby," the clerk said, leaning over the counter and pointing at a pair of ornately etched doors.

"Thank you," Mako said as he walked away, trying to look like he was heading straight for the bar as he looked over his shoulder, still eyeing the lobby for Krista. As he cast a final glance back at the reception desk before going into the bar, he saw the desk clerk on the telephone looking frantic and pointing in his direction. A huge man in a navy-blue blazer and khaki pants emerged from a door behind the counter and began walking briskly in Mako's direction.

Security guard. Shit.

He pulled the bar door open and slipped through. The place was dark and crowded and already noisy. Mako shoved a middle-aged couple out of the way, nearly tripping over a velvet rope that hung between two low posts off to the side. With a sudden flash of inspiration, he unhooked the plush barrier at each end and shouldered his way back to the door, threading the rope through the brass handles enough times to prevent someone from opening it, then hooked the two ends together. More shoving, a series of increasingly loud and annoyed versions of "excuse me" as he passed sweaty businessmen and the women they were trying to seduce and he was at the opposite end of the room. A sign glowing dull red designated the fire exit and he wasted no time pushing himself through and down the stairs to the alleyway. Dumpsters, trashcans and a catering van were placed along the narrow path in what seemed to be an obstacle course someone had designed for Mako to run. He looked behind him and saw no one emerge from the stairway door, but he kept moving. Ahead, he saw the dull gray of the stormy sky. Finally, he emerged onto the boardwalk, looking right and left to make sure they weren't trying to cut him off, and headed to the Church of the New Revelation.

∧∧∧

Eustace settled himself into a booth in the back corner of the Cleaver's directly facing the Church of the New Revelation cathedral across the street, keeping a watchful eye on Yoshi and the Marines waiting in the line for the visitors gallery.

"How you doin' today, sugar?" said a woman's voice to his right. It was the waitress. Damn. He hated to take his eyes away from the line.

He chanced a quick look and was rewarded immensely. She was gussied up in the standard Cleaver's uniform of pasties bearing stylized tomato slices and a g-string resembling a leaf of lettuce. Temporarily tattooed over her left breast was the name Mary. "Good, good. Just coffee right now, please."

"You got it. Anyone else joining you?"

You, if there was any true justice in the world, he thought to himself. "Probably so," he said out loud. "Don't know if he'll be ordering though."

"Good enough, hon," she said with a wink of a false eyelash tinted like a peacock tail. "Back with that coffee right away."

He watched her go and sighed. Unlike at the Final Frontier, he felt pretty safe here in assuming his waitress was in fact a woman with all the standard equipment, and attractively arranged equipment at that.

He turned his eye to the window again, watching Yoshi display monk-like calm while Barry and Lewis horsed around, all according to plan.

"Special Forces, right?" the waitress said, having returned with the coffee. Eustace's eyes shot to his forearms, where the sleeves had ridden up to expose the ink work he worked so hard to hide. Registering his concern, she played it off. "My daddy was Special Forces — Iraq, Afghanistan, Palestine," she said by way of explanation. "Says he saw some shit over there."

"We all did, sweetheart," he said, suddenly grim. But why burden this kid with my baggage, he thought. He then gave her the smile he usually saved only for customers. "Seeing you, though, that's like a bright ray of sunshine on this dreary day."

The kid, standing there nearly in the altogether, actually flattered him with a blush. "You're too sweet," she said, turning her eyes down. She set down the coffee and a dish of little plastic cups of half-and-half. "You need a menu?"

"Won't be here that long, I hope. But tell you what. Keep an eye over here for me, will you? Might need a little backup, know what I mean?"

Her eyes got wide in mock awe. "Ooh, mysterious. Sorry you've got to run off, but don't you worry at all, hon. I'll be sure to keep a close eye on you."

219

^^^

"It will soon begin to rain in earnest," Yoshi said to the woman in front of him as he looked up at the sky from the crowd of CNR faithful and curious gawkers.

"It's comin' up quite a cloud, that's for sure," she replied. She was like many of the *gaijin* he saw here: friendly but suspicious of him, of the way he looked. That was fine. He was paid to observe suspicious people, and were he a small American woman with blue tinted hair and a plastic bandanna, he would find a large Okinawan suspicious, also.

"Everything going okay out there, brother?" he heard Eustace ask over the earpiece.

"Affirmative," he barely said, making the sound for the word by moving his lips as little as possible, just as he had been instructed. He turned to look behind him at Barry and Lewis, who stood talking to a pair of teen-age girls barely clad in equally revealing garments. He grinned just slightly at the futility of the girls' attempts at socialization with the two men, who remained gracious, nonetheless. Yoshi then turned his attention to the Cleaver's restaurant. It was at one time an old-fashioned metal trailer diner, placed on the lot across the street in one piece. It had since been renovated with the suggestive Cleaver's logo – an image of a buxom woman holding two giant hamburgers in front of her breasts, with the Cleaver's name on top and "Bone-Suckin' Good" below. There Eustace waited for Lucas Schaefer. He could see the man's figure in the window as Eustace spoke to the barely dressed waitress, then leaned back and adjusted the rubber band around his ponytail.

"Great," Eustace said in his earpiece. "The signal for you to start the show will be me putting my napkin in my lap. Then I want you to raise all holy hell with Barry and Lewis. Got it?"

Again, he voiced "Affirmative" while keeping a close eye on the diner window. Meanwhile, the woman in front of him kept trying to make conversation.

"You from China, young man?"

"No. Okinawa. It is an island in Japan."

"Oh. I could've sworn you were from China."

He tried to pay attention to the woman and be as courteous as possible, but her talking was distracting him from his job watching out for the signal.

"As a matter of fact, you are correct, ma'am. I am Chinese after all. Congratulations on your perception," he said in an effort to end the conversation.

"Thought so," she said, giving a satisfied nod and turning back to face the front of the line.

"Stand by, Yoshi. Got a dandy coming across the street from the church now in an ice cream suit. This might be our boy," Eustace said in his ear. Yoshi glanced quickly over his shoulder at Barry and Lewis, who both looked up and silently acknowledged their readiness, then turned back to the window of the Cleaver's. He saw the man in the suit as he entered the restaurant and made his way down the aisle to where Eustace sat. The two exchanged a bit of conversation that Yoshi didn't hear. Eustace had turned off the transmitter, he decided. Strategically Yoshi objected, but there was nothing he could do now. He watched and waited. Finally, the man in the suit sat down and Eustace pulled the napkin from around his silverware and placed it in his lap. The man was Schaefer, after all.

"Pardon me," Yoshi said loudly as he turned to Barry and Lewis. "Do you two know those young ladies?" He pushed his way back through the clump of four or five people that separated them.

"And what if we don't?" Barry said. He puffed up his chest and stood nose to nose with Yoshi. "What's an ugly Jap like you going to do about it?"

Yoshi had not expected racial epithets. They did, however, add to the scene's sense of realism. He slid his right foot back, assuming a defensive stance, cocking both his fists back to his hipbone. "Oh, so we're going to play a little kung fu, now are we?" Lewis said from beside Barry, pushing the two girls behind him.

"Perhaps," Yoshi said, bringing his right fist up from his hip in a lightning motion, the pointed tips of his knuckles making sharp contact with Barry's solar plexus, knocking the breath out of him and doubling him over. Yoshi reached down and grabbed his shirt and leaned in close. "Are you all right?"

"Nice move," Barry gasped. "But you pull another punch on me and I really will kick your ass."

"If I did not pull my punches, I would kill you, I am afraid."

"Apparently you underestimate the U.S. Marine Corps," he said, reaching up to grab Yoshi's topknot and slam his forehead into Yoshi's. Yoshi's unconscious response was to unleash a barrage of rapid-fire punches at Barry's midsection, ending with a side kick as the Marine fell backwards.

But when Barry grabbed his foot in mid-kick and turned the ankle hard to the left, Yoshi thought that perhaps he had indeed underestimated the pair. As he spun to keep his ankle from being broken, there was a brief moment of facing the sidewalk and he was face up again, Barry and Lewis each ready to pounce on him

"Okay, okay! What's the problem here," a security guard said as two others came up behind Yoshi's companions. Yoshi got to his feet slowly. It was about time. He had wondered if the church security guards would ever show up.

"I am sorry, officers. These gentlemen were harassing two young women in line and I asked them to stop. They refused."

"Fine. But you boys take your little disagreement somewhere other than my line. This is a church service, for chrissake." The security guards were unarmed, and Barry and Lewis gradually converged on them.

"No, I think we'd prefer to wait inside," Yoshi said, producing from his waistband a Heckler & Koch Silent Stalker, a dainty six-round automatic with a built-in silencer he had found rummaging in Eustace's "goody bag," as he called it. Barry and Lewis discretely produced their own weapons, holding them close to the guards' stomachs as they urged the security men forward. "Keep your hands at your sides and look as if nothing is wrong and take us to the security control room," Yoshi calmly suggested to them.

"You'll never get away with this," one of the guards said to them, apparently believing it himself.

"Wrong, my friend," Lewis said. "We already have."

They walked along the inside of the line, blocked from view of the street by the crowd of people, until they reached the church's doors, where they turned a corner and left the throng of congregation members to walk down a short corridor to a door marked "Security."

"Who's on duty in there right now?" Yoshi asked.

"Just one guy. Name's Doug," one of the guards said. "The rest of us are out on patrol. But nobody answered from here last time we tried to check in."

"You better hope whoever is in there isn't expecting us," Lewis said as he examined the keypad beside the door. "What's the code to get in?"

The first guard, the one who seemed to be the ranking member of the group, stood there silent. "Whatever you guys are trying to do, you might as well give up. The police will be here any minute."

"Bullshit," Barry said, holding his pistol to the guard's throat. "You haven't had time to call the police. And unless they're being alerted by the clenching of your nervous ass, they won't be here anytime soon. Now tell us the code, please?"

"Hold on," Lewis said. "The keypad's a decoy." He then flipped up the face of the pad to reveal a smooth surface with a grid pattern.

"Old fashioned biometrics. Not quite as quaint, but effective," Yoshi said. "Now, officer, if you don't mind?"

All of them stood off to the sides of the door as the guard reached down to press his thumb against the pad. There was the solid sound of a bolt disengaging. Barry reached down to turn the knob and then threw open the door.

Only the video monitors and keys on the control panel lighted the room, but it was enough light to see that someone had already been there before them.

"Holy Christ," the guard said upon seeing what was left of Doug. Yoshi was struck, also, but managed to push the guard in anyway as Barry and Lewis herded their hostages in behind him. The floor of the control room looked like that of a slaughterhouse. Something had either choked him or eviscerated him or both, Yoshi thought.

One of the guards quietly vomited in the corner while the other two just stood in stunned silence and tried not to look directly at the mess of human flesh. "This is most unexpected," Yoshi said to his two companions.

"No fuckin' shit, man. What the hell happened here? This guy's been torn all to pieces, and it wasn't by us."

"No. Someone has obviously preceded us. And I'm afraid whoever it was has provided for us an extra hurdle," he said as he pointed to the bank of video screens. On one was what looked like a passport photo of Krista sleeping, obviously taken recently by the bruises on her face. On the screen next to it was a real-time image from a security camera showing Krista sitting in some sort of hotel room, her leg jiggling nervously.

"Fuck," Barry said. "How the hell did that happen?"

"She said her kidnappers photographed her. This is obviously where they sent the image," Yoshi said. "The person who killed this guard did not want his connection to Krista revealed. Barry, radio Eustace and tell him we are here and to be very careful. It would seem Mr. Schaefer is more dangerous than we first imagined."

"Mr. Schaefer, I presume?" Eustace said from his booth seat, not bothering to make eye contact with the white-suited man who hovered above him. The British accent figured. The ice cream suit, too. The guy was straight out of central casting under "evil mastermind."

"At your service. And you are?" Schaefer responded, seeming not too concerned with the implications of the meeting.

"Someone you should take very seriously. Have a seat." He reached for his silverware, which had been rolled up in a paper napkin like a toothpick joint and secured by a thin piece of adhesive paper, then unrolled it and placed the napkin in his lap, trying for Yoshi's sake to make just enough of a production out of the process.

"I understand you're a busy man, Mr. Schaefer, so we can take care of this very quickly." Still no eye contact, a tactic designed to keep the subject off balance that Eustace picked up during a stint at the training school for Latin American military officers down at Fort Benning. Don't make eye contact until you really mean business. And that was now.

"I have in my possession information that directly relates to you and your organization," he said as his eyes, firm and unblinking, met Schaefer's. Mary the waitress passed next to Schaefer without acknowledging them, but the man ignored the attractive girl's figure.

With about two dozen TVs, a row of VR games and a bar crowded with gawkers gazing out on the CNR line, the place was becoming noisy and warm, and he could feel his upper lip growing moist in spite of the cool he was trying to project. Schaefer, on the other hand, looked like he'd just emerged from a refrigerator. Odd, considering the temperature inside and the level of humidity outside as the sky hovered on the edge of what looked to be a badass thunderstorm. Still, he decided it was best not to think about that and to instead carry on.

Shaeffer fidgeted as Eustace took his time adding sugar and then creamer to his coffee, which was rapidly cooling. Good thing he didn't actually plan to drink it. Slowly stirring, making sure to clink the spoon against the inside of the cup, he continued. "Perhaps you're familiar with this information. Near as my associates and I can tell it connects you to a conspiracy with Nikura International to include a particle accelerator weapon on that communications satellite the Church of the New Revelation has been trying to buy. It also implicates you in a plot with the members of an organization called SHAG to kill a number of Nikura International employees who knew of this plan, the most dramatic of which would probably be Akiro Nikura. Then, of course, there's

Hiroshi Nikura, who apparently helped you acquire this nasty weapon then killed himself when he was about to be discovered.

"I believe the police said he was shot by his errant nephew, mister … ?

"Not out of the question, except that the nephew saw him take the poison that killed him and never fired a shot. Oh, and I almost forgot Andrea Turner, an executive assistant at Nikura who was shot to death in her office two days after her boss died. I would imagine you had something to do with that, considering that's who provided us with much of this information. And that's not to mention the fact that you're likely an accessory to much of the carnage wreaked by SHAG using weapons you arranged to be diverted to them from Nikura shipments."

Schaefer's gaze didn't waver. He just sat there looking eerily at ease, his pale, delicate hands crossed on the table. Eustace maintained eye contact as he tried to gauge the other man's response. But there was nothing to gauge. The man was like animated plastic.

"An amusing yarn you weave. Have you ever thought of a career in fiction?" Schaefer said, the corner of one side of his mouth turning up slightly, apparently his sad excuse for a smile.

"I wish it was fiction and that I could take responsibility for it, Mr. Schaefer. I'd probably be a rich man. Either that or it'd be written off as too over-the-top." Eustace saw in his peripheral vision some commotion on the sidewalk opposite them and knew Yoshi, Barry and Lewis were following the plan to the letter. The next thing he should be hearing from them was that they were in the control room.

"Then shall we pretend for a moment that it is fiction? This particular manuscript – the one that contains this information of which you speak – how much would you ask for it? I assure you that should this prove to be a work of quality, I could be very generous in obtaining exclusive rights."

The offer of money came sooner than Eustace expected. This guy was all business. No beating around the bush, and just barely interested in continuing with the "work of fiction" cover. On one hand, it made Eustace feel more at ease that this was moving along quickly, but it also worried him that Schaefer was so willing to start talking money before he had even seen any evidence that the stick was still in Eustace's possession. He pondered his next move. Well, he thought, since Schaefer was moving along so rapidly, what was there to keep him from moving equally as fast?

"I'm afraid my price is a little higher than you could afford, generosity or not. As it stands the only publishers that are gonna get their hands on this story will be a few federal agencies that I think would be very interested in what you've got going on here. My colleagues and I took the liberty of forwarding that information to them so they could decide themselves what to do with it."

"So," Schaefer said, sitting back and placing his hands flat on the table, "it is not money you seek. Then may I ask the purpose of this meeting? Were you simply interested in idle threats?"

"Not at all, Mr. Schaefer. They're anything but idle. We just want you to realize that whatever you had planned with that orbiting ray gun is never going to happen, because your satellite is going to go up without it. On a more personal note, I and my colleagues would like to make sure you're punished for the considerable trouble you've caused us both personally and professionally."

"Well, then. I have what you might like to call a counter-offer," Schaefer said, his mouth again turning up slightly. "I have already had a meeting with someone who I believe is a colleague of yours. My security personnel said her name was … " He paused to reach inside his suit coat, making Eustace impulsively reach for the sidearm he'd made sure to bring with him. He extracted only a small piece of paper, unfolded it and read it. "Krista. Yes, that's it. I believe that in your story she is no doubt a minor character, but one of some importance, perhaps? Nevertheless, she is at the moment enjoying the hospitality of the Church of the New Revelation. So, sir, if there is any way to reclaim this manuscript you have so hastily delivered to your law enforcement organizations, I would suggest that in the interest of Miss Krista's welfare, you should do so immediately."

He was bluffing. Eustace knew it. Schaefer was using an old trick – taking one known piece of information that he has on his side and using against the enemy in an effort throw them off. He knew Krista had been in the hands of the nuts from SHAG and he knew they had a picture of her. Schaefer had obviously made some connections of his own and was now using them in trying to squirm his way out of a rapidly deteriorating situation.

"I'm afraid it's too late, Mr. Schaefer. Of course, our forwarding this information doesn't guarantee that you'll have every domestic branch of U.S. law enforcement hovering over your church in the next day or so, but I'd say there's a pretty good chance that you can expect some visitors within the near future." Eustace removed the napkin from his lap and threw it on the table, then got up to leave. But as he rose, he felt as if his leg had caught on something underneath.

"I'm afraid that won't be possible," Schaefer said. Eustace suddenly realized that his leg wasn't caught on anything. Instead, something had hold of him, something that slithered up from his ankle and tightened with each passing second. Against his will, whatever it was pulled him roughly back into the seat as Schaefer calmly leaned forward, lacing his hands together on the tabletop. "You see, you and your friends are on the verge of destroying a project that you might say is near and dear to my heart." The tightening grew worse, and Eustace, against his best instincts, found himself grimacing as he felt flesh being compressed between what seemed like steel coils choking off the blood. "That is, of course, if I had what you think of as a heart."

A tingling heat suddenly built up in Eustace's leg – a vibration that coursed through his entire body before he realized what was happening. This thing, whatever had him under the table, was slowly, deliberately electrocuting him. He tried to reach across the table to Schaefer but realized his arms wouldn't move. And there the bastard sat, grinning that sorry, pathetic grin, fully aware of what was going on. And he was loving every minute of it. It was then that Eustace knew it was over – knew it because he smelled smoke. The smoke of his own flesh cooking in the awful grip of whatever it was, burning his brain in his skull as he felt himself twitch uncontrollably.

It was growing dim, Eustace's eyelids fluttering uncontrollably, as Schaefer leaned forward and whispered in his ear.

"I'll tell Krista you said hello."

^^^

Yoshi looked at the clock on the wall and drummed his fingers impatiently on the control panel. What was left of Douglas Rohrbaugh, as his Pennsylvania driver's license had identified him, had been moved into the employee restroom adjacent to the control room with relatively little fuss.

Now, though, he was concerned more with Eustace's fate than whether there were bloodstains on the rug. His transmitter had been turned off for too long. If the man had any sense at all – and Yoshi was positive he did – he would have radioed by now and let the rest of them know what was happening. But there was nothing.

"Any word yet?" Barry said as he pulled his head back in from the door he held barely ajar.

"Nothing."

"I'm sure he's got everything under control," the other man said. Yoshi, as much as he wanted to believe it, wasn't so sure. The whole plan seemed reckless, especially the part about Eustace meeting with Schaefer. If the man was capable of deluding the leaders of an organization as large as the Church of the New Revelation, he was obviously someone of great determination and little concern for the welfare of those who got in his way. And Eustace, sitting there as the three of them watched, could possibly have been a very small barricade in the path of a maglev.

Lewis, who had taken up the security guard's position at the control panel, muttered into the headphones as his fingers flew over the colored buttons and touch-sensitive computer screens. A whole bank of security monitors flickered and changed point of view, now tracking the path of a tall, gaunt man in a light-colored suit as he made his way into the church.

"Yoshi, company's coming," Lewis said. "From the guard chatter, it must be Schaefer heading this way."

Barry closed the door quietly and stepped backwards, drawing his sidearm and aiming at the door. Yoshi followed suit, and between the two of them there was no way anyone would come in that door with the tactical advantage. Lewis stayed seated, his eyes alternating between the door and the surveillance screens, tracking Schaefer's progress.

"He just left the lobby, guys. Took a second to peek in on the sanctuary from a side door. All of the security's still in place there. All right, good… He doesn't look like he suspects anything. Okay, now he's heading in this direction at a pretty good clip."

"Anything we can do to slow him up?" Barry asked.

"Unless you want me to trip the fire alarms and clear the building, no."

"And that would cause the unnecessary distraction of alerting the fire department," Yoshi said. "At this point, I would like to minimize the number of surprises we have to face."

"Cut the chatter guys. He's turning the corner headed this way," Lewis said. "Everyone stand by. He's walking up to the door." Lewis' voice had quieted to a whisper. Yoshi noticed his palms were sweating. He took a deep breath, exhaled slowly and focused.

"Right outside now, fellas. If you're going to take any shots, better make 'em count."

"No shots!" Yoshi hissed. "We need him alive."

"Check," Barry said. "Pulls anything funny, though, he's losing a limb."

They all watched the door, the room silent now save for the electronic hum of the controls and the high-pitched, almost inaudible whine of the security monitors. When they heard the heavy sound of the security bolts disengaging, the tension in the room increased tenfold. A thin sliver of light penetrated the room from the hallway, the door swung wide, and in stepped the gaunt figure in the immaculate white suit.

He looked mildly surprised, but not overwhelmed by their presence. Yoshi would have felt much better if he had responded a bit more dramatically. Such nonchalance indicated that the man was, on some level, expecting them to be there.

"Gentlemen, I don't think we've been introduced," Schaefer said, entirely too calmly for Yoshi's satisfaction. "However, I'll assume you are all associates of the unfortunate fellow with whom I just spoke in the restaurant."

"Where is he?" Barry demanded.

"Oh, still there. I imagine the wait staff has noticed by now that he hasn't ordered a refill on his coffee and has probably alerted the police," Schaefer said, closing the door behind him. "The coroner's report will likely list the cause of death as electrocution, although a source for the shock won't immediately be forthcoming." All this said with eerie calm.

"Motherfucker..." Barry said, sighting down his pistol.

"Barry! Hold your fire," Yoshi said.

"A sensible choice, sir," Schaefer said, turning to Yoshi, not seeming at all concerned that he was seconds away from being shot. "I'm afraid there's been entirely too much carnage of late, and I would like to avoid any more. Now, gentlemen, since your plans seem to have gone awry, I'll ask you to hand over your weapons and accompany me to my office so we might discuss the situation like civilized beings."

"The situation? And what situation would that be?" Yoshi said.

"Please, gentlemen. Your weapons?"

Barry seemed utterly aghast that an unarmed dandy would dare ask for his weapon in such a bold and casual manner. "Who the fuck do you think you are, man?"

"Someone over whom you have no advantage," he said calmly. "Perhaps this will persuade you," he said as he began to reach towards the inside of his suit jacket.

"Put your hands at your side, Mr. Schaefer," Yoshi said. "We will fire without hesitation if you don't." Yoshi grasped the pistol tighter, his knuckles growing white along the front of the grip. But his warning did nothing. Schaefer kept going, pulling the jacket open at the lapel and reaching inside, a bold smirk crossing his lips as if he were enjoying a marvelous, secret joke.

"Hands down!" Barry shouted. Yoshi cut his eyes right to see the man sweating profusely, then over his shoulder to see that Lewis had drawn his own weapon and was also training it on Schaefer, whose hand was now emerging from inside the jacket, the bizarre smirk still on his lips, until he drew his hand out with one, quick motion.

The noise from the three pistols firing inside the small room was like being next to a mine going off, the smell of the charges and the smoke burning Yoshi's nose and filling his mouth with sulfur taste as he watched Schaefer's body convulse with the impact of the rounds, chips of drywall splashing across the room from around him. But the man didn't fall. He stood there, taking each impact is if it were a heavy stone. This despite the fact that each round chewed away at a different part of his body, the flesh erupting in craters and tearing away at the arm that had been reaching inside the jacket until most of the limb lay torn and mangled by his side.

"Stop! Stop! Hold your fire!" Yoshi shouted as he waved the other two off, realizing they were doing no good – realizing that Schaefer was right. They did not have the advantage.

The two men lowered their weapons, still keeping them at the ready, and surveyed the damage, each looking as if they could not comprehend what they were seeing.

"Holy fucking Christ!" Lewis said. "There's no blood."

And there wasn't. Not a drop. Only splatter marks all around the room and around Schaefer's wounds that looked more like pureed lettuce. Beaten but not down, Schaefer leaned against the far wall, still smirking, his remaining hand reaching up to straighten his hair, mussed from the onslaught. In the fingers of the arm that wasn't there, the one that lay there on the floor, twitching in a pool of green ooze that looked like something you'd squeeze out of an aloe plant, was a ripped shred of fabric. A patch. A patch that said "Sunrise Moving."

The patch that was on Krista's shirt when they dropped her off.

It wouldn't have taken a great amount of intuition for Schaefer to guess their thoughts at that moment, as they all grasped the "situation," as the wounded man had called it. A situation that existed on multiple levels, some of which they had no way of understanding. All Yoshi knew at that point was that Schaefer was many things, but he was not human, and that he had definitely captured Krista, all the better to use one of their own against them.

"So you see, gentleman," Schaefer said, nudging himself up from the wall to stand erect once more, "your circumstances are a bit more dire than you might have imagined." For the first time, he looked pained by his wounds, but it only took a moment for Yoshi to realize that it wasn't pain of injury that made him grimace, but the pain of healing. Before their eyes, the holes and divots in Schaefer's flesh closed themselves, even the fabric of his suit growing back over them, a plant-like green stump finally emerging from his ruined shoulder. It sprouted like a spring bulb and formed itself into a new arm. A new sleeve grew back over it to its previously perfect, tailored length.

Even the two Marines were at a loss for profanity to express their shock. Only Yoshi could find the strength to speak.

"What are you?"

"As I said earlier," Schaefer said, straightening his suit again and running his regrown hand through his hair, "someone over whom you have no advantage. Now, gentlemen, your weapons, if you please?"

Rain had begun to fall in fat, loud drops on the limousine roof as it crawled along Ocean Boulevard from Jon's hotel. Had it not been for the lightning directly overhead, he imagined the streets would have looked much the same as on a clear evening. Tonight, however, the sudden downpour and threat of electrocution from above had driven both the tourists and the locals inside. But the neon and traveling lights and holographic ads glowed and blinked as if there were still throngs along the sidewalks interested in strapping on a pair of feelie goggles for a game of Doomsayer in the arcades or hungry for cups of boardwalk fries drowned in malt vinegar.

He drummed his fingers nervously, a complement to the noisy rain, as he pondered the next few hours. He would be required to sit through an entire CNR service, he knew. And he couldn't help thinking how appalled his mother would be if she knew the second church service he'd been to since Easter – the other was his cousin Anita's third wedding, this time to a used car dealer, back in May – was one where alcohol and drug intake was permitted and nudity and sexual partner-swapping were encouraged. Come to think of it, that was a bit like Anita's wedding.

Then there was the question of what to do about Veronica Whitaker, who he knew probably had him targeted as her next conquest. "Larry would never trust anyone he didn't trust to make love to his own wife," Veronica had said of her husband's business philosophy. And given her performance earlier in the day, Jon expected her to pull out all the sexual stops in convincing him of their combined trust.

He realized his trepidation must have shown on his face when he caught the chauffeur's eyes in the rear view mirror. She was typical of the CNR's young helpers he had met earlier in the day – a twentyish brunette with a bright smile and a pair of stunning green eyes. The only difference setting her apart from her contemporaries at the plantation was her outfit, an abbreviated chauffeur's uniform of dark cap, double-breasted Eisenhower jacket and micro-miniskirt. The limo, of course, could have run on its own. But if he had to have a human chauffeur in place of the ubiquitous female computer voice, he wasn't complaining about this one.

"Will this be your first CNR service, Mr. Temple?" she said, her eyes meeting his in the rear view mirror.

"Was it that obvious? I'm sorry," he said to her reflection. "What was your name?"

"Melinda, and yes it is that obvious." He could see by her eyes that she was smiling. "But don't be nervous. For a lot of people, their first CNR service is the best night of their lives."

THIRTY~FIVE

"I can understand that," he said, leaving "If they have pathetic, empty, depressing lives in which bogus religion and rampant promiscuity can fill the gaping maw of their sad souls," unspoken. Then again, he couldn't help thinking about Regina, who seemed even better adjusted now than she did before becoming involved with Whitaker's bunch. And in his dealings with the CNR so far, the creepiest person he'd come upon was Lucas Schaefer, which under the suspicious circumstances was to be suspected. Otherwise, it seemed like a surprisingly well adjusted – if sexually forward and religiously zealous – group of people. Still, he imagined that were it not for his assignment from Eli, he never would have set foot inside the Ocean Cathedral.

"How long have you been a member, Melinda?"

"Oh, it's been about five years. I was one of the charter members at the College of Charleston and hosted the school's first CNR student retreat. Later on I was the one who spearheaded the movement to have us recognized as an official student organization and get First Amendment protection as a religious group." Jon remembered when that happened, back when he was still on staff. Their higher education reporter, a bookish, excessively sweaty man who was used to covering tuition hikes and controversial changes in curriculum was suddenly thrust into an imbroglio that knotted up college academics with mainstream Christianity, sex orgies and church-endorsed substance abuse. At one point he was positive the man would beg their managing editor to be put onto something "less" controversial, like the police or the State House beat. "We were the ones who really got the CNR started on college campuses here. After that, it just spread like wildfire."

"Well, I didn't realize I was in the presence of a celebrity," Jon said, unconsciously turning on the charm and relishing the ability to do so. He had to make a conscious effort to get out of the habit of flirting and schmoozing with every woman he met after he and Linda married. But while for Jon Templeton, married man, this sort of behavior was simply not appropriate, for Jonnie Temple it was exactly what was expected.

"Oh, Mr. Temple. You're so sweet," Melinda said as the limo rolled to stop at an intersection. "I'll tell you what…" Suddenly she was digging inside what sounded like a purse in the front passenger seat, then passing back a perforated strip of stickers. "Try one of these when you're at the service, and let me know if you got over that little nervousness problem."

Jon examined them and found that they all bore the superimposed images of the common male upraised-arrow and female descending plus-sign symbols.

"Are these what I think they are?"

She laughed and caught his eye again in the mirror. "Don't tell me you've never even seen a dermal before."

He smiled back, trying to play it cool. "I guess I'm just not the man of the world you took me for, my dear."

She laughed again, this time imparting an ironic tone. "Oh, don't be so sure, Mr. Temple. I've no doubt you're worldly enough for me." Another come on from another CNR girl? He wasn't sure he could take this any longer. "Just peel one off and put it somewhere on your body where the blood vessels are close to the skin. Some people like them along the jugular," she said, running a long finger along her delicate neck. "But that's a little too obvious for me. Try on your wrist or on the inside of your elbow. It works a little slower there, but that just means the effect lasts longer."

"And what's the effect?"

"Stamina, heightened sensitivity, lowered inhibitions, delayed ejaculation for men while still experiencing all the other sensations of orgasm, that sort of stuff. Basically, it takes everything good about sex and makes it about a hundred times better."

"Well…" he said, folding up the strip and putting it in his jacket pocket as the car began moving again. "I'll have to see if all those claims are backed up. Thanks."

"Oh, don't worry. You won't have any problem finding company tonight. Everyone knows who you are and they're going to be fighting to be your prayer partner. But from what I hear, Sister Veronica has first dibs."

"Funny," he said as he leaned back in the deep leather of the backseat. "I get the same feeling myself."

They slowed as the limo drove them into an alley that didn't seem to be anywhere near the Ocean Cathedral. But a few turns down a few more alleys later they pulled up beneath a covered entryway well-protected by two burly security guards, each in navy blue sport coats and khaki pants. As the limo approached, a door opened and out stepped Veronica Whitaker.

"And speak of the devil herself," Melinda said as they came to a stop. "Looks like you'll be well taken care of tonight, Mr. Temple."

She then exited the car and came around to open his door for him. As he climbed out, the first image to fill his field his vision was that of Veronica Whitaker, resplendent in a shimmering ivory gown that reached from her throat to her feet and nearly matched the color of her china-doll skin. Cut out of the bust was a crucifix large enough to reveal the inside curves of her delicate breasts, and up her left leg ran a slit that reached almost to her waist. But before he could say anything to her, his attention was once again drawn to Melinda, who extended her hand to him.

"It's been a real pleasure meeting you, Mr. Temple, and thank you for everything you're doing for the church." He started to respond, but was quickly pulled toward her and engaged in a deep tongue kiss, her free hand snaking around the back of his head to pull him closer. She finally broke the kiss, leaving Jon in a befuddled state of delight as he tasted the remnants of her lipstick on his own lips. "I'll see you after the service then, Mr. Temple."

And with that, she returned to the limo. "Thank you, Melinda. See you back at the house," Veronica said. She then turned her attention to Jon, gazing at him intently and biting her lower lip. "Well, Jonnie, here we are at last. I thought tonight would never come."

"I've been looking forward to it," he said, finding himself bowled over again by her sexual intensity. It was perfectly clear what she had in mind for him, Jon thought. All that remained was to see how long it would take for her plans to go into effect.

She threaded her right arm around his left and walked him through the heavy paneled doors into what anywhere else would be a tastefully – and probably expensively – appointed living room. "Please make yourself at home, Jonnie," she said, taking her time in releasing him from her grasp. "There's a full bar and you'll find just about anything else you need in the drawers beside the refrigerator. I've got to go check on Larry, but I won't leave you alone for too long." She gave him a final devouring look before going through another doorway.

Jon scanned the room and found the "tasteful" objects were obviously holdovers from the decorating job on the main Whitaker house. Again, each one featured subtle and not-so-subtle patterns and designs alluding to sex. Even the Oriental carpet, upon closer inspection, revealed what seemed to be ornate renderings of Kama Sutra positions like Harvest Moon over Ivory Tower or Hungry Dog Devouring Cucumber.

He carefully regarded the painting behind the bar. Reubens? He imagined it could quite possibly be an original, if it were. Regardless, it was all cherubs and naked fat ladies reveling around some Dionysian character and reminded Jon that a drink would most certainly be in order. He perused the collection of premium liquors lined up there, many of which he'd never been able to afford by the glass, let alone by the bottle, and chose a rare Scotch he'd read about in a magazine. He found he had been mentally congratulating Lawrence Whitaker on his taste ever since their meeting, based either on his home, his wife, his booze or his ability to keep swarms of negligibly clad nubile females around him under the pretense of godly activities. Were he prone to jealousy he might envy the man's circumstance, but given that his third in command was under suspicion by the Supreme Being, Jon found he envied him very little.

Jon swirled the whiskey around the crystal tumbler engraved with an ornate "W" and listened to the ice clink against the side. He took a sip, letting it make its warm way delicately over his tongue and down his throat, and found it sublime. That was more than he could say about his thoughts regarding the CNR in general. Having had the most superficial view of the organization from the inside, he could only say he found it surreal. Of course, he thought, that doesn't mean much coming from someone who has died, been subjected to altered laws of time, space and theology and then reanimated for some heavenly secret mission.

As he enjoyed the drink, he couldn't help but be curious about what Veronica meant by "just about anything else you need." On the bar was an ornate humidor with an ebony inlay of an African man with a ridiculously large phallus being orally serviced by two women. Jon lifted the lid and the sweet, musky smell of excellent tobacco – the kind you had to sell an organ to get in the U.S. – filled his nostrils. Though the craving itch of the recovering smoker had left him when he conked his head on the toilet, he still couldn't help thinking about how good a cigarette would taste right now.

The inside of the humidor was divided into two sections. In one of them were fine Cubans. In the other, which had its own hinged wooden lid, he found dozens of precisely rolled joints, each the width of a cigarette and giving off the potent sickly-sweet smell he recognized so readily from his youth. Having discovered these, he decided to check out the drawer by the refrigerator Veronica had suggested he investigate. In it he found a wide smorgasbord of dermals, all arranged in individual cubbyholes like the lead type he saw in the printer's shop on a childhood trip to Colonial Williamsburg. There were patches similar to the ones Melinda the chauffeur had given him – which he still had in his jacket pocket, he reminded himself – and dozens more, each with its own unique symbol representing its effect or the circumstances under which it would best be useful. One featured a clock face with an erect penis as the hands. That one would be for stamina, he imagined. On others, the symbolism was too obscure for him to immediately assess their use, but he imagined all of them were somehow sexually related.

He closed the drawer and moved to the couch, easing himself into its softness as the liquor did its work. Instantly, the image of the painting on the opposite wall disappeared and was replaced with what seemed to be a live transmission from the church's sanctuary. Hundreds of the faithful had already filed into the hall and were taking their seats in the couch-like pews. As the camera angle changed, each shot revealed more and more the state of undress in which these people showed up for church. Everything was tight, brief, low-cut, high-cut or seethrough. The crowd was mostly made up of people from their teens to their late 20s – the church's core congregation. But every so often Jon would spot an older person in the crowd, usually a well-preserved woman in her 40s or a virile looking man in his 50s. In fact, most of the men looked not unlike the way Jon looked in his new guise. He wasn't sure if that was going to work for him or against him in dealing with the women in the congregation. Then again, he thought, it would seem Veronica wasn't planning to let the other women have anything to do with him.

"Oh, good. I'm so glad you've made yourself at home," he heard Veronica say as she emerged from wherever she had gone to meet her husband. He turned around to look and marveled at the way she moved across the room, her body curving in a series of vertical arcs that only accentuated her painfully evident dimensions. "Oh, and you already have a drink, too. Well, I suppose that just means I'll need to start catching up." She turned to the bar and lifted the humidor's lid, then the inside lid and removed one of the joints, carrying it over to where Jon sat.

She eased into the couch and draped an arm delicately over Jon's shoulder as she held the joint to her lips and gave him an anticipatory gaze. He quickly realized she still needed a light, and spotting an ornately carved and decidedly phallic lighter on the coffee table, obliged her. "Thank you, sir," she said after inhaling deeply. "You certainly do know how to anticipate a woman's needs."

Here it comes, he thought. Everything she had subjected him to before was only a pleasant breeze compared to the tornado she was prepared to unleash on him tonight. He figured the only thing to do was play along and not worry about being one of the trailer parks in the twister's way.

"Yes, I have been accused of being a bit psychic in that regard. I suppose it comes from a world of experience with what women really want." God, he was going to make himself sick if he kept this up.

She exhaled and cocked a delectable eyebrow. "And what would you say that is, Jonnie? Now you've got me all interested and we haven't even gotten our clothes off," she said, grinning broadly as the cannabis worked its mellowing spell.

"What does a woman want? That's a very big question, you know," he said, furrowing his brow with mock seriousness and trying not to laugh at how silly all this was. "And frankly, it's taken years of research for me to come to a conclusion on that question. But it seems to me that every woman, no matter their preference for men or other women, wants only one thing. But it's a closely guarded secret."

"Come on, Jonnie. Tell!" she squealed, reverting again to the girlishness he saw in her performance under the grapevine. Her free hand had moved from its resting place on his shoulder up his neck, then up farther to delicately play with the short hairs over and behind his ear.

He smiled. She was almost too easy. By this time, a thousand other women would have already called bullshit and put out a cigarette in his drink. But with Veronica, there were almost no limits.

"I don't know, Veronica. This is highly proprietary information. There are many other people who would love to get their hands on this sort of thing." She had crossed her legs as she leaned closer to him. At the same moment, her dress fell open at the slit to reveal every square inch of her left leg, the draping material the only thing keeping more from being revealed. He took the opportunity to lay a hand, moist and cool from the condensation on his glass, on the inside of her flawless thigh. "I've been threatened with torture, kidnapping and death and still have kept the secret, you know. It's that valuable."

She responded to his touch just the way he had imagined she would. Her eyes closed to half-slits as she bit her lower lip in anticipation of what he would do next. "Oh, Jonnie…" she said, almost with a moan. "Now you're just teasing."

"I wouldn't really call it teasing, my dear," he said, leaning close and placing the glass on the coffee table, then taking the joint from her fingers and inhaling deeply himself. "I'd call it following up on an unspoken promise. After all, wasn't it you who said your delicious grapes were only a taste of things to come?"

She laughed, low and languid, opening her eyes fully again to meet his. "Yes, I did say that, didn't I."

"Yes, you did. And that was after your prayer demonstration, which had me so filled with the spirit" – he threw that in just for her – "I didn't know what to do with myself. So now who's the tease, Mrs. Whitaker?"

"Well," said a voice from the opposite door. "I'd have to agree that both of you are doing an excellent job at it, and it's encouraging to see. You are indeed a godly man, Mr. Temple."

It was Whitaker, dressed in his pastoral vestments and a multicolored stole depicting Jesus and Mary Magdalene in a number of amorous embraces.

Veronica, meanwhile, didn't break her gaze. "Hello, Larry darling. Are you all ready?"

"Feeling as full of the spirit as I'm likely to get tonight, my love. Jonnie, I trust Veronica has shown you our best hospitality?"

"Absolutely," he said, getting up and straightening his jacket, then offering his hand to Veronica as she stood. "And I can't wait to see what inspirational words you'll be sharing with us during the rest of the evening."

"Thank you, Jonnie. But it would seem from the way you two have been getting on there'll be no need for me to provide you with inspiration. Shall we go?" the Reverend said as he guided Jon and Veronica through the door and down the corridor to the sanctuary.

^^^

Linda felt the eyes of the crowd on her as the suspiciously perfect young man acting as usher led her to her pew in the visitor's gallery. Suddenly she wasn't feeling so sure about her decision to follow Regina's fashion advice. It didn't take many sideward glances, however, to realize precisely what she suspected. She was the most conservatively dressed person here. It seemed even the tourists perched in this voyeuristic vantage point were as into the decadence of the whole affair as the folks down in the congregation.

She crossed her legs and folded the program neatly in half, just as she would have if she were attending church with Jon and his mother on a normal Sunday morning. But this was not Sunday morning and it was certainly a far cry from Carlton United Methodist. The crowd below undulated like a single amorphous organism the color of human flesh, flecked here and there with bits of lace, leather, sheer silk and sequins. She imagined Regina, if she weren't still waiting in line, was in that mass somewhere indulging in God-knows-what. Many of the regulars she passed on the way in already seemed to be in some advanced altered state, and those who weren't had the opportunity to be just inside the sanctuary doors, Regina had told her. Everything from traditional stuff like good weed and a variety of hallucinogens to new-fangled things like custom-made transdermal patches. Linda knew about the dermals, of course, but the closest she'd ever come to one was the nicotine patch Jon used before he switched to Nica-Chew. No telling what those could do, but Regina seemed to have perfect faith in their safety.

Still, Linda couldn't help worrying about the girl – and it was hard to see her as anything other than a girl – and wondering what her grandmother would think. On one hand, she would be delighted Regina was actively involved in church. On the other hand, if she knew that involvement included a drug-induced sexual frenzy, she might not be so thrilled. Then again, it's not like it was impossible to find out what the church was all about, since an edited recording of the service was broadcast across TV and the Web as soon as the live service ended. It didn't take much reading between the lines of Rev. Whitaker's sermons to realize that when he told the faithful to "be one in Christ," he wasn't speaking figuratively.

She unfolded the program and checked the progress of things. Right now, they were in what was called the "social sacraments" portion of the service, which Linda figured involved everyone getting good and lit or stoned. Then came

237

the greeting and introduction of guests from Whitaker, then music, then a responsive reading from Veronica Whitaker, listed in the program as "Deaconess Veronica." At first glance, it all seemed quite traditional. Upon closer inspection, however, everything was skewed toward the sexual. About midway through the order of worship was another musical interlude marked with an asterisk, which referred her to a footnote that said "Worshipers may adjourn to meditation chambers at this time." In other words, she thought, the horny congregants could feel free to grab a stranger and go have anonymous sex in the name of the Lord.

Already the music was stoking the mood, she noticed. It was – well, the only way she could describe it was *funky* – slow but with a heavy backbeat, the kind of music that prompted you to gyrate your hips without even realizing it. She found it interesting that the choir and church musicians were some of the least conservatively dressed people in the church. It was more like an adult musical review than what she commonly though of as church music. Around her she could see fingers and toes tapping and heads bobbing to the beat. She checked her watch just as the lights in the sanctuary dimmed once. Ten minutes to go, which meant she probably only had 10 more minutes of light by which she could try to spy Jon in the crowd. She started at the front row of the main sanctuary, even though she really didn't think she would find him among the rabble of the Rev. Whitaker's congregation. She eyed each face, the back of each head that looked male, quickly and carefully.

Across each row, then back and again. Nothing. No one that looked even remotely like Jon. The next step was to check those around her in the guest gallery. She tried as casually as she could to turn and look behind her, but the angle of the balcony was to steep for her to get a good look at the upper rows without suspiciously craning her neck. Meanwhile, each time she happened to catch the eye of someone in a row behind her – male or female – they would make direct eye contact right back, one woman even being so bold as to raise her brief skirt a little so Linda could see she wasn't wearing anything underneath.

Linda snapped her head forward again. She decided that there was no subtle way to accomplish a survey of those around her and tried not to think too hard about the implications of what just happened. She was sure Regina would have told her to lighten up and appreciate the gesture, especially since Linda was sure she had caught several lingering and appreciative glances from the younger girl. While she should have considered the possibility earlier, the concept of Regina going both ways as part of her service to the Lord had never really crossed her mind. It probably should have.

The lights dimmed again, this time twice, and the level of the noise from the crowd below immediately decreased as the faithful began to find their places and sit, many of them still openly fondling each other in the pews. At the front of the sanctuary, in front of a huge stained glass rendering of an open-armed Christ resplendent in a suggestively bulging white robe and surrounded by nude men and women, a large screen began to descend from the ceiling. A close-up image of the altar appeared there just as the Rev. Whitaker emerged from a door at the far side. After him came a woman with dramatic long, red hair and a wisp of a dress that covered her from throat to her ankles, the slit that ran all the way up to her hip not withstanding. That was "Deaconess" Veronica. Upon their arrival, the music grew louder and the noise from the crowd surged with a smattering of applause.

After them came another man, this one obviously not a member of Whitaker's clergy because he wore a suit instead of the Reverend's elaborate vestments. Something about him seemed vaguely familiar, she thought. Something about the way he carried himself, the length of his step. It ignited something inside her, gave her butterflies for no reason she could put a finger on. Then it hit her.

It was Jon.

His seat on the pulpit was on the outside of a row of three and he didn't have to walk past the camera for the big screen to sit. Still, she knew it was him. She was positive about it. No one walked that way, self-assured but casual, as if he had no particular place to be but knew exactly where he was going. But the questions rushed her brain. What was he doing here? Why had he disappeared and not tried to contact her? What was he doing sitting with the husband-and-wife leaders of the Church of the New Revelation? And why – she suddenly felt the outrage building in her – why was Veronica Whitaker fondling her husband's thigh?

She breathed deeply and tried to compose herself. Damn if that police detective what's-his-name wasn't right about her seeing him here. And damn if Jon didn't scare the hell out of her. Well, at least now she knew he wasn't dead. Now all she had to do was get down there and let him know how much trouble he was going to be in.

She rose and excused herself past the others on her row until she reached the aisle, climbing the steps to the entry door where the hunky young usher stood.

"Is everything all right, ma'am?" he asked quietly.

"Not really," said, trying to choose her words carefully. "It's just that I need to get down to the main part of the sanctuary."

"I'm sorry, ma'am. Only registered church members are allowed there. If you'd like to see the service, you're going to have to stay up here," he said.

"I'm sorry, it's very hard to explain," she said, glancing back at the screen and seeing Jon's face, huge now, hovering above the congregation.

It was strange, though. He looked older, more like his father than the Jon she knew. Was he in disguise? That and the fact that he looked quite happy to be there, chatting and laughing with Veronica Whitaker, made finding him even more imperative.

"Ma'am, I'm afraid I'm going to have to ask you to sit down now."

"No!" she said, a little too loudly. Several of those seated close to her looked around and scowled. "I'm sorry, I just can't. I really have to get down there right now."

"Ma'am, please. Either have a seat or I'll have to escort you to the…"

Linda didn't know when she decided to bring her knee up sharply into the young man's groin, but it seemed that she had and it achieved the desired effect. Pain crossed his face slowly as he doubled over and fell to the floor. She didn't stop to assess his condition, instead hurrying down the long curved staircase she had ascended to reach the balcony. From the sanctuary, she heard the volume of the music increase, signaling the beginning of the service. Good, she thought. Maybe the rest of the security men will be distracted. But coming around the curve of the staircase she saw two more, both burlier than the one in the balcony, and they were both looking straight at her. She turned and looked behind her and saw the usher staggering to the head of the staircase. She obviously hadn't hit him hard enough, because it seemed he was able to alert his colleagues. Damn.

"Ma'am, please stay right there. We don't want to have to hurt you," said one of the guards below her while the other one spoke into a headset.

"That's my husband in there with the Whitakers," she said, backing up the stairs. "I have to get in there to see him."

The guard who had spoken to her looked at his companion, who paused and listened for a moment. "The satellite guy? Didn't Mr. Schaefer say he wasn't married?"

"Yes, he is married! He's MY husband, damn it!" She was getting hysterical again. She knew she needed to calm down. "Look. I don't have to go in there. I won't be a problem, I promise. Just let me speak to your supervisor so I can explain. Will you do that for me?"

The guards were now close enough to grab her if they had to, and she held her spot to show them she wouldn't try to run away. They looked at each other for a moment, regarded her again, probably to assess exactly what she was capable of, and deciding that it wasn't much, quietly consulted each other.

"Ma'am, just stay right there and we'll see what we can do," the lead guard said.

Meanwhile, the other one spoke again into his headset. "Control? This is Peterson. I need Mr. Schaefer."

"What's this guy got against windows, anyway?" Barry said as he completed his fifth circuit around the perimeter of Lucas Schaefer's office.

"It's like a fuckin' cave in here, man. Even the overhead lights are dim," Lewis said as the two passed. Yoshi tried to ignore them, focusing instead on some means of escape. So far, none had presented itself. There were no windows, as the two Marines so astutely noticed, and the locks were electronically controlled with multilayered biometrics. Even stranger, there were no visible sources of ventilation, which not only eliminated another possible avenue of escape, but also contributed to the already sultry room becoming more uncomfortable by the moment.

"He is a mushroom," Yoshi said from his place on the couch, where he sat cross-legged, trying to sort out their next move in his mind.

"A what?" Barry said, stopping in his path.

"A mushroom. He is obviously vegetative in origin, as hard as it might be to believe. Mushrooms aren't vegetables, but they thrive in dank darkness. Perhaps he requires the same environment in which to live," Yoshi said without opening his eyes. He said this only for his companions' edification. He had already excluded the possibility of using that facet of Schaefer against him. There was no way to raise the temperature of the building without setting it on fire – a move which would likely kill many and accomplish relatively little toward their goal. "By any chance, have we tried to contact Krista and Mako?"

"Holy fuck, no!" Barry said, immediately pulling the tracking device from the side pocket on his camouflage pants. "Guess we shoulda thought of that as soon as the Triffid threw us in here."

"The what?" Lewis said.

"The Triffid. It's from an old movie – 'The Day of the Triffids' – where these huge plants start to think and run all over England eating people."

"You watch too much fuckin' TV, man. Got to get you a hobby or something," Barry said, laughing and shaking his head.

"I thought that's what I had you around for," Lewis replied with a conspiratorial grin.

"Gentlemen, if we could please focus on the matter at hand?" Yoshi said, hoping his impatience was clearly audible.

"Hold on, hold on," Barry said. "Wait, man... This is too weird. The tracker says they're both nearby."

Yoshi's eyes popped open. "What are their locations?"

"Keep your shirt on, man. The thing's still cross-referencing with the floor plan Eustace downloaded for us. Okay, here it is. She's on this level, but the room doesn't have a designation. I'm zooming in now." A few anxious moments passed with only their breathing and the electronic chiming of the device breaking the silence. "Got it. Shit, man! She's right down the hall."

"Good. At least we know she's close. And Mako?"

"Checking … Got him out on the boardwalk right on the beach side of the church. Well, that's good. At least Mr. Mushroom didn't get them both," he said.

"True. Perhaps we can use him to help us escape," Yoshi said, reaching up to tap the disk on his throat. "Mako, come in please. This is Yoshi."

"Yoshi-san, baby!" the younger man's voice crackled through Yoshi's earpiece. "Nice to hear from you. What's our status?"

"Eustace, we believe, is dead."

There was a moment of silence during which Yoshi could hear only Mako's breathing. "Shit. Schaefer, right?"

"Yes. Schaefer also discovered us and is holding us in his office. And as I'm sure you know, Krista has been kidnapped and is being held in a room down the hall from us."

"Well, I knew they'd grabbed her, but wasn't sure where she was. I was just trying to figure out a way to get into the church to find her … and now you guys too, I guess," Mako said.

"Good. You will probably have better luck at the main entrance. You will be able to blend in with the crowd and sneak away into the administration wing. We will stay in radio contact and guide you here. But you must avoid Schaefer at all costs. We are not sure how Eustace was killed, but we have seen what he is capable of, and he is nothing to be trifled with."

"Check. I'll keep in touch."

^^^

The rain splattered on Mako's head and soaked straight through his hair, making cold trails as it ran down his scalp to his neck and face. His shirt clung to him and his pants, heavy with water, flapped as he ran down the alley from the boardwalk to Ocean Boulevard. The only piece of clothing that was actually appropriate for the weather was his sandals. At least, he thought, he'd be spared the ultimate uncool of wet, squishy shoes.

But his cool was the last thing he needed to be worrying about, he reminded himself. Eustace was most likely dead, damn it, and Krista had found herself the victim of Schaefer's kidnappers yet again. He was sure that the next time they saw each other she would either kiss him or deck him. More than likely, she would do both, not necessarily in that order.

He splashed along the alleyway, seeming to land in a deeper puddle every time he tried to avoid another one. But the rain didn't matter now. He had to get himself into the church, regardless of what it took.

He could see the street ahead, the line of people waiting to get into the sanctuary still stretching out along the boulevard. He slowed his pace and caught his breath before stopping to tap the disk at his throat and radio Yoshi once more.

"Okay," he said to the air, breathing deeply in and out. "I'm at the front of the church building now, Yoshi. I'll let you know when I'm inside."

"Acknowledged," Yoshi said. "Keep an eye out for Schaefer, Mako. He is a tall, thin Caucasian with closely cropped hair and a severe face. He's also very pale and is wearing an expensive white suit. And whatever you do, do not – I repeat, do not – confront him."

"Ten-four," Mako said, knowing it would aggravate Yoshi. He calmly made his way out of the alley, excusing himself as he passed through the line of waiting faithful, now decked out in identical plastic ponchos that were being handed out by church security. A couple of people stared at him a little too long, prompting him to simply smile back and shrug. "Didn't get here in time for the plastic garbage bags, I see," he told one fellow, who sported a personal viewer on his glasses and seemed to look right through him. He eased his way to the front of the line where the doors stood open and those at the head of the line were clumped together under the marquee to keep dry. There were two security guards in view – at least the ones in uniforms – who were busy keeping an eye on the street and the length of the que.

Examining the situation, Mako decided the only way he would be able to get inside the building would be to buy his way into the line, but he would have to be casual about it. What remained on his cash card was likely more than most of these folks had ever seen in one place. After all, nice people didn't deal in anonymous cash any more. It was the currency of grifters and dealers and black marketeers. It still bought and sold the same as any electronic transfer ever would, though, and without leaving a neon-lit electronic trail from buyer to seller and back again.

Luckily, his target immediately presented herself. She was a lithe blonde, probably 19 or 20, with an open smile and a killer body, which was glaringly obvious through the ensemble she wore, consisting mainly of a pair of thong panties and a sheer wrap tied in back. She was talking to another woman behind her, but he gathered that they didn't really know each other. Then he heard her introduce herself – Regina was her name – then mention something about the University of South Carolina CNR chapter. She was the leader in getting the chapter established on campus, it seemed. Good things to know, Mako thought.

She reminded him of all the good things he'd remembered about the CNR girls from when he was back in Florida. Jesus, it seemed like months ago. But counting backwards he realized it was only a few days.

As he stepped forward, however, the line surged ahead. He saw her take a program from one of the ushers, and then she was gone, pulled inside by the irresistible forward motion of the rest of the crowd. The next likely target was the Web head with the remote viewer. Upon seeing the blonde, Mako began to think he might be able to keep his hands on his bankroll, but he knew he'd have to sacrifice it now. As casually as he could, he strode up to the fellow and smiled.

"Evening, buddy," he said, rocking back and forth from heel to toe. "Pretty shitty night, huh?"

"Yeah," the Web head said, eyeing him suspiciously. "Something I can do for you?"

"Now that you mention it, yeah. See, I need to get into this service more than you could ever possibly imagine," he said confidentially, determined not to upset the people directly behind him and instigate a riot.

"Sounds like you've got a problem then, dude," he said, turning away.

"Tell me about it, man. Standing out here, soaking wet while all those folks are in that nice, dry sanctuary. Hell, man … Even you've got one of those nice ponchos. Church give those out to everyone?"

"Yeah," the Web head said flatly.

Mako just let the reply float there as he kept his spot, moving ahead as the line lurched forward again, pacing his target. Finally, Mako broke the silence again.

"So, whatcha running there, my man?" he asked, nodding towards the headset the fellow wore. "That a 4000 XE?"

The Web head's face brightened. "Shit no, man. This is the 4500. It's got the full spatial rendering in 3-D, wireless sound, kinetically recharged power cell and optically activated menus. And that's just the bells and whistles. This thing's got enough memory right here," he said, holding out his forearm to reveal the nylon-covered processor wrapped around it like an old blood pressure cuff, "to totally smoke those clunky old 4000s."

"Aces, brother," Mako said. "I hear they're coming out with the 5000s before too long. You looking at upgrading?"

"I wish, dude. Had to nearly sell my soul to get this one. Plus, they're taking a major price jump, I hear. The 5000 is gonna go for close to twelve." Mako knew he meant thousands of dollars. Rigs like that didn't come cheap. "Definitely too rich for my blood."

The Web head was grinning and shaking his head now, acknowledging the futility of even considering such a move. "Besides, the new model's gonna have direct sensory inputs, and I hear you might have to go in for surgery just to use one."

"Still, though, man. Direct sensory inputs. That's some killer shit," Mako said. "No more clunky glasses, totally integrated viewing, sound piped in directly to your cortex. I'd pony up if I had the cash."

"That's just the thing, dude. Gotta have the ducats. Can't do anything without it."

"Amen, bro," Mako said. He paused for a moment, scoped the scene and caught the guards looking away. Turning back to his neighbor, he pointed down at his shoes. "Hey, dude. Shoe's untied."

"Aw, thanks, man," he said as he kneeled to check the laces, just in time to see the cash card as Mako flipped it out of his pocket, the tiny liquid crystal readout blinking the remaining balance. The fellow stopped what he was doing and just looked. Just like Mako thought … never seen that much cash in one place. Mako kneeled next to him and leaned close.

"Yeah, buddy. I know what you're thinking. That *is* a lot of money.

About $50,000 at my last count. And all you need to do is let me ease right here in front of you," Mako said in a voice low enough to be just barely audible above the sound of the rain.

"Dude, I don't know…" Damn, Mako thought. This guy had more scruples than he gave him credit for. "There's a lot of people in line behind me. They won't be too happy."

"It's easy, my man. I hand you the money and you just let me slide on in. Look, we're almost to the door, anyway. No one will notice. They already think we're together since we've been chatting so nicely for the last few minutes. And as if I needed to say it again: Direct sensory inputs. You thought the porn feelies were good on that system?" Mako said, tapping the side of the eyeglass viewers. "Just wait till the feeling of that virtual honey riding your pole is piped right into your spinal cord."

That seemed to seal it. "Deal," the fellow said, quickly unburdening Mako of the card, then standing and allowing Mako to ease in front of him just as the line began to march forward again. He eased inside the doors, keeping his head down in an attempt to avert being identified by the guards or over the video cameras. Up the steps, where the red artificial turf changed to rich carpeting, and he was through the doors. No problem so far, he thought. He just wasn't sure when the other shoe was going to drop and someone was going to recognize him and throw him out. Or more likely, throw him in with Yoshi, Barry and Lewis. He tapped the disk at his throat and tried as much as he could to do the ventriloquist thing like Eustace showed him.

"Yoshi, it's Mako. I'm in the building," he said, trying not to draw to much attention to himself.

"Good work," Yoshi said in the earpiece. "Now we need you to find a way to get to us. Facing the sanctuary, we should be down the corridor to your left. It's a plain door, fourth or fifth on the left, with Schaefer's name on it. We used the trackers to pinpoint Krista in another room just down the hall from us."

"Right. Be there as soon as I can."

Suddenly, there was a loud commotion on the staircase that flanked the left side of the main sanctuary entrance.

"Where are you taking me?" an upset woman's voice said. "You have to take me to my husband! He's in there with the Whitakers!"

Two guards descended with a struggling woman held between them. She was dressed a little less provocatively than the rest of the faithful and was a little older, but was still as hot as most of the other women he'd seen. She was, however, clearly pissed off.

"Get your hands off of me, you bastards! I'll call the police! You can't do this to me!" she shouted, obviously trying to cause as much of a scene as possible. Behind her came a tall, severe-looking man in a white suit. He leaned forward and said something into the woman's ear and she quieted for a moment, seeming to struggle less. On their way around the corner, however, he caught the woman's eye, then saw her look directly at the girl Regina ahead of him in line.

"Regina? Regina! Come tell them it's Jon in there! I found him!" the woman shouted, the desperation evident in her eyes.

The girl was torn from her conversation when she realized what was happening. They obviously knew each other, because Regina immediately bolted from the line and tried to follow her around the stairway and down the corridor before being stopped by another set of guards. Mako saw this as a golden opportunity. He charged forward like a bull towards the guard on the girl's left. Mako's head landed in his gut, knocking the air out of him and landing him on his ass, gasping and wheezing. The other guard still held Regina by her arm as he turned to face Mako, who righted himself and planted a firm kick at the side of the guard's right knee, a painful move he'd found effective when dealing with toughs on his delivery routes in Florida. The guard crumpled to one side and released the girl, landing on his back and pulling the injured joint up to his chest as he grimaced and rocked back and forth.

"Come on, follow me," he said to her as he dragged her from where she stood staring at his handiwork. Tapping the disk at his throat again, he said, "Yoshi, I'm on my way. But we may have some company pretty soon."

"Fine," Yoshi said. "There is a utility closet directly across from the door to Schaefer's office. I want you to go in there first."

Mako was baffled. "Sure. Whatever. Just hold on."

"Who are you? Who are you talking to?" Regina said, running by his side now.

"My name's Mako. Nice to meet you, Regina," Mako said as he counted off the doors he passed, looking for Schaefer's nameplate.

"How do you…?"

"Overheard you talking in line. I'll explain everything else later. Are you with that woman who was just taken away?"

"Yes," Regina said. "She's a friend of mine. She was supposed to be watching the service from the visitor's gallery."

"Fine. Go ahead and follow them," he said as they arrived at the utility room door. "I've got to help some friends first."

"But…"

"Just follow them. Maybe we can help each other, okay?" he said as he tried the lock on the door and found it open. Then, touching the radio disk, he said, "Yoshi, I'm at the utility room. What do we need?" Regina still didn't move.

"Good," he said. "A can of spray cleaner and a bundle of rags – can you find those?"

"Got it. What now?"

"Place the can against the door knob to Schaefer's office and tie it on with the rags. Then find some matches or a lighter." Mako did as he was instructed, managing to force the can of commercial-grade Glass Brite! into the space between the knob and doorjamb.

The first two were easy, but he didn't smoke. Then he turned to Regina. "Lighter? Matches?"

"What? Oh! Yeah," she said, digging into the tiny purse she carried and producing a pink disposable lighter.

"Okay, Yoshi. Now what?"

"Light the rags and get into the utility room. The heat from the flames should explode the can and blow the lock, but there will be shrapnel," Yoshi said.

"Shrapnel. Great," he muttered as he lit the longest end of the dangling rags. But motion down the hall caught his eye, and looking that way he saw Krista and the other woman being roughly removed from another room by Schaefer, then forced through another door. God damn it. Too late to put out the fire. Just going to have to hope I can catch up.

"What?" Regina said, still befuddled. "What are you doing?"

"Nothing," he said, taking her arm and pushing her into the closet, then closing the door behind them.

"I hope you don't expect …" Regina said, backing to the far corner but not sounding very adamant about not being taken advantage of. As a CNR girl, she would've ended up in the same situation with someone else toward the end of the service, anyway, so he didn't know what she was getting so upset about.

"Please," he said, giving her his best "Who are you kidding" stare. "I've got better things to worry about right now than a piece of CNR ass, regardless of how tasty it may look."

"Why, you bastard motherfucker!" she shouted, clearly upset. "You have no right to talk to me that way. Let me out of here right now!"

Mako leaned hard against the closet door. "Sorry. I don't think that's a very good idea. Ever wonder why spray cans always say not to throw them into a fire or keep around an open flame?"

The explosion that followed not only felt like it would puncture Mako's eardrum, but very nearly punctured his head when a shard of charred metal with the word Brite! on it emerged through the door and lodged itself about three-quarters of the way through.

"Would that be why?" Regina asked, staring stunned at the interrupted missile.

"That would be why," Mako replied. He opened the door to the overwhelming scent of vaporized commercial glass cleaner and the sight of Yoshi, Barry and Lewis standing in the hallway. He pulled Regina out and made quick introductions. "Guys, this is Regina. Regina, this is Yoshi, Lewis and Barry."

Yoshi couldn't suppress his bow. "I am honored, Miss Regina. Now Mako, which way?"

They bolted down the hallway and through the door through which Mako had seen Schaefer, Krista and Linda's friend pass, which led to a flight of stairs going up. The sounds of footsteps and muffled cries could be heard down the stairwell, then the sound of a door opening and a fire alarm going off. "They're on the roof," Yoshi said. "Hurry."

The group sprinted up the narrow stairway nearly single-file, slowing as they rounded each flight, but keeping up the pace regardless. Finally, on the fourth floor, Mako caught a sign as he passed by that read "Aircar Pad," with an arrow pointing in the direction they were headed. That can't be a good sign, he thought.

Lewis was the first to burst through the door to the roof, left ajar by Schaefer's hasty exit, and Mako saw the wind and rain catch him as soon as it swung open. Once he reached the top of the stairs, it seemed to be raining horizontally, cutting across the roof like everything had been tilted 90 degrees and the rain was still falling down. It only took a moment for him to realize what was causing it – one of two skycars parked on the roof was powering up, the powerful engines adding to the already stiff wind blowing from the storm.

"They can't take off in this," Barry shouted across the roof. "The wind's too strong!"

"I don't think Mr. Schaefer will be taking all the safety checkpoints into account, and there doesn't seem anything we can do to stop them," Yoshi shouted back as the skycar lifted off and quickly became little more than blinking lights in the rain. "Back downstairs everyone!"

"What now, big guy?" Mako said as he passed Yoshi, forsaking his usual sarcasm for genuine concern.

Yoshi paused a moment, his topknot drooping from the rain and his face soaked. Then the giant Okinawan actually grinned. "We take advantage of the fact that Mr. Schaefer obviously doesn't know he's carrying with him a spike-haired homing beacon."

"So would anyone mind explaining to me exactly what's going on here?" Regina said as the rest of the group piled into a crappy old Humvee parked about three blocks down from the Church of the New Revelation. And as if the day couldn't get any worse, she had had to walk those three blocks in the pouring rain, which just didn't mix with an already see-through white outfit.

"We must leave immediately if you want to help your friend," Yoshi, the huge Japanese man, said from the driver's seat.

"But who was that taking her away?" Regina said, needing answers quickly. She was suddenly in the company of four strange men and wasn't sure at all what to expect. Yoshi, meanwhile, started the engine and whipped the huge vehicle out into traffic while he muttered instructions to the guidance system. He compared the screen to the image on his paperback-sized electronic reader. Yoshi tapped a few buttons, performing what looked like a sync between his device and the Humvee's map. A blip then appeared on the sat-map's screen, slowly moving south along what looked like the coast of the state.

"Guy's name is Lucas Schaefer and he only gets nastier the more we find out about him," Mako, the skinny one who she decided must also be Japanese, said as he reached across her to draw the shoulder strap down across her and fasten the buckle into place. For a moment as his forearm brushed her left breast she thought about what she would miss by not being at the service. But then she remembered Linda and forced herself to reprioritize. "Have any idea what they might want with your friend – what was her name?"

"Linda Templeton," Regina said. "We've been looking for her husband, Jon, and a detective told us we might find him at the service. I was going to be there anyway, so I just got Linda to come along with me. I thought it might help her get her mind off her husband, too. Deep down she's worried something really terrible has happened to him." She stopped short of saying, "Deep down we both think he's dead in a ditch somewhere." No use putting her problems or those of Linda on these guys, who seemed to have enough worries of their own.

"Wait a minute," Mako said, wincing as he tried to remember. "She was shouting something about seeing her husband in the sanctuary. That's why they wouldn't let her in. They thought she was crazy and would start a disturbance."

"I guess. But he couldn't have been in there. Especially not where she said he was," Regina said, trying not to sound too incredulous.

"Where was that?" Yoshi asked from the driver's seat.

"On the pulpit with the Rev. Whitaker and Sister

249

Veronica. There would be no way he could have gotten up there."

"Was the church featuring any guest speakers tonight?" Yoshi asked.

"Well, there was the satellite guy."

"The who?" all four men said at once as they turned toward her.

"The guy from the satellite company. Y'all do know we're getting a new satellite to broadcast into China, don't you?" God, she thought. What rock have these guys been under?

"Yes. We know all too well about the church's new satellite. Was there an order of service or a program?" Yoshi said, meeting her gaze in the rearview mirror.

"Hold on," she said. She knew she sounded frustrated, but she needed answers and no one was telling her a thing. She unzipped her tiny purse and pulled out the folded program, printed in a deep pink, opened it and began to read. "The special guest tonight, seated on the pulpit with the Rev. and Deaconess Whitaker, was a representative from Orbital Technologies named Jonnie... Oh my God..." She couldn't believe her eyes, but there it was in print right before her.

"What?" Mako sounded alarmed. "Who is this guy?"

"It says his name is Jonnie Temple. My friend Linda, her husband's name is Jon Templeton. You don't think that could be some sort of weird coincidence, do you?" She was close to tears. Linda was right, and for some reason the CNR people wanted her out of the way because of it.

"I doubt it," Yoshi said. "What does you friend's husband do?"

"He used to be a reporter, but now he does PR for some firm in Charleston, I think. But I can't think of any reason he'd be at a CNR service. The last time I talked to him, it seemed like he didn't even know that much about the church." That was evident from the way he fought against her friendly kiss on the beach. "And I'm sure he doesn't know anything about selling satellites."

"Could he be working undercover for some agency without your or his wife's knowledge?" Yoshi asked.

"Jon? No way. He and Linda didn't have any secrets from each other," she said.

"As far as you knew," Barry, the tall Marine, piped up. "Honey, if you knew the people we knew and the secrets their wives didn't know, you'd blush enough to burn through that flimsy little thing you're wearing."

"I know all about that, but still. They had one of the best marriages I've ever seen." And she was adamant about that. She'd never known another couple that got along as well as Jon and Linda did. They seemed to understand and respect so much about each other, she thought. She'd often doubted that she would be able to ever find someone who loved her as much as Jon loved Linda. "I can't imagine that Linda wouldn't have known about something like that. Or at least suspected."

"Fine," Yoshi said. "We have determined that the satellite representative is likely the missing husband of your friend. And now Schaefer is holding your friend and our companion Krista hostage. We know why our friend is being held, and we now have a theory about why your friend was removed. Now..."

"So why was your friend kidnapped? If I'm coming with you guys, you've got a lot of explaining to do," she said, curious as to how a group such as this one would end up trying to waylay a CNR service.

Yoshi wove through Myrtle Beach traffic and breathed deeply. "My late employer – Mako's father – was killed in a car bomb explosion early Thursday morning. His company, Nikura International, manufactures, among other things, aerospace technology. We have reason to believe that Lucas Schaefer, working through intermediaries, purchased an orbital weapon from others in the Nikura organization without my employer's knowledge. We believe agents of Schaefer killed Mr. Nikura when they learned he was investigating the purchase. We also believe those agents of Mr. Schaefer have killed several other people, including my late employer's secretary, and tried to kill Mako himself, to keep this purchase a secret until Schaefer is able to have the weapons technology integrated into the church's new communications satellite."

Holy shit. She had contributed $500 of her own money – money she busted her ass for in a seafood buffet restaurant full of stupid Northern tourists – to help pay for that new satellite. "But what does he want a weapon on our satellite for?"

"Schaefer may intend to exploit the deteriorating relationship between the United States and several nations by placing this weapon into space. He may be considering blackmail, or perhaps something more insidious."

"How could anything be worse than that?" Regina asked.

"He may simply use the weapon. Space-based weapons were made illegal in the SALT IV treaty in 2015 after a North Korean missile platform accidentally targeted San Francisco. The only thing that kept war from breaking out was the North Koreans' willingness to alert U.S. officials of the situation so they could shoot the missile down. This weapon Schaefer has acquired, however, does not use missiles, so an attack from space would be completely unexpected. Schaefer could use it to fire on any number of nations encircling the Pacific rim, further enflaming animosity and perhaps bringing all-out war."

"But why? What would he get out of that? He'd just end up getting everyone killed."

"We do not know his motives, only his methods. And perhaps we will never know. All that we are sure of is that he must be stopped," Yoshi said, again meeting her gaze in the mirror. "And hopefully, in the process, we will also be able to save the lives of our friends. Krista has on her a small homing device, which shows her moving south. Do you have any idea where they might be headed?"

"Well, the Whitakers have another estate close to Hilton Head that they use as a private retreat. It's another one of those old plantations, except this one is way out on an island and can only be reached by boat."

"Or air," Lewis said. "I'd bet my last money the place has a lovely little landing pad."

It began as a church service just like any other, only much more underdressed.

Eventually, the novelty of the congregation's partial nudity had less of an impact on Jon, who found himself slipping into the idle mental wandering church often induced. There were the hymns (some of which Jon actually recognized), the responsive reading, the Lord's Prayer – with a few bawdy additions – and a pause for the passing of the plate.

Even Veronica managed to behave herself after an initial grope. Up until now he had only heard her referred to as "Sister" Veronica by the members of the congregation, but once inside the sanctuary, she became "Deaconess," a tribute, no doubt, to the power she held within the church and her influence in its creation in the first place.

Of course, Jon remembered to keep Veronica's good behavior in clear perspective. At the same time she was sitting next to him on the alter, playing the good preacher's wife before his faithful flock, he noticed a change other than her title came over Veronica when she, Jon and her husband entered the sanctuary to rousing applause from the congregation. Her face glowed and she couldn't resist touching her hair and straightening her dress to emphasize her evident curvature. It was as if she were flirting with the hundreds of people crammed into the cavernous tabernacle, attempting to woo them even further into her fold with the sheer power of her sexuality.

It was something Jon had never witnessed on such a scale. Certainly, he knew women in his life who had had such an effect on a room of people. He'd even had the simultaneous pleasure and displeasure to date at least one. He knew the power of a beautiful woman on both sexes, particularly in a setting where the mood was light and the social lubricants flowed freely. But in Veronica, he saw it amplified hundreds of times. Her edge was, he imagined, that she knew she didn't have to work for this crowd's adoration. She and her husband had created around themselves such a cult of personality that the faithful didn't think twice about the fact that they were worshiping two humans – two humans that were obviously being used by Schaefer for some nefarious purpose – instead of a deity. Lawrence and Veronica Whitaker had cast themselves as Jesus and Mary Magdalene living out the earthly destiny that Christ wasn't able to fulfill, and everyone bought it. And if anyone needed any evidence as to how much, all one had to do was gaze out into the rows and rows of young, beautiful faces rapt over the words of a man with a mighty good scam going. Although he was ashamed to think such a thing in the context of religious worship, Jon felt as if he were watching a porn feelie that was trying to legitimize itself with interminable and bogus dialogue and seemed like it would never get around to the good part. He wondered why Whitaker even bothered with all the trappings of an actual religious service, when everyone knew the only reason anyone came to this church was to get laid.

Jon checked his bulletin, flipping it over to peruse the end of the order of worship and see at what point they were in the service. Close enough, he realized, for him to start considering his next move as far as Veronica was concerned. He knew only that he was a marked man, and that at some point very soon he would be expected to accompany her to a meditation chamber and let her lay her special kind of evangelism on his heathen and unworthy body. As a result, for the first time in his life, he felt something akin to what must have been performance anxiety. What was she really expecting, anyway? Had she assessed, through their few brief meetings, some hidden sexual capacity in him? If Veronica consulted Linda on the matter, he was sure he would get nothing but glowing reviews. But the reviews of one's wife, who in addition to being a sex partner also had to deal with the day-to-day business of marriage, wouldn't really mean much to someone like Veronica. Jon imagined she no doubt had taken at least one bite off every piece of candy in the sexual sampler.

Jon was broken from his thoughts when he saw Whitaker rise and move to the altar, which Jon had failed to notice earlier simply because whatever was on it was covered with crisp, white vestment cloth. He realized at once what was going on. Whitaker was preparing the sacraments for communion. The next item on the bulletin, Jon noted, was the "meditation period," to be followed by church fellowship, which would likely go long into the night.

"Lord, we approach your alter humbly, full in the knowledge that we are not worthy of your boundless love and bountiful blessings," Whitaker said. Jon could see from his somewhat obscured point of view that Whitaker's eyes were tightly shut, the intensity of his prayer coming across vividly on his tanned face. The orchestra, meanwhile, kept up a slow gospel organ solo similar to what Jon had heard at Aunt Lil's funeral, which she demanded be held at the all-black AME Zion church in Carlton. Nothing pissed Lil off more than a boring church service, and as she faded into her last days of life, he had actually heard her say she wanted her funeral service to "Rock the rafters."

"Let these, your sacraments, bring to us the insight to see your love and open our minds to accept it into our hearts during this time of worship. In your name we pray, Amen."

With that, the music swelled and resumed its slow, grinding rhythm. The worship attendants, who would've been called ushers in any other church, then made their way up to the altar where the vestments were removed and neatly folded. They revealed about two dozen trays of tiny plastic communion cups filled with what Jon imagined was wine and others stacked with what seemed to be traditional cardboard-tasting communion wafers. As the attendants moved down the aisles, alternately passing down the wine and wafers, members of the congregation busied themselves by taking strips of dermals stowed on the backs of each pew and applying them to one another. Most of the congregation had at least two of the patches pressed along their jugular veins. As the wine was drunk and the wafers dissolved on tongues, it would seem the drugs were taking effect. Hands that had been caressing arms and shoulders quickly moved to breasts, chests, buttocks and genitals. When one of the attendants approached Jon after the rest of the congregation had been served, he thought he might initially wave him off. Somewhere, deep down inside where there was still a respectful 10-year-old who got gold stars on his Sunday school lessons, he felt that taking communion under such circumstances would be sacrilegious. Then he felt Veronica's hand on his thigh as she reached over to take her wafer and wine and realized that to refuse the sacraments would be seen as a blatant affront to his hosts' hospitality. So, as reverently as possible, he placed the unleavened disk on his tongue and let the sweet wine wash over it and down his throat.

Then he realized it wasn't just the drugs from the dermals that were kicking in among the congregation. Jon felt his mind go immediately through some drastic chemical change, every nerve ending in his body suddenly tingling in only the best possible way. Were he not in the presence of so many beautiful, willing women, he'd feel compelled to touch himself, the better to speed along the overwhelming desire for immediate and intense sexual gratification. Luckily, though, he wasn't alone in his feelings.

Where Veronica had obviously been aroused before, it was glaringly evident that she was somehow feeding on the energy from her husband's followers as well as getting the same effect from the "sacraments." She sat more erect, if that were possible, which only emphasized even more the shape of her unencumbered breasts beneath the sheer material of her dress. In his peripheral vision, Jon sensed her moving closer to him, not exactly squirming so much as deliberately pressing her thighs together, indicating quite clearly that there was something going on between her legs worthy of encouraging. Her hand, having left his leg after she received her wine and wafer, returned to trace a slow path over the light material of Jon's trousers from his knee up to his crotch. Despite his efforts at maintaining some decorum in front of all these people, there was growing evidence of his chemically enhanced arousal. Without moving her hand, Veronica leaned closer, her other hand finding its way to his chest, lightly slipping beneath his jacket and heading straight for the inside pocket where Jon had stowed the 'dermals.

"Mrs. Whitaker, may I remind you that we are in the house of the Lord?" he said, trying to be funny to stave off his increasing anxiety under the drug's influence. She ignored him and slowly removed the strip from his pocket, taking special care to graze her long, lavender fingernails against his chest. She then delicately peeled away one of the dermals with tiny flames and pressed it against his neck.

"This may be the Lord's house, Jonnie, but I've got the key," she whispered in his ear. Again, she peeled away a dermal – this one featuring the clock with penis hands – and pressed it below the first one.

Never, not even in the midst of his most heated sexual encounter, had Jon actually felt the blood leave his brain and reallocate itself to his crotch. But that is exactly what happened no more than 30 seconds after the application of the second dermal. Initially, he thought he was feeling both patches.

That is, until he felt his toes. It was like someone was holding him over a low-level radiant heater, the warmth coursing upwards, enveloping his legs, then his groin, then up through his torso and finally to his head, where the drug took full effect. Without realizing what he was doing, he found himself pressing his lips against Veronica's. He held in his hand a thick mass of her red hair, tightening his grasp gently as he kissed her hard and deep and relished the sound of her tiny moans as she fought for air and for domination over his insistent and invasive tongue. Somewhere in the peripheral parts of his hearing, there were cheers and applause and loud shouts of "amen" and "praise the Lord." But he didn't care. He'd forgotten where he was and why he was there and what he was supposed to accomplish and instead had in mind one single purpose: to take this woman.

Jon held her lips to his tightly, releasing her only enough to flick his tongue over her lips, teasing her by treating her mouth as if it was her other, even more delicate set of lips. His free hand he found trailing its way up her exposed legs toward the top of the slit in her dress. Her hands, meanwhile, cupped his face, caressing his jaw and stroking the back of his neck before sliding down his shoulders and chest, where they paused to stroke and lightly pinch his nipples through his shirt's thin material.

Suddenly, she pushed his face away just far enough for her to speak, her breath quick and labored, her voice rough with the sweet rasp of sex. "I have somewhere for us to go," she said.

"What about…"

"Larry won't mind, Jonnie. He wants it. He knows you're a godly man."

Godly? Perhaps not. But he had never felt more like what he had often jokingly referred to as a love god. And he planned to make good use of the feeling. The weight of his Linda guilt remained, but had been sent by the drugs to somewhere deep in his consciousness. He tried to summon trepidation about taking Veronica, but it wasn't happening.

Jon stood, realizing that his excitement was then even more evident, but not caring. Veronica offered her delicate hand and he took it as she stood, slowly and languidly, emerging from her chair like a cobra coiling upward. She led the way down the steps from the high stage toward a peaked door with a tiny crucifix-shaped stained-glass window set near the top. Jon felt as if he would burst before he could get through it and on to whatever surface awaited them. There could have been a block of ice inside, for all he cared. He'd simply lie down and, like some overheated cartoon character, melt into it a Jon-shaped impression. Veronica opened the door far more slowly than he would have preferred, especially since his prominent erection felt like it was about to tear through his trousers, then finally led him inside.

The meditation chamber wasn't exactly what he had expected, but it was close. The room was round, and at the far end from the door was another stained-glass window, this one stretching from floor to ceiling and dimly backlit from some artificial source. It depicted a couple that he took to be Mary Magdalene and Jesus, engaged in something more reminiscent of the Kama Sutra than the Bible. A benevolent God hovered above them that looked exactly like the God everyone expected to see – all flowing white hair and beard. His leer made him look more like some aging rock star than the ruler of all creation. The rest of the chamber was a bed, also round and made up with white linens and covered with purple throw pillows, each bearing the church's cross-and-flaming-heart insignia. It left just enough of a walk space for two adults, who at that moment included only Jon and Veronica Whitaker, to stand shoulder to shoulder.

But they were not standing shoulder to shoulder. They were pressed as close together as two human beings can be without actually merging, though Jon imagined if they could at that moment they would have. But there were clothes still barring the merger, and Jon sought to make things easier on both of them by removing that barrier. Veronica was obviously thinking along the same lines. While Jon fiddled with the clasps of her dress – which he found entirely too complicated considering its diaphanous nature – Veronica quickly undid the buttons of his shirt, stripping it and his jacket off at the same time. She immediately placed her lips upon his chest and sucked his left nipple hard into her mouth.

The sensation — spread along, he imagined, by the sensitizing drugs — coursed down to his toes and back, taking a quick detour at his groin while traveling in each direction. He heard himself gasp as he pulled her head tight against him, again clasping a handful of her thick crimson tresses. The only sounds filling the room were those of their breathing, coming in short rasps and abbreviated sighs, and of material sliding against skin. Somewhere in the background, the music from the sanctuary filtered through, but it served only as a muted soundtrack to the meditation chamber's activities. Jon was aware only of Veronica's lips and fingers and tongue and breasts and the sensations that gripped his body and refused to let go until they reached some sort of dramatic physical climax. And it was in precisely that direction that Jon was headed.

Veronica's dress loosened at the shoulders finally and allowed Jon to pull it forward. The tiny sleeves slithered along her arms, which she had wrapped around him, drawing her long fingernails along his back as she worked her way downward. She kissed from his chest, along his ribs (which suddenly felt as if they were primary erogenous zones in themselves) and on down to his navel. He looked down and found her looking up at him, her eyes wide with desire and her tongue anxiously licking her lips as she undid his belt and fiddled with the top button on his trousers. He could gaze down past her face to her unencumbered breasts, now almost entirely revealed by her loosened dress. Then, before Jon even realized, his trousers were open and the full measure of his excitement was glaringly evident. Veronica took him delicately in her hand and stroked his length, gazing at it lovingly and planting small kisses on its tip. He was momentarily concerned that he couldn't contain himself, but the effect of the drugs held fast and, despite the level of his stimulation, he knew somehow that he would be able to maintain enough control to last through whatever sweet torture Veronica had in mind for him.

Then, without any warning, her mouth was on him, her rose petal lips surrounding him, drawing him in with gentle suction as her tongue, which seemed to somehow operate independently of the rest of her mouth, toyed with him. He heard himself moan through the haze of drugs and frenzied passion as his hips began to respond to her delicate ministrations. Only her mouth handled him, her hands free to roam up and down the parts of his legs now left exposed, trailing along the crease of his ass and then back down to his taut calves. He looked down again just as the angle of Veronica's arms allowed the gossamer threads holding up her dress to fall forward, completely revealing her abundant breasts, the nipples taut from excitement and the cool of the room. His nerve endings raced even more at the sight as she once again gazed up at him, her mouth fully engulfing him and her fingers now delicately encircling him as her head moved slowly back and forth.

He could stay like this for days, he thought, wallowing in delicious, decadent sensations at the hands and lips and tongue of this woman who seemed little more than pure, distilled passion issuing endlessly forth from an exotic fountain. But while one part of him wanted to simply bask in her attentions, another part was urging him to forsake his passive role and drink thirstily from this fountain.

As if she had read his mind, she gradually released him from her mouth, her hand staying in place and continuing a slow stroking, her thumb lingering at the ridge between shaft and crown. As he bit his lip and suppressed the urge to shout out in his pleasure, she stood, the rest of her dress falling from her entirely, and leaned forward to plant tiny bites and kisses along his neck and shoulder.

"You know, Jonnie, for this to be a truly effective evangelistic experience, we must minister to each other," she said, pausing with her lips excruciatingly close to his ear. "We must share our pleasure, both giving and taking equally, for the true power of God to operate within us."

He was surprised she maintained the façade of worship in all this, but he figured he probably shouldn't be. Still, it was much easier to focus on what she was doing to him when she wasn't treating it as if it were a pornographic Sunday school lesson. He'd have to do something about that, he decided.

His arms encircled her, sliding down to the small of her back as she continued to whisper her pseudo evangelistic nonsense. However pleasant the sensation of her breath against his ear, he decided he must take action against it immediately. He pulled his head back to look her in the eye.

"I liked it much better when your mouth was full," he said, then pressing his mouth hard against hers, his tongue pushing inside, eliciting a long moan that came from deep inside Veronica.

And somewhere along his ear canal, past the rushing his own blood and the beating of his own heart amplified by the aphrodisiac substances coursing through his body, he was sure he heard cheering.

^^^

"Brothers and sisters, looks like we've got ourselves a deal!" the Rev. Lawrence Whitaker said into the microphone at the pulpit. His exuberance was barely contained as the congregation cheered on his wife and Temple in their equally exuberant coitus, broadcast for all to see on the towering screens above the altar.

"Children of the Lord, it's time to rejoice!" His arms were thrust upward in a triumphant "V" as his flock, full of the spirit at the sight of his gorgeous wife, his very own vessel of the Holy Ghost, sealing the pact between the Church of the New Revelation and Jonnie Temple of Orbital Technologies. The moment guaranteed that the Lord would have a way, through the church, to convey His word to the people of China whether or not their leaders wanted them to hear it. If they wanted to insist on their godless ideology – godless unless you count their worship of that long-dead Mao – that was fine with him, but he would be damned if he wouldn't give those billions, those teeming masses aching for spiritual release, something to grab onto.

The music rose higher now, bringing with its infectious beat the desires that allowed God's word to course through these innocents before the Lord – these lambs not headed to slaughter but to salvation in the arms of each other. They were off to make the music of their bodies, just like Veronica and Jonnie up there on the screen, impressing their faith on each other through their flesh, their juices and their delicious, holy sweat.

The Reverend looked out on them, a sea of faces eager for each other and for the Lord. But tonight he would be without his sacramental partner, and that was a situation that had to be rectified immediately. Fortunately, more than a few of those eager faces were aimed in his direction – figures of nubile passion, their need for the blessing only he could give them shining in their lovely faces. In just the first row of pews, he picked out three likely candidates, none of them up to Veronica's heavenly standards, but who would do for now.

"Friends, I ask you now to retire to a meditation chamber or remain in the sanctuary in reverent celebration for the remainder of the service," he said, raising his hands and reverently closing his eyes as he delivered the benediction familiar to all his flock. "Now, may the peace and passion of the Lord go forth with you in all its glory."

"And also with you!" the congregation shouted back, ending in a roar of cheers that filled the Reverend's heart with pride in what his faith had wrought. Whitaker stepped down from the pulpit and into the congregation, his lovely match-pair boy and girl acolytes leading the way. At the first row of pews he stopped and pointed, one after the other, at the three women he had spotted from above, motioning for them to follow him into a meditation chamber. Into the loving arms of Jesus.

^^^

Veronica Whitaker loved the male body. She could drink it in in all its forms. And she was at the moment drinking in that of Jonnie Temple, satellite salesman. She was on the outside edge of sleep, just conscious enough to be aware of her surroundings, but so relaxed that it might as well have been a full slumber. It was in this state that she found she could fully enjoy all the accessory pleasures of a man's form – the warmth of his flesh against hers, the definition of muscle beneath skin, the sandy scratch of a beard. It was nothing like being with one of the boys from the youth group, she thought, with their fumbling insecurities of adolescent sex. With Jonnie, as with Larry, all that was replaced by the assured touch of experience.

And oh, what a difference that experience made. Veronica had found that even with the help of the dermals, a clumsy lover was still a clumsy lover, made only more tedious by the drug-fueled endurance. But Jonnie wasn't like that at all. Even with the drugs urging his libido on, he had paced himself, his body continually recharging like a solar cell left out in the desert. Finally, after the fifth time, when he knelt behind her and slipped inside, reaching forward to take her long hair in his hands as he moved deeply in and out, keeping up a slow steady pace that made her crazy with desire, after he had driven her to orgasms she had lost count of, she realized he was truly someone special, someone for whom she could find a place in the Church of the New Revelation. And better still, someone of whom her husband already approved.

The light chiming of the intercom system woke her from her contented dozing. She let her eyes adjust to the dim light of the meditation chamber before quietly answering "yes" to the soft noise.

"Deaconess, I'm sorry to disturb you, but there have been some developments I thought you should know about," the voice said. She recognized it as that of Bowers, one of the lower ranking members of the security team.

"Why isn't Mr. Schaefer handling this?" she said, trying not to sound too perturbed.

"Well, ma'am, that's part of the problem. We can't seem to find Mr. Schaefer. And Doug Rohrbaugh from Security Control is dead."

Dead? She sat up, completely awake now. "What happened?"

"We don't know, ma'am, but it's a mess down here in the control room. We think it might have something to do with the woman we were holding."

She was confused. "What woman?"

"The woman from the visitors' gallery, ma'am. The one who claimed to be Mr. Temple's wife."

She rested her forehead in her hands, trying to sort if all out in her mind. "But Mr. Temple isn't married," she whispered, remembering that he still lay sprawled next to her, naked and so far oblivious to the conversation. "We checked on his background and we didn't find anything about a wife, Bowers. Do you have any idea who she is?"

"She gave her name as Linda Templeton. She just stood up before the service and started hollering about Mr. Temple being her husband. Then when we tried to take her out, she just lost it. We decided to take her to Mr. Schaefer because she was being so disruptive. Then the next thing we knew they were both gone."

Templeton. It's almost too close, she thought. "Did you try contacting Mr. Schaefer?"

"Yes, ma'am. No luck. He's apparently turned everything off. Either that or he's just not answering."

"And we don't have any idea where he might have gone?" This was very unlike Lucas, even under the direst circumstances. Normally he was the most annoyingly calm person in the room. For him to be thrown by an unstable woman in the congregation was entirely out of character.

"No, ma'am... Wait a minute. We just got the results of another security scan. Apparently one of the skycars from the roof landing pad is missing. But I can't imagine that anyone would take off in weather like this. It's coming down in buckets out there."

Veronica felt motion at her side and saw that Jonnie was beginning to stir. How she hated for such a lovely service to end on such a down note. And in such an odd way, too. "Just keep trying to find Mr. Schaefer. He's got to know something about all this. And don't worry the Reverend just yet. We'll fill him in when we know more."

"Yes ma'am. I'll let you know if anything changes."

Another chime signaled that he had signed off as Jonnie rolled over, his hair all mussed, making him look like an innocent little boy. "Everything okay?"

"Just a little disturbance in the visitor's gallery earlier," she said, purposefully angling her naked body to the light and pushing her shoulders back to emphasize her breasts — a classic trick she learned while working the feelie site before she met Larry. It achieved the desired effect and prompted Jonnie to lean forward to touch her, his finger making long strokes against her right thigh. She reveled in the sensation for a moment, then leaned down to kiss him. She'd determined early on that he would be a good kisser, and she was right. She then caught him looking at her in a way that said he knew something was wrong, but he was too polite to ask.

The problem was, as soon as Bowers had told her about the woman claiming to be Johnnie's wife, all the things Lucas had told her, all the suspicions he had about Jonnie not being who he said he was, came rushing back into her mind. At first, she had of course thought Lucas was being entirely too suspicious – paranoid, even. But the woman appearing at the service, the similarities of their last names and all the things Lucas said seemed to converge in a storm of doubt in Veronica's mind. She knew she probably shouldn't bring it up, but she had to know. She and Larry both had put so much trust in Jonnie, not only for themselves, but for the future of the ministry and spiritual lives of all those lost souls suffering in China. And what if Jonnie was someone sent to destroy them? Someone whose sole purpose was to infiltrate the ministry and expose everything that went on there as if it were something… bad? Something that the Lord would disapprove of? Then she couldn't not bring it up, if only for her and Larry's safety.

"You know, it's the funniest thing, though. The disturbance? Apparently it was some crazy woman claiming to be your wife. Can you imagine? You don't have anyone out there stalking you, do you?" she said with a dismissive laugh.

But something about Jonnie's expression changed. Just the slightest bit, but Veronica noticed, and she recognized the look. It was the slightest shift that takes place when someone not very adept at lying is caught in a lie and tries to keep up the front. This worried her, but prompted her to continue.

"And the strangest thing – you won't believe this – is her name. I mean, she must know you and had it changed to sound like yours, because it really is an odd coincidence. I'm just glad she didn't hurt anyone, you know? I mean, people like that, they're sometimes capable of anything."

"So what was her name?" Jonnie said, the odd expression gone now but some tension added to his voice. He continued to stroke her thigh – which she was not complaining about – but he seemed distracted now.

"Templeton," she offered, watching him closely. His jaw ever so slightly clenched in response. "Linda was her first name, I think." And then, before she could gauge his reaction, the intercom chimed again and Bowers' voice filled the room without waiting for her acknowledgement.

"Deaconess, we've found the skycar. We've tracked it heading toward the compound off Beaufort with three people aboard. We're pretty sure two of them are Mr. Schaefer and the Templeton woman. We still can't establish contact, though. And the storm isn't helping."

"Thank you, Bowers. Keep trying," she said as she turned back to address Jonnie. But he wasn't there. He was already up and dressing, his face now a grim mask of determination as he buttoned his shirt and zipped up his trousers. "Jonnie, dear, what's wrong?"

"Is there another skycar on the roof?" His voice had lost all of its smooth, salesmen veneer. Suddenly he was a different man from the one who had just made expert love to her. Lucas was right, after all. She realized that with Lucas gone and her husband occupied with the responsibility of the church, the job of finding out who he was fell to her, just as Lucas had warned.

"I hope you know how disappointed I am in you, Jonnie ... Or whatever your name is." She couldn't help pouting over losing such a talent, not to mention over endangering the church by deciding he was trustworthy. But obviously, he didn't care. He picked up her dress from the floor and threw it at her.

"Answer me! Is there another skycar on the roof?" He looked then like he could kill her without a second thought. Saving the church, she decided, would just have to wait a while.

"Yes," she said, resigned for the moment to helping the unexpected enemy. "I'll show you the way."

They called for thunderstorms today, not a hurricane, Jon thought as Veronica pushed open the door to the roof of the Church of the New Revelation. The wind howled like death and the rain flew sideways, stinging his face and drenching his clothes as soon as he stepped out. In the distance, barely visible through the swirl of the downpour, Jon could see the faint outline of the other skycar, the landing skids occasionally rising a fraction of an inch from the landing pad. The machine was held there only by heavy hinged clamps overlapping the skids, and at that moment it seemed as if the thin supports holding the aircraft to its landing gear might snap and send the craft careening into the churning Atlantic.

While he could think of far better circumstances in which to escape, at that point he was simply glad they had made it as far as they had. As Jon suspected, there was a discreetly hidden second door to Veronica's meditation chamber that led directly to a service stairwell. The stairs took them directly to the roof, allowing them to avoid the suspicions of twitchy security guards and curious members of the congregation.

"Jonnie, you can't expect me to go out in this," Veronica shouted over the wind. He ignored her whining, grabbed her hand and pulled her from the doorway out onto the roof. Her dress instantly became drenched and, consequently, transparent. But he didn't care any more. He'd had about enough of the charms of Deaconess Veronica Whitaker. Her preening, pouting temple whore bit had worn thin immediately after the aphrodisiac drugs wore off, and his mind was now completely focused on Linda. She was with Schaefer, and Schaefer knew Jon wasn't who he said he was. That in itself presented more danger to her than she could possibly imagine. He only hoped she didn't know that.

Jon pushed her in the direction of the skycar, both of them fighting against the wind to maintain a straight course. Guide wires supporting the massive neon crucifix on the cathedral's roof hummed and groaned as the obnoxiously lit icon tilted ever so slightly with each gust. He only hoped they could take off before the wires snapped and sent the giant cross plummeting towards their only means of pursuit. Veronica reached the aircar first, pressed her hand to the ID pad on the side of the door and stood back as the craft opened up like an alloy flower, the gull-wing door rising with a slow, mechanical whir as a stepped ramp lowered itself to the landing pad. She nearly dove in as Jon looked behind him just in time to see a lightning bolt crackle down from the sky and strike the towering crucifix, sending up a shower of sparks before the blue and red neon flickered and went out.

The doors closing made the skycar feel like being trapped inside a giant, well-appointed bivalve. The seats were arranged limousine style, like comfortable couches facing each other, without any sign of a command cockpit or manual controls. The vehicle's thick insulation immediately sealed out the sound of the storm, and when they were completely closed, the inside sprang to life. Dim lights were activated and various discretely placed control panels flickered on.

"Good evening, Mrs. Whitaker," said a disembodied female voice. The onboard computer was taking the initiative. "Would you like to choose a pre-programmed flight plan?"

"Well, Jonnie? Would we?" Veronica looked miserable, her hair dripping on her already saturated wisp of a dress. She sat, whiny and pouting, with her hands held up as if touching her wet hair or clothing would cause acid burns. Finally she reached up to take a handful of thick hair and wring out nearly a half-cup of water that she let run on the aircar floor, then whining more with each drop extracted.

"That depends. Do our choices include Mr. Schaefer's destination?"

"Of course they do," she said. The "you idiot" at the end of the statement went unsaid but was clearly implied. "But he's quite a ways ahead of us. We'll never catch him before he gets there." She went back to making small pouty noises as she fussed over her condition.

"And where would that be, Veronica? We don't have all night for you to worry about how you look." Jon could feel himself becoming even more agitated. He'd been at this point with women before, where the façade created by their beauty and desirability shatters and reveals the loathsome person underneath. But with those women he had usually made some emotional investment, only to be dejected when he discovered what everyone else was telling him about the object of his affections was true. With Veronica, the investment was only his time and energy in trying to resolve Eli's assignment. So far, though, that investment was providing increasingly diminishing returns.

She sighed dramatically and rolled her eyes. "Barstow said they were headed toward the plantation on our private island off Beaufort."

Jon waited for her to take some action, but there was none. As patiently as he could, he said, "Then would you mind please telling the car to go there. We're on a bit of a schedule here."

She was on the verge of another extended sigh when she caught Jon's withering gaze. He wasn't sure if he would hit her, but he'd be damned if he'd let her get away with this without a believable threat. It wasn't necessary though. In a voice suddenly smaller and more childlike than he had ever heard it, she said, "Lillith, please take us to the Beaufort plantation."

"Very good, ma'am," the skycar said. "Please prepare for takeoff in two minutes."

Immediately the vehicle's powerful turbines began to whine, only a decibel or two of which bled through the hull. "Mrs. Whitaker, there seems to be some unpleasant weather at the moment. Are you sure you'd like to leave now?" the computer asked.

"Yes, Lillith," Veronica said as if responding to a persistent child.

"Very good. Please be aware that there may be some turbulence before we reach cruising altitude."

"Thank you, Lillith."

"You named your skycar?" Jon asked as he searched behind him for something resembling a seatbelt.

She immediately was on the defensive. "And what's wrong with that? I find it makes life much easier to name my inanimate objects. Especially when they talk back to you."

"So you don't just name the cars?" Jon knew she was powerful, influential, oversexed and generally a little askew from the rest of the world's women, but she was beginning to seem downright nutty.

"Of course not, silly." Much of her malice had disappeared, as the focus was once again on her and a topic she enjoyed talking about. "Nearly everything. My grapevine, for instance, is named Dionysus, and my personal car I call Zephyr. And the two skycar limousines are Lillith and Eve."

"Interesting." He regarded her for a long moment as she returned to fussing over her appearance, then decided to lay on the table all his thoughts about Deaconess Veronica Whitaker, Mary Magdalene to her husband's Jesus and temple whore to what he imagined were more than a few young CNR novitiates. Jon figured that since he was toeing the line of kidnapping, he might as well dispense with the fake social graces. "You're an absolute nutbag, do you know that. Not that you aren't beautiful and sexy and an excellent businesswoman, but you strike me as being a few sandwiches short of a picnic. Do you think that's an unfair characterization?"

Veronica looked up, a sharp movement she seemed to make only with her eyes until the rest of her head followed along. "What's that supposed to mean? I'm not the one pretending to be someone I'm not and ruining the plans of a national religious movement, am I? Larry and I are just exercising our rights as free citizens of this country, practicing our religion and running a business. That's all. I don't know that anyone could say that was crazy."

The argument sounded genuine but rehearsed, as if she has sat down with a team of lawyers – or perhaps just her husband and Schaefer – and gone over it repeatedly until it sprang forth from her mouth without a thought. Jon fully realized at that moment how defensive she and her husband were about all this. Rather than running a scam operation thinly veiled as a religious movement, as was the case for so many other TV preachers, the Whitakers genuinely believed that what they were doing was good and decent in the eyes of God. It was then that he knew that Veronica likely would be the key to finding out about Lucas Schaefer.

"Of course not. Not when you put it like that. But spending as much time with you and your husband as I have, I wonder if there's not something a little more sinister going on here. I mean, do you actually believe that you're going to start beaming your channels into China, which has lately taken an even greater dislike for all things American, without some political ramifications for somebody? To someone who didn't know better, it might seem like you're just going out of your way to piss the Chinese off."

"It's nothing of the sort, Jonnie. And it's certainly not …" She paused as if the word tasted bad in her mouth. "It's not sinister at all. The Chinese are terribly oppressed people. They're not allowed to practice their religions, and since the last Cultural Revolution, they've been hunting down and killing anyone that might breathe a word of Christianity. It's our duty to try and spread the word, even if some shortsighted politicians think it might be a bad idea."

"I wouldn't call it shortsighted to worry about the Chinese lobbing a few hundred nuclear tipped missiles this way. And if you've been following the news, it would seem that's not out of the realm of possibility. All it will take is the right … or wrong move on our part. And that's why I get that sinister feeling. It seems like the Church of the New Revelation is going out of its way to be provocative. I don't keep up with the pundits, but I'm sure there are plenty of other people out there saying the same thing."

"Provocative or not, it's the right thing to do, Jonnie. Being a good Christian isn't about doing what's convenient or easy. It's about oppression and opposition, just like those poor people in China. They want to believe, but their government won't let them. And meanwhile, our government looks at what we do and says it's wrong, too. For all I know, you could be someone from the FBI or something checking into our church to try to catch us doing something wrong."

"Oh, you mean besides statutory rape, corruption of minors, illegal drug trafficking and the raft-load of other things the police could potentially charge you with? I can't imagine why they would think that."

"There's no need for sarcasm, Jonnie. See, you're just like everyone else. You just don't understand what kind of spiritual fulfillment people find in the arms of God."

"I don't know about spiritual fulfillment, but I saw plenty of people getting good drugs and some easy sex in the arms of God. Why do you think the porno industry is about to crash and burn? I mean, why go to all the trouble and expense of downloading a feelie to use alone when you can show up at church once a week and get all the easy tail you want? Your church is moving in on their turf. And don't try to dispute it. I've seen your catalogs and your home shopping shows. And I'd venture to say you're the first mainstream religion offering genital jewelry and vibrators to its congregation."

She balled her tiny hands into fists and banged them in unison on her knees, her eyes scrunched up in frustration. "You just haven't been paying attention, have you Jonnie? It's all about doing everything in the eyes of God," she said as if it were the most obvious thing in the world. "It's all about doing the things humans are supposed to do because it's the way God designed us. If He didn't want us to have sex and enjoy ourselves, He wouldn't have made it so enjoyable, would He? We just take those things and bring them into a safe, sanctified place where they can incorporate it into their celebrations of the Lord. Is that so hard to understand?"

Jon realized he had her totally off kilter now, savagely defending her most precious turf with every ounce of righteous indignation she could muster. Now was the time to slip in the blade a little deeper.

"So what about Schaefer? Where does your creepy aide-de-camp fit into all this blessed activity?" he posed to her, meanwhile maintaining a calm demeanor that contrasted starkly with her agitated state.

"What do you mean?" she asked, caught off guard as he knew she would be. "Every organization needs someone to focus exclusively on the business of running it, and that's what Lucas does."

"I see. And you trust him implicitly to know and run all the inner workings of the church?"

"Of course we do. He came to us highly recommended."

"I would imagine so. I've seen his resume and it's quite impressive. Lots of prestigious schools and jobs. But what if I told you that all that information he gave you, all the good recommendations and the stellar grades and the winning performances on the cricket field over at Oxford, were fake."

Veronica paused for a moment, her mouth dropping open as her brain tried to process the information. "No, no... That's impossible. We did a very thorough check on everyone we considered for that position. All of his information checked out. I know it did."

"I'm sure it did. But a true investigation of someone's background goes beyond checking their curriculum vitae and their police records. You have to interview people who knew him, find out what he was really like. That's how you really get to know someone, not by looking at his credit history. And I've tried to do the interviews," he lied. "And came up with nothing. Nothing at all. No one from his graduating class at Oxford, no one from what he claims was his hometown and no one from his previous places of employment. His references, as wonderful as they were, were stooges impersonating people with impressive sounding names and positions. Up until the moment he met the Reverend and Veronica Whitaker, he exists only in expertly crafted and exquisitely detailed computer records. So I ask you again, Veronica, doesn't something about all of this seem a little sinister?"

She crossed her arms, pouted and slouched back into the seat, regarding him angrily the entire time. Jon simply sat there, trying not to look too smug, waiting for her to finally come to her senses and help him. In the course of their discussion, Jon had decided Veronica knew as little about Schaefer as everyone else did and was not feigning surprise at Jon's unpleasant revelations.

"Jonnie, who are you working for?" she asked, as pitiful as she had been the entire trip. "Who are you working for and why are you trying so hard to destroy everything that Larry and I have created?"

He leaned forward and placed a hand gently on her knee. "Veronica, I'm not trying to destroy anything. And as for who I work for, let's just say it's someone who has the best interests of you and everyone else in mind."

She seemed to soften, and her expression went from one of obstinance to one of overwhelming sadness as she reached forward to caress his cheek. "Jonnie, darling, I appreciate your honesty. And I can understand why some people might be concerned about the evangelical direction the church is taking, but you really have to understand where I'm coming from in all of this." Still maintaining her gaze and her touch, she changed tack. "Lillith, please initiate security protocol two."

And with that Jon felt a stabbing pain in his buttocks followed by a slow numbing that progressed from his hips down to his legs and up to his torso. He found it harder and harder to maintain his position, feeling his body losing control. His toes went numb as his abdominal muscles gave out and allowed him to slump forward into Veronica's lap, where she gently stroked his hair and spoke close to his ear.

"You're really quite lucky, Jonnie," she said. "Lucas had that feature installed himself. The injection is sea anemone venom that's quite deadly to smaller creatures. Of course, if you were underwater, you'd be dead from drowning anyhow. But luckily for you, you're safe here with me."

She then grabbed him by the neck of his suit jacket and lifted him back into a sitting position, straddling him to hold his torso and head upright so she could speak directly into his face. "You're also quite lucky I like you as much as I do, because it would have been so easy to kill you rather than just paralyze you. But I just find killing so messy, Jonnie. And un-Christian. And so terribly unnecessary, too. So instead I'll just thank you for a lovely evening and let Lucas and Larry know when I see them that the satellite deal fell through. If there ever even was a really satellite, Jonnie."

She then reached under his arms on either side of him and pulled out two more seat restraints, these configured to let the arms pass through and then secure the upper body with one buckle. She fastened them together with a solid click and slid back into her seat, in the process giving Jon an extended glimpse up her dress, a move he imagined was designed to remind him of what he would miss by not being favored in the eyes of Deaconess Veronica Whitaker. He wanted to yell, wanted to somehow struggle to make some attempt at escape, but his muscles and nerves were no longer on speaking terms, and their differences at the moment seemed quite irreconcilable. All he could do was sit there slack-jawed, his body a mass of useless meat, and wait for her next move.

"And as much as I'd like to keep you around simply for my occasional amusement, Jonnie, I'm afraid we're going to have to say good-bye now," she said, seeming to have already dismissed his existence as annoying but temporary. "Lillith, please remove Mr. Temple from the vehicle."

"Protocol initiated, Mrs. Whitaker. There will be a momentary stop to ensure safe ejection," the computer said as Jon felt his portion of the couch receding into the hull of the aircar as the space closed in front of him. He was plunged into darkness and could just barely hear Veronica's voice in response to the computer's last statement.

"Oh, Lillith, must we stop, really? I so want us to be on our way without any more delays."

The aircar didn't stop. He could still hear the air rushing against the vehicle's outer skin, more distinct and violent than from inside the cabin. And it was cold where he was, away from the insulation and climate control. This must be what it feels like to be a dog in the belly of a jetliner, he thought, trying to force himself to smile at the notion, anything to distract him from the fact that he was about to be dumped at a few thousand feet. But the disagreement between the cognitive centers of his brain and the lower echelons of his motor functions was still on, making his whole body feel like his lips after a major dentist visit.

Then the space, which must have served as a mini-airlock, depressurized and an outer hatch opened as Jon felt his ears pop violently and the cold wind and rain whipping around him before whatever was holding the seat fast released him, sending him twirling end-over-end towards the earth.

Where Jon Templeton's clothes had been only wet before, now they were soaked through, sopping, heavy rags, the weight of which seemed only to speed him faster towards the ground. Had he been able to, he probably would have struggled in a desperate act of self-preservation, but in his paralyzed state, he realized that if the chair was equipped with a parachute, he was safer being confined. For all he knew, though, he could hit the ground in seconds and not even be prepared for it. The cloudbank over which they had been flying now engulfed him, obscuring his view of anything but his own limp, pitiful form.

Then, somehow, the chair began a slow deceleration. Jon had never skydived before, but he knew that the release of the parachute was accompanied by a sudden jerk upward as the canopy caught the air. There was no jerk. It was more like the smooth stop of a maglev train, coming to an easy rest on its electromagnetic cushion. Still surrounded by clouds and the rain still stinging his face, he hovered in midair, completely still, as he watched the raindrops go from multitudinous streaks to individual drops, a reverse evolution that left glistening blobs of water suspended before him.

A familiar voice then echoed from inside the mass of water vapor. With it, the welcome figure of the younger Aunt Lil took shape in its nondescript linen pants and top.

"Dear Jonathan, what have you gotten yourself into now?"

Jon found that his muscles were once again responding to his command, allowing him to speak. "Seems like you have a little more influence than I thought, Lil. So now you're stopping time?"

"No, dear. There's no stopping time unless our Eli does it. You've simply been stopped in the middle of time. You're suspended between moments, between fractions of a second. All around you time goes on. I've simply slowed your motion so much that you can't see time moving forward. Not a bad trick, eh?"

"Very impressive. But what are you doing here?"

"Let's just say we needed a quiet moment together. You remember when you used to come over to visit me during the summers when you were a little boy?"

"Yes, ma'am," he said, unable to avoid the honorific out of sheer habit. "You'd make lemonade for us and spike yours with a little vodka, then we'd sit on the back porch of your house and talk."

"Yes, and you'd ask me all sorts of questions. I remember some of them I could actually answer every once in a while," she said, gently laughing as she sat cross-legged in mid-air in front of

F
O
R
T
Y

him. "So inquisitive. Your other grandmother thought you would be a preacher some day because you had charisma, but I knew you'd never take to dogma. Too many questions. But I'm here to answer some questions for you that I know you want to ask – questions that have plagued you during the course of this assignment. You're almost finished, you know. And when you're done, there's nothing but happiness that awaits you," she said.

Again with the pleasures of eternity. "If I hear one more person tell me how great it is to be dead…" He struggled against the restraints now.

"Ah, ah, ah," Lil scolded, patting his knee. "Remember, you are still falling, only very, very slowly. Getting out of that chair will only mean trouble for you later, sweetie. And there's too much for you to do to have you end up a splatter mark on the pavement."

"Please, Lil, just let me know what's going on," Jon said, finally resigning himself to remaining in the ejector seat.

"First, let me tell you something in the interest of full disclosure. I was the chairman of your temptation committee."

"My what?"

"Now I understand that it sounds a little … incongruous, given the normal human concept of paradise, what with all those angels flitting about and such, but the fact remains that such groups are often called together in matters such as this. Usually it consists of a deceased family member who knew the subject well and a party from another time who doesn't know anything about him. Our job was to investigate you, your life and your relationships, gather together information on what would or would not 'lead you into temptation,' so to speak, and then report that information to our Eli. We are not responsible for how that information is used thereafter."

"Very interesting. So what's the point," Jon said, taking a tone he normally wouldn't have with Lil when she was alive.

"Patience, honey. Most of the time we have no idea how this information is used. We report to Eli and that's it. Your case, however, has been quite different. Because we – that is, the members of the committee – have been close witnesses to how the information we gathered on you has been used, we've realized the methods have been not only unfair, but also genuinely deceptive. Maybe we were naïve, but we took for granted that the information we provided would be used positively, rather than destructively."

"Lil, you're talking in circles. Just give it to me straight," Jon said. Though time had slowed, he still found himself growing impatient to move on, especially with Linda's life likely in danger from whomever or whatever Schaefer turned out to be.

"Yes, I know – the point. The members of the committee found that you were highly unlikely to be led astray from your assignment by sex. It's not that you were unlikely to fall for women, it's just that you've displayed a tendency to be very particular when it comes to the women you fall for. As a result, it was unlikely that you'd deviate from the mission for just an easy lay.

"Then, of course, starting out in a low-pay, low-respect field like journalism made you acutely aware of the limitations of material satisfaction. As a result we decided you'd be unlikely to be tempted away from your duty by money or gifts. And because you have never sought power, it was unlikely that ambition or offers of power would lead you astray. But there was something that would tempt you, we found. We saw in your relationship with Linda a love so deep, so ingrained in your very being, that we were obligated to report it as the largest potential stumbling block. I, for one, didn't expect this information to be used... well, in a manner inconsistent with the goals of the mission."

"And what manner might that be," Jon said, the suspicion rising to the surface.

"I'm afraid that because of information we provided, you've been duped. We were worried this so-called weakness might be exploited by someone or something that would prefer to see our mission fail. We hardly imagined it would be used to ensure the mission was a success."

"Eli?"

"I'm afraid so. And worst of all, there's this whole mix up with Robert. Even for the Supreme Being, cutting deals with demons can be a risky prospect."

"That was why he sent me to see Robert, then. They both conspired for Robert to offer me that contract because he knew I would do anything to see Linda again," Jon said, feeling the grim weight of universal despair descend on him like a leaden rain. "And the clause in the small print?"

"Oh, that had its own grand purpose. The clause bound you to an arrangement both Eli and Robert knew was impossible for you to keep. So they conspired again to make sure you and Linda would cross paths, negating the terms of the contract and letting Eli off the hook of having to insert you back into the corporeal plane. It was just coincidence that Yeshua – Mr. Zabarra – filled you in that the clause was even included. If it weren't for Alex being there, your grief over the whole thing might have done you and the mission in."

"So why tell me all this now? We could have had this talk already and I wouldn't even be in this position," Jon said.

"I'm afraid not, Jon. From the perspective of an omniscient being, this sort of strategizing is like the blink of an eye. If Eli had wanted to, he could have plotted out a thousand variations that would have ended with a successful mission."

"So I will find out what Eli wants to know? Well, at least there's that."

"Yes, but remember, all Eli wants to know is Schaefer's true identity and purpose. Beyond that, anything else you accomplish is for yourself. And that's the main reason I'm here," Aunt Lil said, looking as if what she was about to reveal caused her genuine pain.

"Finally we're going to get to the point. I thought you were going to keep me hanging here all night."

"You must remember that Eli, or the being that manifests as Eli, has no basis in morality as we know it. It is composed of the energy from the entire universe, acting as a sentient being that both controls and is controlled by that energy. And as such, this being has what you might say is a minimized regard for individual lives. To Eli, we are all part of the universe no matter what state we exist in.

271

It is only for the purpose of a mission such as this that a distinction between living and dead even occurs to him. And because of that, certain things may be… overlooked in his planning for matters such as this."

"Lil, I love you like my own mother, but you need to make yourself very clear right now. With all this dancing around the subject I might have thought you were a lawyer when you were still alive," Jon said. He was growing increasingly frustrated by the moment. An unexpected hand caressing his face from behind, a delicate touch that calmed him from his agitated state, startled him. It could only have been Alex.

"What Lil wants to tell you, Jon," she said quietly in his ear, "is that we acknowledge your obligations beyond those of the mission, because Linda is in grave danger."

"I knew that," Jon said, his head lolling back against the seat in the glow of her empathy. He knew he should be far more upset, but it was impossible with her around. But it did help him focus rather than let himself be overcome by the rage he knew he should feel.

"We know you did, and we don't blame you for wanting to save her. Just don't worry about contracts or obligations to Eli. If you save Linda, everything will be revealed. Just remember that. Can you do that for me?"

"Yes, of course…" he said through the calming haze with which she had surrounded him.

"And do you trust that I'm telling you the truth about this?"

The empathic mojo she had put on him was going beyond calming him, acting almost like a truth serum to his battered psyche. "I do trust you, Alex. Because you love me, and you wouldn't lie to me."

She laughed and sniffed back tears. "That's right, Jon, and that's why I want you to be happy. So find her, and everything will be all right."

Then, at his side, Lil again. "Jonathan, I've always been so proud of you, and I know you're going to make me proud again." The soft drawl of her voice lifted his soul as Alex's touch had absorbed his anxiety. "We're behind you all the way. Don't forget that, Jonathan."

"Yes ma'am," he murmured.

"There are people who are going to help you, do you understand? You won't have to do this alone. Others have been on the same trail as you and they'll cross your path soon. So don't fret, child. Everything will be all right."

"Jon, you're a brave and resourceful man," Alex said, moving around on a wisp of a cloud to face him. "We know you're going to be a success, but it's still going to be dangerous. We're counting on you, the solitary warrior, to protect us all from danger, and you have all of our faith and hope."

Alex then smiled broadly, tears welling in the corners of her eyes, then leaned forward to give him a quick, solid kiss on his left cheek. "May your journey be safe," another kiss on his right cheek, "and your victory swift," a final long, soft kiss on his lips.

Then the rain again bit into Jon's face, cold and piercing like moist darts, as he resumed his plummet, the mist of the clouds swirling around him with the rain and wind. Still basking in the glow of Alex's touch he found it hard to be concerned about his fate, despite the fact that he was hurtling towards earth with no visible means of deceleration. Then something popped on the chair and there was the sound of fabric against the wind. Metal clinked behind him, as if something heavy then passed his ears on the way up. Then, with a spine wrenching jerk, he felt the descent seem to stop. No, not stop, only slow. He was hanging now, suspended below some blessed canopy he could not raise his head to see. In his peripheral vision, however, he caught sight of two straps dangling from above. Those are to steer, he thought. It wasn't like some World War II paratrooper movie, where there was no control. He could decide where he wanted to go. But he was still paralyzed, still limp from the effect of Veronica Whitaker's sneaky trick with the anemone venom. So he was left to the wind. Left to the forces of God, he thought, and that made him laugh. It wasn't God. It wasn't even Eli. It was the earth cleansing itself by rain and by wind and by rising rivers flowing faster, all happening quite on its own without any influence from fickle deities. And so he left it to the earth, to the Great Mother, as he'd heard the Indians called her in the TV documentaries. He would leave himself in her hands.

The clouds below were breaking, but there was only blackness beyond. No city lights, no traffic, nothing. He would have braced himself if he could, because he knew the storm clouds would be low and for him to be through them would mean he was close to the ground, but he was safe, flying with the pelicans and the seagulls.

A gust then blew up from below, bringing a spray of rain at him in reverse. He felt the parachute catch it, then pull him backward hard. He could hear his feet grazing the tops of high sawgrass or bulrushes, the canopy above him flapping violently in the tempest, dragging him closer and closer to the ground. Occasionally his limp feet hit firm earth, then water, dragging and bumping, until he felt himself become horizontal to the ground, being dragged along by the fierce breath of the Great Mother.

Then, another mighty gust, and he felt his head strike something hard. A utility pole? A tree? He couldn't decide, and before he could ponder the matter further, the blow took its toll, and all around him went from dark of night to deep black.

"Lucas! Lucas, where are you?" Veronica Whitaker shouted as she entered the front door of the massive plantation house. She'd never been here alone before, and she found that the property, which she always thought a little creepy anyway, became even more ominous in the early morning mist. The Spanish moss hung from the live oaks like grim theater curtains that refused to reveal the brightly lit stage behind them.

The door stood open and Veronica remained rooted there, gazing into the dim entryway. The skylight above had been darkened, the curtains were closed and a dank odor, which she at first attributed to the surrounding marshland, emanated from inside like must from a crypt. Then somewhere from the place in her mind where she stored away unpleasant things she didn't want to remember came a sensory template that she could lay over the smell – it was that of Lucas Schaefer's office at the house in Myrtle Beach. She felt herself shudder at the realization, knowing then that he was near.

"Lucas! It's Veronica, Lucas. I really need to talk to you." Again, nothing but the rustle of the sawgrass and the symphony of crickets and frogs from across the expansive yard. Damn this house, she thought. The lights should have come on as soon as she spoke, but the interior remained lit by only the gray of the morning. She stepped inside, trying not to be spooked by the statuette of the Polynesian fertility god that she personally chose on a trip to Tahiti just before taking it upon herself to educate the dark, strapping young artisan in the ways of Western Christianity, CNR-style. She smiled at the memory, recalling how the mat of palm fronds had left an elaborate pattern on the skin of her back, knees and elbows and how the craftsman's mighty totem had left an indelible impression on her most sacred spot. Imagining the scene again gave her some comfort as she proceeded, but that comfort quickly dissipated after she tried the closest light switch. Nothing.

"Lucas, if you're playing a joke on me, it's not very funny," she said to the air. Then, in the hope that assuming a more managerial tone would get his attention, she changed tactics. "Lucas, damn it! Come out and speak to me right now. We have a very big problem, you know! Lucas? I found out about Jonnie, and you're right. He really was up to no good."

Still, no response was forthcoming. Her fright was quickly being unseated by anger, and she steeled herself for a determined walk straight into the house, looking into each half-lit room and calling out for her wayward employee. Emboldened by her frustration, she combed the entire house, finally seeing through the window of the master suite the sun's orange rim peeking over the edge of the Atlantic. After searching upstairs, she realized the one place she hadn't looked, probably the result of some subconscious sense of dread. She then left the relative comfort and safety of her bedroom and headed downstairs again, to Lucas Schaefer's private office.

Long shafts of light now lay across the oak boards of the downstairs floor as she approached the room on the house's northern end. When she came to the heavily paneled doors, she was at first compelled to knock. But had Lucas been around, he certainly would have heard her by now, so she ignored the urge to be polite and turned the brass handle. She half expected the door to be locked, but it opened almost without any effort on her part. As she stepped inside, she was nearly overwhelmed by the dramatic change in atmosphere. While the morning was certainly humid, stepping into the office was like walking into the greenhouse at the Myrtle Beach plantation's botanical gardens. She could almost feel her hair frizzing further, prompting her to whimper over the seeming impossibility of her clothes ever being dry. And the smell – it was as if some sort of exotic flower were in an advanced state of rot, its perfume mixing with the scent of its own deteriorating parts. She had to back out of the room for a moment to catch her breath in the comparatively fresh air of the hallway. Stepping in again, she tried not to breathe through her nose as she called out to Lucas once more, still receiving no response. She wanted to search further, but the overwhelming odor prevented her from staying in for much longer than a few minutes. She held her nose and gave the room a visual once-over. Other than the smell, there was nothing unusual. From the looks of things no one had been there since the last time they were all in residence back in the spring.

She turned and was on her way out when a faint noise stopped her. At first it was just a soft thump, something she might otherwise attribute to something benign like the house settling. But this was different. It was rhythmic and definitely was coming in a pattern that had to be created by someone or something that knew what it was doing. Still breathing through her mouth she stopped and turned, thinking of the way a cat's ears cock towards a noise behind it. She stood and listened as the thumping continued. Then she detected in unison with the thumping a voice – muffled – but definitely a human voice. Veronica walked back to the center of the room and it grew louder and more distinct, so much so that she was able to make out words, the two most surprising being "under" and "floor."

She was struck for a moment, paralyzed in a sudden fit of panicky indecision. She knew what was happening, but something in her mind still wouldn't quite let her believe it. The thumping and muted shouting came again, and Veronica shook herself free of her fear and hurried to the edge of the Oriental rug, pausing for just a moment to admire the craftsmanship that went into creating the surrounding pattern of ancient Persian fertility symbols before she knelt to roll it up. As she approached the middle of the room, the voice grew louder and more desperate. Whoever was calling thought she had left, Veronica thought.

"Calm down! I'm coming!" she shouted at the floor, trying not to sound too exasperated by being subjected to much more physical activity than she was used to outside the bedroom. Veronica then rose and with some effort slid the heavy coffee table with the mahogany penis inlay off to the side. Her path now clear, she continued rolling the rug, gradually revealing the edge of some sort of doorway, the seams visible against the grain of the boards. More rolling uncovered two such panels, each with a smaller, six-inch-square panel set to its right.

"I've found the door. It'll just be a few more minutes!" she said to the floor, hoping she was being heard. The shouting and banging had stopped, so she imagined she had been. Either that or… No, she didn't even want to think about that possibility.

She felt around the seam of the doors and found no way to open them. But around the first smaller panel she found a notch obviously designed to allow someone to lift the door but to not be too obvious. Lifting it she saw in imposing metal handle, like something she might see on an antique refrigerator door or an old-fashioned safe. Her hand hovered over it for a moment as she thought about what might lie beneath. This was certainly more than she had anticipated when she landed. But it took only one more muffled cry from below to prompt her to reach down, close her eyes and turn.

It was hard at first, but once it gave way it slid up with machined precision and gave forth a sudden fury of electronic and gassy-sounding noises. She started and jumped to her feet. She inched backwards as she watched the outlined section of the floor drop about three inches, then slide away, revealing a bluish glow that made the early morning half light that much eerier. Then all was still. Again she had to steel herself to look over the edge. She stepped forward, her hands clasped tightly in front of her, the fingers fidgeting over the knuckles as her trepidation grew. At first she could see only the glow and nothing from which it might be emanating. But as she grew closer, she began to make out a shape, moving as frantically as one might expect someone trapped under the floorboards of an abandoned house to move. The shouting was more discernable now, and moving closer, Veronica could make out a face. As she expected from the muffled voice, it was a woman, but no one she had ever seen before. Moving closer still, she saw that she was uninjured. When the two of them made eye contact, the other woman almost bowled Veronica over with a look that was nothing close to fear – more like a furious intensity, she thought.

"What are you waiting for?" the woman shouted, her voice now perfectly clear. "Get me out of here!"

"I'm trying!" Veronica shouted back. "Just hold on a minute, okay?"

Veronica drew closer, finally kneeling down at the trap door's edge and looking inside. There she saw that the woman was not uninjured after all, but was encased from the chest down in what looked like a giant mass of roots, moist and green in the pale light from below. At first she thought she was going to be sick, then after a moment got herself and her rebelling stomach under control.

"I don't care what you have to do to this root ball, just get me out," the woman said. "Find something sharp. These things aren't as tough as they look."

Veronica nodded and scurried to Lucas' desk, just as antiseptically neat as anyone who had met him might expect it to be. Everything was in perfect order, allowing her to immediately spot the CNR letter opener the church had sent (along with discreetly small campaign contributions) as a "get acquainted" gift to state legislators. She grabbed it and quickly dropped to her knees, raising the piece of sharpened silver high above her head.

"Wait!" the woman shouted. Veronica then saw fright. "Try to be a little less enthusiastic, honey. I'm still under here somewhere. Push the letter opener in slowly and I'll let you know when to start cutting down."

Veronica did as she was instructed, sliding the letter opener in like a meat thermometer into a roast, bringing forth a thick glob of something green and viscous around her hand. When she saw the woman wince, she stopped.

"Are you okay?"

"Well, I don't think you drew blood, if that's what you mean. Just drag it down and try not to force it any deeper. I'd like to come out of this thing with everything I had coming in."

Veronica complied, although the dull edge of the letter opener didn't smooth her way. She might as well have been using a plastic picnic knife, she thought. As a rough seam opened behind the implement, more of the green goo oozed forth, covering her forearms as it dripped from her hand. It was all she could do to keep from getting sick at that point. She fought every second to suppress her gag reflex, which wanted so much to send her dinner back the way it came and all over the woman she was trying to save.

"Hold on there, sister. You're looking a little green around the gills. You okay?"

"Fine. I'm fine," Veronica managed to mumble, worrying that opening her mouth too wide would be an open invitation for the contents of her stomach to exit. Up on her knees, leaning deep into the chamber, she pulled the letter opener with even more determination then, lest she lose her resolve and give in to nausea.

"Just a little farther," the woman said, who already looked as if she was preparing to shield her face from a fountain of partially digested food. Veronica couldn't imagine, though, how that would be worse than being trapped inside a giant pea pod surrounded by gelatinous goo. The woman was now splitting the cocoon further from the inside, wriggling her body and using her feet to force her way out before finally struggling into a sitting position, supporting herself by leaning back on her arms and breathing heavily. Veronica couldn't help but notice that the woman was naked, covered only with a thin sheen of the substance that coated her own hands and arms. She was one of those women Veronica described as good at being naked. Her breasts sat high, their curves emphasized by the glistening on her skin. She would do well in the church, if she chose to.

Veronica raised herself up, her arms straddling the hole in the floor as she, too, caught her breath. She closed her eyes, feeling the sweat from her brow trickle down the bridge of her nose. It was rare that she perspired while doing something other than indulging in the highest sacrament with Larry or someone else from the church. But she felt better about herself for having freed the woman from her vegetative prison. She didn't even mind the sweating. The satisfaction of having done her Christian duty for another poor soul satisfied her enough.

The other woman finally stood, trying in vain to scrape the slime from her skin, looking as if she felt as sick as Veronica thought she might be earlier. "You look familiar," the woman said, giving Veronica a quizzical look as she stood there without any apparent regard to her lack of clothing.

Veronica felt herself beam. She loved it when she was recognized by her viewers. Larry teased her that, whenever that happened, her entire demeanor changed. She flicked her hair, threw her shoulders back and straightened her posture, emphasizing her breasts and – were she standing – the curve of her bottom. Larry found it particularly intriguing that she did this as often with women as she did with men.

"Well, I imagine you recognize me from television. I'm Veronica…"

She had never been truly punched before. Veronica remembered being slapped, spanked, pierced, bitten, anally penetrated, having her nipples painfully twisted and the feeling of a man with an 11-inch penis grinding inside her, but this type of pain was a different sensation altogether. The knuckles of the other woman's hand cracked against her face, half of them making contact with the soft flesh of her cheek and the other half with her delicate cheekbones, over which so many fashion and personality magazines had gushed. It knocked her head sidewise and forced the rest of her body down to the ground. When she looked up again she found the woman out of the compartment and standing over her, goo now dripping into a puddle all around her.

"Nice to meet you. I'm Linda Templeton, Jon Templeton's wife. I saw you with him at the church service. I want to know what he was doing there."

Veronica slowly sat up, rubbing her face where the Templeton woman's fist had made contact. She would have a bruise there, definitely. Examining her fingers, she saw blood, then looking up saw the ring on the one of the fingers of her attacker's right hand – the one that had obviously taken a substantial gouge out of Veronica's cheek.

"I'd say there's been a slight breakdown in the communication between you and your husband, then," Veronica said. "Your husband – if he really is your husband – told me he was single and that his name was Jonnie Temple. His company is supposedly selling us the satellite we've been raising money to launch."

"Oh, that's right," Linda said, looking around and taking in her surroundings. "I forget the most well-to-do TV preachers are always the ones who go begging for cash. What's it going to be next year? Money to sponsor evangelists on the moon colony?" She looked back and caught Veronica eyeing her appreciatively, then quickly made her way to the window, where she proceeded to tear down the thin curtain behind the heavy tapestry drapes that upon which Lucas had insisted. She then deftly fashioned it into a makeshift toga, the material overlapping just enough to hide the areas Veronica was admiring most.

"Sorry about the modesty, Ronnie, but you seemed to be enjoying yourself a little too much, and I don't swing that way."

"Please don't call me that," Veronica said, the vulgar nickname wounding her almost as much as the blow to her face. It brought back a flood of horrible memories – feelie suits and tiny hidden cameras, the pathetic affection of all those sad men and their panting desire for her, no matter what it might cost them in money or reputation.

"Not fond of that name? Well, my Jon isn't fond of the name 'Jonnie,' so either we're talking about a different person or something has gone terribly, terribly wrong with my husband." She knelt at the edge of the second trap door. "Come give me a hand with this. We've still got someone else under here we need to get out."

"There was someone else with you?"

"Yeah, some little punk girl. That freaky friend of yours, Mr. Schaefer, brought us both here in his nifty limo," Linda said as she lifted the smaller door and turned the handle, prompting the door to lower and slide back.

"Do you know who she is?"

"No clue." The girl lay there, out cold, encased up to her throat in a duplicate cocoon. "She was unconscious when I saw her, and Schaefer knocked me out before she and I could try to wake her up. Hand me that letter opener."

Linda repeated the process Veronica had performed on her, being more careful because the girl couldn't tell her when she'd gone too deep, finally slitting the pod from top to bottom and pulling the two sides apart with surprising strength. The girl, too, was naked beneath the layer of liquid oozing from the mass of green, and Veronica again found herself drifting into thoughts of carnal pleasure when she knew she should be focusing on other things. And again, Linda caught her looking.

"Oh, for God's sake, could you get your mind on the job here? I'd like to get her out of here and I can't do it by myself," Linda said, her temper obviously growing short. Veronica resolved to concentrate.

Linda placed herself at the girl's head, grasping her under her arms, while Veronica knelt at her feet and wrapped her hands as tightly as she could around her ankles. "I'm ready," Veronica said.

"Okay, on three," Linda said before counting off. They both grunted with the strain, but managed to lift and drag the girl free with what Veronica hoped was a minimum of damage, especially considering the bruises that were already healing on their unconscious companion's face. Linda leaned down over her and gently patted the cheek not mottled by purple and shades of yellow-green.

"Honey, wake up. Hello?" Linda then took the girl's wrist and checked her pulse. "Well, she's not dead. And it's probably been a couple of days since whoever he was did that to her."

"Well, I'm sure it wasn't Lucas," Veronica said, indignant on her employees' behalf. "He's a very responsible man and certainly doesn't go around hitting women."

"Then that's one less thing I can hold against him. But the fact remains that he did drag me out of your church service against my will, kidnap me and sedate me, then seal me up in a giant ball of... something," she said as she looked over the pod from which the younger girl had just been removed. Her expression was one of disgust mixed with a touch of fear about what might have happened to her had she remained inside.

A slight moan drew their attention back to the girl, whose head now lolled from side to side. Linda again leaned over her and stroked her cheek in a maternal fashion. "Sweetheart, wake up. You're okay, now."

"Where am I?" she murmured.

Linda laughed lightly and shook her head. "Beats the hell out of me. Let's ask our hostess. Sister Veronica?"

"This is our estate on Palm Island. We're about two miles off Hilton Head." Veronica couldn't help feeling proud every time she said "estate." It had such a regal, opulent ring about it that she couldn't imagine others not being impressed.

"No kidding. You're the ones that bought this place after Senator Garland's development deal dried up?"

"Yes, but how did you know?" Veronica felt even more confused. The land deal was supposed to be highly confidential, accomplished through a number of dummy companies.

"No reason, really. It's just that the deal died in the first place because my husband is the reporter who exposed it."

"A reporter? I knew it," Veronica muttered under her breath.

"So, let me guess," Linda said, not hearing. "Your desire for the utmost privacy for your little porno church means no bridge?"

Veronica winced inwardly but chose to ignore the comment. "No, but we do have the limousines."

"True. Nothing like making our escape in high style," Linda said, sarcasm dripping off every word.

"I'm afraid that won't be possible, Mrs. Templeton," said a voice echoing from the hallway outside the room. It was Lucas, and he was acting even more ominous than Veronica would normally expect. Both she and Linda watched him enter the room slowly, his hands clasped formally behind his back and an uncharacteristically smug look on his normally blank face.

"Speak of the devil," Linda said, almost under her breath.

"Not quite, Mrs. Templeton. But perceive me as what you like."

"Lucas, what is the meaning of all of this?" Veronica said, standing with her hands on her hips. "As your employer, I demand an immediate explanation."

"Mrs. Whitaker, your petty demands and your childish temper-tantrums are growing quite tedious. Please sit down before I'm forced to restrain you."

Veronica felt the heat rise in her face. "Restrain me? Restrain *me*? Who do you think you're talking to, your dog? It's me, Lucas. Your *employer*? The woman you work for?"

"It will soon become quite clear, Mrs. Whitaker, that it is you and your husband who have been working for me," he said, still as calm as before. "Now, there is the dilemma of Mrs. Templeton, here."

"And what dilemma would that be," Linda said, sounding even more deadly serious than Lucas.

"It would seem that if you are indeed the wife of the man from whom we believed we were buying a satellite, then a number of things he told us were untrue. In fact, I'm beginning to doubt whether he is in any position to provide for us what we need so desperately."

"I'd say probably not," Linda said. "The closest my husband has been to a satellite was a trip to the Air and Space Museum. As for misleading you, that, I'll grant you, he can do. He does work in public relations for a living, after all."

"Really," Lucas said, a cocked eyebrow conveying his only expression. "Fascinating. So, to your knowledge he works for no intelligence or law-enforcement agencies?"

"I told you. He's a former news org reporter turned PR hack. He's lucky I believe him when he tells me he loves me," Linda said, laughing at her own joke.

Just then, the younger girl began to rouse further. "And then there's our young friend here. Whereas you, Mrs. Templeton, seem blissfully unaware of the various elements aligned against myself and the Church of the New Revelation, I believe she can shed some light on what might be in store for us."

Keeping her eyes on Lucas, Linda kneeled next to the younger girl and nudged her in the shoulder with a finger. "Honey, you need to get up now. Dr. Bizarro wants to ask you a few questions."

She stirred slightly, lolling her head from side to side once more, then finally peeled her eyes open and slowly sat up. "What's your name, honey?" Linda asked.

The girl rubbed her head and it seemed to take her a moment to gather her thoughts enough to answer. Finally she mumbled, "Krista."

"Good. Krista, you remember Mr. Schaefer."

At the mention of his name the girl started, her eyes popping open in obvious fright as she squirmed backwards towards Linda.

"You get that sort of reaction a lot, Mr. Schaefer?" Linda said, looking back up at Lucas. "Seems you have a talent for giving people the heebie jeebies."

"Yes," Veronica agreed, unable to shake the humiliation of him rejecting her advances. "Lucas' shortfall always was his lack of interpersonal skills."

"And there will be no need to worry about that particular failing any longer, Mrs. Whitaker. My disinterest in whatever carnal pleasures you choose to offer me should be the last thing on your mind."

Linda and Krista both turned to her, each with her own distinct expression of disgust. "Carnal pleasures?" Krista asked. She was apparently growing more lucid by the moment. Veronica felt herself flush with embarrassment.

"Not that it's any of your business…"

"Hah! This from the woman who screws her entire congregation and has it beamed around the globe by satellite," Linda said. "Now, if you two are finished with your little lover's spat, do you think we might be able to get Krista something to wear without ruining another set of drapes?"

"I'm afraid that won't be possible, Mrs. Templeton. The three of you are far too valuable and, with your combined intellects, I imagine far too resourceful for me to leave alone," he said as he walked to the edge of the trap door and peered in.

"It seems you've already taken it upon yourselves to destroy my larger plans, and I imagine you won't be content until every small detail is ruined."

"Plans? Lucas, whatever are you talking about?" Veronica heard herself

281

becoming shrill but didn't care. She simply couldn't have someone like Lucas – a paid employee – treat her this way, regardless of what he might have done for the church.

"I believe our young friend, Miss Krista, would be the best to tell you. She and her cohorts, over the last few days, have systematically plotted to destroy everything I've worked for since arriving in your employ, Mrs. Whitaker. Haven't you?" he asked, directly addressing Krista.

The girl was obviously still groggy but was now in perfect grasp of her senses. She addressed Veronica directly. "The satellite you've been raising money for? Smiley here was planning to add on a particle accelerator he bought on the sly from Nikura International."

"A what? I don't know what you mean…" Veronica was confused. She'd never heard of such a thing and had no idea why anyone would want to fiddle with something they were going to put to such good use.

"A death ray, okay? We figure he was going to threaten to use it to fire on China or Taiwan or somewhere like that. A bunch of lame-ass James Bond shit, if you ask me," Krista said, directly addressing Lucas.

Again, the only expression that registered on Lucas' face was one of curiosity, indicated by an arched eyebrow. "Impressive. But I assure you I make no threats. My intention always was and remains to use that weapon alternately on the People's Republic of China, North Korea, the United States, England, India, Pakistan, Iran, South Africa, Israel and a number of smaller nuclear states around the Russian Republic."

"Mind if I ask what you expect that to accomplish, besides the extermination of the human race?" Linda asked.

"Only that, Mrs. Templeton. Only that," he said. "Consider me a real estate agent of sorts. My employers are investors in a rather large trans-dimensional resort project, for which Earth was deemed an ideal location because of its friendliness to multiple species that serve as its wealthiest customer base. While their timeline is a bit longer than you might anticipate, they were unwilling to wait for the planet's inhabitants to die off naturally. I have been hired to make sure that event takes place a bit sooner."

Veronica sat hard, dumbfounded by what her trusted advisor was telling them. He really had no concern for the success or failure of the Church of the New Revelation, only for the ways the church could help him further this crazy scheme of his. All they had achieved together, everything he had helped them build, he was throwing away. Veronica couldn't conceive of it.

"Lucas, really. It's quite obvious you need help and have seen far too many – what was that?"

"James Bond movies," Krista said.

"Right. There's no way you could really want to destroy everything we've worked for, is there?" She was trying her best to sound caring and maternal, but Krista and Linda didn't look as if they were buying it. She doubted Lucas was, either.

Still, for a second Lucas seemed to soften. He sighed deeply. "I'm afraid our young friend is only too correct. I must admit my talents lie in sales more than demolition, and the popular entertainment of your silly little race has provided me with a number of highly viable methods of eliminating it altogether. But we are all inspired in different ways, are we not? Some by emotion," he said, glancing at Linda and Krista, then straight into Veronica's eyes, "and some by blind lust and greed."

Then a noise rumbled through the room, too indistinct to be called a voice, but at the same time not so random that it could be attributed to noises from the house. To Veronica it sounded like an amplified version of the noises her stomach made when she skipped lunch. Both of the other women clutched their arms close to them as Veronica felt goosebumps break out on her skin.

"Ladies, I do apologize, but I must excuse myself from this delightful conversation to attend to other matters," Lucas said, obviously responding to the noise. "But I must emphasize that attempts at escape would be quite futile."

The three of them watched, frozen, as each of Lucas' arms changed shape and reconfigured themselves into something green and vegetative, similar to what Krista and Linda had been encased in but on the move, expanding and reaching out to them. Veronica heard herself scream as she tried to crawl away, but something wrapped around her ankle and tugged her back. The green tentacle wound itself up, binding her legs together, then her arms against her, her arms folded up against her chest in an effort to protect herself. Finally, another shoot sprang forth and slithered around her mouth, muffling her screams to forced grunts of protest. Krista and Linda were in the same state, squirming against the living restraints.

"They're coming for you, you know..." Krista shouted out before she was gagged, leaving her writhing and angry like fly caught in a spider's web.

"I have no doubt that your friends will try to rescue you, ladies, but I'm quite prepared for that. Now, if you'll pardon me, I'll see you again when your friends arrive."

FORTY~TWO

The singing, far away at first, eased its way into Jon's subconscious, breaking up the fog in his brain prompted by the blow to his head. Beyond his closed eyelids was sunlight, dim, but sunlight nonetheless. At least the storm cleared, he thought as he peeled one eye.

A hermit crab, going about its crabby business, stood not three inches from his face, picking through the mud in search of whatever crabs search for at this hour of the morning. He knew it was morning now – Sunday morning, to be specific – because he finally nailed down the singing. It was a church choir, coming from nearer by than he originally thought.

The other eye he kept closed, for it wasn't long before he realized that half of his face was nearly submerged in putrid swamp muck, his body still strapped into the ejector seat on the bank of a marsh. The sawgrass and reeds rose all around him, blocking his view of anything more than a foot away. It was just him and the hermit crab. For all the critter in its limited experience knew, this is what people did on Sunday morning. He imagined his tiny clawed companion heading home with the news that laying half-buried in goo was one of those odd things they could only attribute to humans, much like collecting their brother and sister crabs and selling them in cheap Grand Strand gift shops to children from Ohio and Michigan.

But before Jon could kindly explain that this wasn't typical human behavior, the tiny beast skittered away, disappearing into a quarter-sized hole at the edge of where a clump of cattails grew. There was another sound then, one he attributed to a being like himself, unless he was unaware of the presence of some very large crabs.

"Boy, get your sorry ass up," the voice said. It was Eli, and he was perturbed.

"If I could, don't you think I would? I can't move. Come down here and get me out," he said out of the side of his mouth above the sand level. Still he felt a trickle of grainy water cross his lips.

Eli made a frustrated sound and scrambled down the bank, trying to avoid the more saturated spots of sand so his feet wouldn't sink under. Jon saw him reach down and grab one of the chest straps and lift him upright. It was then he saw the trunk of the palmetto he must have earlier struck with his head. His head should have been sore with a growing knot at the point of impact. But there was only the remaining weakness from the toxin Veronica had administered. "I have to say you're a welcome sight."

"I oughta be your worst nightmare, boy," Eli said, kneeling so his face was at the same level as Jon's. "There's no reason we should even be having this discussion right now other than the fact that you've screwed yourself something awful."

It was the first time in their short relationship Jon had heard him this angry. The lines between his eyebrows were creased in a deep scowl. Jon spat out the last of the dirt from his mouth and took a moment to assess the blue seersucker suit and white shoes Eli was wearing. His dreadlocks, which he normally wore loose, were tied up neatly, dangling in a ponytail of dark ropes at the back of his head, which was topped with a white pork pie hat. "What are you all dressed up for?" Jon asked, trying to avoid the subject, the subject obviously being his gross incompetence.

"Boy, don't try to avoid the subject," Eli said, poking Jon hard in the chest with a long index finger. "You know exactly why I'm here. So far you have signed a forbidden pact with a demon, pursued your wife at every turn in violation of my explicit instructions and made absolutely no progress in discovering anything about our Mr. Schaefer. Not to put too fine a point on it, but you've failed, boy, and miserably, if you've got to know."

"You're going to *church*," Jon said, making the connection. "That's why you're all dressed up. It's Sunday morning and the Supreme Being has come to praise the Lord at a little sea island chapel. I think that's about the sweetest thing I've ever heard. How exactly does that work, anyway?"

"Boy, you know my policy on divine intervention, but I'm about three seconds away from laying a bolt of lightning on your pathetic primate head. Yes, I'm going to church, and what of it? I don't care how much those good people in there claim that room is full of the Holy Spirit. I haven't known Casper to personally show up at services in a thousand years. But what those folks have in there – all that singing and praying and love for each other – that's human spirit, boy, and there's nothing like it in the universe. So you just shut your mouth and take your scolding like you should, all right? What we have right now is a situation, and I'm at a loss as to how this situation's going to resolve itself."

"Then this is only the second time I've seen you at a loss," Jon said, growing impatient with his continued captivity. "The first was when you gave me this asinine assignment in the first place. So I don't want to hear any more about how *I* screwed up the mission. You're the omniscient one. You should have figured out ahead of time that I was wrong for this sort of work."

Eli stood and turned away, plunging his hands into the pockets of the suit pants. "Yeah, I suppose so. Blame it on my inherent lack of understanding of human nature. But it's too late for us to worry about that now."

"I agree," Jon said. "Let's worry about how you're going to explain to me the little scam you and Robert have been pulling all along."

Eli turned slowly to look at Jon. "Figure that out for yourself, boy, or did someone tip you off?"

"Oh, please. Like you don't know."

"Sorry. Haven't been paying attention. Even omniscience needs focus. But it doesn't matter who it was, they were right."

Jon had no doubt it was true, but somehow hearing confirmation from

Eli's lips made it worse. "Oh, don't look so hurt, boy. What did you expect? I needed you to work hard for me and I found out how to get you to do it. I don't see anything wrong with that."

"That's because you obviously don't give a rat's ass what happens to us. You don't care if we blow ourselves to hell or not. You're just looking after the greater welfare of the universe."

"And pardon me for that. Want to know the truth? The truth is humans aren't special. Your planet is just one of millions overrun with perfectly intelligent life. I could show you a hundred planets right next door, cosmically speaking, that would have taken all your little sci-fi assumptions and blown them to bits. All this business about these little gods and religions and holy books doesn't mean a damn thing to me. But I'm the only one I know running the show around here, and with that job comes certain responsibilities. It just so happens that one of them is protecting what's mine.

"But humans are notoriously narrow-minded, so I just broke it down a little for you. Simple enough, right? I needed you motivated, so I had to make it personal."

"Then why weren't you just honest with me in the first place? You don't think the imminent destruction of the universe is motivation enough?"

"Not according to your profile. Remember your grade school report card, boy? 'Displays lack of respect for authority,' it said. Three years in a row. We knew your rebellious side would come out, so I had to give you something to rebel against."

"Thus the contract with Robert, right?" Jon said with no shortage of malice in his voice.

"Now, it's not like I was trying to get you tied up with that sort of crowd…"

"Oh really?" Jon said, struggling against his restraints to get up and shake Eli violently. "You just sent me in there under the pretense of him being able to help me with this bogus business, with Robert already armed with all the weapons he needed to lead me right off the path of whatever righteousness I might attain, that's all. Then you convince him to dangle a very tempting offer in my face using my wife as bait."

"Boy, you just don't…"

"No. Just shut up and get me out of here and let me find Linda. Either that or send me some Supreme Being who's got an ounce of compassion. Hell, I'll take Zabarra at this point. He at least seemed to give half a damn."

"Don't let the Kid fool you. Don't forget, when he puts on his Jehovah hat he's the same one who laid down a bet with the devil over just how much abuse his boy Job could take. You might think you've got it bad, but that ol' boy got it a thousand times worse. So quit your whining. And I'm not completely devoid of compassion, or at least what you folks consider compassion. I did give you Alex to watch over you during all this."

"Oh, yeah. She and I have already discussed your role as cosmic pimp."

"And as I recall, she didn't appreciate the way you cast her in that particular relationship, either. Girl's got a mean arm on her, eh? Look, I know it looked like she was meant as a distraction…"

"You mean she wasn't?"

"Not entirely. If that's all I wanted to do I could've hooked you up with any number of little honeys. But I knew that wouldn't work for you, and I knew Alex would take good care of you. So lay off her. She didn't do anything she didn't want to do. That's what's so funny about love, boy. If you're not human – or weren't human at one point – you really have no concept of it. I don't think I could have predicted the way Alex responded to you, and without the help of your temptation committee, I certainly couldn't have predicted how you would have responded to being separated from your wife."

Jon pondered that for a moment, then recalled what Alex had told him as he hovered in the stilled rain. It was the first time Eli had agreed that Jon's quest to contact Linda was somehow legitimate. He appreciated that, but still couldn't quite bring himself to trust Eli completely.

They both were quiet. As the breeze shifted, the sound of the church choir intermingled on the wind with that of seagulls and sawgrass. Across the marsh the sun rose higher, the heat building among the reeds and swamp mud.

"So," Jon began. "It seems everything isn't such a failure after all."

Eli turned and looked down at him from the bank above. He actually looked conflicted about his thoughts. And how many thoughts, really, must an omniscient being have? Something with so much on its mind couldn't possibly be sure about everything, especially when it was responsible for so much and had so little to go on. At least all the gods of humans had a framework in which to work, even if they were laid down by the humans they were supposed to rule and control. Eli had only – what? Instincts? And it couldn't be easy for him.

"Not yet, boy. Not yet. You've still got a chance to do two things – one for me and one for yourself. We still have no idea what our man Mr. Schaefer has up his sleeve. And as fortune would have it he happens to be holding your wife prisoner hoping you will show up."

"I know. And what worries me is that sounds exactly like what you earlier described as a failure."

"There's where the opportunity lies, boy. Find out about Schaefer and save your wife. You've got a chance to do both."

"But the contract…"

Eli sighed. "Forget the contract. We've got to get both our priorities straight, and I think under the circumstances negotiating over legal details isn't on the top of the list. Don't you agree?"

Dumbstruck by Eli's sudden acquiescence, Jon simply nodded in the affirmative. "Oh, absolutely. But that's not going to cause you any problems, is it?"

"Not to worry. Just keep in mind that if demons were as smart as everyone thought, they'd have better working conditions." With that he turned and walked off. "Just try to stay on the path, boy. At this point the fewer screw-ups the better."

Watching Eli leave, Jon struggled again against the restraints in the ejector chair. "But I'm still stuck here! And I have no clue where the hell I am!"

"Relax, boy. Relax. You're on your way out of the wilderness, but don't forget that bright, shiny city up ahead – it could be paradise or it could be Babylon."

And with that he ambled away, quickly disappearing over the low horizon of the marshy bank. The last thing Jon saw were the ropes of his dreadlocks bobbing as he walked, the breeze shifting again carrying the voices of the church choir over him.

Jon laid his head back against the seat and closed his eyes, listening to the slow stomp-and-clap rhythm. Babylon is what they sang about. It was the old reggae tune "The Rivers of Babylon," reworked for a gospel choir and using the whole building as an instrument. He remembered it now, the verses about God's people being forced to sing while in bondage. Of course, their bondage was on a larger scale, but trapped in the straps of the ejector seat Jon felt just as helpless.

With Eli's departure, it seemed the normal insect life of the wetlands had returned, a black swarm of gnats hovering close enough to his face to tickle his nose. He shook his head from side to side to try to prevent them from setting a course up his nostrils, finally reaching up and swatting at them, an effort he knew would be futile but would at least make him feel better.

Then he stopped, catching himself with his hand frantically waving in front of his face, and came to an important realization. "I moved my arm!" The return of motor functions prompted an impromptu celebratory dance on his part, consisting mostly of arm waving and butt wiggling in what was formerly his prison. He then set upon looking for some way to release the restraints, finally settling on the large metal buckle in the center of his chest. A hard strike there loosened it and the leg straps came free. He lifted the heavy assembly over his head and stood for what seemed to be the first time in weeks. His legs were a little wobbly at first, a predicament not helped by the slippery foundation, but they were strong enough to propel him scrambling up the bank, parting reeds and sawgrass as he went, until he saw the white clapboard church and the road just beyond.

Eli had disappeared, either literally or inside the church to join the congregation. He could imagine them through the walls, a sea of dark faces, the men in immaculate pastels or seersucker and the women sporting a feathered aviary of elaborate hats, heads bobbing along with the rhythms of the choir, nodding in agreement with the practiced, hypnotic cadences of the pastor. As Jon made his way past the church, its trimmed lawn a sharp contrast to the nearby marsh, he was able to discern the name written in an arch of plain black, block letters: "Dewees Island AME Zion Church."

He recognized the name immediately from his work on the Garland land development story. He had come here on a weeklong trip to do research, taking a day to go out on a boat with the local elementary school principal, whom his father knew from college. They had sailed across a narrow sound from Dewees to Garland's coveted Palm Island, a tiny dot on the way to Bermuda that promised exclusive golf privileges, a luxury spa and accommodations that rivaled those of Europe's finest hotels.

The native inhabitants had long since succumbed to the twin-pronged assault of the Europeans — smallpox and the long musket – leaving only the curse that was rumored to bring any of the island's later settlers to ugly and mysterious deaths.

Jon's most vivid memories of the trip were the oppressive heat, the jet liner-sized mosquitoes and snakes that dangled from the cypress branches on the banks of the island's inland swamps. Then there were the Venus flytraps – they seemed to be everywhere, their toothless but savage-looking mouths poised open, waiting for some hapless insect to light upon their vegetative whiskers and become a slowly digested snack.

At the time, there was no way to know that these tiny survivors of some evolutionary aberration would be Garland's undoing, but Jon was happy they were. The signs posted around the island – who for, he couldn't imagine – announced the resort's arrival and made Jon feel physically sick.

He remembered he attended this very church the next morning, his a single pale face standing out among a room of brown, and prayed that tiny Palm Island would somehow be spared further ruination.

Then afterwards was lunch, a two-hour covered-dish affair that featured two of every Lowcountry standard. He ate shrimp, fried chicken, biscuits, collards, and macaroni and cheese until he thought his abdomen would erupt.

Despite what Eli said, this did bode well. Jon knew this place, these people. He knew how to get back home. All was not lost. Not yet.

Though the church parking lot was full, the adjacent road seemed abandoned, so when he heard the rumble of tires coming from behind him Jon turned quickly and tried to wave the vehicle down. Even from a distance he could tell it was a military Humvee, the distinctive profile seeming to take up the entire lane of the two-lane blacktop. Jon saw the headlights blink and stepped back off the road, concerned that the reservist at the wheel might be lost or late getting home from weekend maneuvers and speed past him without much regard for his welfare.

Jon turned and shielded his eyes as the vehicle blew past. He didn't even have enough time to properly stick his thumb out for a ride. But as he looked back up to follow the course of the vehicle, he saw it stop suddenly and a blonde head emerge from the back window.

"Jon? Is that you?" the head said. The voice immediately registered as that of Regina Holiday. How they had come to cross paths again on this barren little spit of land he didn't even want to speculate about. But he didn't question his good fortune and ran towards the Humvee as it slowly reversed course in his direction. They met halfway, the military vehicle parked in the middle of the empty road.

"Jon! What are you doing here?" Regina asked, leaping out of the car to give him an enthusiastic hug.

"I could ask you the same question. You join up when I wasn't looking?"

Then the vehicle emptied of its occupants. There were two men of Asian descent and two Caucasian men who were members of some branch of the military, Jon judged by their haircuts and garb and by the fact the group was traveling in the Humvee.

"It's a long story," she said as Jon noticed what she was wearing, which wasn't much. The dress, if you could call it that, covered very little of her front and almost none of her back, giving Jon a view of Regina that somehow seemed more provocative than seeing her in a more revealing bikini. "But I think we're going to the same place, if you can believe that."

She then stepped back and studied him. "You're a mess."

"I know. Your girl Veronica Whitaker pushed me out of her skycar and I spent the night strapped in an ejector seat."

"But there's something else. You do something different with your hair?"

Jon realized that she noticed the aging Lil's work had accomplished. He self-consciously ran his hands through his hair and tried to smooth out his rumpled clothes, still damp and muddy. "No, no. It's just been a really rough couple of days."

"You're telling me," she said. "Linda and I were running all over the Grand Strand trying to hunt you down. What happened to you?"

The relief he felt knowing that Linda was looking for him almost overwhelmed him. "That, my dear, is also a long story," he said, reaching out and taking her hand in his. "Now introduce me to all your friends."

She ran down the list. First was Mako, the young Japanese fellow in the surfer garb who looked like someone had grafted occipital folds onto the face of a very tall Native American. Jon immediately recognized him as the heir to the Nikura fortune whom he had read about in the paper what seemed like a few months ago. He reminded himself that it was only a few days before. "Pleasure to meet you, Mako. Sorry to hear about your father."

The young man looked surprised as he shook Jon's hand. "I appreciate that, man. I really do."

Next was Yoshi, the larger of the two Japanese men, who Jon learned was Nikura's head of security now operating as something of a rogue samurai on behalf of Mako and his father. Then there were Barry and Lewis, Marines and – from as far as Jon could tell, possibly lovers. He decided he wouldn't even broach that subject lest he be killed barehanded in one of 50 ways in a tragic case of mistaken sexual identity.

"We understand our destinies and yours have unfortunately crossed paths," Yoshi said, his face an inscrutable mask of non-emotion.

"What my friend is trying to say is that he thinks we're both after the same guy," Mako interrupted. "His name is Lucas Schaefer, and we're pretty sure he's holding one of our friends hostage."

The name hit Jon like a brick. He remembered what Aunt Lil had told him, that there would be people who would help him. "Funny you should mention that. I think he's got my wife."

"*That's* what happened to Linda," Regina said. "I saw her getting dragged off by Schaefer, and by the time we got up to the roof of the church the two of them were gone."

"I'm sorry to interrupt, Jon, but time grows short. And I'm sure you would not want your wife to be in danger any longer than necessary," Yoshi said.

"Small problem, Yosh," Barry said, looking around. "We have no fucking clue where we are."

"You guys are lost?" Jon wasn't so sure if this could officially be qualified as help.

Yoshi looked frustrated, the first emotion he'd seen the man register. "Not lost. More accurately, at a loss."

"What he's trying to say," Lewis cut in, "is that our GPS system died on us back up in Beaufort and we've been following a homing beacon without a map for the last four hours. All we know is that our friend Krista is somewhere east of here. So if there's anything you can do to help us, we'd really appreciate it."

"There's nowhere east of here except Palm Island and Bermuda," Jon said. Then it struck Jon – the Whitakers' estate off of Hilton Head. Palm Island wasn't much, but it did lie east from where they stood, and it would be the perfect place for Schaefer to hide from those who were following him.

"I take that back," he said. "Everybody in the truck. I'll tell you where to go."

Once Yoshi was behind the wheel and the rest of the group had squeezed in – he, Jon and Mako in front and Barry, Lewis and Regina in the back – he directed the huge man to continue along the way the vehicle had already been headed. If he remembered correctly, there was only a private ferry maintained to Palm Island, and even that was intermittently manned. With luck, the ferry master wouldn't be too hungover from a Saturday night at the local juke joint and would be manning his post.

The road cut an asphalt strip across a swivel bridge that had been knocked askew by the same hurricane that flooded the island, then rebuilt to some day endure the same fate. On the other side, the only structures were a bait shop/saloon and a seafood stand, the owner of which was just opening up for the day. Otherwise, there was only the road and the rushes on either side, giving way farther out to the brackish water of the marsh, then the ocean.

About a mile and a half along, they saw a crude sign nailed to a utility pole saying the ferry was a half-mile distant. "You been here before, Jon?" Mako asked.

"Yeah, but it's been a while. You'll find, though, that down around here things don't change very much."

A small grove of palmettos flanked the dirt road that took over where the blacktop ended and eventually gave way to a gravel parking lot where a ramshackle wooden shed stood off to the side.

Down at the dock they saw a small launch bobbing and knocking against the old tires hanging from the posts. The ferry master was seated in a tattered aluminum lawn chair with green plastic webbing. As they parked, he watched their approach with some interest and evident amusement.

The group piled out of the Humvee as the man stood, walking toward them with an off-kilter, arthritic gait. He stepped straight to Yoshi, sizing up the huge man and his topknot without a word. He then moved to Regina and took her in, shaking his head as he realized the young girl was half-naked. He reached into the pocket of his short-sleeved madras shirt and fished out a pack of Newports, tapping one out and lighting it before walking over to Jon.

"Y'all need de ferry, den?"

"Sure do," Jon said. "How much for all of us…"

"And our gear," Barry interjected.

The old man looked them over. "Six, eh? Dat be 300 dolla. Fifty apiece," he said, taking a drag on his cigarette. He then looked over the group again, a bit more suspicious this time. "You goin' to Palm, right? You got bidness deah?"

"You could say that. When can we leave?" Jon said, growing impatient.

"Next ferry ain't till church let out. Twelve-thirty."

Off to the side, Jon saw Mako kneel and pull something from his ankle. He wasn't sure who Regina had fallen in with this time or what kind of scam they might be pulling, but there was no way he was going to let some trust fund brat pull a gun on this old man. Jon turned with speed that surprised even him and grabbed Mako's arm as he rose, finding only a wad of cash as big around as a soda can.

"Hey, man, why so jumpy?" Mako said, giving him a slow, knowing smile. "Just trying to offer this gentleman a little extra incentive."

Jon kept his eyes locked on Mako's as he released his grip. He had felt the bands of taut muscle in the younger man's arm and, upon reflection, imagined Mako could likely outmatch him in any physical confrontation. Still, Jon wanted Mako to know that he meant business. Mako strolled up to the ferry master and peeled off three $100 bills, then laid an extra two on top. "Mr. Franklin says he'd like to leave a little bit earlier than that."

The old man took a deep drag on his smoke and snatched the money out of Mako's hand. "That Mr. Franklin, I always say he's a smart man. You get what you carryin'. I'll get a blanket to cover up dis nekkid chile. De wind get cold out there on the water," he said, giving Regina another once-over.

Yoshi, Barry and Lewis were already back at the Humvee rolling back the green canvas tarp covering the back bed of the vehicle. They hefted out what Jon immediately recognized as a military gunney sack. As he watched, Mako sidled up to him and leaned close.

"Hey, dude. You didn't actually think I was going to shoot the old man, did you?"

"Sorry. There's already been too much weirdness over the last few days," Jon said.

"You're telling me. This is not how I planned to spend my weekend," he said as he shook his head and laughed.

The ferry dock had apparently been a busier marina at an earlier time, and there were at least a dozen empty slips up and down the dock. One, however, remained occupied by something long and low to the water, its deck covered entirely by a spotless white tarp.

Jon leaned in close to Mako. "You see what I see over there?"

Mako nodded. "She looks a whole lot faster than the ferryman's dinghy, whatever she is."

"If he's got the keys, you have enough bills there to take care of the extra he's going to gouge us for?"

"Absolutely. As many as it takes."

Jon raised his voice so the ferryman could hear him. "'Scuse me, sir. We're in a bit of a hurry. You have anything faster at your disposal?"

"At my disposal? What you think this is, boy? A boat show?"

"No, no. It's just that Mr. Franklin thinks that boat would be *much* faster," Jon said, pointing toward the mystery vessel.

"Oh, do he?"

Mako peeled off five more hundreds and fanned them out in front of his face. "Yes he do."

"Well, all right, chullen. Looks like we're changing vessels. C'mon, now. Let's get dat gear over dis way. Time's a'wastin'."

Regina appeared once again, this time wrapped in a green Army blanket Jon imagined was part of an ancient Civil Defense first-aid kit. Barry, Lewis and Yoshi approached quickly from the Humvee, Yoshi carrying the huge bag like it weighed half of what it probably did.

"Let's cut the chitchat and get going, folks," Barry said. "We'll get this stowed and then the rest of you come aboard."

"Hey deah', sweetheart," he called to Barry as he unfurled the tarp to reveal a Cigarette speedboat worthy of a billionaire playboy or an international narcotics trafficker. "Change of plan. We're takin' the express. You good to get that gear squared away?"

Barry looked up slowly, his lips in a thin smile. "Sweetheart? What do you mean by that, sir?" The Marine was suddenly, menacingly official.

"Aw, boy. Don't get your panties all bunched up. It ain't like you're wearnin' a neon sign on yo' head. I just pick up on that kinda stuff. My granddaughter call it the 'gay-dar.' You ever hear dat?"

"Yes sir, and I'd say yours is pretty damn good," Barry said, hefting the bag over the side before the old man began shoving it into one of the under-seat compartments.

"Well, mostly. Picked up on my son early. Now the boy makes his livin' dressin' up like Diana Ross at some honky-tonk up in Charleston. I'm proud of him, though. Boy's a dead ringer."

Lewis boarded the craft and found a seat. "Allotta Greens is your son? We saw that act last year. That guy's good." Yoshi and Mako, who had been talking alone up in the tiny parking lot, walked down the dock and joined them, Regina following behind and trying to swat away the cloud of gnats that swarmed around her head, likely attracted by her shampoo or some styling product.

"We ready to go?" Mako asked.

"All y'all in 'cept you, boy" the old man said, addressing Mako. "I'll get her fired up, 'den you cast us off and hop in, okay?"

Mako nodded and stood by the bow line. The old man turned the key, prompting a thundering aquatic roar from the rear of the boat. Mako unlooped the heavy line from around the dock piling and stepped aboard. "Y'all all hold onto somethin'. 'Dis won't take long."

The wind whipped his hair and took what was left of Regina's hairstyle and turned it into a long blonde contrail twirling and twisting in the breeze. Sitting behind her on the boat's bench seats, he got the full impact of what was left of the scent on her hair. She always did smell good, even as a child, he remembered. Her grandmother would regularly let her Regina rummage through her makeup kit during the girl's visits to the beach, and she would inevitably spritz herself with her grandmother's Shalamar or Chanel No. 5 before coming over to visit him and Linda. He leaned close to her ear to speak but couldn't help breathing in deep while he was there.

"What was Linda doing at the service with you?" he asked, raising his voice so she could hear him over the noise.

She turned to him, holding the blanket close against the wind and sea spray. "We were looking for you. She came down to the beach house because she figured that's where you would go after your fight. When you weren't there, I let her stay at my place and we looked all around town for you the next day. Finally I convinced her to go to the police. We talked to this little detective guy – Detective Robert – and he told us he'd do everything he could. I was going to the service anyway, so he suggested that Linda come along to get her mind off of things."

"Wait a minute. Robert?" Jon knew immediately who their "detective" was. Robert had set a trap for him and for Linda as well. Figures, he thought. Eli was covering all his bases from the get-go.

"Yeah. He must normally do undercover work, because he looked a little ratty for a cop. You know, hair short in front and long in back, scruffy beard, beat-up shoes, know what I mean?"

"I know exactly what you mean. Then what happened at the service?"

And she told him. All about them splitting up and Linda heading to the visitors' gallery, then being approached by Mako as he saw Linda being dragged away by church security guards. "The next thing I knew, surfer boy over here was blowing stuff up and dragging me out into the rain to look for someone named Krista. I figured Linda went to the same place the other girl did, so I came along with them."

"Well, it looks like you picked the right crew to travel with," Jon said.

"Depends on how you look at it, I guess," she said. "Apparently one guy that was with them when they got to Myrtle Beach was killed. They think Schaefer did it."

That didn't make Jon feel any better about Linda's safety, but it was good to at least have some idea of what he would encounter. "Well, I'm glad you're okay, and I'm glad you were there to look after her."

Regina cast her eyes downward. "I didn't manage to do a very good job of it."

"It doesn't matter. You were there when she needed somebody to help and I'm sure you did a great job," he said, rubbing her back in consolation. "All this other stuff that happened – that was totally beyond your control, okay?"

She smiled weakly. "Okay. You're such a sweetheart, Jon. Linda's a really lucky woman."

Jon sat back and gazed out to the shoreline growing on the horizon. "I guess we'll see how lucky before long."

Jon heard the engine throttle down and looked up to the ferry master, who glanced back and waved him forward. "Where, 'zactly y'all goin', anyway?"

"The Whitaker place, I think. Is there even one?"

"Oh, yeah. But you don' wanna go there, boy. That's the old plantation house. It haunted somethin' bad."

"Really?" This just got worse, Jon thought. "Haunted how?"

"Been bad spirits 'round there since the Indian times, even before the white folks came. You know how the Indians got names for all the spirits and know what they do and what animals they live in? Well, this ol' spirit didn't seem to have no use to them. It only did bad. Folks from the tribe come out here to get oysters and crabs and such, and they just disappear ... poof," the old man said, his gnarled hand waving through the air like he was erasing the long ago native from existence. "When the white folks came and set up the plantations, it didn't get no better. Slaves start disappearin' just like the Indians did. Then folks from the big house would go missin'. Didn't nobody want to live there full time 'til the Whitakers bought the place. No more disappearin', but ain't nobody there half the time to go. Just that one fella' that runs the show for the preacher."

"Schaefer?"

"I guess. Don't nobody hardly know his name. Never takes the ferry. Just come and go by skycar. Only folks that ever sees him much is the fishermen out on that side of the island. Everybody that seen him, though, they say he's kinda creepy lookin'."

"They're right," Jon said. "Do you know how to get out to the plantation house?"

"Sure do. Take the road from the ferry landing straight across. Takes you right to the front door." The old man throttled the engine back to a slow gurgle as they approached the shore. Their pilot turned to assess the baggage they carried and reconsidered. "But since I'm guessin' you folks ain't on any Meals-on-Wheels run, I suppose y'all don't want to pull up at the front door."

This gave Jon pause. No, they didn't want to show up at the front door. If anything, they wanted to show up at the back door, and very quietly. He looked astern and waved Yoshi forward. "I could make a tactical decision here, but I figure you've got a bit more experience at this sort of thing. You think it's a good idea to dock at the ferry landing?"

Yoshi was quiet a moment. "You are willing to take us elsewhere?" he said to the ferry master.

"I got enough green in my pocket that says y'all can go wherever you want to go," he said with a laugh.

"From a strategic standpoint, I would prefer that we land somewhere secluded, but closer to the plantation, if possible," Yoshi said.

"I got just the spot." The old man gunned the engine again and they turned sharply away from shore, heading around the island to the right. "Dey a little lagoon just south of the plantation," he shouted over the roar. "Current cuts up the coast, so I'll kill the engine before we get there and we'll float in. Ain't no dock down there, but the lagoon's only a few feet deep. Y'all can walk in to shore with no problem. After that there's a path through the woods takes you right onto the plantation."

"That sounds acceptable," Yoshi said, stoic as ever. Then to Jon: "Do you know how to fire a gun?"

Jon should have known that question would arise eventually, but he had no ready answer prepared. "Do you think we'll need to?"

The huge man's face tightened. "I did not share this with Regina, but we are facing something that is only masquerading as a human."

"Yoshi, I've met Mr. Schaefer, and I'll admit he's eccentric. But inhuman?"

Yoshi pulled him close, his massive hand wrapping almost entirely around Jon's bicep. "I have seen what this creature is capable of. He possesses the abilities of a sentient plant. Barry, Lewis and I shot his arm off at the shoulder, then watched as it regenerated itself, suit jacket and all. Wouldn't you agree that this is not the behavior of a normal human?"

Jon gulped. "Yes. I think I'd have to agree."

"Fine. I repeat: do you know how to fire a gun?"

It tasted like broccoli, Linda decided as she began gnawing on the green, fleshy root covering her mouth. Not entirely unpleasant, but considering the source not something she'd wanted to swallow, either. Once she got far enough for her to open her mouth all the way, it only took three good bites to snap it in half. She spat viciously once her mouth was free, wishing for the first time in her life for a vigorous dental cleaning. The taste lingered, and she wasn't sure if she would ever be able to look at anything in her vegetable garden quite the same way.

But she had far to go. Her legs and arms were still tightly bound, and it would take more than some well-kept incisors to get herself loose. Meanwhile, Krista and Veronica, watching her work her way through the gag, had begun to do the same. Great, she thought. Krista she didn't mind, but she preferred that Veronica stay speechless for as long as possible. Linda was surprised that the woman had the resolve to even give chewing her way out a try. She seemed relatively intolerable but easy to ignore when she was on television. Sitting here next to Linda, though, she was little more than a constant stream of prissy demands blurting out of her china-doll face. That worked very much in her favor, Linda imagined, since in her experience men sought to alternately protect and possess women who looked that way. Linda was thankful that genetics and her own style hadn't conspired to turn her into one of them.

She looked around the room again, trying to find anything she could use to help free them. The closest thing was the letter opener Veronica had used to cut her out of the cucumber coffin in which she'd been trapped. That might work, she thought, but it would require someone with enough leverage to drag the dull edge through the thick branches. She tried again to squirm loose, to at least free a hand or an arm, but it was no use. Then Krista commenced an encore performance of Linda's spitting, looking as if she'd eaten something dead.

"What's the matter?" Linda asked. "Not a big fan of vegetables?"

"No," Krista said, spitting violently again and nearly gagging. "And I think I hate broccoli the most."

Veronica, continuing her pained chewing, was still muffled and only made indistinguishable noises around her gag, interspersed with an occasional and very distinct whine of discontent.

"Any ideas on how we get out of this before Glamour Kitty there gets her voice back?" Linda asked, still squirming with her bonds.

"Nope. But he worked for her," Krista said, cocking her head in Veronica's direction. "Think she would have any idea?"

Linda snickered. "If it's not about her, I don't think she

cares about it. When you're the center of the universe you don't pay much attention to the insignificant orbiting bodies."

Veronica scowled and made an angry noise of protest that, if she could speak, would translate into, "Hey!" and only prompted her to chew away faster.

"So how did you end up in this, anyway?" Krista asked.

"Domestic dispute," Linda said, rolling her eyes at the very thought of being involved in anything so common, as her mother would say.

"Been down that road," Krista said, laughing.

"Is that what happened…" Linda's voice trailed off.

"Yeah, but that seems like years ago now. Hopefully he's enjoying the hospitality of the city of Philadelphia and some of its finest criminals now."

"What about your friend, Mako? Where did you two meet?"

"Well, as I was hitchhiking my way down I-95, he stopped and picked me up. I needed a ride out of town, but I never thought it was going to end me up in something like this."

"Tell me about it. I've been looking for Jon for the last three days. He came home Thursday saying he'd been fired. Then I found another woman's panties in his pocket. Of course I went off the deep end and kicked him out. Then the woman I thought he'd slept with called me and told me what really happened. By that time Jon was already gone. I didn't hear a thing from him, and then I saw him sitting next to her majesty here on the altar at the Church of the New Revelation."

"So … he wasn't having an affair."

"Thankfully, no. The office slut tried to seduce him and he refused, so she accused him of attacking her. Jon's boss was her uncle, so of course she got the benefit of the doubt," Linda said.

"What about the panties?"

"Just a little reminder of what he could have if he wanted, I imagine. Didn't help his case with me, though. I was pissed. But I should have known Jon would never do anything like that. He might be a flirt, but he's no adulterer."

Then there was frantic spitting and coughing as Veronica finally worked away enough of the root to allow her to speak. "Bullshit," she said with a haughty lilt instead of the declarative vigor anyone else would allow the word. "I call bullshit on you and your husband and your perfect little marriage."

"This from the woman who screws her way through church every Saturday night," Linda replied. "Who made you qualified to judge the quality of anyone's marriage, sister?"

"I'm not saying that mine's any better than anyone else's. I'm just saying your husband didn't seem so devoted when I had him in my meditation chamber last night."

Every muscle in Linda's body tensed. If she could have, she very well might have killed Veronica Whitaker at that moment, and it was only by the virtue of her vegetative bonds that she didn't try.

"Be careful what you say, honey. We're not going to be wrapped up like this forever," Linda said, glaring at the other woman. "And I won't hesitate to hit you again."

Krista looked back and forth and realized a catfight at this point could seriously jeopardize their chances of escape. "Ladies, I hate to interrupt, but we've got other things to worry about than each other's sex lives, don't you think?"

"I suppose," Linda said, in no way withdrawing her threat. "Freak boy works for you, Veronica. Any theories on how we might get out of here?"

"What would I know about that?" she said. Linda couldn't decide if she was playing dumb or innocent or just really was that stupid. Half the civilized world knew she wasn't that innocent.

"Because you're around him all the time, that's why." Linda was growing frustrated already. "Ever notice anything odd about him, besides the fact that he tends to sprout plant parts and hide people in giant pea pods?"

Veronica pondered for a moment, biting her lip as she did. Another trick to draw the men in, Linda thought. God, did the woman have any shame? "Well, there were his preferences about the light."

"The light. Great. What? He likes sunlamps?" Krista broke in.

"No, no. He doesn't like bright light. He hardly ever comes outside during the daytime, and even in his office it was very dark and dank. I always thought that was creepy."

"Good. That's a start," Linda said. "Can everyone move their legs?"

All three of the women move theirs together, looking like a group of mermaids who found themselves trapped in aggressive seaweed. "Okay, let's try to get over to that window where I pulled the drapes down," Linda said, motioning with her head. "The sun is moving around enough to come in the window pretty bright, so maybe that will do some good."

Linda was sure the image of the three of them squirming across the floor propelled by their bound legs would have been absurd to anyone watching them. They each made their way around the huge desk, Krista reaching the dim patch of sunlight on the rug first. She lay there panting as Linda and Veronica joined her on either side.

"Is there a chance in hell that this might work?" Krista said, lying on her side and facing Linda. Underneath the remnants of bruises around her right eye there was a lovely young woman. Probably a thousand times more street smart than Linda would ever be, too.

"At this point anything's worth a try, don't you think?" Linda said. "Check every so often to see if that thing is loosening up."

Krista squirmed, succeeding in freeing her right hand from where it had been wrapped up tight. "Hey, maybe this wasn't such a bad idea after all."

The smell of decaying vegetation wafted from her as Linda watched the thick roots slowly brown and shrivel in the sunlight. After more squirming, Krista was free, quickly rolling away from the rotted stalks and standing up to pull down another set of drapes, imitating Linda by wrapping them into a makeshift toga. She then reached down to help Linda by dragging her into the patch of sunlight as she scooted her way over. Veronica made an impatient noise when she realized she wasn't next. "Relax, Miss Thing. You'll get your turn," Krista said as she pulled drying stalks from around Linda.

"Thanks, hon," Linda said once she was freed. She could now safely say that the two most disgusting experiences of her life had both taken place within an hour of each other. She adjusted her toga to fully cover herself once again and knelt to face Veronica on her level. "Now, then. I don't know if you're lying or telling the truth about fooling around with my husband. But given the circumstances we're in, I'll forget you said anything if you agree not to bring that up again. Does that work for you?"

Veronica looked to Krista for help, but she only stood with her arms crossed. "It might be a while before someone finds you after we kick your flunky's ass. I'd hate to have to just leave you here."

"Fine, fine. I won't bring it up again," Veronica said after quickly assessing her options.

"And we have a winner. I'll resist the urge to move you over to the window by putting my hands around your neck," Linda said, then grasping the heavy stalk around Veronica's shoulders and, with Krista's assistance, dragging her toward the light. The two freed women then went about their business trying to find a way out as Veronica's bonds gradually loosened.

"Door's locked tight," Krista said after turning the knob and examining the bolt. "And we've got alarm-sensitive micro-mesh running through the windows, too, so that's not an option."

"How the hell could you tell that?" Linda said as she rummaged through the contents of the desk drawers.

"My highly attuned sense of deduction and the little sticker on the window that says, "This residence protected by the Micro-Mesh Alarm System," she said, breaking into a laugh.

Veronica, still seated and looking offended at being ignored, looked back and forth between them. "Well I don't think this is very funny. I just found out one of my most trusted has been running some sort of... scam on the side and using the ministry my husband and I worked so hard to build to do it."

"It's not a scam, sister," Linda said. "Three-card Monty is a scam. Pyramid investment plans are a scam. This, it seems to me, is a plot to initiate global thermonuclear war or something equally nasty. We can bet that whatever Mr. Schaefer is, his type doesn't have much regard for the human race."

"But we're sorry," Krista said with mock sympathy. "Obviously worrying about the human race would take attention away from you and your porno priesthood."

Veronica rose and headed toward Krista. "You obviously have no knowledge of who we are or what we do, so I'd appreciate it if you'd refrain from commenting on it."

"Ladies," Linda said, interrupting. "We all promised to behave so we could get ourselves out of here, didn't we? So let's start thinking of how we can do that."

Veronica threw herself into an antique wingback chair, scowled at Linda and began chewing on her pinkie fingernail. "I can assure you we'll never get out of here through a door or window. Lucas' security precautions have always been too thorough for him to let that happen."

"I'd have to agree," Linda said. "Unless there's some hidden way out, which we really don't have time to look for, I'd suggest we think of something else."

"So, what? Do we just wait for the freak to come back and tie us up in weeds again?" Krista said.

Linda thought a moment. "If we got him back here and we were ready for him, it wouldn't be that bad. There would have to be some way we could take him by surprise enough to immobilize him."

"Not to be the pessimist, but how do you expect to get the jump on some guy who probably lives on Miracle Grow?"

"Well," Veronica said. "We do have the light."

Krista and Linda both looked at her as if she'd just recited a bit of quantum theory. "What?" she said. "The pretty one always has to be stupid, is that it?"

Linda suppressed the urge to agree with her and instead offered congratulations. "No, no. That's a really good point. If we can somehow get him in here, then expose him to the sunlight, we might have a chance of at least weakening him."

"And even though the mesh will keep us from breaking the windows enough to get out, it will at least set off the alarms and maybe get him back in here," Krista said.

"Right," said Linda. "But first we need to get all the drapes out of all these windows, so we need to get up high."

Wordlessly, the three of them surrounded a nearby Queen Anne loveseat with the inlay of 18th century women fellating their lovers, which they dragged toward the window. Veronica was tallest, so she was assigned the job of pulling down the highest drapes.

When they were finished, the room was bathed in the warm light of the morning sun, somehow offering them some hope in what Linda realized was a situation that didn't have much hope to spare.

"I suppose I get to do the honors, then?" Linda put forth, glancing back at the other two. "Fine then. Krista, hand me something heavy and let's get this party started."

^^^

Jon found the rifle much heavier than he remembered from his days in basic training, but pure muscle memory immediately threw him back into the routine of being armed. So much for being able to brag that as a member of the Fighting 53rd Public Relations Corps he never had to fire a shot other than on the target range.

Meanwhile, the machete the old man had given him – a gift for folks he thought were destined to kill the monster of the island – slapped against his left thigh. As if to demonstrate the worthiness of the weapon to the vanquishing knight, the ferrymaster had lifted a croaker from his bait box, tossed the fish into the air and sliced it in half with one quick stroke.

Coming off the boat, he imagined that he, Mako and Yoshi must have looked like a pretty sorry excuse for an assault team, all of them in their damp and inappropriate clothes, holding their weapons high above their heads to avoid getting them wet. But if what Mako had told him about Schaefer's plans for the satellite was true, it would seem this little group was the last chance anyone had to stop them.

Yoshi, who led them, motioned for the group to stop as they left the beach and stepped into the native bramble and underbrush of the island. They all knelt as the huge man leaned toward them. "The old man said that beyond this there is a swamp to the east and clearing just ahead on which the house is located. We will travel single file along the edge of the swamp to get as close to the house as possible, do you understand?"

Jon and Mako both nodded. As Yoshi began to move ahead, Jon leaned forward and whispered to Mako, "Tell Yoshi to be careful of the water moccasins."

"The what?"

"Water snakes," Jon said as calmly as he could. "Poisonous water snakes." He then watched Mako lean forward to relay the information to Yoshi, who immediately signaled for them to stop.

"You know of these snakes?" the huge man said over his shoulder. "Intimately," Jon said. "Just stay away from the edge of the water and watch in the branches above you. They usually don't strike if they're not agitated."

"Fine. Let us do our best not to agitate the poisonous water snakes," he said to Mako before giving the signal to resume.

They crept along, staying low and using the abundant cypress trunks for cover. They traveled so for what Jon estimated to be about ten minutes before rounding a curve in the edge of the swamp to see the plantation house about a half a mile away from them. It was even more a picture of the stereotypical old South than the Whitakers' place in Myrtle Beach. It was of the same antebellum style, with a huge double stairway leading up to the second level and at least five dormer windows set along the roof on each side he could see. It sat in the center of an manicured lawn and looked to Jon as if someone had decided to build the massive home in the center of a golf course, of which there was no short supply along the coast. The only things missing were some contrived rolling hills, a few sand traps and some old men in ugly pants.

Yoshi signaled for them to stop and turned back to Jon and Mako. "This lack of cover is unexpected," he said, looking as frustrated as Jon imagined the expressionless man ever did. "Our approach will be visible to both security systems and the human eye from all angles. We will be putting ourselves and our friends at grave risk should we attempt to reach the house."

The three of them crouched in silence for a moment as they all ruminated on the latest challenge. Jon looked ahead along their path to gauge whether a sprint from the swamp's nearest point to the house would be a good idea or suicide. He was perfectly willing to put his life – or what amounted to a life in his semi-deceased state – at risk for Linda, but not in a manner that might jeopardize her rescue.

"I am unwilling to attempt to approach the house from here. Let's continue and perhaps we will find a place closer to the house," Yoshi said, reluctantly signaling them forward. Jon felt his feet sink slowly into a thick boggy muck. The Argentine loafer now irretrievably mired in the black slime of the swamp, he pulled his damp foot free and stripped off the sock, then repeating the same process with the other foot. He had always felt more sure of himself in bare feet, anyway. He just had to remember to watch out for those snakes. And the leeches, of course. Jon figured it was best not to mention those, lest his two companions turn around and give up the hunt.

To their right, through the stand of cypress trees, Jon could see that they were moving closer to the house. He was surprised – and he imagined Yoshi was also – that they hadn't already tripped some sort of alarm or been picked up on a surveillance camera or some other sensing device. If they had, it seemed as if no one cared, which was fine for Jon at the moment. He was perfectly capable of using the rifle for its intended purpose but wasn't interested in actually doing so.

They rounded a bend in the swamp, bringing into view what passed as the front of the house, since it was this side that faced the driveway. Two skycar limousines were parked in plain view on a gravel patch apparently reserved for that purpose. "I'm guessing one of those is the skycar Veronica pushed me out of," Jon whispered.

"And the other one likely belongs to Schaefer," Yoshi said.

"Boy, you fellows don't miss a trick, do you?" Mako said, rolling his eyes. "I've about had enough of this sneaking around. It's obvious no one knows we're here. Why don't we just rush the joint and get everyone out?"

"Your impatience is understandable, Mako, but measures must be taken to ensure not only our safety but that of Mr. Schaefer's prisoners."

Jon studied the exterior of the house, wondering if there was some way, some loose window or unused door that would allow them discrete entry. Movement in one of the windows caught his eye, and he poked Yoshi hard in the arm to interrupt him. "Hey there, big guy. I think I see what room he's keeping the ladies in." Jon pointed across the lawn to a tall window on the first floor where figures that could have been female seemed to move in and out of view.

"It could be a trap," Yoshi said, squinting as he tried to see.

Jon found himself in an intense internal argument with his rational and emotional sides. The rational side told him to stay put rather than run the risk of endangering Linda. But the emotional side came up fast and blindsided reason, insisting that the worst course of action was to take no action at all.

"I'm willing to find out," Jon said to no one in particular as he bolted from the cypress stand, splashing out of the water and running fast and low along the lawn toward the window with the figures. The rifle slowed his progress, but he'd be damned if he was going to leave that behind. He was stupid, he thought, but not nearly that stupid.

Jon arrived at the latticework surrounding the foundation exhilarated and out of breath. After throwing himself against the side of the house just beneath the targeted window, he took a moment to catch his breath. Back towards the line of the swamp he could barely see the figures of Mako and Yoshi crouched in the grove of palmettos they had been approaching when he broke away. They remained still, unwilling, he imagined, to draw any more attention to themselves than Jon already had. He was sure Yoshi was at that moment muttering something dry about Jon's impetuous move, but Jon didn't care. He turned slowly and inched his body up the wall to allow himself to peek inside.

The first thing he saw was wire mesh running through the window pane, a confirmation of Yoshi's speculation on the level of security. There would be no breaking in here, he thought. Then, as his eyes focused, he caught another glimpse of movement over the top of a huge wooden desk. He raised his fist to the glass and paused a moment, considering his rash actions. Then he rapped lightly.

Three women's heads popped up from behind the desk like a trio of lovely, startled prairie dogs. There was Veronica looking disheveled and exhausted, a younger woman he didn't recognize whom he assumed was Mako's lady friend, and – like the face of an angel sent to bring him forgiveness and redemption – his beautiful Linda. She was a mess, but as was always the case she shined through it, lighting the room the way no other woman he ever knew could.

Linda leapt to her feet, followed closely behind by Veronica, whom Linda elbowed without guilt back behind her.

"How can I get in?" he said, half whispering and trying to exaggerate the words with his mouth, the better to allow her to read his lips. Veronica angrily muscled her way next to his wife as Linda shook her head that she didn't know.

"The front door," he saw Veronica mouth. "The front door is open." That was a relief. His breaking and entering experience was limited to a childhood incident using a wooden skewer to jimmy the lock on his best friend's sister's bedroom door so they could read her diary. Unlike some of his newsgathering contemporaries, more advanced lock picking was a skill he'd never felt the need to learn. He imagined the security here would have taken more than an oversized toothpick to breach.

"Can you make a distraction?" he asked.

"We're on it," Linda said as Veronica held up an anvil-shaped doorstop to show him how well armed they were. He wasn't sure what that was going to do for them, but it was clear they had sorted something out among themselves. Linda held up her hand and pantomimed a toss at the window.

He nodded in agreement as Veronica and the other woman returned to the center of the room. Linda's eyes, however, remained fixed on his, and it took every bit of his resolve not to break down and beg her forgiveness right there. Her hand, which had closed slowly, opened again, to Jon blossoming like a delicate flower. She pressed it against the window and leaned forward, her eyes welling up with tears, and mouthed "I love you."

He pressed his hand opposite hers and said quietly, "I love you, too," knowing then that regardless of how things turned out – even if he couldn't wrangle his way out of the mess he was in, she would know that he hadn't forsaken her. Linda then turned away to join the others, leaving Jon to slither back down to the ground and wave for Mako and Yoshi to join him. A moment passed before he saw the two men burst from their cover and repeat his squatting run across the lawn.

"Your willingness to take unnecessary risks is unsettling, Jon," Yoshi said as he and Mako pressed themselves to the wall on either side of him. Jon took that to mean that he had succeeded in scaring the bejeesus out of the man. Mako was more complimentary.

"Man, that was some crazy kamikaze shit you did," the younger man said, clapping Jon on the back in congratulation.

"Okay guys, we're going in the front door. You ready?" Jon said, not wishing to waste any precious time.

"Jon, from a strategic standpoint I must object..." Yoshi said, actually beginning to look worried.

"It's okay. Veronica said she left the front doors wide open. And the rest of the place is sealed up tight."

"Unless, of course, you've got any better ideas," Mako said, smirking as he looked around Jon to address Yoshi. He was clearly enjoying watching Jon get the best of the huge security specialist.

"No, I do not," Yoshi said, the stoicism returning. "I will lead the way."

They hunched over again, running from window to window in short bursts as Yoshi checked the way ahead and then waved them on. When they arrived at the corner, he stopped them.

"We will use the skycars for cover after we round this corner. Then I will approach the door from the side as the two of you cover me. I will make sure everything is clear inside before waving you in. Is that understood?"

Jon and Mako nodded their heads that it was, after which they scurried in a low single-file line to the skycar from which Jon had been propelled hours earlier. They all scanned the surrounding terrain – more neat grass and a gravel driveway stretching deep into the live oaks and lobblolly pines. At the front of the house, the left of the two massive panel doors sat open, revealing a sliver of the foyer that lay beyond.

Yoshi looked at Mako and Jon to confirm that they were ready. Each man then took his weapon and laid it across the angled nose of the skycar aiming toward the house. Then, in a surprising burst of speed for a man so large, Yoshi bolted across the slice of lawn between the house and parking pad, then backed up against the closed of the two doors. They watched him as he turned his head like a startled bird to look inside and assess the situation inside. Looking back, he waved them on with a moment of eye contact and a tilt of his head. Jon's rifle made a quiet rattle as he ran and prompted him to cringe at the thought of some super-sensitive security device hearing it and setting off an alarm. But none sounded, and both he and Mako made it to Yoshi's position without arousing any suspicion – at least as far as he could tell.

Yoshi checked the foyer once more and led them inside, each step a silent ballet of soft heel-to-toe. Even in the halflight of the low morning sun, Jon was impressed by the splendor of the entryway. It was as if the Whitakers found it physically impossible to live in anything other than understated opulence. As Jon surveyed the vaulted ceiling with the high windows designed to fill the room with light, he heard Mako snicker at something on the floor. Looking down, Jon realized that everything that had held true for the Whitakers' other private spaces held true for this one. Inlaid in the center of the gleaming hardwood floor was a ring of silhouettes of nude men and women, sexually gratifying themselves and each other in a variety of ways. Yoshi looked back to shush him, but after Mako pointed out the source of his amusement, even the stoic bodyguard couldn't help but crack a minute smile. Jon simply shook his head. Veronica was here somewhere, and he found it almost a shame that he had arrived under such dire circumstances. A guided tour of the house led by Veronica would be something Linda could turn into 15 different articles, from home and design magazines to the snarky humor newsletters that showed up free, whether requested or not, on everyone's readers.

A noise startled them all. It was a low, repetitive throb – most likely an alarm sounding in response to the women breaking the window. Yoshi turned and surveyed the foyer, silently ordering Jon and Mako behind two person-sized planters that flanked the front doorway. Yoshi, meanwhile, crouched behind a long, dark table that sat against the foyer wall. Then there were hurried footsteps coming from above. Jon's eyes remained glued to the top of the stairway, which curved from them up to a second-story landing. At the sight of feet he felt his muscles tighten, his finger easing back from the trigger guard onto the trigger as his thumb disengaged the safety. A figure rounded the curve of the stairs and all of them saw that it was indeed Schaefer, unarmed as far as Jon could tell. But that meant nothing for someone who could sprout roots, he reminded himself.

Yoshi waved back for them to hold their fire as he watched Schaefer descend. He seemed to have no idea that they were there. Jon realized that whatever distraction Linda had in mind, it must be working. Still, he was sure no good awaited the women should he be forced to visit them again.

Jon stood and leveled his weapon. "Schaefer!"

He stopped as gracefully as if the moved were choreographed. "Ah, Mr. Temple, if that is indeed your real name. Come to find your women, have you?"

"That would be woman, thanks. And yes, among other things."

"I'm sure Mrs. Whitaker would disagree with the singularity of that comment. You and she seemed to have a lovely time in her meditation chamber last evening."

"Dude!" Mako whispered from the shadows. "You nailed the redhead?"

"And I see you brought friends, as well," Schaefer said, looking behind Jon to where Mako and Yoshi were hidden. "How nice. Although I can't imagine what any of you might expect to accomplish at this late time."

"Not sure what you mean by late. Your satellite deal is off. Veronica is pretty sure that your inherent weirdness isn't just some personal quirk, and we're prepared to do whatever is necessary to find out who you are and what exactly you had in mind."

"Fascinating. I had no idea that my destruction would come at the hands of such a rag-tag assemblage," he said straight-faced, but with palpable sarcasm. "Please pardon me while I tremble in terror."

"Not nervous at all?"

"Not in the least, Mr. Temple, because everyone who could potentially do my little project any harm is either dead or on this island. The non-existence of our satellite arrangement is a small detail that will be easily overcome, because the weapon has already been purchased. The only two people who would be able to stop it are hiding behind you and, like you, will not be leaving this island alive. As for the girl Krista and the woman you claim is your wife, even if I were to allow them to live no one would believe them anyway."

"What about your high priestess, Sister Veronica? I doubt you'll be able to keep her quite so easily."

"A small matter. Her interests in the church supersede all others and she is disinclined to believe anything that goes against its ultimate goals."

"Maybe that's just because she hasn't seen you turn into a giant killer cauliflower," Mako interjected.

Schaefer cocked his head to regard the younger man. "Your self assuredness is ill-placed considering the ease with which your uncle agreed to sell me a weapon that would likely destroy his entire planet. But I see you possess your father's hypocrisy, as well. For a man who dealt in instruments of death, it was interesting to see how only the scale of those deaths affected his decision to work against me."

Mako chuckled. "Why, you mother…"

A low murmuring that seemed to reverberate through the house interrupted him. Schaefer paused and cocked an ear, then turned his attention back to the three men.

"But I have wasted too much time with this discussion, as the women are likely up to no good and are long past the point of necessity. Please enjoy what is left of your stay."

Three new appendages then sprouted forth from Schaefer's torso, forming themselves into thick vines that launched towards each of them. Raising their rifles, the men fired, but the only effect of each bullet was to take a small nick out of the branch of vegetation headed straight for them.

Each tendril first entwined their rifles, rendering them useless, then moved on to their arms, encasing them along with the weapons. Yoshi began to shout, but found himself immediately muffled by another branch of Schaefer's quickly expanding appendages. By the time Jon could even begin to assess Mako's condition, he was nearly encased himself, with only a slit in the surrounding branches left through which to see the younger man squirming on the shiny floor.

Then an electrical current stronger than anything Jon had ever felt in the course of his occasionally misguided home electrical work shot through every muscle and nerve, making his body rigid with pain. Schaefer wasn't kidding about any of what he said. He fully intended that none of them would leave the island alive, and he seemed to have reserved the most painful fate for him.

Jon fought against the pain, determined to remain conscious before finally losing himself to the agony. Then, from the deep recesses of his mind, a memory came through in the form of a mellow, deep and lilting voice – a voice that echoed through the heat of the stars and the nucleus of the tiniest microorganism.

"Relax, boy," it said. "You're already dead."

As soon as Jon agreed in his own mind that this was the case, the pain subsided. His physical form still twitched and thrashed on the mansion floor, but his mind was freed. He found he was able to ride the currents now, and they ran straight back into Schaefer, opening the being's mind to his own.

The thoughts and emotions were foreign to him at first. But as if some internal translator was at work, the images and feelings gradually clarified to the point where Jon could interpret them. He saw great, glowing plains of antimatter surging with blue bolts of electricity. Above the horizon floated clouds that resembled chunks of brightly colored coral and smaller structures that, in any other circumstance, Jon would have sworn were spineless sea urchins.

Inside one of the urchins was a being he somehow recognized as Schaefer, or at least what Schaefer was originally. It was as if someone had taken raw electrical current and fashioned into a shape, although it was a shape for which he had no reference. Others of the same race were there too, and by the conditions, the number of beings and the palpable level of boredom, Jon couldn't describe it any other way than to say it was a meeting. What began as nothing more than the wordless noise he had heard echoing throughout the mansion eventually evolved into language he could somehow recognize, and the topic of the gathering was obviously Earth.

The Schaefer creature was presenting to the rest of the group statistics and studies detailing how Earth's atmosphere could, within a short span of time, be altered to accommodate their race for purposes of – and Jon could hardly believe the words – a vacation resort. A hovering diagram of Earth seemed to track its evolution from steamy ball of volcanoes and an ammonia atmosphere to what it was today. "With the proper post-purchase management, this planet would offer resort amenities that our customers didn't even know they desired," it said. "Granted, there are a few issues leading up to that point will have to be addressed, but I predict that at the end of the development period you all will be pleased with the results."

"What sort of issues?" said another of the beings.

"An emergent culture of low-evolution-level beings will have to be addressed and managed, but I don't anticipate any trouble there. Their awareness of trans-universal travel is purely theoretical, so the plan will be able to proceed without interference."

Trans-universal travel? No wonder Eli was so clueless about Schaefer. The guy didn't exactly come from the same neighborhood.

Another being spoke up. "All the necessary studies on this species have been done regarding any long-term impact its loss would have on the planet, yes? We certainly don't want a repeat of the Mars incident. And as you are aware, this planet's dimensional shift will soon be inaccessible for quite a long time."

The mention of Mars seemed to deeply pain the Schaefer being, but it covered. "I'd like to assure you that the dimensional shift zone, which is already in a remote area, is well protected. Also, Earth has a 99 percent rate of viability in a post-human environment, and recovery time to allow for rapid construction of the necessary facilities and resort areas will be minimal," it said. "Please keep in mind that in the Mars incident the impacts of various foreign bodies and the subsequent shift in the planet's magnetic field were entirely unpredictable."

But something in the back of the Schaefer creature's mind nagged at it. There was a step he had skipped or a detail he had failed to mention. Jon probed deeper, forcing himself beyond the upper layers of the creature's consciousness into the place where it kept thoughts it hid from itself.

And there he saw it. A glimmer of guilt over not revealing a fact to its employer and the knowledge that should this fact be revealed, his entire plan would end in disaster.

Humans, it seemed, were on the endangered species list.

"You forget that you are employed to anticipate the unpredictable. Another such failure will have unfortunate consequences, do you understand?"

"I do, and I will not fail you or our investors. Please feel confident leaving all the details to me."

"Excellent," said still another being. "We will adjourn, and please proceed with the plan as outlined. Report back when you anticipate construction can begin."

Then, from somewhere outside the realm of Schaefer's mind, came a female voice. It was calling his name.

Somewhere far off he once again became aware of excruciating pain, of his body jerking and convulsing, his mouth foaming and his eyes rolling back in his head. The voice was achingly familiar and echoed across the dimensions like that of an angel. It was Linda.

Jon realized in the time it took him to probe Schaefer's thoughts only seconds had passed. He forced himself back into the present and beyond the pain coursing through his body, gaining just enough control to see Linda standing at the far end of the mansion's immense foyer, then watching her run straight toward Schaefer.

Jon struggled to free his right hand as he watched another weedy extension shoot out from the creature's body straight toward his wife. He continued to strain against his bonds, until finally he extended his right hand from the shoulder enough to reach the handle of the machete the ferry master had given him. He found that he couldn't remember rejoicing at anything quite so much as the feel of the electrical tape the old man had wrapped around the handle or the whispering sound of the blade as it slid from its sheath.

He raised his arm above his head just as the narrow end of the vine reached Linda's ankle, then brought it down with more force than he was aware he could muster. The slice went deep, and a spurt of green goo issued forth across the floor as Schaefer screamed and shifted his attention to Jon. One more downstroke severed the tendril completely, allowing him to stand and shake off the now dead extensions. Jon looked up to find Linda again, but she had disappeared. She wasn't in Schaefer's grasp and he couldn't see her hiding anywhere. It was as if she hadn't been there at all.

Jon ran to Mako and Yoshi, again bringing the machete down hard and swift, slicing them free and allowing both men to roll away to where they could unravel their weapons.

"Schaefer, I've got bad news for you, my friend. Your little plan is going to fail," Jon said as he shook the blade hard, slinging a stream of gelatinous slime.

Schaefer's face caught most of the splatter, and he spat with contempt. "You have no idea what you're talking about, Mr. Temple. My plans are far beyond the scope of your feeble imagination."

"Oh, I don't know, Schaefer. Considering you talk like the bad guy from a lousy movie script, you shouldn't be too hard to figure out," Jon said as he hacked off the end of another vine slithering his way. The whole room was starting to smell like raw broccoli. "Besides, my imagination's pretty damn good. Why don't you try me?"

Mako and Yoshi wrestled the last of the dead and dying vines from their bodies and ran to his side. "What now, boss?" Mako said.

"Good question. Any thoughts, Yoshi?"

"This creature prefers dark, moist environments. I would imagine the bright sun might help weaken him, if nothing else."

"Great. I'll cover the two of you while you pull down these drapes," Jon said. He looked up at the darkened skylight, slivers of morning sun barely visible at the edges of each pane. "Suppose we better save that for last."

"Agreed," Yoshi said. "And it might be best that we alert Barry and Lewis for purposes of back-up."

"Good thinking. I'm pretty sure we're going to need it," Jon said. "And Mako, see if you can get past Schaefer to find out where the women are."

"Right."

The two other men began their work while Jon leveled the rifle at Schaefer once again. He heard Yoshi calling the two Marines as he jogged away, and Jon hoped nothing had happened to the two of them to keep them from riding to the rescue, because he wasn't sure how much longer he could hold Schaefer off.

Still, he was going to give it his best shot.

"So, Mr. Schaefer, tell me about this dimensional door. Is that why there's always been some legend about people mysteriously disappearing from this island?"

For the first time since Jon met him, Schaefer looked genuinely confused. "How did you ...?"

A curtain came down and he shielded his eyes, even if small patches of his vegetative flesh began to smolder and shrivel where beams of sunlight were striking him.

"And the real estate project, that's very interesting. I'm a huge fan of real estate projects. Did I tell you about the one that was planned for this site before you bought it? It was going to be nice – nothing but golf courses and marinas and fancy restaurants with ass-kissing waiters and old men in ugly pants. But you know what happened?"

Another curtain came down and Schaefer winced. Another tendril shot out toward Mako, who was edging around the foyer wall to the far door, but Jon fired quickly enough for it to explode in green pulp before it reached him. Mako slid through and disappeared.

"The guys behind the development were too focused on their own greed to pay attention to the little details – especially the one about a tiny little plant that eats bugs. Turns out this is one of the last places you can find that plant, and the government was very upset that the golf courses and marinas would probably destroy all of them. So the government stepped in and said, 'Sorry, you can't build here. We're keeping the old plantation house but otherwise it's going to be a wildlife preserve.' How upset do you think those investors were that the developer didn't do his homework? I'm sure they lost a lot on that deal."

Schaefer only grunted and moaned as the brightening sunlight continued to sizzle away at his flesh. "You're probably wondering how any of this relates to you, right? Well, considering your little development project involves destroying human life as we know it, don't you think a study on humans would have been in order? Because I have it on pretty good authority that we're something of an endangered species."

"Oh, dear," was all Schaefer could say. Jon imagined what must be going through the creature's mind right now. Failure was imminent, and worst of all it had come at the hands of the insignificant race he sought to destroy. His employers and investors, all of whom were monitoring his progress closely, would be furious and would likely inflict on him a fate worse than anything Jon or his friends could dream up. But that didn't mean he wouldn't try.

Just then, movement across the foyer caught his eye. It was Mako with the women crouched behind him. Among them – thank God – was Linda, intact and unharmed.

"So, Mr. Schaefer, I'm offering you a new deal. We'd like you to vacate this planet, and preferably this end of our dimension and slither on back to your own to face the music from your employers. If you don't, we'll just be forced to terminate you ourselves."

Jon knew it was big talk for three guys armed with weapons that had very little effect, but if there was one thing he'd learned from both life as a reporter and a PR hack, it was how to bluff.

"You're all too correct, Mr. Temple," said Schaefer, his voice noticeably weaker. "But I have put far too much into this project to let insects like you destroy all my work. If I succeed in stopping you, there will be no one left to stand in my way. So I do believe you are the ones who should be concerned with termination."

A low, rhythmic thud drew Jon's attention away from Schaefer's ramblings. Yoshi, in the midst of pulling down the final curtain, craned his neck to look into the sky.

"It is a helicopter," he said, flatly. "An Army helicopter."

Again the nearly subsonic murmuring shuddered throughout the house, but this time the words seemed to make more sense to Jon in much the same way Schaefer's native language did as he probed the being's thoughts.

"His computer is activating the security protocols and trying to open the dimensional door, and it sounds like that involves some sort of self-destruct," he yelled to Mako. "We need to get out of here."

The thudding grew almost deafening behind him. Jon looked behind him through the mansion's front door and saw that the helicopter had landed in the front yard a few dozen yards away from the aircars. "What the hell?" he muttered to himself.

Yoshi ran to his side. As Jon watched to see who would disembark from the vehicle, the huge man pointed to a spot in the air just above where Schaefer stood. "The air, Jon. It is shimmering."

And it was. Jon's knowledge of any sort of physics stopped at the law of gravity, but he imagined this was the beginning of the transportation process back to Schaefer's home dimension.

"We've got to get everyone out now!" Jon shouted again.

Behind him, the door burst all the way open. "Good idea, buddy, 'cause things in here are gonna get kinda hot," said a man's voice.

"Eustace?" Yoshi said. The man looked as if he was seeing a ghost.

"Back from the dead and ready to rumble, kids!"

Jon turned to see a middle-aged man with a graying ponytail holding a makeshift flamethrower that seemed to involve a Zippo lighter affixed to the nozzle of a pressurized plant sprayer. He was flanked by a tall, shirtless man in – Jon really couldn't believe his eyes – pink camouflage pants and a petite blonde woman in jeans and a Cleaver's t-shirt. Both of his companions seemed to be carrying water balloons.

Yoshi looked at Jon and, for the first time in their short association, smiled. "The cavalry has come."

"I don't know who you are, man, but you'd better do what you've got to do right now," Jon yelled. "This situation's going south fast."

"On it, partner. Ladies?"

At that both of his companions lobbed the first of their four water balloons each at Schaefer. When they splashed open, Jon immediately recognized the smell of gasoline.

"All right, You," said the tall man with a flourish. "Light this bitch up."

The man stepped forward and pulled the trigger, sending an arc of fire at exactly the points where the balloons had made impact. The way the flames erupted from Schaefer's surface reminded Jon of archival footage of napalm attacks in dense foreign jungles.

"Mako, now!" He waved the younger man over and watched him convey the message to the women. He sent them over first, hanging back to cover them with the rifle, but he saw that Linda was insisting the other women go first. You are such a selfless pain in the ass, he thought, smiling to himself.

The flames licked higher now, and Linda finally made her move. Mako came close behind, his back to her as he kept the rifle pointed at Schaefer.

Then, to Jon's horror he saw another weedy branch emerge from Schaefer's more human body and whip like a loosened fire hose toward Linda. When it made contact, it encircled her waist and dragged her down to the ground. Linda only had time to shout his name before he saw her grimace and twitch. But Jon was sure that Schaefer's latest effort at self preservation would be his last.

"Mako, the skylight!" Jon said as he ran toward Linda, who was also showing the effect of the electrical current coursing through his body. Jon unsheathed the machete as he ran, bringing it down hard in two slices before freeing Linda. Jon looked back helplessly at Yoshi, who grabbed Eustace's male companion and sent him forward to help. He ran alongside Jon and scooped up Linda like she was a bag of feathers. "C'mon, honey. Time's a' wasting," he said. And he was right, Jon realized. There was no time for sorrow. They had to get out. He ran back toward the front double doors.

Barry and Lewis were there now, each brandishing his weapon and marveling at the spectacle of Schaefer's flaming half-man, half-plant form.

"See, man. I told you," said Barry. "Fucking triffids."

Yoshi surveyed the room to make sure everyone was safe, then motioned them back to the doors. He then unleashed a fusillade of bullets straight at the blacked out skylight. The glass rained down on Schaefer, shards of glass piercing his flesh as the morning light streamed in upon him with devastating force.

The shimmering in the air above the wailing creature that was Schaefer grew more evident, and the background murmuring indicated to Jon that whatever was going to happen with the dimensional door was going to happen soon. "OK, everyone. Time to go."

The effect grew stronger, now looking as if the entire scene before them was being viewed through some funhouse mirror reflection of reality. Then, in the center, the world seemed to twist inward, as if space were suddenly water slurping down a bathtub drain.

They exited to the foyer into the yard, where Jon laid Linda on the moist grass. Eustace's female companion ran to their side, swinging around a small bag she carried over her shoulder. Jon saw her extracting a stethoscope while checking Linda's pulse. He ran to her side just as she was waving Yoshi over. "She needs CPR," she said. Jon heard himself say, "OK" before attempting to manually force life back into his wife.

The man with the ponytail kneeled down next to Jon and put his hand on his shoulder. "We'll take her in the helicopter. She needs a hospital."

"No time," Jon heard himself say as he compressed Linda's chest. "The nearest hospital is 50 miles away."

He saw Eustace look up at the girl, who shook her head "no."
"I understand, my friend. Still, we'd best skedaddle," he said gently.

"Just one second," he heard the man's male companion say. "Lewis?"

The Marine handed him a canvas backpack, from which the man, who Jon noticed still wore the faintest hint of eyeliner, drew a single grenade. He gripped the business end tightly in his left hand and pulled the pin with his right. He then dropped the live explosive into the backpack and gave it an underhand lob into the center of the warp between their dimension and Schaefer's.

"That's for blowing up my nightclub, bitch. Enjoy your trip."

They ran then, Jon sprinting across the lawn with Linda in his arms. When they all thought – or at least – hoped they were far enough away, Jon placed Linda in the grass again and resumed CPR. He looked up in time to see the exact point where the vortex had been centered bulge back out at them like the skin of their universe had worn thin and something had erupted from the other side. The bulge stretched to its limit, again distorting the sky, only this time back in their direction, then snapping back into place like it was a painting on a rubber canvas.

Jon imagined that was exactly what had happened, the explosives going off and hopefully wreaking as much havoc as possible on the interdimensional real estate speculator and his kind. If nothing else, Jon imagined, it would be unlikely they would employ this particular access point again.

There was no noise, though – only the sound of an island morning, full of bird and frog songs and sound of waves lapping against the far shore.

"I have to congratulate you folks," Barry said as he rose from where they had crouched to survey the peace around them. "You're all in some small way responsible for the oddest fucking weekend of my life."

The woman in the Cleaver's T-shirt ran to Jon and knelt beside him as he finished another round of compressions. "My name's Mary Dargan. I'm in school to be a nurse," she said.

"Thank you for your help, Mary," Jon said. Then, considering the situation, "Things don't look good for her, do they?"

"I'm sorry," she said, here eyes turned down. "She got a pretty bad shock."

"We must at least get everyone off this island," Yoshi said. "I suspect this area is still highly unstable."

Veronica stormed ahead of the entire group, her delicate fists clenched in frustration. She then turned around and addressed them like the lady of the manor she perceived herself to be.

"When is someone going to be kind enough to explain to me what has happened and who all these strange people are?" Jon watched as everyone else paused and looked at each other, silently choosing to move on past her and pretend they didn't hear what she just said. "Didn't you hear me? I have no idea what's going on here!"

Jon heard Veronica stomp her foot on the creaky dock as they passed her, the glamorous first lady of the Church of the New Revelation reduced to a temper tantrum worthy of a 6-year-old. He shook his head and laughed. Otherwise, he thought, he would burst into tears.

The tall man who had thrown the grenades helped Jon get Linda aboard the chopper, treating her as if she was the most precious cargo he had ever carried. Once aboard, Jon continued compressions on Linda while Mary checked her pulse.

"It's back," she said, looking up at Jon and smiling. "It's not strong, but it's back."

"What can we do now?" Jon asked, feeling as helpless as he ever had.

"Keep her comfortable while we get her somewhere safe," she said.

"On it," Eustace shouted over the increasing whine of the rotors. "Everyone grab some headphones and buckle in!"

The helicopter rose as they watched the ferry master's Cigarette boat growl out of the small bay.

Only now did Jon realize he was covered with bug bites and his clothes had barely dried from the trip ashore. It wouldn't surprise him if among the bites were some from snakes, but he knew that he had no need to worry. According to the cosmic rules that governed Eli's universe – and by extension his own – Jon was still dead. All this work on behalf of Eli had made him no less dead. And now the disaster that it had become was ready to claim his wife, too.

FORTY~FOUR

"You folks OK back there?" Eustace said, crackling over the headset.

Jon nodded yes.

"Where's the hospital? We can call ahead and use their landing pad."

Jon pulled the tiny microphone closer to his mouth. "There's a clinic on the other side of the island," Jon said. "It's not much, but it's closer than any hospital."

"You sure?"

"That's going to be best," Mary said in his ear. "They can stabilize her until she can get her to the mainland."

"Just follow the main road inland once we get above the island," Jon said. "I think there's a field next to it where we can land."

"You got it," Eustace said as he banked the helicopter right and accelerated past the speeding Cigarette boat below them.

Jon leaned forward to the co-pilot seat. "I just realized, I don't think we've been officially introduced."

The man reached a huge hand out for Jon to shake. "Roth, honey. I own the Final Frontier nightclub in Florence, may she rest in peace. This cowboy here is my number one bartender," he said, putting his arm around the guy with the ponytail and the tattoos.

"Eustace Conway, at your service," he said.

Jon finally picked out the Special Forces ink on the man's arm and laughed to himself. "The cavalry…"

"Well, as close as you were going to get today, my friend," Eustace said, smiling. "And you?"

"Jon Templeton," he said, relieved that he could safely use his real name. "I'm a reporter."

"A hell of a story you've got here, my friend. Only problem is I don't think anyone will actually believe it."

"Honey, somebody ought to be writing a story about you. It looked like you were kicking some serious ass in there," Roth said.

Were he to reveal the true nature of his involvement in all this, the awe would turn to pity or reproach and the congratulations would ring hollow. But Jon appreciated it nonetheless. It was one thing to have your good work noted by long-dead ethereal beings, but he realized it meant so much more for the sentiment to come from the living, those who could feel the pains and aggravations and joys with which he was so familiar.

The rhythm was barely perceptible beneath the thin flesh on Linda's wrist. Damn. There's not going to be enough time. He felt like asking Eustace if the craft could go any faster, but he knew that if it could, he would make it do so. Eustace looked back at him then and nodded as if to say he was doing his very best, and Jon nodded back in thanks. Somewhere in the dark recesses of his guilty mind, he thought that perhaps this was the best way. He, after all, had little to no chance of ever returning to the mortal plane, so perhaps it was better for the two of them to end up in eternity at the same time. But he decided that was unforgivably selfish, and the thought was overwhelmed by the other option – the option of both of them somehow living, having children and growing old together, having shared all the

316

joys and sorrows of a complete life. And they would die, as everyone does, but they would die when they were supposed to. In spite of all that Jon had seen and learned from Eli and Alex and Aunt Lil, despite all the evidence against fate and predestination and having one's "time" divinely ordained, he still held on to that small bit of faith. This could absolutely not, he told himself, be the end.

"You did a pretty good job yourself," Jon said to Eustace, "especially for a guy who was supposed to be dead."

"For that you can thank my little angel of mercy back there. Figures that the first time in fifteen years I get the gumption to flirt with a waitress she ends up saving my life. I seriously thought I was a goner."

Mary grinned and actually blushed as she kept her fingers on Linda's wrist. "Just call me a sucker for lost causes," she said.

"You and me both, baby girl. How do you think I got roped in with that crew?"

"But how did you find everyone all the way out here?"

"Krista got snatched along the way by these geezers who work for Schaefer and they sent him her picture. Then they made the mistake of stopping off to try and blow up the Final Frontier because they don't play shag music."

Jon made an expression that said, "Huh?"

"I know, honey. I'm still trying to figure it out myself," Roth said.

Eustace went on to explain the following day, the planned "action" on the Church of the New Revelation and the need to keep track of Krista. "After Schaefer zapped me, everyone naturally thought I was a goner. But Miss Mary back there brought me 'round."

"Turns out Mr. Tough Guy here had this old queen as his emergency contact," Roth said, acknowledging himself with a flourish. "Kinda sweet, don't you think?"

"So Roth shows up and wants to take me to the hospital, but I get him to drive me to Myrtle Beach Air Force Base instead. Took a little doing, but I managed to convince the National Guard guy on duty that I was on some Black Ops mission to put down lingering Castro-ites in Cuba."

"Mmm, I do love the military. No stealing, just 'requisitioning,'" Roth said.

"All I had to do then was lock on to the signal from the tracking device Krista had on her, and it brought us right here."

In a blink the water below them changed to land, the marshes of Deewees flashing past as Eustace followed the main road from above. Through the cockpit window Jon pointed out the miniature form of an ancient ambulance.

The reeds and rushes whipped outward as the craft landed, and Jon immediately removed the headphones and unbuckled his seatbelt, cradling Linda in his arms as he climbed gingerly from the helicopter with the other three passengers right after him.

The clinic wasn't much – whitewashed cinderblock on the outside with a red cross painted on the building. A roll-away marquee sign with faded red and yellow lights running across the top announced "Emergency Doctor's Care, 8-5 daily" in a variety of mismatched letters. Along another wall was a wooden bench, an ancient pay phone and a not-so-ancient Coke machine where Jon saw a figure feeding coins into the slot. From that distance it could have been anyone else from the island, but for Jon, the familiar suit and the tangle of dreadlocks gave the identity away. Eli turned in their direction, looked straight at Jon and smiled.

"Where you folks going in such a hurry?" he said, adopting the accent of the island locals. "Everything all right?"

"'Scuse us, friend," Eustace said before Jon could answer. "Got a lady here who's pretty badly hurt."

Jon interrupted, trying not to be too rude in light of Eustace's concern. "You might want to let me handle this."

He turned and regarded both Jon and Eli in turn. "You know this guy?"

"All too well," Jon said. Then turning to Eli, he said as politely as possible, "You and I have a lot to discuss, don't you think?"

"I do, boy. I do indeed," he said, slapping Jon on the back and drawing him away from the group. "You nice folks excuse us please. We've got some business to work out."

"But Jon, what about your ..." he heard Mary say before he was cut off.

Jon blinked and the landscape changed from that of sea island South Carolina to the green expanse of Eli's pastoral eternity, the flickering vision of New Jerusalem shining its light down from above them. Jon looked behind them, finding all that remained of the clinic site was the Coke machine, bench and the dilapidated pay telephone. Jon, holding Linda's nearly lifeless form, stopped and calmly regarded Eli.

"My wife is dying," he said in a more flat and emotionless fashion than he ever thought he could say such a thing.

"I know, boy. And it's a shame, too, because if you'd just done what I'd told you to do, things would have been so much easier."

"Bullshit!" Jon shouted, his voice echoing through the small valley in which they had materialized. "This whole bogus operation of yours has been a farce from the start."

"I got news for you, boy," Eli said. "The universe is a farcical place. Look at everything that's gone on here. You have to laugh at it, even if it is in the middle of all this tragedy. Unfortunately for you, though, that's just the way it works. Now why don't you quit worrying so much and let me debrief you on this mission."

"Oh, now you want to debrief me. Now that you've gotten me and all these other people wrapped up in this you want to just carry on as if we're tying up some tidy little business deal."

"Well that is what we're doing, isn't it?"

"And as I recall I made another deal with Robert that alters a few of your plans," Jon said.

"Oh yeah. What do you say we don't worry about that right now. You just tell me what happened down there and what you found out and we'll discuss particulars when you're finished."

"Wrong. We'll discuss particulars now," Jon said. "First off, you render our arrangement null and void. Second, you agree to abide by the terms of my contract with Robert, minus the clause that nullifies it should I come into contact with Linda."

"Boy, you have no idea…"

"Oh, I think I have some idea," Jon said. "I think I have a pretty good idea that you, in all your omniscience, had no clue what happened down there in that house. You don't know what happened, what was said or by whom it was said. In short, you are absolutely clueless, and right now I'm the only source you have that will allow you obtain that clue you so desperately want."

"What makes you think you know what you're talking about, boy?" Eli said, growing more cross by the minute. "What makes you think I need you any more at all?"

Jon lips turned up in an easy, relaxed smile. "Because if you didn't, I wouldn't be here. You'd have sent me along to my reward without a thought and I'd be powerless to do a thing about it. But here you are, and the only thing keeping you from getting on your knees and begging me to tell you what I know is your almighty pride. So let's deal, Eli, so we can both get on with what we should be doing."

Eli stared at Jon hard. There was more menace in his eyes then than Jon had seen during the course of their acquaintance. "I could zap you into non-existence, you know that, boy? I could remove you from the continuum altogether. You would have never existed."

"Blah, blah, blah, Eli. Do you want to know what happened down there or not? Because I know you're not going to violate your precious non-intervention policy just because I've pissed you off."

Jon almost thought he could see Eli clenching his teeth. "Okay, boy, here's the truth. Whatever that thing was, it had some shield or cloak or some pain-in-the-ass sci-fi piece of hardware that kept me from seeing what was happening inside that mansion. Now if you were still wondering why this joker scared me as much as he did, now you know. He could do things and keep things from me that should-n't be kept, at least not from an omniscient being. I may not pay attention all the time, but when I do I like to see what I want to see."

"Fine," Jon said. "Thanks for finally being honest with me. I just wanted to confirm that I was still as useful as you thought I'd be. Now I'm going to be hon-est. You're not getting a bit of what you want to know until you agree to cut me a new deal."

Eli was dumbstruck. "Until I what? Boy, obviously you have no idea of the gravity of this situation. Do you know what kind of stuff you're playing with here?"

"I know exactly what I'm playing with. Or did you forget that I just spent the morning playing commando all because of my 'mission from God?'"

"Just remember who you're talking about when you talk about God, Jon," he said, pointing a sharp finger in Jon's chest. "The Kid is what you mean when you say God, and you keep forgetting that I'm the boss. The Kid will cut deals with you all day long. Remember what I said about that bet with the Devil? Well, which do you think is worse, a business arrangement to save the universe or a sporting bet to test one man's faith?"

"I think they both suck, if you want to know the truth," Jon said. "And I think you're avoiding the question. Are you going to cut a deal to find out what you need to know or not?"

"Boy, I'm gonna…"

"Because I'm ready to give you what you want if you can meet my terms," Jon said, staring at Eli with stony resolve.

Behind Eli there was a clunk from the Coke machine, and both of them turned to see Alex insert the top of the bottle into the opener then take a long sip after the cap tinkled down somewhere inside the contraption.

"He's got a point, Boss," she said. She looked radiant as always, clad again in her cutoff jeans and plain white T-shirt, her auburn hair draping over her shoulders. Lil stood by her side.

"Ladies, I thought I told you not to interfere with this anymore," Eli said. "You've done all you needed to do as far as this mission is concerned."

"She already has interfered, haven't you, Alex? She's the one who brought me back," he said, turning to her. "It was you calling my name after Schaefer grabbed me, wasn't it?"

She hung her head, contrite. "I know you told me never to impersonate your wife again, Jon, but I figured you might forgive me this one last time."

"Absolutely, you're forgiven. You saved us all …"

Lil broke in. "Eli, we feel like the information we provided for you about Jon was used in bad faith, and that you lied to us about why we were gathering it in the first place."

"Lied? Lil, you have gone way too far over the line this time," Eli said. "I do not lie. I was straight with Jon from the very beginning. I told him flat out he'd come back here after the mission was over and he wouldn't be reunited with his wife."

"True. But you did arrange with Robert to do your lying for you by setting up that bogus contract. Then you lied about your 'policy of non-intervention,'" she said, making quote marks in the air with her fingers.

Alex continued for her. "And now you're lying to him again by telling him that you can't cut him a deal. Now I know you don't have much respect for your afterlife subordinates, but right now you're not any better than any of them are."

"Why you ungrateful … We are all going to have one serious sit-down when we get finished with all this. I can't believe that you two would be this disloyal."

"Disloyal? I wouldn't call it that, Boss. Jon's not the only one you hired because he doesn't always play well with others. Unless you've forgotten, the world's oldest profession isn't exactly taken by people on the high road to social conformity," Alex said.

"You bunch of monkeys are going to be the death of me," Eli said, shaking his head.

"On the contrary. Schaefer could have easily been the death of you, or at least made your duties that much more difficult," Lil said from behind Jon. "To treat our boy with such disrespect would be doing him a disservice, don't you think?"

"Oh, I get it," Eli said, turning to look alternately at Alex and Lil. "It's gang up on the Boss time, is that it? Well here's a news flash, kids: Peer pressure won't work. You can't shame me into doing what you think is the right thing here. You forget who's the one who determines what's right and wrong around here."

"You don't have anything to do with determining right and wrong," Lil said. "All you have to do is determine what *is*. And if that approaches the existential a bit too much for your taste, consider that to you there is no morality beyond what you've absorbed from we mortals. If it weren't for us, you wouldn't even have a concept of how to truly appreciate your own creation or your place in it."

Both women converged on Eli like a couple of hyenas to a wounded wildebeest, but Eli wasn't backing down.

"There's nothing any of you can do to convince me on this, understand? This is far beyond what any of you can comprehend, and I don't have the time to sit around explaining it to you."

"Cut the crap, Boss," Alex said. "You can do anything you please any time and any place and it will automatically fit back into the continuum. Because you are the continuum, and it is you. You're woven through time and space and everything in between and you move through it effortlessly. So don't play the 'poor old Supreme Being' part with us. We know better."

"Yes, and that being the case, we, acting as duly appointed advisors to you in your capacity as Supreme Being, highly suggest that you return Jon Templeton and his wife to the corporeal plane," Lil said.

"Whatever you think of me, keep in mind that I have other obligations," Eli said. "There's an agreement I have to keep with Robert. Jon did sign a contract, after all."

Lil rolled her eyes. "We all know all this legal falderal is just for our benefit, so why don't you rise above it? Linda here is still alive, and it's not like anyone ever found Jon's dead body."

"You're both kidding, right?" Eli said.

"We aren't kidding," Alex said. "Despite the fact that you think you're so very above us, you seem to have absorbed one of our most identifiable traits. As a result, for you to deny Jon his requests simply to save face makes you no better than we monkeys who've … How did you put it? Oh, yeah – learned to drive and have sex in the missionary position. In short, it makes you a hypocrite."

The women had closed in around Eli to within three feet, and each stood her ground, their faces pictures of determination and conviction. These people believed in him so much, believed in the purity and nobility of his cause, that they would challenge the Creator on his own turf to put things right. Had Jon not been so absolutely terrified that Eli would simply zap them into nonexistence he might have wept.

The jingle of the antique pay phone interrupted them, and all of them turned to stare at it as if it had sprouted legs and begun to tap dance. They gawked through three, then four rings. "You gonna get that?" Jon said.

"Yeah," Eli said without moving. "Yeah, I'm gonna get it. But I think you and I both know who it is."

Eli stormed over to the telephone and picked up the receiver. "Hello? Oh, hello Robert," he said as he turned to glare at Jon. "Yeah, we've got him back. What? No, I don't have it yet." There was a long pause on Eli's end. "Yes, he understands perfectly the terms of the contract. The Kid showed up yesterday and did some pro bono work for him, so he got all the fine print spelled out. Now we've got Lil and Alex here arguing on his behalf."

There was another long pause, during which Jon knelt and placed Linda gently on the lush grass. He checked her pulse and found it still weak. But it was good news that there was even one to find at this point. He reclined on the ground and stroked the ringlets of Linda's hair as he waited and Lil and Alex watched.

"Just listen to me. The boy's got the information, but he's holding out for a change in the contract. What do you mean, what kind of deal? You know what he wants," Eli said. "He wants everything to be back like it was, no strings attached." A pause again. "Oh really? Well aren't you in the gracious mood today. Fine. Tell your boss we'll work out the details later. Oh, and don't ever call me at this number again."

Eli hung up and turned back to Jon, then slowly cast his eyes over the rest of them. "A fine, loyal bunch you are," he said, shaking his head. "I have to admit I expected more of you. Especially you, Alex. My right hand, my good little helper. I couldn't have done any of this without you."

Lil made a disgusted noise and stepped up nose-to-nose with Eli. "Give it a rest, will you please? Who do you think you're dealing with here, a bunch of Catholic schoolgirls? You can't guilt us out of this. We know we're right and you're wrong and there's no more arguing to be done about it. Are you willing to meet Jon's demands or not?"

Jon stood to await the decision. Eli saw that he had been outflanked by the temptation committee's earthly street smarts and Robert's willingness to deal. He gazed at them all, resigned to giving up this battle. "Yeah," he said under his breath.

"What was that?" Alex said, cocking an ear in Eli's direction.

"I said yes," he said in a firm, strong voice. "Yes, I will agree to the terms you've laid out. No more arguing. And you're released from the constraints of your contract with Robert. The little bastard's been nothing but a burr in my butt since this started, anyway. Nothing worse than an underworld ass-kisser."

Alex and Lil's arms were around Jon, squeezing him in a tight, celebratory hug. Lil then took his face in both hands and kissed him on the cheek. "Congratulations, hon. You have done something truly remarkable, and my only wish is that there were some way for the world to know about it."

"There is," Jon said. "I suppose I have just one more condition for you."

The old man threw up his hands. "Name it, boy. I'll just add it to the list."

Jon Templeton remembered the precise moment he earned his soul back. It began with a question in the parking lot of a sea island medical clinic.

"Please tell me I didn't see you back there with a machine gun and a machete?" Linda said as she squinted and pinched the bridge of her nose.

He shook himself. He was back, standing in the exact same spot and still holding Linda close to him. He staggered, overcome once more with the switch between realities. Strong arms steadied him from behind.

"Hold on there, sugar," Roth said. "Why don't you sit? Don't want to drop that pretty lady, now do you?"

Jon, still bleary, followed his instructions, allowing himself to be guided to the bench where he sat with Linda's head on his lap.

The Humvee skidded into the parking lot and Yoshi, Mako, Krista, Regina, Barry and Lewis all climbed out. Regina ran forward.

"Linda! You're OK!"

"Really? I thought OK would feel better than this."

"How're you doing, man?" Eustace said to Jon. "Seemed like you dropped out on us for a second after we got off the bird. Airsick?"

Jon gave a weak laugh. "Something like that," he said.

Linda leaned up on her elbows to take in the sight of the helicopter. "You brought me here in that?"

"Yes, I did," said, laughing at the obvious absurdity of it all. "Nothing's too good for my lady."

She smiled at him with every muscle in her face. "Not bad for an out-of-work PR hack. Think I might let you come home now."

They kissed the way Jon imagined kissing her again when he thought he had lost her for sure. The softness of her lips, her hair in his hand and the smell of her filling his nose made everything seem that much more worthwhile. If after all they had been through this was his only reward, he decided he could be perfectly content with that.

Their lips parted, and they looked up to see everyone else trying to look somewhere other than at them.

"Thank you guys for all your help," he said. "I couldn't have done any of this without you."

Mako looked confused. "Dude, it's not like you didn't help. What, exactly, did we do, anyway? I mean, did we really save the world?"

Jon laughed. "I'm pretty sure we did. I just don't think

anyone will ever believe how."

"Oh, it was nothing, really," Barry said, feigning modesty.

"Yeah, all in a day's work for the U.S. Marines," Lewis added, with an aw-shucks grin.

A woman in a white lab coat emerged from the door and acted as if seeing an Army helicopter in her parking lot was an everyday occurrence.

"What's the trouble with all you, then?" she said.

"This woman has received a significant electrical shock," Yoshi said as he ushered Jon and Linda past her into the building. "We need you to do whatever you can."

"I'll see what I can do, but this girl needs to be at hospital."

"I don't need a hospital, and please put me down," Linda said.

"I still think she needs to be looked at," Jon said.

"You come on in, honey," she said, her hand on Linda's shoulder. "We'll get you all taken care of."

Jon carried her into the single examination room, followed by Mary, and laid her on the table, the white paper crinkling under her. "How you feel, girl?"

"Weak, but OK," Linda said. "This really isn't necessary."

"She was shocked really bad," Mary said. "I'm a nurse, by the way."

"Good thing," the doctor said as she began her exam. "Yes, your pulse is still a little weak, but there. All right, you step out and let me do my thing," she said to Jon. "You, girl, you can stay. My regular nurse don't come on till church lets out."

Jon stepped back out into the morning heat to join the rest of the group. The first thing he noticed was the absence of Veronica and Regina. "Did they not come along?" Jon asked Yoshi.

"Mrs. Whitaker thought it best under the circumstances that she returned to Myrtle Beach to let her husband know what had happened," Yoshi said. "I believe Miss Regina felt it her duty to accompany her."

"I'm sure that'll go over well," Krista said. "'Sorry, sweetie, but our loyal assistant is actually an evil plant monster who was sucked into a wormhole with our island plantation house.'"

"I'm sure she'll find a way to get by, if only on pure denial," Jon said.

Gravel crunched in the clinic parking lot, and Jon turned to see a battered turn of the century pick-up truck pull up.

From it emerged the ferry master. "How dat pretty girl?" he said, walking toward them with his peculiar gait.

"Better," Jon said. "She's in with the doctor now."

"Oh, she be fine, den. The lady doctor does good work," he said. He then reached into his back pocket and extracted an envelope. "Say, any y'all leave something on the boat? Found this on one of the seats. It's addressed to just 'Templeton' and I figured that was one of you."

Jon stepped forward and took it, thanking the old man. He examined it, feeling two oblong lumps under the rough parchment paper, then unwound the red string from the cardboard disk and extracted the letter. Obviously composed on an ancient manual typewriter, it read:

TEMPLETON:
OUR ARRANGEMENT HAS BEEN EXECUTED,
PER THE ENCLOSED.
DON'T FUCK IT UP.
STAY COOL,
ROBERT

The second "o" in "cool" was hand-embellished with a tiny set of horns and a pointed tail. From the envelope Jon tipped first a cheap red plastic cigarette lighter. On it, in tiny letters, was scrawled, "Garland Vacation Video." He slipped his fingernail between the base and body and pulled. Out came a camouflaged memory stick. The other object Jon immediately recognized, and the simple mathematical symbol it bore filled his heart more than anything he could have seen that day.

All eyes turned to the clinic door then as the doctor emerged, draping her stethoscope around her neck and shoving her hands in her lab coat pockets.

"You Mr. Templeton?" she asked.

All Jon could do was nod.

"Well, child, I got some happy news for you all around."

Linda was transported by military helicopter to Charleston Medical Center, where she was treated for her injuries and released two days later. There, it was confirmed that she was eight weeks pregnant. Upon returning home, she discovered that she had been hired by South Carolina Home magazine to write a spread on "Veronica Whitaker: Southern Style Icon," which she politely declined. Instead, she pitched a story titled, "Veronica Whitaker: Nothing Succeeds Like Excess" to Vanity Fair, in which she proposed profiling the Church of the New Revelation's co-founder as a spoiled, overly ambitious sex addict. The story ran three months later to wide national acclaim. That spring she gave birth to a healthy baby girl (seven pounds, five ounces), whom she and Jon named Lillian Alexandra.

The memory stick Jon received from Robert included not only the video rumored to be circulating about Senator Garland, but also hundreds of other videos, e-mails, fiduciary statements and falsified tax records implicating the owners of the *Charleston Gazette* news org in various unsavory and illegal schemes and business relationships. Ironically, the same two underage dancers as in the Garland video turned up regularly in the others, as well. They went on to have successful careers as hosts for a teen music show.

When Jon's story appeared on NewsHound, an independent news org site, three months later those implicated, including Garland and Jon's former employers, were forced to resign in disgrace. Buck Mays, Jon's former city editor, used a cash infusion from his restaurateur brother-in-law (and one of Cleaver's most successful franchisees) to buy a controlling interest in the *Gazette*, after which he hired Jon back as managing editor for investigative reporting. His next major story was a four-part expose on the Church of the New Revelation. His mother, meanwhile, is delighted to have a beautiful granddaughter and that Jon attends church a bit more often.

Ashley DuBose left Hampton, DuBose and Associates a month after Jon's initial disappearance to write a book, titled "Winning Against the Other Woman." The self-help book was designed to help married women keep their husbands from having affairs. It was released a year later and immediately went to No. 3 on The New York Times' nonfiction best-seller list. She continued her "research" by preying upon husbands whose wives obviously did not read her book.

Her uncle "Dub" DuBose struggled to recover from losing Senator Garland as a client, but his fortunes rose again after his niece engaged the firm to represent her upon the launch of her

E
P
I
L
O
G
U
E

wildly successful book. Dub's wife, who *did* read the book prior to its wide release, subsequently suggested that her husband and his mistress might be more comfortable living full-time in the company's Isle of Palms condo.

Barry and Lewis returned to Camp Lejeune, N.C. where two months later they were deployed as part of a multinational peacekeeping force to the Niagara Falls DMZ, where they were both cited for exemplary performance after stopping a bomb-laden RV before it entered U.S. territory. Upon their discharges two and a half years later, they married in a civil ceremony at a bed and breakfast inn in Stowe, Vermont. They later opened a science fiction-themed battle simulation park, which included regenerating human-plant hybrids as holographic targets.

Mako remained a majority shareholder of Nikura International, leading the movement to divest the company of all its defense and weapons holdings, instead focusing on civilian space development and terrestrial technological advancement. He chose not to return to Florida, instead drastically overpaying for a city block of land in Folly Beach, near Charleston, already purchased for the construction of a new Cleaver's restaurant. On the site he built a two-story retail building, which included a surf shop and a restaurant, both of which he and Krista manage together from their immense loft apartment on the second floor.

Mako also bought, then deeded to the state of South Carolina the remaining private portions of Palm Island, with the understanding that the only additional construction on the island should be at the ferry landing and that visitation should be strictly limited "to preserve the natural integrity of one of the state's last completely natural habitats." The legend of random disappearances from the island persists, though no more are documented.

Mako arranged for Yoshi's lucrative "retirement" as security chief of Nikura International, after which Yoshi returned to Okinawa to study under the masters of Ishinryu karate.

He later opened three highly successful dojos – one in the ground floor of the Nikura Building in Center City Philadelphia, one in the well-to-do Philadelphia suburb of Bryn Mawr and the other in a poverty-ridden neighborhood of North Philadelphia, where he now lives and helps mentor neighborhood kids. To his students and mentees, he regularly says, "Preparation is crucial, because no one can ever know all the challenges we might face. Always have an open mind, because the universe is full of surprises."

Harlan and Dwight, the surviving members of the SHAG cell that blew up the Final Frontier, were charged with a variety of crimes related to the bombing and Krista's kidnapping. At their trials four months later, they renounced the SHAG organization, placing the majority of the blame on Monique, their cell's leader. After being convicted of 18 of the 24 charges against them, they now offer shag lessons to fellow inmates at the Atlanta Federal Detention Center. Denied access to youth-enhancing drugs and treatments, they began to look a little worse for wear.

Eustace Conway and Roth returned to Florence, where Roth used the insurance money from the destruction of the Final Frontier to open an upscale restaurant and nightclub, the Next Dimension, and named Eustace the general manager. While the club aims at a more diverse clientele, Roth still holds court on Thursday nights as drag queen Formica Dinette, regularly engaging Diana Ross impersonator Alotta Greens as a featured performer.

Mary Dargan transferred from the University of South Carolina-Myrtle Beach to continue her nursing studies at Francis Marion University in Florence. After moving in with Eustace, she eventually convinced him to donate his extensive collection of military memorabilia to various museums throughout South Carolina, North Carolina and Georgia. Eustace, meanwhile, convinced her to leave Cleaver's. She is now head hostess at the Next Dimension.

After returning to Myrtle Beach with Regina Holiday, Veronica Whitaker offered her young congregant a job in the recruiting offices of the Church of the New Revelation. After spending nearly an hour conversing directly with her idol, Regina was disappointed to discover that she behaved more like a rich heiress than the leader of a global religious movement, and declined the job offer. A month later she left the Church of the New Revelation congregation in Columbia and offered to serve as a named source in Jon's story on the church. At the same time she began volunteering with the University of South Carolina Women's Crisis Center, where she is now considered one of the top counselors.

After she recounted the weekend's events to her husband, Veronica Whitaker was quietly transported to a discrete, upscale rehabilitation center on the Caribbean island of Anguilla. Her absence was explained by the Church of the New Revelation's public relations apparatus, of which Hampton, DuBose and Associates was a part, as a 40-day "spiritual retreat."

Three months later, after the simultaneous appearances of both Jon and Linda's stories, the church became the subject of two Congressional hearings based on violations of various space treaties detailed in Jon's story and at least three FBI raids resulting from the story's accounts of underage sex as a part of the church's youth program.

The seemingly negative publicity resulted in the church's popularity growing exponentially. As a result, the church continued its fundraising campaign to finance its satellite purchase and launch, which took place three days before Jon and Linda's daughter was born. Publicly, the governments of China and North Korea vehemently denounced the launch as an attempt by the U.S. government to undermine their countries' cultural purity. Privately, the leaders of both nations are described as "huge fans" of Veronica Whitaker.

The being that was Lucas Schaefer returned to his home world, partially wounded from the grenade explosion, to face the consequences of his failure to properly prepare Earth for colonization as an interdimensional vacation resort. As punishment, his employers stripped him of his status as a developer. He now sells mid-level time-shares along the methane seas of a tiny planet orbiting the star Betelgeuse via another worm hole. Irreparably damaged, the Palm Island worm hole was never used again.

Alexandra Chaumont, Lillian Templeton, William Z. Robert, Jesus Zabarra and Eli are. And will continue to be.

FINIS

Immaculate Deception
is the inaugural title for Codorus Press.

This book is set in Palatino for body copy, and Gill Sans for titles.
Designed by Hermann Zapf, Palatino emulates the humanist fonts
of the Italian Renaissance, which mirrored the letters made by a broadnib pen.
It is named after Giambattista Palatino, a 16th century master calligrapher.
Designed by Eric Gill, Gill Sans is a humanist sans-serif font inspired by
the Johnston typeface developed for the London Underground.

Printed in the United States of America on 10% post-consumer recycled cover stock
and 30% post-consumer recycled acid-free paper using soy-based inks.